DRONE MARAUDER

A Sci-Fi LitRPG

Kyle Johnson

*To Keri, my inspiration for pretty much every
strong female character I write.*

FOREWORD

A note about profanity

The future of the Collective has cured many of mankind's ills. There is no more poverty, normal disease, hunger, or really physical wants of any kind. However, it hasn't cured humans of their capacity to swear, and profanity abounds in the language of the Collective. These words have shifted over the millennia, though, so here's a glossary of profanity. Enjoy!

Flork – /flōrk'/ One of the more profane swear words, it refers to the act of sharing one's body with others, specifically with strangers one isn't attracted to. Used generically for emphasis or as an interjection. Ex. "What the flork are you doing?", "You florking son of a whore!"

Gassucker – /gas' suk er/ A pejorative term used only by those who spend their lives planetside or in some of the larger stations. Refers specifically to people who travel constantly through space, as these people are 'sucking gas', or hydrogen. Used to denote someone who is foolish, reckless, or stupid. Can be used as a noun or adjective. Ex. "That gassucker flew his ship right into the sun!", "Listen here, you gassucking moron!"

Hole – /hōl/ Refers to the interior of a stellar singularity, or black hole, specifically meaning a place that is deadly and terrifying even to Citizens. Usually capitalized and called 'the Hole'. Can also be used as an adjective, in which case it is not capitalized. Ex. "What in the Hole is wrong with you?", "We are totally holed!"

Hole Florker – /hōl flōrk' er/ Refers to someone so idiotic and absurd that they tried to 'flork the Hole'. Possibly the worst insult you can give someone, this phrase is also used by itself to express extreme discontent. Ex. "I'm going to send you to respawn, you hole florker!", "Hole flork!"

Plantrash – /plăn' trash/ Similar to 'gassucker', above, but only used by those who live away from planets and large stations, especially those who travel the void. Indicates that an individual is a piece of trash deposited on a planet. Usually used to imply someone is clueless, naïve, unintelligent, or unsuited for life among the stars. More generically, used as an insulting but not deeply pejorative term toward another. Ex. "I'm not letting a piece of plantrash like you on my ship!", "You're just a plantrashing hole florker!"

Scrit – /skrĭt/ An expletive that refers to human waste. Most often used to indicate generic displeasure or unhappiness, it can also be used as an insult. In this case, the individual is usually called some variant of 'a scrit'. Ex. "Aw, scrit, I can't believe you did that!", "You little hunk of scrit!"

Generally, none of these phrases are acceptable in polite company. However, 'hole' is mild enough that few people take offense over it, and 'scrit', when not being applied directly to someone, is rarely a cause for outrage. 'Flork' is considered quite offensive, however, and calling someone a 'hole florker' is a good way to get sent for respawn.

Time in the Collective

Time is not a constant in the Human Collective. Ships moving at a tock or more, speeds exceeding a tenth of the speed of light, experience time dilation that can range from half a percent up to almost five percent for standard cruising velocities. Stations far removed from a star or planet's gravity well experience time contraction, where the passage of time is faster compared to that closer to a star or planetside, on a planet's surface. Because of this, the System dictates specific rules about measuring time in the Collective.

The passage of time in the Collective, by long tradition, is Earth standard. The 'correct' calendar date and time is based on that of Earth's rotation and revolution around Sol star. A standard day consists of twenty-four hours, seven standard days constitutes a standard week, four standard weeks make a standard month, and 364 standard days or thirteen standard months make a standard year. All starships and space stations use these definitions to measure time, regardless of location.

However, individual planets often adhere to a more localized standard. Some have a day that corresponds to that planet's rotation and a year that equals one revolution of that planet about its star. Many use a calendar that is linked to the founding of the first colony in that system, or the Collective's arrival in that system. Because of this, an Earth-standard day is often called a "solar day", and similar nomenclature applies to weeks and years, while local measurements may be called "planetary", or they may have more specific nomenclature such as a "Centaurian day" or "Barnard year" to distinguish them.

CHAPTER 1

The starry void rushed past the *Resolute Hammer*, speeding by at a velocity of three tocks, 30% of the speed of light. The destroyer-class vessel raced into the darkness of space, pushing a wave of excited hydrogen before it that glowed faintly against the CMB, the cosmic microwave background. Those blue-shifted photons sped out ahead of the 640-em-wide, spherical warship at the speed of light, a clear warning to anyone in the area that the *Hammer* was on the hunt. Every ship in motion pushed just such a bow wave, no matter how well shielded their drive or power plants, rendering the idea of a stealthy approach moot.

Of course, even without the wave alerting those around it, the *Hammer's* beacon radiated its presence constantly. The ship's 'net broadcast that signal to any ship, planet, or station with scanners able to pick up a beacon at that range, so everyone within a light-hour of the destroyer would know of its presence soon enough. It was impossible to turn it off; even if a ship stopped beaconing, the Overnet would pick up the lapsed signal and carry it to anyone who should be able to detect it. Stealthy starships simply didn't exist in the Human Collective.

Benning knew all that, of course. Her Starship Captain training taught her the nuances of traveling in space, and that included how to detect other ships traversing the void nearby. She knew that the brightness of the bow wave went up by the cube of her ship's velocity – doubling her velocity would double the number of particles her ship impacted per second and square the energy of those impacts, resulting in cubing the net brightness of her wave – and that the ship she was currently stalking would pick up those warnings long before she arrived. At least, that would have been the case if not for the *Hammer's* dive engines.

"All hands, prepare for dive," Benning ordered, her voice carried automatically over the ship's 'net to each of her crew members. "Repeat, prepare for dive." With her Better Captain than Crew ability, she could practically see her crew members locking themselves into place, grabbing hold of things, and staring fixedly into space. Within seconds, every member of her crew was in position, and she turned toward her pilot, Brialle Caldwell.

"Dive," she instructed shortly.

"Aye, Captain," the blonde-haired woman replied. "Diving."

The ship's negmass power plant suddenly poured energy into the dive engines. Those engines pumped negative energy into the fabric of spacetime, flooding the compacted fifth dimension lurking below the horizon of reality with that energy. In response, the Calabi-Yau manifold expanded around the ship, swelling until it encompassed the entire vessel in a bubble of five-dimensional spacetime. The three normal spatial dimensions flattened around her, spreading out so that she could see the entire ship at once as if looking down on it from a height. If she wanted, she could examine the hull of the destroyer from every direction at the same time, peer into closed lockers and vaults, even see into the bodies of the crew members around her.

Of course, Benning didn't allow herself look at any of that. She kept her focus squarely on the pistol strapped to her hip, watching it and nothing else. That was the key to riding a dive through CY-space; the human mind, even the augmented and enhanced one of a Citizen, couldn't handle seeing the entirety of three-space at once. To stay sane and undamaged, she had to narrow her focus as much as possible. That also helped her remain still, a necessity since small distances in five-space could translate out to much larger ones in three-space. A shift of a finger during a dive could result in that finger tearing free of its hand and landing an em or more away when the dive ended. While any Citizen's nanofield could repair that sort of damage, it still hurt, and Benning wasn't interested in experiencing that pain again if she didn't have to.

The world sprang back around her as the ship exited the dive, resurfacing in normal spacetime with a wash of hyper-energized photons. These exploded out from the ship in a ring, forming a dive splash that could be seen even by the naked eye, much less sensitive ship scanners. Her prey now knew that she'd exited a dive – or they would in six seconds, when the ring of light reached them. Fortunately, by then, it would be too late.

"Weapons, fire fusion salvo," Benning instructed. "Staggered burst pattern. Follow it with the new missile."

"You got it, Captain!" Charlo Herrick replied from the Weapons station, her voice excited as it always was when she got to use a new weapon. The Weapons Engineer took an almost childlike glee in new and exotic weapons, and the new warhead was something that she would never have gotten to use with any other captain. It was a prohibited item, and its usage against manned vessels or stations was a Fleet crime, one punishable by execution, the loss of levels, and imprisonment. For most Citizens, that was a powerful deterrent.

Benning simply didn't care.

The *Hammer* soared forward, racing toward its victim. Benning's skin warmed slightly as her fusion missiles exploded like miniature supernovae, one after the other in a line toward her target, bathing her ship's hull in weak bursts of gamma radiation and neutrinos. The blasts cut a line across the enemy's evasion cone, forcing them to either curve above or below the missiles, narrowing that cone and limiting their maneuvering options.

"Captain, enemy vessel moved above the ecliptic," Jezper Shields spoke in his usual calm, laconic voice. Her head of Ops rarely got excited or ruffled, a valuable trait for the man who was essentially her eyes and ears in a battle. "She's powering her dive engine. Her escorts are moving to intercept us."

"Not for long," Herrick muttered almost under her breath, and Benning felt a small smile curl her lips. Hopefully, her Weapons Engineer was right.

"Captain, I'm reading four escorts," Shields added. "Two frigates, a fast frigate, and a destroyer."

"Just as you said, Captain," Caldwell said, shaking her head. "All four are moving toward us, four leconds distance, bearing zero-one-four, six degrees declined."

"Begin evasive maneuvers, pattern seventeen," Benning instructed. "Weapons, time to impact?"

"Seven seconds, Captain," Herrick replied eagerly.

"Engineering, prepare to shut down on my mark," Benning instructed.

"Aye, Captain," Graesen Barry's voice replied through the ship's 'net.

Benning's skin warmed slightly as the first of the enemy escort vessels opened fire, bathing the area around the *Hammer* with gamma radiation. The wide blast lacked the power to do much to the destroyer, but that wasn't the point. The enemy ships would try to bracket her with their attacks, narrowing her evasion cone and making her an easier target. She felt another flash warm the hull as something exploded far below the ship; her enemies were using missiles, as well.

"Glancing graser blast, Captain," Shields informed her. "Fusion warhead exploded 4500 kims declined, no damage."

"Weapons, target the destroyer with grasers, wide spread," Benning instructed. "Fire an AM battery at the fast frigate, starburst pattern."

"On it, Captain," Herrick replied.

"Engineering," Benning spoke, watching the timer in her vision, "Shut down... Now!"

Instantly, Benning's sense of the ship dimmed as Graesen Barry cut power to both of the ship's plants and dropped the engine offline. The bridge's holo-screens went dark, and information stopped flowing into her from the ship's 'net. For a moment, the *Hammer* floated totally helpless, its shielding down as it moved on an inertial track that any negaputer could target easily. That moment seemed to last forever to Benning even though she knew it was only seconds. The ship rumbled and shook in those brief seconds as a nearby explosion rocked the hull, and Benning's skin burned and seared as grasers painted the ship mercilessly.

Suddenly, a wave of white light flashed in her vision, rippling through her bridge. The light slipped through the ship's bulkheads but illuminated nothing as it traveled through higher-dimensional space, flaring with searing radiance before disappearing as it spread out into the distance in all directions. A moment later, her power plants came back online, and she felt the engine whir to life as it slammed gas and anti-gas together, channeling the high-energy photons thus created into momentum to propel the ship. Screens popped back to life, and data began flooding her brain even as her crew called it out for her to hear.

"Captain, the Planck warhead exploded zero-point-two seconds early," Herrick informed her. "It must have been intercepted by the *Orion*."

"Captain, engines are down to 61%," Barry spoke through the 'net. "Power plants are down to 73% and 68% respectively."

"We took a close fusion impact and three graser blasts while the power was down, Captain," Shields added from Ops. "We're venting gas in two places, but all other systems seem nominal."

"And the escorts?" Benning asked.

"Getting images now..." Shields turned and offered her a rare smile. "The warhead worked, ma'am. All four have their power plants spiking with engines offline." Benning felt a sudden flash in her mind as the power plant of one of the frigates' ruptured, letting all its energy loose in a single blast, and the man added, "The *Interdictor* has gone photonic. The others will have to shut down their plants or do the same."

"Captain, incoming message from the *Orion*," Caldwell spoke.

"Ignore it," Benning said. "Weapons, we've got three ships with no shielding on ballistic trajectories. Hit each of them with a fusion barrage."

"Absolutely, ma'am!"

"Helm, make for the *Orion*," Benning instructed. "Plot a parallel course. Weapons, when we reach one lecond, hit her with our neutrino beams."

Benning felt the ship shudder as three volleys of fusion missiles raced outward. The warheads quickly accelerated to nine tocks and streaked across the leconds toward the hapless vessels. The missiles impacted their hulls directly; without engines, the ships could only move in a straight line and constant velocity that made hitting them easy. Explosions lit Benning's inner vision as the warheads converted their hydrogen payloads into helium, carbon, and oxygen, exploding not once but repeatedly as each stage of fusion ignited. When the flashes of energy faded, nothing but shattered hulks of dead ships remained. One of these, the destroyer, quickly exploded into a blaze of light, but the other two soared through space, their inertia carrying them away from the area of engagement.

"Captain, the three remaining escorts have all been opened to space," Shields confirmed. "The *Red Javelin* went photonic; reading multiple hull breaches and no power generation from the frigates. They appear to be dead ships."

"Keep an eye on them just in case, Ops," Benning instructed. "We might want to pick them up for salvage after this."

The *Hammer* roared past the drifting ships, heading toward the huge carrack that was her main target. The *Hammer* slowly curved under the pressure of a thousand g's of acceleration, moving into position near the 1.6-kim-long cargo ship. The *Orion's* captain continued to bombard Benning with messages – most likely pleas to surrender the ship's cargo in exchange for safe passage – but Benning ignored them. She wanted the ship, not just its cargo. Besides, the *Orion* had something like a fifth of a cubic kim of cargo space. There was no way the *Hammer* could carry even a tiny fraction of that.

The destroyer raced alongside the carrack, bathing its hull with glaser and neutrino blasts. The gravity lasers slowed the larger ship, dropping its momentum and making it pass more slowly through time than the destroyer. The neutrino beams pierced the carrack's neutronium hull and exploded into blasts of photons that tore through the ship, knocking electrons and neutrons free from the hull. Those within swam in deadly radiation, while the free electrons played havoc with the ship's 'net and thus slowed any possible repairs.

The *Hammer* docked with the cargo ship at last, and Benning led her marines into the ship's interior. The ship was dark, the only illumination a series of chemical lights along the floor that gave off a dim, green glow, just enough to allow someone to walk without running into bulkheads. The ship sounded strangely silent without the constant hum of its engines and the power running through it, and it creaked and groaned softly as it rotated slowly, providing about a tenth of normal gravity without its shroud. The marines moved slightly awkwardly in the microgravity but compensated swiftly as they boarded the doomed vessel.

A Sojourner-class ship like the *Orion* typically had impressive defenses, including a contingent of over sixty marines, dozens of bot defenders, and emplaced graser turrets that would target anyone the ship's 'net didn't recognize. Benning had twenty marines plus herself, a large contingent for a destroyer but nowhere near what she would normally need to take a ship the size of the *Orion*. At least, that would be the case if the ship's power plant wasn't offline, disabling its automated defenses, and if her barrage of the ship hadn't killed half its soldiers and left the other half unable to communicate or access the 'net to track boarders.

As it was, Benning's forces slaughtered the eight marines who tried to defend the unlocked airlock, then split up to move into the ship, piggybacking off the *Hammer's* 'net and comm system to stay in contact. Geraldine Dickerson took a squad to secure the marine quarters and armory, while two squads moved to take the engine room, a fourth moved on the forward bridge where the ship's pilot and weapons officer were located – a feature common among cargo ships – and Benning led the last to the main bridge to meet the captain. They encountered minor resistance along the way as a few mobile squads of the carrack's marines struck at them, but the neutrino beams left those marines badly wounded and weakened, and Benning and her team slaughtered them without too much difficulty.

The bridge stood open and unsecured thanks to the lack of power to the vessel. A handful of marines defended it, and Benning led her attack with a pair of graser flash grenades that bathed the bridge in lethal radiation. She and her marines moved in behind the grenades, setting up portable neutronium barriers from behind which they could fire safely on the defenders.

Benning's nanofield filled the bridge, linking to her helmet visor and giving her clear information about the positions of her foes despite the darkness of the unlit bridge. She popped up and leveled her Foehammer rifle at a marine hiding behind a microthene barrier. The rifle jumped as she pulled the trigger despite its inertial dampeners, and the heavy tungsten-coated bullet wrapped in dark matter to give it extra mass punched through the barrier effortlessly. The bullet shattered against the marine's armor, but the impact cracked the chest plate and knocked the marine back, allowing Benning to send a second bullet through the broken armor and into the defender's chest cavity. The marine's aura flashed from green to dark orange in Benning's sight, and she fired a third bullet that dropped the aura to crimson before it winked out entirely.

Benning took out a second marine before replacing her rifle on her back and grabbing the long metal rod strapped to her right thigh. She tossed another grenade to keep the defenders down for a moment before leaping over her barrier and charging the defenders, the rod quickly lengthening and expanding into an em-long hammer with neutronium spikes on the back and top and a glowing, anti-matter-coated striking head. Bullets slammed into her liquid metal armor as she crossed the bridge, and her left leg burned as a round pierced her defenses and plunged into the meat of her thigh. She ignored the injury, leaping over the defenders' barrier and lashing out with her hammer.

The marines reacted at once, one whipping out a heavy, spiked mace and moving to engage her while the others stepped back, giving themselves room to fire at her safely. Benning slid a heavy mace blow, guiding the weapon toward the floor, then slammed the back spike of her hammer into the marine's side. The neutronium spike punched through their armor and slid into their lung, dropping their aura to medium orange. They stepped back, but Benning lengthened her hammer by half an em with a thought and jammed the top spike of the weapon into the marine's throat.

Bullets cracked against her back, and she spun to face her attackers, leaving the dying marine behind. Her hammer lashed out, crashing into armored bodies. She shattered elbows and knees, shoved the top spike into microthene visors and buried the rear spike in spines, legs, and chests. She lost herself in the sheer savagery of melee combat; in that moment, the ache in her chest that never seemed to fade receded into the background. For a while, she was Benning Kidd the Stellar Corsair once more, glorying in battle and bloodlust, not Benning the Drone, a mistake given eternal life and hunted throughout the systems of the Collective.

The battle ended too soon as her marines used her distraction to bring down the remaining defenders. Benning's hammer found no foes to strike, and the frenzy of combat that filled her ebbed and faded, leaving the ache in her chest to slowly return. That place deep inside her had always been empty, but with the return of her memories, it had filled at last. Unfortunately, it pulsed with pain, anger, and hatred for the System that gave her this life by trying to steal her previous one from her.

I'd almost have preferred the emptiness, she thought

bitterly, not for the first time.

"Squads, report," she spoke aloud, pushing the discomfort aside. Despite living with the feeling for the past few months, she still wasn't used to it, but she found she could ignore it if she had to.

"Second squad, marine barracks are secure," Dickerson's voice spoke back through the *Hammer's* 'net. "Nine enemy dead, one casualty."

"Third squad, engine room secure," Keanna Lucroy added a moment later. "Seven enemy combatants dead, fourteen noncombatants captured. Two casualties."

"Fifth squad, forward bridge secure. No enemies, pilot and weapons officer both DOA."

"Good work," Benning replied. "Keanna Lucroy, execute all Citizen captives. Bind any Workers. We might need them later."

"Aye, Captain."

"What?" one of Benning's captives demanded, a man of about Benning's height with lighter skin, pale blonde hair, and dark eyes with very faint epicanthal folds. "You can't just execute...oof!" The man grunted and spasmed as one of Benning's marines drove the toe of their boot into his side. Benning glanced at the man and activated her helmet's scanner.

> MAZEN GONG
> Level 21 Starship Captain
> Damage Rating: 8
> Defense Rating: 7
> Resistance Rating: 19
> Highest Stat: Social (10.55)

Lowest Stat: Physicality (8.3)

"Mazen Gong," she said, walking over to the command console, the only place on the bridge still receiving power. "You're not exactly in a position to tell me what I can and can't do, are you?"

"I'm empowered by Laserline Shipping to negotiate in the event of the ship's capture by pirates," the man replied slowly. "Spare my crew, and I could..." He fell silent as the nearby marine jammed the muzzle of their rifle into the back of his neck.

"Why would I need to negotiate?" Benning asked curiously. "I already have the ship and cargo. What else could you offer me?" As she spoke, she extended her nanofield into the console, pinging it and sending banal requests to it. Gong had been able to lock it down, but with most of the power to the ship cut off, he hadn't been able to secure it adequately. It took her only a few seconds to unlock enough functionality to get a damage readout of the ship and a manifest of what it carried.

"Your destroyer can't tow the *Orion*," Gong pointed out a bit scornfully. "And you might be able to take a few gigs of our cargo, but nothing more. I'm willing to offer you two hundred credits, far more than you'd get from what little cargo you can take, if you leave my ship and crew in peace."

"You're right, Mazen Gong. I can't tow the *Orion* – at least, not in any reasonable amount of time." She smiled at the man as she unlocked the basic level of the console before her and used it to turn the power plant back on, running it at the bare minimum necessary. The command screen flickered to life along with the bridge's emergency lights and life support. "I don't have to, though. I can just fly her where

I want her to go."

"How – how did you do that?" he demanded. "Step away from that console at once, or my offer...aaiigh!" Gong screamed as the marine beside him shot him in the shoulder, the sound echoing in the otherwise silent bridge.

"Again, not in a position to give orders, here," Benning reminded the man as she worked on the command console. She keyed her comm system and reached out to the *Hammer*. "Graesen Barry, I've got enough power for a damage readout," she told her Engineer, sending him an image of the *Orion's* damage control screen. "What kind of repair time are we looking at?"

"The Planck warhead basically blew out the main engines, Captain," the man replied after a moment. "The power plants are down to 6% capacity, not enough to even power the engines, much less make headway, and she won't be able to dive."

"Repair time, Engineer?" she repeated.

"Approximately eighteen hours, Captain."

"What if I instruct the nanofield to prioritize repairing the engines and power plants exclusively?"

"That might cut it down to twelve, ma'am. Without a full team onboard working on the engines, though, there's no way to get it below that."

"Thank you, Graesen Barry," she replied, cutting the communication and issuing some commands to the ship's 'net to repair the engines and power plants at the expense of everything else on board. "Keanna Lucroy, how many Workers are left?"

"Seven, ma'am."

"Have them get to work repairing the power plants," she instructed. "Let them know that if they do a good job,

I'll be willing to let them keep serving on the *Orion* once it reaches port."

"Yes, Captain."

"What – what are you doing?" Gong gasped, panting with pain and his dark eyes wide. "You can't just take the *Orion*! You'll never be able to crew her, and you can't possibly sell a thousand gigs of heavy metals! Any buyer will know it's stolen from a corporation and refuse to deal with you!"

"Not all at once, no," Benning agreed. "But I'll be able to sell the four gigs of anti-iron you've got hidden in the hold in a heartbeat, and I'll be able to ship the rest to various systems and sell it off piecemeal. Plus, then I'll have the ship. I can think of some solid uses for a carrack."

"If you do this, Laserline will…"

"Laserline will put out a bounty on me, yes, I know," Benning cut him off. "I can add it to the list of ones I've already got." She nodded to the marine, and they lifted the cringing man to his feet, dragging him over to the command console.

"Now, Mazen Gong, you're going to unlock the real cargo manifest," she told him with a smile. "I want to see what you were really carrying that required that kind of escort."

"The – the anti-iron," he stammered, but she shook her head.

"No, while that's a valuable cargo, there's something else here," she said. "Something hidden behind a containment field and blocked from the manifest. You're going to save me the trouble of getting a deep scanner in here to figure it out."

"What?" he demanded, shaking his head. "I'm not helping you! Send me to respawn if you want, but…"

Benning held a hand over the man's, and he fell silent. A moment later, his eyes widened, and he began screaming as the skin on the back of his hand began to dissolve, bubbling and liquefying to run down onto the floor in a steady trickle. Cartilage, bone, and muscle gleamed beneath the ministrations of Benning's nano-disassemblers, and as she withdrew them from Gong's body, he shrieked in pain, clutching the maimed hand to his chest.

"I'm going to send you to respawn, Mazen Gong," Benning said, speaking loudly over the man's pained sobs. "The only question is, will I send you quickly, or will I slowly dissolve your body into liquid?" She shrugged. "The choice is yours, but choose quickly. This is only going to hurt more the longer it lasts."

Ten hours later, the *Orion* – now beaconing as the *Wild Orchid* – moved forward under its own power, run by the ship's 'net as it dove toward the distant Frostwise system. The ship floated along, empty of all life, its surviving Workers in the *Hammer's* hold and its Citizen crew sent for respawn.

All in all, it had been a good day.

CHAPTER 2

"Can I be blunt, Benning Kidd? The *Orion* was a waste of time and resources."

The tall, slim, blonde woman sitting behind a microthene desk colored and patterned to look like wood took her hands off the smooth desktop and turned to face Benning, her face simultaneously attractive and severe. Her crimson Molex suit with silver piping was high quality and expertly fitted to display her lithe curves without being crass or revealing, and she was one of the few Citizens working for Benning who lacked a sidearm or weapon of any kind. As Benning's chief administrator, Tereza Erdeli had little need for a pistol; she fought different kinds of battles for her employer, and words were her chosen weapons.

A flash of irritation passed through Benning at Erdeli's words, but she tamped it down. Erdeli had previously worked for Nikita Mosin, the man who'd arranged for a group of Benning's enemies to join together to take the Corsair down. While Erdeli had agreed to work for Benning, the administrator hadn't really wanted to do so and only signed on to avoid the wrath of Fyodr Mosin, Nikita Mosin's father and a powerful Noble of the Collective. Erdeli's contract forced her to look out for Benning's best interests, but it didn't require the woman to like her new employer. Benning supposed the fact that she had captured and tortured Erdeli for information on a shipment probably didn't help matters much, as well.

However, Benning couldn't argue that the woman was good at her job. When Erdeli had come to station IS-39267, the place was a disaster. The strangelet bomb Benning used to take the facility from Mildred Joyce did enormous damage to its systems, and the station's nanofield was still working to repair it. Half of its docking bays were nonfunctional, and entire sections of the station lacked life support. Benning and later Charlo Herrick had done what they could to patch the damaged systems, but the station was barely functional. Erdeli fixed that; she hired Systems Engineers to come and oversee the repairs, purchased a few dozen Workers to run the daily operations of the station, and brought in crews to man the station's repaired defenses. IS-39267 had gone from a near-ruin to a fully functional space station, and Erdeli's competence and efficiency were in large part the reasons for that. Benning could deal with the woman's attitude so long as she continued to do her job effectively.

"Why?" Benning asked in reply, staring at the large holoscreen that made up the back wall of the administrator's office and not giving her employee more than a brief glance. "Didn't you say that I should try to turn the station into a transport stop?" The screen could show just about any view that Erdeli wanted; for some reason, the woman had set it to display the twin brown dwarfs of the nearby Frostwise system. The failed stars barely glowed in the background, lacking the mass of hydrogen needed to ignite stellar fusion but still possessing enough gravity to heat themselves until they shone a dull reddish-brown.

"Yes, but that doesn't mean you need a vessel like this," the blonde woman shook her head. "Look, ships already stop at Frostwise for gas so they can avoid losing cargoes to us, right?" Benning nodded; that was part of her contract to lease the station from Frostwise, the true owners of IS-39267. "Well, that's an arrangement of which previous inhabitants of this place never fully took advantage, Benning Kidd. If you set up the station with extremely low taxes on all transfers, representatives from the Far Systems like

Cygni, Ross, and Teegarden could set up shop here, buy goods from the Near Systems, and ship them rimward themselves. It would save them credits in the long run since gas at Frostwise is cheaper than it is most places, and you'd collect on every transfer. You could be looking at thousands of credits per standard day, Benning Kidd!"

"So, why wouldn't having our own carrack make us even more money? If those brokers didn't have to bring their ships here but could pay us to ship their goods for a reduced rate, wouldn't they be even more likely to send their representatives?"

"No, and for two reasons," the administrator shook her head. "For one, it's far larger than you could realistically use for that purpose. In most systems, only corporations can transport more than an h-cube of goods into or out of the system, and the *Orion* can transport 160 h-cubes easily."

Benning wasn't used to thinking about h-cubes, cubic hectometers, each h-cube equal to a million cubic ems. It was a ridiculous amount of cargo, equal to almost ten of the *Heliopause,* her first ship, and only large corporations dealt in those sorts of quantities.

"That means you could only carry an h-cube of goods for any one buyer, and to get it to them, you'd have to park the *Orion* out-system and ship it in with a smaller ship. You'd either need a clipper – which you don't have – or make eight trips with a brigantine like the *Heliopause.* Either that, or you'd need a corporation to send a carrack to dock with you out-system, and if they're going to do that, why wouldn't they just carry the goods themselves?

"Finally, there's no way you can hide the fact that you stole this ship, Benning Kidd. Even if you change its registry, only corporations can buy carracks or barges. To have it, you must have stolen it, and that means anyone can attack it and take it from you without consequences. Hole, if they figure out that it belonged to Laserline, they could get a substantial reward for returning it! It's basically a giant target, begging every bounty hunter, privateer, and Fleet ship that sees it to come take it..." The woman's words drifted off, and her eyes widened. Benning still wasn't good at reading facial cues, but she recognized surprise when she saw it.

"Exactly," Benning nodded, turning away from the screen and looking at her administrator with a cold and predatory smile. "Tereza Erdeli, I'm not opposed to your plans because they'll bring me credits, and credits are useful – but they aren't the point of my path. I'm not a Merchant Captain or Trader, looking to accumulate as many credits as possible. For my path, I need battle, and the *Orion* is a way to bring that to me."

Benning looked back out toward the holoscreen, staring into the starry void that surrounded the dimly glowing binary system. "I want you to get the *Orion* refitted," she instructed. "Double its offensive and defensive capabilities, even if that cuts into its cargo capacity. Have Erix Adelsson arrange to sell off its cargo piecemeal to pay for the upgrades; it's carrying two gigs of unstable helium-6 and four of anti-iron that will probably pay for everything by themselves."

"Helium-6 and anti-iron?" Erdeli repeated, her eyes growing wide once more. Helium-6 was an incredibly rare isotope of helium with a half-life of less than a second, but it greatly increased the power of any fusion reaction into which it was injected and was thus a primary ingredient of the most potent fusion explosives. Anti-iron, on the other hand, was the most stable and energy-dense form of anti-matter that could be easily created. It could power an anti-matter plant, but it was routinely used in the highest-grade AM weapons. Both materials were restricted substances, ones whose sale was regulated by the Fleet, but that also made them extremely valuable.

"With the credits from that, you could completely overhaul the ship and still have some left over," Erdeli shook her head. "However, refitting the *Orion* will take time – unless you want to attract the kind of attention Nikita Mosin did by rapidly upgrading ships in an attempt to trap you. I'll have to bring in different engineers to work on individual systems, upgrading things slowly so that no one thinks to remark on the changes."

"How long?"

"Six months at the minimum," the blonde woman shrugged. "A standard year at the outside. The longer it takes, the less likely it will be that people realize what you're doing."

"Aim for six months, Tereza Erdeli. People will figure out what I'm doing eventually anyway." Benning turned back to the woman. "How is everything in the station?"

Benning listened as the administrator spoke about the day-to-day details of running IS-39267, something about which Benning had practically no interest. The woman talked of repairs, upgrades, new crew she'd brought on, and ideas she had for further expansion of the station. Benning nodded and asked occasional questions, but for the most part, she barely took note of the woman's words. She'd already gotten this information from the station's 'net when she entered it, so none of it was new or interesting to her. However, her social training taught her that underlings often enjoyed the opportunity to show off their accomplishments, even when those accomplishments were nothing more than doing their job at the bare minimum level. Benning didn't understand why Erdeli took such delight in proclaiming that she'd performed adequately, but she did know that if the woman felt appreciated, she'd perform better.

After their meeting, Benning took an elevator up to

the Owner's Suite, a set of rooms set aside for the leaseholder of the station. The suite was larger than Benning needed or wanted, with three separate spaces. One of these was apparently meant for hosting guests and sported fancier décor and seating for up to ten; Benning had removed all the furniture and now used it as a training center. A second space had an enormous tub that her AI guide Tiddly told her could be filled with hot water in which to soak and get clean. Benning didn't understand the point of that since her nanofield kept her clean at all times, so she simply ignored that space and pretended it didn't exist.

The third room was her sleeping chamber. When she'd taken over the station, she'd found the chamber dominated by a large, soft bed, three ems wide and two long. She'd demolished that and replaced it with a ship's cot, a simple bed just large enough for her to lay on with a curved covering that could be latched over her to keep her from moving around during high-g maneuvers. She'd always preferred to sleep with the cover down, even while the ship was docked, but before she regained her memories, she'd never understood why. Now, she did: the cover reminded her of a Drone's sleeping capsule, something she'd rested inside almost every night of her life. Like most Drones, she'd eagerly awaited rest periods since rest meant using her game credits from her day's labors. Even without being able to remember that capsule, she'd recalled the comfort of being within it at a fundamental level.

She placed her kits into the room's safe and locked it, then lay down on the bed and locked the cover into place. She closed her eyes and pulled up her menus. Instantly, whirling icons spun before her eyes, each icon representing a different menu she could access. She touched the first, a rotating image of her own body that showed her short orange hair, deep blue eyes, and light brown skin along with a figure that was athletic but not slim. The figure expanded until only her face was visible on one side of her vision with her current status floating beside it.

BENNING KIDD
Citizen Path: Stellar Corsair
Level: 9
To Next Level: 15%
Credits: 30,922.4 Standard Credits

Physicality: 12.9
Coordination: 12.7
Resistance: 12.9

Acuity: 11.5
Willpower: 18.5
Social: 11.1

Renown: +/- 56
Nanodefense: 19.1

SKILLS
Conditioning: 19.8
Cyberwarfare: 16.2
Leadership: 19
Martial Combat: 20.3
Nanoresistance: 2.5
Naval Tactics: 22.5
Sense Deceit: 4.7
Starfaring: 18.8
Weapons Expertise: 19.2

ABILITES
All is Lost
As It Should Be
Better Captain than Crew
Blitzkrieg

Critical Strike
Declared Enemy
Flurry
Focused Attack
For Fame
Honor the Fallen
I Have the Bridge
I Will Not Fall
Inspiration
On My Command
Strength from Pain

She grimaced at the slow pace of her progress. Since reaching level 9, she'd struggled to advance her career significantly. Despite capturing or destroying over a dozen ships, she'd only gained 12% to her path over the last few months. In fact, her biggest progress was with her skills and stats, and she'd managed to bring her Martial Combat skill to over 20 several weeks ago.

SKILL UPGRADES!
You have achieved rank 20 in one or
more of your skills. With this increase,
your skills achieve a new tier, and
you can use them in unique ways.

MARTIAL COMBAT
+2% x rank melee damage
+2% x rank melee defense
+1% x rank armor penetration
with melee weapons
Flurry: Increase melee attack speed
by 50% but suffer -25% penalty to
attack rating for 30 seconds.

She closed her status and selected the icon that looked like a series of golden spheres all whirling about one another. The spheres expanded rapidly, filling her vision, and with a flash, she found herself standing in the center of a space that seemed to stretch out infinitely in all directions except the featureless white deck beneath her feet. Once, her Overnet domain had been entirely empty, but she'd changed that. A glowing pedestal occupied the center of the domain, and glimmering doors shimmered and hung around her, each leading to one of her training modules. When she didn't concentrate on the doors, they spun slowly, looking like rectangular slabs of mercury gleaming in the light of her domain. By focusing on one, though, she could halt its rotation and cause it to show an image of its content, allowing her to select any training exercise she wanted.

"I like your plan for the *Orion*, Benning Kidd," a familiar voice spoke. Benning glanced to her right and saw Tiddly standing beside her. The AI was in her usual guise as a gnome, about an em tall with honey-colored hair that hung from her head in dozens of tight braids. She wore her usual leather smock and goggles, and her blue eyes shone brightly in her wide face. Once, Tiddly had bounced around with seemingly endless energy, her voice always perky and upbeat. Since Benning unlocked her memories, though, Tiddly had become somewhat more reserved and cautious in both her words and tone. "It'll make good bait."

"I hope so, Tiddly," Benning sighed, ignoring the spark of anger she felt as she looked at the gnome. "My path hasn't been advancing much recently." Benning knew why Tiddly had become more cautious, and she didn't blame the AI. Tiddly had known Benning's true identity the entire time and had kept it from her, prevented from telling Benning by the overarching System that controlled everyone and everything in the Collective. The System still constrained Tiddly, Benning was sure, but she could never know how much influence the System had on the AI. That made Tiddly untrustworthy, as far as Benning was concerned, and Tiddly, tied closely to Benning's thoughts, had to know that.

The gnome seemed to ignore Benning's spike of irritation as she nodded. "You're approaching level 10. That's a significant milestone, and it takes longer to reach it."

"Significant how?" Benning asked almost woodenly. She was curious, but at the same time, she found it hard to care about the peculiarities of the System anymore. It had tried to kill her; it let the Nobility hunt her. As far as she was concerned, the System was her enemy, and Benning always found a way to punish her enemies.

"Most paths give you the chance to choose from a few different abilities at that point, Benning Kidd. That choice will help you further define your path and differentiate it from others pursuing the same path."

Benning frowned. "What choices will I get?"

"Who knows?" Tiddly shrugged. "There's no standard for any path, much less a unique one like yours. The System offers choices based on how a Citizen has walked their path up to level 10. The point is to let the Citizen decide exactly how they want to continue their path in the future." Seeing Benning's confusion, the gnome smiled.

"It's not really that complicated, Benning Kidd. Take a Starship Captain like Argus Leon, for example. He's a cautious man who likes to run from danger, but he's also a creature of habit. The System might offer him a choice between an ability that improves his ship's speed or dive range, one that boosts defenses, and one that lets him take a predetermined action at a large bonus. He'll have to decide what's most important to him: running, being safe in a battle, or staying in his comfort zone. What he chooses will then guide the System's offerings for abilities for his next ten levels."

"So, I'll get offered a choice of abilities based on what I've done as a Corsair so far?"

"Probably, yes. That's not always the case – some paths offer the choice at a higher or lower level, and a very few don't offer the choice at all – but both Starship Captain and Arena Gladiator do, so I'm guessing Stellar Corsair will, as well."

Benning nodded. "So, what do you think I should do to advance my path faster?"

Tiddly frowned. "I know you don't like to hear this, but you're actually advancing at a pretty decent pace, Benning Kidd. Most Citizens take a couple years at least to go from level 9 to 10. In fact, most Citizens don't reach level 10 until they've been at their path for a decade or so; you're way ahead of the curve already."

Benning shook her head. "I don't care what everyone else does, Tiddly. I don't care what the System thinks my progress should be, or if it thinks I'm going too fast. How do I force the System to speed up my advancement?"

Tiddly sighed. "The System has total control over the speed of your advancement, Benning Kidd – except in one case. There's a protocol called 'Great Progress Unchecked', Benning Kidd. It forces the System to recognize when a Citizen expands their horizons or pushes themselves beyond their normal limitations. If you do that, the System will have to acknowledge it with a huge bump in your progress."

"So, how do I do that?" Benning asked. "Do I need to put myself in another unwinnable scenario? Beat a foe that I shouldn't be able to?"

"That might work, except…" Tiddly made a sour face. "You've already done that, Benning Kidd. The System has already acknowledged it once. It might not do it a second time." She shook her head, her braids bouncing as she did. "No, Benning Kidd, what you need to do is stretch yourself. You need to do something that doesn't come easily for you."

"Any ideas?" Benning probed.

"Well, I've got one." Tiddly looked hesitant. "You're a great captain, Benning Kidd, and a great fighter – but you're still working on being a great leader. I think that's the direction that will give you the most gain."

"You mean more training exercises?" Benning sighed. "Like the Kobayashi one?"

"No, I mean actually leading people in combat. Not just coming up with a plan, but directing and commanding them in battle."

Benning looked at Tiddly dubiously. "I do that all the time, Tiddly."

"No, you lead them *into* combat, not *in* combat. There's a difference." The gnome sighed again. "Benning Kidd, because of who you are – and what you were – you're very independent. You don't trust others, and you prefer to do everything yourself. That's worked for you so far, but if you want to grow in your path, you need to learn how to fight alongside others as a team, how to command them so that they all fight in unison. If you can do that, the System will have to acknowledge your growth. It might even be enough to push you to 10th level years ahead of schedule."

Benning looked at the gnome and thought quietly. Tiddly was right; Benning did tend to try to win every battle on her own. She was the first into every boarding action, she led every assault on enemy ships. Even then, though, she didn't command; she just trusted her subordinates to do what they were supposed to while she acted on her own. She used strategy plenty, but she rarely used tactics to control the battlefield – mostly because she had no idea how to do that.

The other issue was part of what Tiddly said. Benning didn't trust others. She'd never had a reason to develop trust. Drones didn't trust because Drones could barely recall anything beyond the last few hours of their existence. The other Drones around them weren't people, they were just things, objects they could interact with. Drones didn't need to trust because their entire lives were tightly controlled by the System.

Benning couldn't help but see every human around her the same way. They were tools to be used, objects she could interact with, nothing more. She didn't trust them any more than she trusted her rifle to shoot on its own or her ship to fight its own battles. If she handled things herself, she knew they were being done correctly; if she let her ship's negaputer make its own decisions, she couldn't be sure it would make the best ones.

Humans aren't like negaputers or rifles, though, she told herself firmly. *They can be trained and taught to do things correctly. I've trained my crew to respond the way I want them to; I can train my soldiers and commanders to do the same thing.* She snorted. *Not that I have the faintest idea where to start.* Fortunately, that at least was fixable.

"Okay, I'm going to need some training modules," she said after a few moments. "I don't really know much about tactics or fleet warfare. I don't know about training or teaching others. Can I learn those things?"

"Absolutely!" Tiddly said, perking up slightly. "I can help you pick out some great training programs that will help with all that! It'll be fun!" The gnome paused, and the joy seemed to slide from her face.

"Benning Kidd – how are you doing?" she asked softly.

"I'm fine," Benning shrugged. "Frustrated with my

path advancement, but otherwise..."

"No, Benning Kidd. You know what I mean. How are you feeling?"

Benning stopped and considered her response for a few seconds before speaking. "I don't know," she admitted at last. "Tiddly, there used to be something inside me that was just – empty. It was a place that didn't feel anything, and it was the reason I always thought I was broken. I knew that place was wrong, but I never knew what it was or why."

"Do you now?"

Benning nodded. "When my memories came back, that place filled up. It's not empty anymore. Now, it just – aches all the time. It hurts." She shook her head. "I almost wish that it was empty again."

"Almost? You don't want to go back to the way things were?"

"No, Tiddly," she said firmly. "No, I don't. The System was controlling me by keeping my memories from me. I never want to be controlled again. I'd rather hurt every moment for the rest of my life." She straightened. "And there are times when it doesn't hurt. When I'm angry, it stops for a while. And when I lose myself in battle or training, I don't notice it anymore."

"I wish I could tell you that it'll go away, Benning Kidd," Tiddly said sympathetically. "I don't know if it will, though. So much was taken from you – I don't know if you'll ever fully heal from that loss." She smiled, and even Benning could tell that it was forced. "In the meantime, though, if training helps, that's what we should do! Come on, Benning Kidd. Let's find you some tactics modules. I can't wait to see what you're offered at level 10!"

CHAPTER 3

The *Hammer* raced through an infinite tunnel of space without moving a fraction of a cim. Red light flooded the bridge, each photon hanging in midair, vibrating endlessly but remaining utterly still at the same moment. The light shifted to amber and then green without changing wavelengths as Benning's mind hung in the space between moments, her senses linked to the ship's 'net and her brain fed the information she needed to survive. Space contracted around her and spread out infinitely at the same time, but nothing changed in that timeless space inside a singularity. The entire universe seemed to spread out before her, stretching away into infinity, and she sped toward it without moving through a single second of time.

The photons slid from green into blue, indigo, and violet, finally becoming something more violet than she had words to describe as the destroyer approached the end of the wormhole. Space slammed back into her as time expanded infinitely, and in that moment, Benning ceased to exist. Her consciousness spread out across eternity, experiencing every moment of time at once as she slipped through the temporal singularity that sealed the wormhole. She hung in an infinite expanse of time for what felt like an eternity before the universe formed around her and her mind crashed into reality once more.

Her body shook and shivered as the *Hammer* exited its deep dive. Tears threatened to leak from her eyes, and the ache in her chest stabbed at her like a knife. She'd traveled through wormholes dozens of times, but she never got used to that moment of nonexistence, when only the negaputer kept her from being utterly unmade by the temporal singularity. She'd been undone, all that she was and could ever be unraveled in that instant and rendered meaningless, and that realization shook the foundation of her reality.

Fortunately, she recovered swiftly. While she couldn't seem to ignore the terrifying passage through a deep dive, she had learned how to put it from her thoughts and let it fade into the depths of her memories. She knew that the 'net helped with that; each passing moment, the memories of the dive faded and lost their sharpness as the 'net helped her mind process them and push them behind her. That was a necessity since if she recalled that moment of nonexistence with perfect clarity, she suspected it would damage her sanity – and it would certainly make her terrified to dive again.

While she recovered, the GPS or galactic positioning system reconnected, getting the vessel's exact location. Deep diving allowed a ship to travel light-days or more in mere seconds – technically, the passage was instantaneous, but it took seconds to enter and leave the wormhole – but it wasn't particularly accurate. Quantum effects dominated within the singularity, and no negaputer could predict the exact point a wormhole would exit because of the uncertainty relation between time and energy. Longer dives required more energy, and that energy caused larger fluctuations in time inside the wormhole. Passing through the exit singularity transmuted those time fluctuations into spatial ones, shifting the exit randomly in space. Longer deep dives had exponentially greater uncertainty, so a dive of a full light-year could put a ship anywhere within a light-day's radius of their intended exit, and a kiloparsec dive, while theoretically possible with sufficient power, could land a ship anywhere within a several hundred light-year radius. That was the main reason the Collective hadn't colonized the entire galaxy or even those beyond. Reaching the edge of the galactic disc in light-year-long dives would take centuries; reaching Andromeda would require millennia.

The crew slowly awoke and returned to their stations. Benning was the only officer onboard the *Hammer*, and only officers could use the As It Is ability to shrug off the effects of deep diving by linking to the ship's 'net. Benning's As It Should Be ability wasn't quite as good as a true officer's would be, only reducing the negative effects of the dive by 50%, which was why dives shook her more deeply than they did someone like Fodor Hendricks or Britella Holland. Staying awake and conscious for a deep dive would kill anyone else on Benning's crew, though, so they spent the passage in deep sleep, basically comatose with only minimal brain function.

"Captain, we are three light-hours from the system edge of Tau Ceti," Brialle Caldwell stated. "Bearing to the star is 322 degrees, four degrees declined."

"Set a course for Gaia Station 86, Helm," Benning instructed. "Two tocks, shallow dives only."

"Aye, captain. Estimated arrival time is forty-eight minutes."

Despite being almost twelve lightyears from Sol, Tau Ceti was one of the first systems colonized by humanity using massive, sub-light generation ships. The reason for that was the star's eight planets, none of which were gas giants and two of which were close to the star's habitable zone. The main sequence star was three-quarters the mass of Sol and remarkably stable, without significant solar activity. It also had a massive debris disc that extended hundreds of AUs and provided plentiful material to build Dyson stations around the star, giving colonists ample living space and shielding the nearby planets from solar radiation until six of the eight were habitable. The swarm also left the star far less visible, reducing its brightness to around 15% of what it should have been and making it invisible from Sol.

The debris disc also left the outer parts of the system essentially empty, though. Tau Ceti didn't have a Kuiper Belt or Oort Cloud the way Sol did; the outer debris had never clumped into larger bodies. That was primarily due to the nearby flare star YZ Ceti, only 1.6 lightyears distant. YZ Ceti wasn't large at just 13% of Sol's mass, but its gravity and periodic flares of radiation were enough to tear apart larger bodies forming in Tau Ceti through tidal action. The few that had managed to form were the first bodies mined when humans arrived in the system, clearing out the debris and leaving the Gaia Stations in their wake.

Gaia 86 didn't look like a typical space station. It was a massive cylinder a hundred kims long and fifty wide, but it lacked the usual orbital rings surrounding it. Instead, long filaments extended from each end of the station and connected to a series of disc-shaped platforms that served as docking bays. The Gaia Stations were old and obsolete, unable to accommodate any ship larger than a clipper or destroyer, but for some reason, they'd never been replaced with more modern designs. Since larger vessels had to bypass these stations to dock at the larger, updated ones orbiting the planets and star itself, the Gaia Stations were inhabited by smaller merchants and brokers – exactly the kind Benning wanted, considering her current cargo.

"Gaia 86, this is *Dawning Glory* requesting docking instructions," Caldwell said as the vessel drew near the station, using the spoofed name Benning had the ship's 'net beaconing.

"*Dawning Glory,* this is Gaia 86. Please confirm your cargo manifest and standby."

"Roger, Gaia 86. Retransmitting our manifest."

Benning watched silently as Caldwell guided the

Hammer to its docking platform, then waited for customs. When the inspector arrived with a single Soldier to oversee the operation, Benning was surprised to see that the woman looked vaguely nonhuman. She was tall, several cims taller than Benning, with thin limbs that seemed almost spindly. A face that was rounder than normal held overly large cobalt blue eyes with wide pupils, set farther apart than Benning expected. Her nose was also large and bulbous, while her mouth had thin, purplish lips. Her exposed skin had a faint magenta tint, and her short blue-white hair looked more like a mane atop her head than anything.

Perhaps even more concerning, a sealed, transparent suit made of flexible microthene covered her from head to toe, including her face. The suit seemed to be of one piece and lay against the woman like a second skin, overlaying her beige spacer suit with lilac trim along the arms and legs. Only the face of the suit protruded in a bubble-like visor that somehow allowed sound to pass through.

<It's an environmental suit, Benning Kidd,> Tiddly said silently in Benning's mind. <It's designed to protect the person wearing it from chemical or biological contamination.>

Wouldn't a standard space suit do the same thing? Benning asked.

<Sure, but an environmental suit is lighter and easier to move in. Plus, you can see through it, so you know who you're talking to.>

"Your manifest says that you're carrying thirty gigs of beryllium-8 and ten of genetic stabilizers," the inspector spoke, her voice oddly layered but not muffled in the slightest by the bubble wrapped about her head. "Do you have anything else you'd like to declare before the inspection?"

"No," Benning shook her head, then hesitated. "The suit you're wearing…"

"A standard envo," the woman replied almost mechanically. "All Cetans wear them in the Gaia Stations to prevent biological contamination."

"Contamination?" Benning asked curiously, but the woman shook her head.

"I'm here for an inspection, not as a tour guide," she said shortly. "You'll find out if you board the station. Now, let's check this cargo…"

The woman performed her scan. Benning watched quietly, hoping that the inspector wouldn't find the gig of genetic mutagen Benning also carried hidden beneath her declared goods. The mutagen wasn't precisely illegal, but the customs duties on it in Tau Ceti were enormous, and Benning didn't really want to lose that much of her profit. She'd hidden it well, scattering it among the less profitable stabilizers so that the inspector would have only about a one in thirty chance of choosing a random container that held the mutagen.

While the inspector checked the cargo, Benning ran some checks of her own to distract herself. It took her only a few minutes to hack into the station's 'net and run a search through it for people of interest to her. She used to check against the station's directory, but a Noble who apparently despised her for being an elevated Drone had overridden her search protocols, so she used less obvious methods, instead. A check of every transaction made on the station in the last thirty standard days took a lot longer than scanning the directory, but she doubted that even a Noble would be able to suppress transaction records without good cause.

"It looks good," the official spoke after several minutes. "I've sent you a list of owed duties. You'll need to pay those before you can board the station or offload your goods."

"I will," Benning assured the woman. "Thanks."

The long filaments connecting the docking platforms to the main station were, as Benning suspected, elevator shafts. As she, Keanna Lucroy, and a second Soldier stepped into the elevator, a voice sounded in Benning's ears.

"Welcome to Tau Ceti, Citizen," a smooth, male voice spoke, seeming to come from nowhere but sounding like the speaker stood right in front of her. Judging from her crew's startled reactions, they heard it as well, but it seemed that most of the elevator's passengers either heard nothing or had heard the voice enough times that it didn't affect them.

"Our system is fairly unique in the Collective, as it was the first system discovered that held extraterrestrial life," the voice continued. "This life still flourishes in protected preserves on each planet, and our system has stringent protocols designed to protect that life from the effects of non-native biological contamination. Please note that failing to observe these protocols is a criminal offense punishable by fines, expulsion from the system, loss of levels, and imprisonment depending on the severity of the offense."

Benning had started to tune the voice out, assuming it was some sort of tour guide designed for tourists, but the warning about the possible consequences of failing to follow the system's rules held her attention firmly. She'd come to Tau Ceti to advance her path – just traveling to a new system moved her a couple percentage points forward – and losing a level because she'd failed to hear what the rules were would just be foolish.

"...native Cetans have integrated into the local biology through genetic therapy," the voice continued. "Any Citizen wishing to become a permanent resident of Tau Ceti must undergo similar therapies. Contact a biological counselor in any station for more details.

"To prevent xenobiological contamination, all visitors must undergo decontamination before entering a station.

This decontamination will kill any non-human biological organisms brought into it and may be harmful to those who have experienced extensive genetic modification. If you have genetic modification, please speak with security before entering decontamination. Bypassing or subverting decontamination procedures is a punishable offense.

"Cetans in the Gaia Stations wear protective environmental suits, or envos. Similarly, all non-Cetans must remain in sealed suits in any planetary station or on any planetary surface. Tampering with or deliberately damaging a Cetan's envo outside of self-defense is a punishable offense, as is unsealing a space suit in a planetary station. Unsealing or removing a space suit on a planetary surface is a major offense and will be punished harshly."

They're serious about keeping out contamination, aren't they? Benning asked silently.

<It sounds like it, yeah. Probably best to be extra careful, just in case.>

The decontamination procedure wasn't an especially intrusive one. Benning had to retract her armor, and a combination of radiation and the station's nanofield scrubbed her skin, hair, and exposed orifices to remove all non-human organisms. That almost caused her a huge problem: when the station's nanites approached her, her nanodefenses rose immediately to block them. She scrambled to suppress them, forcing them to ignore the intruders, but before she managed to gain control of them, her nanofield seized control of a few hundred of the station's nanites, binding them to her control. She waited for an alarm of some kind to go off, but apparently, the station didn't notice the loss.

<It's more likely that the 'net expects to lose some nanites during decontamination,> Tiddly suggested. <Everyone's nanofield provides some defense against nanite

intrusions, after all. That's why nanoweapons aren't very effective or widespread.>

Wait, so why is my nanodefense ability such a big deal, then?

<Because you can defend yourself against nanoattacks that others can't, Benning Kidd. Nano-disassemblers are a good example: they're designed to bypass a nanofield's natural defenses. No one's sure exactly how, though, since the technology is proprietary, and disassemblers usually self-destruct if they're caught. That's why Emmed Oswald was so excited to get some from you; if he can work out their programming, he can figure out how they get through a nanofield and maybe counter it.

<These decontaminators are the same, but they're not as effective as a disassembler, so the 'net knows that it'll lose some with every decontamination sequence. Now, if you coopted most or all of them, you'd probably set off an alarm.>

Benning nodded to herself. She'd wondered why disassemblers were so dangerous when everyone had a nanofield that could theoretically be programmed to destroy them. *I'll bet Emmed Oswald would be happy to get some of these decontaminators, too, then, wouldn't he?*

<Probably, but not as much as he was with the nano-disassemblers. A lot of people would pay for a way to shield themselves against disassemblers; not as many would be interested in getting through decontamination without being affected.>

Good point.

The station beyond the decontamination chamber wasn't laid out in a standard fashion. Most stations used dark matter and energy to generate gravitational fields, allowing them to stack their decks vertically. The Gaia Stations had been designed to use rotation to simulate gravity, though, so "down" meant toward the outer hull. The lowest deck lay closest to the hull with each higher deck moving inward toward the center. A central shaft sealed off from the rest of the station contained the station's engines, power plants, storage, and negaputers. The overheads were lower than normal, only three ems high in most places with a few taller passages to accommodate large cargoes, and the design was less open and more compartmentalized. Benning could see the utility in that, at least for an older station, since a hull breach in one area could be easily sealed off without the entire station losing atmosphere.

Benning wound her way through the mazelike corridors to deck fourteen. She stopped before a coral hatch with a holographic image of a large, squid-like creature sticking out of a spiral shell floating above it. The hatch opened swiftly as she approached, dissolving as its nanofield turned it into vapor then reforming behind her as she stepped through. The room beyond was a typical receiving area in Benning's experience; an extremely attractive woman with dark skin, and light brown hair sat behind a faux wood desk, surrounded by green plants and illuminated by a light that was bright enough to see clearly but gentle enough to avoid eye strain. A faint scent wafted into Benning's nostrils, something barely detectable that caused her pulse to quicken slightly, and faint sounds in the background soothed her at a deep, almost fundamental level.

"Hello, Citizen," the receptionist said brightly. "Welcome to Nautilus Mercantile. My designation is Marenda Shou, and I'd be happy to help you in any way I can." She smiled winningly at Benning, and the Corsair felt her body react to the woman's presence. She ignored the sensation, though, pushing it aside as easily as she would a minor injury.

"My designation is Rane Cava," she replied, using the spoofed ID she radiated. "I have an appointment with Jardan

Eberl."

"Ah, yes, Rane Cava," the woman said, an expression of what Tiddly assured Benning was disappointment flashing across her face for a moment. "Jardan Eberl is expecting you. Please, follow me."

Jardan Eberl, like the customs inspector, was obviously a native Cetan. His short, stiff-looking hair was mostly white with streaks of brown, and his orange eyes had large pupils. His body, though, was more muscular than the inspector's had been, and his features were closer to human. He rose as Benning entered the room, and she felt his presence reaching out to her, stimulating her body and causing her heart to pound as he smiled in a friendly fashion. She pushed the artificial stimulation aside with only a minor effort. Argus Leon, who'd originally taught her how to deal with merchants like these, had shut down part of his endocrine system to ignore these effects, but Benning's huge Willpower made sweeping them aside practically trivial.

"Rane Cava," the man said warmly, inviting her to sit before he returned to his chair. "Welcome to Gaia 86. I would ask how the trip was, but deep diving…" He shuddered.

"I believe Erix Adelsson contacted you about my shipment," she said, pushing past banalities. She wasn't good at the sort of pointless chat the man was trying to engage her in, and she suspected that he'd find a way to turn that weakness to his advantage if she gave him a chance.

"Ah, yes," Eberl nodded after only a moment's hesitation. "He did, and I admit to a certain interest. Beryllium isn't that valuable here – we lift it from Tau Ceti, after all – but the genetic materials you're carrying have decent value."

"You lift beryllium-9," she corrected. "Beryllium-8 isn't easy to make, even with fusion reactors, and it decays in attoseconds if not kept in containment, but it's the most useful isotope for neutron and gamma shielding."

"True," the man nodded. "But Tau Ceti doesn't have a huge fleet, so that sort of shielding isn't in high demand here."

"Really? My understanding was that you use beryllium-8 extensively to shield your nature preserves from the neutron background." Benning shrugged. "If you're not interested, I'm sure I can find someone who is."

"I didn't say I wasn't interested," Eberl said quickly, "just that it's not as valuable as the rest of your cargo. I could probably offer you five credits a gig for the beryllium."

"The Namaat stations are currently offering twelve," Benning snorted. "That's across the system, sure, but I'll eat the gas for more than double the credits."

He looked at her, his wide eyes narrowing slightly for a moment. "You're well informed," he noted.

"Knowledge is a captain's most valuable cargo," Benning grinned, repeating one of Fodor Hendrick's sayings. A system's exchange rates were usually confidential information to prevent captains from skipping middlemen like Eberl and selling directly to buyers. Not much information was truly hidden from someone with the Cyberwarfare skill, though.

"I could do eight," Eberl said after a few moments.

"Ten," Benning countered. "Anything lower, and I'd still make a bit more by going to Namaat and eating the gas and higher customs duties. Plus, you can sell at the native rate, which we both know is higher."

The man sat quietly, his eyes unblinking. "Where did you hear that?" he asked softly.

"Does it matter? The point is, you can sell for more than I can, so you'll still make plenty of credits. That doesn't even touch the genetic materials that only natives are allowed to buy or sell. With the recent native plague on Tian, the mutagens will be especially useful, since they'll help the lifeforms there adapt to the disease more rapidly."

He stared at her for long moments before shaking his head. "I'm not sure how you know about that, Rane Cava, but you're right. There is something of a market for mutagens right now – which is why they're taxed so heavily. Tian's government is buying mutagens and stabilizers at ridiculously low rates, but they're waiving the taxes if you sell to them directly. It makes it hard to turn a profit on them."

Benning nodded. "So, what are you offering?"

"I can do sixty per gig for the stabilizers," he said thoughtfully, then hesitated. "And – ninety for the mutagens."

She chuckled and rose from her seat. "That's half of their value, Jardan Eberl, and we both know it. 120 and 200."

"Ha!" he laughed. "That would destroy my profit. I could go eighty and 100, I suppose."

"100 and 160. They'll sell the moment you have them in hand. It's fast, easy credits."

"Ninety and 140. That's my best offer."

"Done," she agreed, sitting back down and pulling up the contract he sent her, reviewing it silently. As she read, she fixed him with a glance. "What are the arenas around here like?"

He shrugged. "Like most other places, I assume. Gladiators fight and spectators bet. There aren't any arenas on the Gaia Stations, only farther in-system, so I don't get to them much."

"Do they level the fights, or are they random? Any

tournaments going on?"

"Oh, the fights are always fairly equal, I think. I'm not sure about any tournaments, though. At least, not since the Fleet crackdown on them."

"The what?" Benning asked, freezing for a moment. "What crackdown? The Fleet has stopped allowing tournaments?"

"No, nothing like that," the man laughed. "The Citizens would revolt if they did. No, they've just started putting a Fleet presence at every tournament. Something about a wanted fugitive who's a gladiator. I guess they committed some sort of crimes against the Collective, and now the Fleet is hunting for them."

Benning's heart began to pound, but she forced her face to remain calm. "I go to a lot of tournaments," she said as casually as she could. "Maybe I've heard of the gladiator. Do you know their designation?"

"Of course. She's got a Collective-wide bounty on her head, after all – one that any number of people would jump to collect, I'd imagine. Her designation is Benning Kidd, and the Fleet wants to capture her alive. They've got ships looking for her in every system."

CHAPTER 4

<This seems like a bad idea, Benning Kidd,> Tiddly said worriedly in Benning's thoughts. <If the Fleet is monitoring gladiatorial arenas looking for you, maybe heading to one isn't the best choice.>

Benning walked calmly and confidently up to the competitor's entrance of the Tian 2 Arena despite the nervous energy swirling in her stomach. As she did, she double-checked her spoofed ID one more time.

AMALISE DOYLE
(BENNING KIDD)
Citizen Path: Mercenary Soldier (Stellar Corsair)
Level: 11 (9)
To Next Level: 17%

Physicality: 12.9
Coordination: 12.7
Resistance: 12.9

Acuity: 9.3 (11.5)
Willpower: 8.7 (18.5)
Social: 8.3 (11.1)

SKILLS
Combat Tactics 17.4 (0)
Conditioning: 19.8
(Cyberwarfare: 16.2)

(Leadership: 19)
Martial Combat: 20.3
(Nanoresistance: 2.5)
(Naval Tactics: 22.5)
(Sense Deceit: 4.7)
(Starfaring: 18.8)
Weapons Expertise: 19.2

Upon arriving at the station orbiting high above Tian, the fifth planet in the Tau Ceti system and the closer of the naturally habitable ones, Benning had immediately hacked into the local 'net. She ran her customary check to make sure no one of any significance to her was present on the station, then worked her way into the respawn list. Amalise Doyle was fourth on that list, a Mercenary Soldier who'd fought recently in the arena and died in the process. Benning shifted the woman's respawn to happen in several days, then assumed her designation as closely as she could. She left her physical stats alone since they were appropriate for a Mercenary Soldier of Doyle's level but hid her advanced mental stats and most of her skills. She'd had to pretend to possess Combat Tactics, a skill that every Mercenary Soldier had according to Tiddly, but otherwise left her existing skills alone.

She'd used her infiltration suite to modify her appearance significantly, as well. Her armor and helmet both gleamed deep blue with dark red highlights, now, and beneath the shaded visor, her skin and hair both shone a dark, chestnut brown. She still couldn't change the shade of her eyes, but her face was slightly rounder than before, with a protruding chin and plumper cheekbones. The process of using her nanofield to rebuild her features was uncomfortable and time-consuming, but Benning felt reasonably certain that she would fool anyone familiar with her current true appearance.

<The Fleet wants to take you alive, Benning Kidd,> Tiddly reminded her. <You know what that means.>

Yes, I do, Tiddly, Benning sighed silently. *They either want to imprison me or spawn-camp me down a few levels – or both, most likely.*

<Exactly. Why risk it? You can advance your path through marine combat, too, after all.>

I can, Tiddly, but not as quickly, and we both know it. I have to fight for glory and renown to really push that side of my path forward, and I think that's part of what's been slowing me down lately. I've avoided arena combat and focused on fighting onboard ships.

<But Benning, you could always go back to somewhere like Wolf or the Oort Cloud, someplace where the Fleet doesn't have much of a presence…>

But those places aren't great for someone low-leveled like me to advance their career. I'd end up fighting people too strong for me again, just like the last time I was there. There's no glory or renown in fighting a level fifty gladiator and getting beaten to scrit, Tiddly.

Benning could feel the AI about to argue, but she cut the gnome off. *Tiddly, I have to do this. If I'm too scared to face the Fleet, how will I handle those Nobles hunting me? We both know that eventually, I'm going to have to deal with them, and they're more dangerous than the Fleet. And how will I confront the System itself if I can't face a few Fleet soldiers? I can't start hiding, or I'll spend the rest of my life doing it.*

<Okay, Benning Kidd,> Tiddly said quietly at last. <I understand, and you're right. You do have bigger enemies than the Fleet. Let's hope that your disguise holds up, I guess.>

"Welcome back, Citizen Amalise Doyle," a man greeted

her as she passed through the competitors' entrance into the arena. The man wore a bright pink suit with lime green tracing along it and was obviously a native Cetan from his appearance. Unlike in Gaia 86, though, the native wasn't ensconced in an envo suit; on the planetary stations, foreigners had to remain sealed in their space suits, while natives roamed freely.

"Are you back to compete in the Arena already?" the man asked, blinking his large, copper eyes, his purplish lips spread in a smile.

"Yes," Benning nodded.

"Excellent! I'm sure this time will go much better than your last match." The man turned to his screen. "As you've already completed the arena contract, I'll just need you to reaffirm that you'll abide by its terms."

"Can you resend those to me?" Benning asked. "I make a habit to always read them before agreeing, just in case."

"Wise of you," the man agreed. "Although if the terms changed, we'd have to get you to sign a new contract, of course. Still – here you are."

The details of the arena's contract appeared in her vision, and Benning scanned them briefly. While it would have taken her a minute or more to completely read through the agreement, Tiddly's digital brain took in and analyzed the document in under a second.

<It's standard enough, Bening Kidd,> the gnome assured her. <It does say that the prohibition against destroying an envo suit or space suit is lifted within an arena battle, though.>

That's good. It would be hard to fight if you couldn't damage the opponent's suit in any way.

<I guess the arena agrees. It looks like you'll be fighting inside a biocontainment field, and there's an

addendum that prohibits you from altering, tampering with, or damaging the field in any way. There's also more stringent penalties for using bioweapons, but that's about it. Everything else is standard: no nanoweapons, gravitational devices, heavy weapons, or high explosives.>

Benning closed the contract and nodded at the man. "I agree to the terms," she told him.

"Good." He touched his holoscreen with an affirmative nod. "Also, you'll need to submit to an intrusive scan, I'm afraid."

"An intrusive scan?" Benning echoed, slightly alarmed. "Why?"

The man shrugged. "New Fleet regulation. All entrants must submit to an intrusive scan to confirm their identity."

"That seems awfully invasive," she protested.

"You aren't the only competitor who feels that way, Amalise Doyle. Participation has dropped by almost thirty percent since the new regulation, and we've had to change all of our tournament entry policies to accommodate the rule." He shuddered. "You wouldn't believe how long it takes to do an intrusive scan of thirty thousand contestants."

<It – might be okay, Benning Kidd,> Tiddly said slowly. <This might even be a good way to train your Nanoresistance skill.>

What do you mean?

<Well, unlike deep scanners that use negative energy to bypass armor and shielding to ping your 'net, an intrusive scanner sends nanites to link directly to your 'net and hack into it. Your nanodefense rating should help shield you from it.>

Won't that just set off a separate type of alarm when the

scan returns nothing? Benning asked skeptically.

<It would, unless you can cyberhack the scanner's nanites and force them to return the profile you want. You did it to the nano-disassemblers; there's no reason you can't do the same thing to these.>

"Okay, I agree to the scan," Benning said after a long moment. Part of her wanted to refuse and walk away – that would probably be the smart choice, really – but if the Fleet was doing this in every system in the Collective, she'd have to either face it eventually or abandon this entire side of her path. Besides, caution and restraint weren't what made a Stellar Corsair; her path was all about taking high risks for high rewards.

"Excellent," the attendant said with a smile. "Just relax. This will only take a few seconds..."

Benning closed her eyes and reached out with her nanofield, touching the fields and 'nets surrounding her. She felt the station's 'net pulsing through the air, as well as the personal 'nets of the attendant, the two guards hidden just out of sight, and those guards' armor and weapons. Each of those was surrounded by a nanofield that repaired and maintained its originator, as well as connecting it to not only the station's 'net but the space-spanning Overnet. The arena podium pulsed with its own 'net and field, and hidden inside it, she felt the intrusive scanner powering up as it activated. A cloud of nanites swept out from the podium and raced toward Benning, descending on her from all directions.

Her field responded instantly, lashing out at the intruding nanites. Her disassemblers tore the invading nanites apart, but her hacking field latched onto the invaders, their tiny 'nets connecting with the scanner's nanites. When she'd connected to the nano-disassemblers, she'd barely noticed it, but the scanners were designed to link to her system. Instantly, she felt millions of tiny pings echoing against her skull as the scanners tried to connect to her 'net through her own nanofield.

The pressure of so many new linkages was almost too much for her. Her 'net activated instantly to hold out the intrusive attacks, but they kept slamming into her, their presence almost physical pain in her thoughts. Had she not already dealt with two nano-disassembler attacks and the unspeakable agony that accompanied them, the sheer force of all those new connections might have rendered her unconscious. She had, though, so she stubbornly pushed aside the sensations beating against her mind, trusting her 'net's upgrades to hold out the nanites' attacks. Instead of defending against them, she reached out and sent her own pings at the scanners, assaulting them with her Cyberwarfare skill.

To her surprise, like the disassemblers, the scanning nanites had practically no defenses against her skill. She wasn't sure why, but it didn't matter; she took control of as many as she could and had them echo back her beaconed status. The rest she simply held until her disassemblers could destroy them. Eventually, the scan ended, and she gathered the remaining hacked nanites. She could feel their presence in her 'net, not really under her control but no longer connected to the scanning device, either.

I need to go visit Emmed Oswald sooner rather than later, she mused. *If I keep collecting nanites like this, I'm going to be stopping by to see him regularly to incorporate them into my nanofield.*

The entire process had taken only a few seconds, but judging from the frown on the attendant's face, that was a bit longer than he'd been expecting. At last, though, his expression cleared. "Ah, there we go. Okay, the scan confirms your designation, Amalise Doyle. Please report to check-in for opponent selection."

"Thanks," Benning nodded, moving past the man, trying to hide the relief that flooded her body. She didn't know if the hidden guards were normal, or if they were from the Fleet, there hunting her. It didn't matter, though; either way, if her designation had become public, it would probably have gone badly for her. She might have been able to escape, but once the station's 'net was alerted to her true identity, it would undo her hacks, and she'd beacon correctly to everyone in sight. She could probably handle a couple guards; an entire station's worth of defenders was a different story.

To distract herself from her worries as she headed deeper into the arena, she sent her thoughts toward Tilly. *Tiddly, why were the scanners so easy to hack?* she asked curiously. *I mean, I get why the disassemblers were – no one's supposed to survive long enough to hack them – but that reasoning doesn't really work with an intrusive scan.*

<Well, unless you're a Nano-engineer or Nanomancer, you aren't supposed to be able to sense them, Benning Kidd,> the gnome explained. <They don't radiate the way most nanites do until they've connected to their target's system, so most people don't even know they're there.>

Does that mean that a Nano-engineer or Nanomancer could do what I just did?

<An engineer with the Cyberwarfare skill could, which is why Emmed Oswald wanted the skill. Really, anyone with Nanoresistance and Cyberwarfare could do what you did, I suppose, but I've never heard of anyone else with the Nanoresistance skill.>

What about a Nanomancer?

<Do they get Nanoresistance? No; they have a Nanodefense rating as a normal part of their path, so they don't need the skill.>

No, I mean, could someone like Veera Meijers have beaten that scan?

<Oh! Well, yeah, sure. A Nanomancer of sufficient level gets the ability to cloak themselves from scans. They don't beacon falsely, though; they just aren't there as far as a scanner's concerned. It helps them to attack from hiding, which is a big part of what they do. They conceal themselves and send their nanites out to do their bidding, then slip away without anyone knowing they were there.>

Benning frowned at that thought. If Veera Meijers could hide from scans, she could technically enter a station without leaving any record of her passage so long as she didn't spend or earn any credits. Stations logged things like who passed through checkpoints or used doors, but Benning was certain they relied on scanners for that information. A skilled Nanomancer might be like a ghost, slipping into and out of a station totally undetected – which would render Benning's scans for Veera Meijers moot.

She headed to the check-in station, where she was told that she'd be fighting a Citizen named Reesha Divakar. Benning looked up what information she could on the woman while she waited for her match to start. Divakar was a Stellar Marine, a soldier who specialized in attacking heavily defended targets like space stations and outposts. She wore heavy armor and carried weapons that were highly effective against similarly armored foes, but she lacked flexibility and maneuverability.

When Benning stepped into the arena and found herself in the middle of a wide, metallic platform, she couldn't help but grin. Clouds of thick gas swirled past her, blocking her vision, and her 'net informed her that the external temperature was about 250 Kelvin, within her suit's tolerances but cold enough that wounds would add a new danger: frostbite. Gravity felt lighter than normal, but even so, the heavy atmosphere pushed against her on all sides uncomfortably. The wind screamed past her, driving to her left with significant force.

Despite all that, she was perfectly happy with the arena. The clouds would hinder both competitors' visibility equally, but Benning's ability to scout with her nanofield would expand her senses significantly. The heavy air pressure would make Divakar's standard loadout a serious burden, and the high winds would make even the Marine's usual 30mm rifle highly inaccurate. The arena didn't totally favor Benning, but it hampered Divakar more than it did the Corsair.

<Uranian sky mining platforms,> Tiddly observed. <Judging from the gravity and wind, just above the mantle. There should be a system of tubes connecting this platform to those nearby and collection towers that suck in gas and compress it into liquid that's stored beneath you.>

Benning switched her loadout from her heavier weapons to her lighter, more rapidly firing ones. Her Arcbar rifle lacked the penetrating power of the heavier Foehammer, but it could fire up to 2,000 24mm slugs per minute compared to the Foehammer's single shot capability. With the chaotic wind, more bullets would be better than heavy ones.

Her nanofield reach out and touched the area around her, and immediately, her visor flickered to life, displaying the objects her field detected. As Tiddly said, a tower stood no more than five ems to Benning's right, its top lost in the swirling clouds as it extended beyond the reach of her nanofield. Benning began to move forward slowly, heading toward the tower – if the arena had put Divakar close to her, she'd need the cover. As she approached the structure, though, her nanofield began to tingle strangely, and her skin crawled as if thousands of insects swarmed over her.

She stopped immediately and stepped back; the tingling faded slightly, but only a moment later, a massive explosion ripped through the air and filled her vision with white light. Her ears rang with the roar of the explosion, and she fell back as something impacted her chest. A glance at her resistance bar told her that it hadn't dropped, so whatever just struck her wasn't powerful enough to damage her, but it certainly left her stunned for a few seconds as her vision and hearing cleared.

What the Hole was that?

<Lightning strike, I think,> Tiddly replied. <Uranus has a lot of lightning storms, Benning Kidd. The mining towers are designed to attract the lightning and use it to help power them. You might want to avoid them just to be safe.>

Good call.

Benning made her way to the edge of the platform, carefully avoiding any towers she encountered on the way. She quickly learned that if she came within three ems of a tower, her skin would start to tingle; at two ems, it would discharge into her, not harming her but certainly throwing off her equilibrium. Even worse, each static strike sent her nanofield into chaos for several seconds, causing her visor's view to spin and swirl chaotically even after her vision returned. The platform ended at a simple railing that she followed around until she found a microthene tunnel that led her to another platform.

She continued across two more platforms until she felt the presence of a strange nanofield enter her perception. She dropped to the ground at once and turned her rifle toward the new threat, waiting patiently. As she lay still, though, she felt her skin starting to prickle once more, and she quickly rolled sideways, scrambling to her feet as a blast of electricity arced through the air behind her. The noise blasted her ears, but she'd managed to squeeze her eyes shut, so at least she still had her vision. Her nanofield buzzed in the aftermath of the strike, though, obscuring her sense of her opponent.

Okay, so the arena isn't going to let me sit in wait for her. Got it.

A red warning in Benning's visor caused the Corsair to dive to the side. A crack rang in Benning's ears as something flashed past her, and she realized that the lightning strike must have alerted Divakar to her presence. She moved sideways quickly, trying to stabilize her nanofield, and another bullet raced past her, the wind and her movement throwing her opponent's aim off. Benning rushed into the clouds to escape, but another bullet followed her, this one racing ahead of her by a full em. Divakar must have had a scanner of some kind to track Benning, but it obviously wasn't very good, or she'd have already hit the Corsair.

Benning's nanofield crystallized, and Divakar's form flashed in her visor. She leveled her rifle and fired a five-round burst, tracking her slugs as the wind carried them wide and to Divakar's right. The Marine responded instantly, rolling sideways and coming to a knee, then tossed something in Benning's direction. The Corsair's visor flared red once more, and Benning leaped away from the flying object as it struck the platform and exploded. The impact of the grenade sent Benning hurtling through the air, rolling her perilously close to a tower and dropping her resistance bar by 7%. She managed to halt her momentum before her skin tingled and scrambled to her feet, locating her foe a moment later.

She unleashed a series of three-round bursts, walking her fire to her left as her bullets swung right. She saw three of her bursts strike her opponent, but Divakar simply absorbed the impacts and tossed another grenade in Benning's direction. Benning dove sideways again, rolling swiftly, and this time, the grenade explosion passed mostly above her. She fired again, once more walking her bullets into her opponent and unloading twenty rounds into the woman's chest. Divakar staggered back at that and reached for another grenade, forcing Benning to stop firing and flee the incoming explosion.

The two stalked each other across the platform for several minutes. Benning moved swiftly, using her lighter weight and the lessened gravity to stay ahead of Divakar, while the Marine advanced steadily toward the Corsair, obviously trying to press Benning against the platform edge and nullifying her greater maneuverability. Divakar alternated between her rifle and grenades, using both to herd Benning along. Benning, in return, alternated between firing her Arcbar and her Razor. The little pistol fired a beam of unstable neutrinos that passed through Divakar's armor and decayed into gamma radiation and fast-moving electrons that played havoc with her 'net. The handgun barely darkened Divakar's health aura, but it kept the woman off-balance and gave Benning the space she needed to stay ahead of the Marine.

Benning saw her chance at last as she dove away from another grenade blast, knowing that she was closing on the edge of the platform. If she reached it, Divakar would rush her, and in a melee fight, Benning suspected she would lose. She came to her feet and noticed that her new position placed her in a line between her foe and a tower, a vantage that Divakar had been careful not to offer so far. She lifted her rifle and fired, unloading half a magazine into the woman in a matter of seconds, and Divakar stumbled back, the sheer force of the impacts driving her backwards. She took a step back, then two – and Benning quickly ceased fire and turned away as the Marine stepped just too close to a tower.

The flare of lightning was far less deafening at twenty ems, but Benning spun back to see Divakar staggering, shaking her head as the blast stunned her briefly. Benning switched out her Arcbar for her Foehammer and rushed forward, getting to only five ems distance before firing directly into the Marine's visor. Divakar's head snapped back, and a second bullet cracked her visor. As the woman stumbled, something fell from her hand to the ground between the two.

The grenade's thunderous explosion knocked Benning back and slid her across the ground. Her resistance bar plummeted to forty percent as the blast pummeled her internal organs, and Benning felt her autoinjector send a shot of medigel into her bloodstream to rapidly patch the internal bleeding. She pushed herself up to one knee, her left leg sticking stiffly out to the side, unable to bend. She blinked as her vision cleared and froze as she saw Divakar standing above her, holding what looked like a saw-bladed polearm pointed directly at a gash in Benning's breastplate. The spike of the polearm blazed with the blue energy of plasma, and it hovered cims from Benning's chest. Even as the medigel worked inside her, Benning knew she wouldn't heal in time to stop Divakar from killing her.

"I – I yield," Benning said after a brief pause. Instantly, Divakar stepped back, lifting her polearm and offering Benning a hand up as the arena manager announced the Marine's victory to the sound of sudden cheering.

"Good fight," the woman said in a monotone voice.

"Not good enough," Benning shrugged as the gas began to fade and the arena lights shone above them.

"It almost was. One more shot to the visor would have ended it." Divakar shrugged. "If you had better armor, you would have won. Liquid metal's fine, but it's better with a neutronium underlayer to stop things like my grenade getting through." She touched her chest plate, which was scarred but not breached by the blast.

"I'll look into that," Benning nodded.

The Marine hesitated. "You're not Amalise Doyle," she said briefly. "Are you?"

"What are you talking about?" Benning replied, trying to keep her voice and body language as calm as possible.

"You don't fight like her; you're better. In an environment like this, I'd have ended her the moment we met. You fought smart, staying back and kiting me around." The woman shrugged. "I don't really care, but I thought you should know that if you want to impersonate someone, you have to copy how they fight, as well."

Benning grimaced inside her helmet. She hadn't thought of copying another person's fighting style before. She wondered if she'd given herself away by the way she fought; if she had, the Fleet would be waiting for her when she left the arena.

"That's good advice," she finally said. "Thanks."

"As I said, I don't much care one way or the other. I'm just glad it was a good fight." She clapped her hand on Benning's shoulder. "Now, let's clear the arena for the next pair. Maybe we'll meet again – and next time, maybe you'll get that third shot off."

"Maybe," Benning laughed. "I look forward to finding out."

As the woman walked away, Benning watched her curiously. The ache in her chest had vanished during the battle, as it always did, but it was returning in force once more. Alongside it, though, she felt something new, an odd warmth that she didn't remember feeling before. It wasn't unpleasant; in fact, it felt similar to winning a battle or defeating an enemy.

She shook off the strange feeling and headed out of the arena. As she walked, she glanced at her status, and the warmth in her chest vanished at once. Her path progress had only gone up a single percent, and her renown stood unchanged.

Tiddly, why didn't my renown drop from that loss? And why didn't my path increase more rapidly?

<Because you were hiding your designation, Benning Kidd,> the gnome explained. <You can't gain renown if no one knows it's you, and without that renown, your path doesn't advance as quickly.>

Benning halted just past the exit to the competitors' area. *But if I reveal my designation, the Fleet will try to capture me.*

<It sounds like it, yeah.>

Benning frowned. *Wait, I thought that the System always allows Citizens to advance their paths if they want to. Isn't there some kind of protocol about that? It's got me trapped so I can't advance, Tiddly!*

<Yeah, there is. It's not the System that's the problem, though. It's the Fleet that's stopping you.>

Still, the System has to have a way out, doesn't it? I mean, there has to be a way for me to fight and gain renown without being spawn camped back to level one. Otherwise, the System's allowing the Fleet to halt my progression.

Tiddly was silent for a moment. <I suppose – I suppose that's true,> she admitted after a moment. <There has to be a way for you to do this, Benning Kidd. You'll just have to figure it out.>

I will, Tiddly, Benning vowed grimly. *I have to grow if I want to become a Noble, and not even the Fleet is going to stop me.*

CHAPTER 5

"Entering Struve System, Commodore," the young man sitting at the helm of Benning's battlecruiser said in a bored-sounding monotone. "Initial scans are clear."

"Set course for the rally point," Benning instructed a bit nervously. The battlecruiser was a titan of a ship, a massive sphere over three kims across, large enough to fit almost two hundred destroyers like the *Resolute Hammer* inside it. Over two million Citizens, Soldiers, and Workers made up its crew, not to mention the unknown number of Drones Benning knew had to be present thanks to the respawn center located on board.

She also knew that she'd never find those Drones, no matter how hard she tried; the system would keep them from her the same way it kept her from revealing their existence to anyone else. She'd gone searching for the Drones aboard her station – IS-39267 had a respawn facility so it had to have Drones aboard somewhere – and she'd never come close to finding it. In fact, she couldn't recall seeing a Drone in a respawn center before; surely, she would have seen one entering a facility to be prepped for respawn.

<No, you won't, Benning Kidd,> Tiddly said softly. <Remember, the System controls what you see and experience through your 'net and nanofield. It won't let you see or hear a Drone, even though you've probably passed by thousands of them without knowing it.>

Benning's jaw tightened at the thought of the System manipulating her like that, but she forced herself to relax.

One day, she promised, she'd find a way to stop being controlled, but until that day, there was no use getting angry over things she couldn't change.

Besides, she knew that part of her frustration stemmed from sitting in the command chair of the massive battlecruiser. She'd never commanded anything so large and complicated before. The sensory input from Better Captain than Crew was almost overwhelming as she felt the entirety of the massive ship, including the bay full of cutters waiting to be deployed and the millions of missiles, bombs, and torpedoes all ready to be fired. The ship had thousands of graser banks, antimatter emitters, glasers, plasma generators, and neutrino beams, all powered by four separate negmass plants dedicated to the weapons array. Two more plants maintained the ship's enormous shroud and EM shielding, while three others ran the huge engines and internal systems such as life support – and she could sense the statuses of all those systems and plants in an instant. She had to deliberately ignore most of the information coming her way; it was just too much to take in all at once.

"Commodore, would you like an update on the fleet status?" the older woman sitting at one of three Ops stations spoke up, interrupting Benning's thoughts. The Corsair flinched slightly; protocol dictated that the commander of a fleet check its status upon entering a new system. She was getting distracted and flustered from the sheer size and complexity of the battlecruiser, something she couldn't afford.

"Go ahead, Ops," she nodded, forcing herself to focus.

"Battle groups one and two are intact and moving toward the rally point," the woman intoned. "Battle group three came out of dive near a gravity well and will need several minutes to reorganize."

"Thank you, Ops," Benning nodded, seeing the same

picture in her own thoughts. Each battle group consisted of a single battlefrigate, a warship a third the diameter of her battlecruiser, ten destroyers, thirty fast frigates, and sixty corvettes. The groups moved in a standard formation with the battlefrigate in the center surrounded by the fast frigates in a sphere, the destroyers in the vanguard and rear, and the corvettes spread out along the flanks. The battlecruiser's scanners could pick up the individual ships, but Benning's tactical display showed each group as a single icon, far easier to track.

"Any updates on our target?" she asked.

"Negative, Commodore. Last readings showed our target at Lagrange L4 around S-Beta at point-four AU."

Benning nodded; L4 was a stable point where the gravity of the small red dwarf star S-Beta and its second planet, Praxis, would hold an object at a constant distance relative to both bodies. L4 moved along the planetary orbit of Praxis ahead of the planet and was typically filled with dust, ice, and small, rocky bodies that accumulated in the Lagrange point, but her target would have had no difficulty clearing that debris.

The battlecruiser hurtled toward the rally point, where her fleet would regroup and prepare for the assault on their target. Battle group three still trailed far behind in her display; they'd come up from a dive near a massive object circling around the edge of the binary system, and the object's gravity well scattered the ships, forcing them to take time to return to their formation. She never dealt with that sort of issue when flying her own ship – she could point the *Hammer* in any random direction and fly it across the galaxy secure in the knowledge that she'd never come close to hitting anything in the vastness of space – but with battlegroups and fleets spread out over linutes, encounters with massive bodies were something she had to consider.

As the fleet approached the rally point, the L2 Lagrange point near the inner planet Fortes, on the opposite side of the planet from its star, flashes suddenly erupted in Benning's vision.

"Dive splashes!" the woman at Ops said, her voice tense. "Hundreds of them, Commodore! We're being attacked!"

"Give me a readout, Ops," Benning ordered at once. "What are we facing?"

The woman stared at her in disbelief. "Of each vessel, Commodore?"

"Numbers and types," Benning replied, her voice slightly frustrated.

"I'm reading 384 corvettes, 288 frigates, and 128 destroyers, ma'am. And the *Dauntless Lion*."

Benning heard the numbers, but they meant little to her. The hundreds of specks swarming around the vast dreadnought that was their target filled her display like a cloud. It was too much information; she couldn't order her battle groups to target individual ships, after all. She needed to combine the enemy ships into groups, the same way her own were. Precious seconds passed as she compartmentalized her foes into distinct groups, but finally, her display cleared, showing three red, flashing icons representing the enemy battle groups. Each group represented thirty-two destroyers, seventy-two frigates, and ninety-six corvettes.

"Acknowledge, Commodore," Ops nodded. "Designating enemy battle groups as Tango 1, 2, and 3."

"Group 1, target Tango 1," Benning ordered her fleet. "Group 2, target Tango 2. We'll handle Tango 3."

"Aye, Commodore," the reply came back over her 'net as the captain of group 1 acknowledged her response.

"And what of the *Lion*, Commodore?" the captain of group 2 asked.

"We'll have to deal with her escorts before we can tangle with her, Captain."

"As you say, Commodore."

"Helm, move to engage Tango 3," Benning instructed.

"Aye, ma'am," the young pilot replied.

"Weapons, target the vanguard destroyers first. AM warheads, fan dispersal. Break up their formation. As they scatter, hit the corvettes with wide grasers followed by a battery of fusion warheads, starburst pattern." The ship shuddered slightly as dozens of warheads leaped from it, streaking toward the incoming group of ships. A moment later, her skin flamed as what felt like dozens of enemy grasers painted her all at once. The ship trembled, and pain flared in her arms and stomach as explosions ripped through space all around her as over a hundred fusion warheads went off at the same time.

"Evasive maneuvers!" she ordered. "Max g!"

"They have our evasion cone, Commodore," Ops reported, shaking her head. "They're covering our entire cone. We can't avoid getting hit."

"Commodore, our shielding plant is down 7%," a young man at the second Ops station spoke up. "Main engines down 2%."

"AM battery into the heart of their formation," Benning ordered. "Spherical pattern. Force them to disperse. Grasers at the destroyers, narrow dispersal. If they're staying in formation, their evasion cones are limited."

"Damage report from our first salvo," a younger woman at the last Ops station said. "Close hit on three destroyers. One is venting gas but maintaining headway.

They're holding formation."

"Fusion battery around the formation. Box them in. Keep grasers on the lead destroyers." Benning winced as her skin flamed once more, and she felt a sharp pain in her side as the ship rumbled beneath an explosive blast.

"Fusion warhead strike to port," the man who was apparently Damage Control reported. "Minor hull damage."

"Commodore, second salvo impacted one frigate directly. It's venting gas..." A flare lit Benning's screen. "It's gone photonic. Three other frigates severely damaged. Group is maintaining formation."

"Weapons, keep the batteries targeted on the heart of the formation," Benning instructed. "Keep grasers on the lead destroyers. Once we have their cone, hit them with medium-dispersal AM beams." As she spoke, her skin burned with the feeling of graser fire bathing her hull in high-energy gamma rays.

"Commodore, shielding plant down 14%. Main engines down 6%. Engine power plant down 1%."

Another flash lit Benning's screen as Ops reported in. "Fusion battery impacted, Commodore. Seven corvettes badly damaged; three went photonic."

"Repeat the fusion barrage, Weapons. Do we have their evasion cone?"

"Within 13% accuracy, Commodore," a young man at one of the six Weapons consoles replied.

"Then target them with a singularity warhead. That should break them up."

"Aye, Commodore." The ship shuddered as the larger singularity missile fired. A moment later, the ship rumbled again, and pain raced down Benning's left side as multiple explosions tore through space near her ship.

"Three AM explosions, seven hundred kims to port, Commodore," Damage Control reported. "Damage to the outer hull; we're venting gas. Sealing that cell off now."

"Full evasion, Helm," Benning ordered.

"Commodore, graser hits on seven destroyers. One is dropping back; the others are spiking power but remaining in formation."

"Fusion battery on the center destroyer, starburst pattern. Follow it with an AM torpedo on that destroyer." Benning's skin seared again as she gave her orders.

"Commodore, they're blanketing our entire evasion cone with graser fire," the older woman at Ops reported. "We can't evade."

"Then we'll just have to take it," Benning said. "Once we break their formation, we'll be able to pick them off in small groups."

"Commodore, shielding plant down 23%. Main engines down 9%, and engine power down 4%."

A huge flash lit Benning's screen, followed by dozens of smaller flashes. "Singularity warhead impacted, Commodore," the younger woman at Ops reported. "Massive damage; twenty-seven frigates and five destroyers went photonic; forty-three frigates and six destroyers are critically damaged. Their formation is breaking up."

"Good," Benning grinned. The singularity warhead was nothing more than a modified Kugelblitz power plant, a contained black hole that hovered on the edge of flashing to Hawking radiation. When the missile exploded, the black hole's entire mass converted to energy in less than a second, bathing the area around it with an explosion similar to a few hundred AM warheads going off at once. "Now, we can..."

She froze as her skin flared with liquid fire, and stabbing pains shot into her shoulders and chest. "What the

Hole was that?" she demanded as she looked at her screen.

"The *Lion,* ma'am," Ops replied quietly. "Battle group 2 is gone, and the *Lion* and Tango 2 are targeting us."

"Gone?" Benning echoed, stunned. Her battle group should have easily dealt with the more numerous but far less powerful Tango 2 – the battlefrigate at its heart would have seen to that. And, she supposed, it would have, had the massive dreadnought not been assisting its forces.

Just as she could have fit a couple hundred *Resolute Hammers* inside her battlecruiser, almost a hundred of her battlecruisers could have nestled within the *Lion.* The spherical warship stretched over sixteen kims across, and it bristled with powerful weaponry. Tiny dots poured out from the dreadnought: the vessel's stored fleet of cutters and corvettes, swarming out to engage the battlecruiser and keep the approaching third battle group at bay. Benning swore as she recalled that she had a similar fleet of cutters – one that she'd never bothered to deploy.

"Deploy cutter fleet," she ordered. "Have them intercept the *Lion's* cutters."

"Aye, Commodore," Ops replied.

"Weapons, target the *Lion* with everything we have."

Benning's skin burned again as more graser fire bathed her ship. "Commodore, shielding plant is down 49%, weapons plant is down 17%, and main engines are down 31%. We've lost 10% of thrusters."

"Commodore, Tango 3 is reforming around the *Lion,*" Ops reported. "Our evasion cone is still covered. We can't avoid their fire."

The ship shook, and Benning's entire body screamed with stabbing pain. "Multiple AM explosions from all directions, Commodore. Seven different hull breaches. We're starting to list."

"Commodore, AM battery impacted less than a thousand kims from the *Lion*. No detectable damage."

"Shielding plant down 71%," Damage Control reported in an alarmed voice as Benning's skin burned once more. "Main engine down 53%, and main power down 28%!"

"Weapons, singularity warhead at the *Lion*!" Benning commanded. "AM battery at the center of Tango 2! Fusion battery at Tango 3!"

The cruiser shook again, and more pain rippled through Benning's body. "Four fusion warheads impacted within five hundred kims! List has increased to 6.2 rpm. We've lost atmosphere in decks 117 – 119 starboard."

"Graser fire on Tango 3, full dispersal," Benning ordered. "Their evasion cone is smaller than ours; flood it with gamma rays."

"Commodore, singularity warhead impacted twelve hundred kims from the *Lion*," Ops reported. "They're venting gas in two places, and their plants are down 4%." Flashes lit Benning's screen. "Fusion volley impacted. Eight corvettes and three frigates went photonic; fourteen corvettes, seven frigates, and two destroyers significantly damaged."

The battlecruiser rocked once more, and pain roared across Benning's body. "AM impact against the hull! We are venting atmosphere; list increased to 19.8 rpm. Main plant down to 31%. We've lost our shielding!"

"Commodore, battle group 1 has broken free and is en route," the older woman at Ops reported calmly. "Battle group 3 is forty-one seconds out."

Too late, Benning shook her head as the ship shuddered once more and her entire body screamed with the impact. "Commodore! Singularity warhead exploded 240 kims below! Main plant is spiking..."

A flash of white lit Benning's vision as the battlecruiser's power plant exploded, its containment failing and allowing the negative mass within to race unimpeded to a tiny fraction of a percent below the speed of light. Energy washed through the ship, overloading its other plants in turn until nothing was left of her mighty vessel but a sea of photons speeding off into the void.

Benning blinked as the simulation ended and her Overnet domain formed around her once more. "Well, that went to the Hole fast," she muttered, shaking her head.

"Are you okay, Benning Kidd?" Tiddly asked, appearing in front of the Corsair, her eyes wide and a frown covering her face.

Benning sat down on the floor of her domain and wrapped her arms around her knees, leaning her forehead on them tiredly. "Yes, Tiddly. And no, I guess."

"That seemed really hard," the gnome offered. "Expecting a battlecruiser to go up against a dreadnought? That's not exactly fair."

Benning shook her head. "It wasn't the dreadnought that killed me, Tiddly. It was the two battle groups. They could blanket my entire evasion cone; I had nowhere to run. They could put hundreds of missiles all around me so that one of them had to be close enough to damage me. There was no way for me to avoid getting hit."

"Do you think it's like the Kobayashi simulation? One that you can't win?"

"Maybe, but..." Benning took a deep breath. "I think it's more that I kept making mistakes. I didn't keep an eye on my battle groups; I didn't wait for the third group to catch up to us." She snorted. "Scrit, I forgot about my cutter fleet. One cutter isn't all that powerful, but with a couple hundred,

I could have done the same thing to them that they did to me. Four hundred grasers bathing their fleet constantly would have done more damage than that singularity warhead over time."

She shook her head again. "I think – I think that I was trying to fight the way I always do with the *Hammer*," she admitted. "I was trying to do everything myself. I should have been using my fleet to my advantage, instead. If I had, I might have been able to win that." She chuckled wryly. "Or at least not died so badly."

"Then you know how to handle it better next time, and that's important. Did you get anything from it, at least?"

Benning pulled up her status sheet and couldn't help but smile at the screen that appeared before her.

SKILL UPGRADES!
You have achieved rank 20 in one or
more of your skills. With this increase,
your skills achieve a new tier, and
you can use them in unique ways.

LEADERSHIP
+2% x rank to skills of all under your
command
+2% x rank to Social stat with
all under your command
From Hell's Heart: Those under
your command gain triple your
Leadership bonus to all actions when
threatened with likely death or
defeat. This lasts until the threat is
ended or has become a certainty.

"Yep. I got a bonus of 1.2 to Leadership, 1.1 to Naval

Tactics, and 0.3 to Starfaring." Benning laughed. "Plus 5% to my path. And that was by losing, Tiddly! Imagine what I'd get if I won."

"I guess you just need to try it until you can, then," Tiddly said eagerly. "It was certainly exciting to watch! I can't wait to see you do it again!"

CHAPTER 6

"Benning Kidd," Fodor Hendricks smiled as Benning walked into the dining compartment with Tereza Erdeli at her side. "Welcome back to Kidd's Rest."

Benning frowned at the dark-skinned man and his wide, gleaming smile that seemed somehow too bright. "Kidd's Rest? What is that?"

"It's the designation we decided to give this place," the man replied, holding his arms out expansively and turning from side to side so that his tightly braided, black hair swung back and forth. "We can't keep calling it 'IS-39267', after all."

"It's the designation that you gave it, Fodor Hendricks," the blue-haired woman beside Hendricks clarified. "No one else calls it that." Avaeyana Roble, captain of the *Merciless*, was shorter and wider than Benning, heavily built with wide shoulders. Her electric-blue hair stood out starkly against her medium brown skin and curled down to frame her light brown eyes.

"They will," Hendricks shrugged. "Give it time."

"Why would they?" a man with strawberry blonde hair, bright blue eyes, and medium brown skin snorted. Trephor Sando, lieutenant in command of the *Silent Scoundrel,* one of Benning's corvette-class ships, snorted fairly often, Benning had noticed. The man seemed to hold the entire universe in some level of contempt.

"Because it's easier to say, Trephor Sando. Sure, if this place were IS-3, we'd just keep calling it that, but no one wants to keep saying '39267' over and over again."

"IS-3 is a defense station along the trade route between Sol and Barnard's," Saavi Boguna, another lieutenant commanding Benning's other corvette, the *Grim Streak*, observed in a calm voice. Her long, purplish hair fell in a ponytail to the middle of her back, and her bright yellow eyes didn't look at the others as she spoke. The woman seemed to delight in random trivia for some reason, and Benning suspected that Boguna wanted to command a ship to explore and discover new things rather than fight in combat.

"You're wrong, Fodor Hendricks," the muscular woman with short, green hair sitting across the table from the Pirate Captain shook her head, ignoring Boguna's pointless observation. "No one's going to go along with your idea for a designation until Benning Kidd agrees to it, and that's that. No one in her fleet is going to risk crossing her." Raelle Muckley, captain of the troop transport *Merry Messenger*, tended to be abrupt, blunt, and honest, and Benning found her company somewhat refreshing.

"And she'll agree to that designation if I use it enough," Hendricks agreed. "Problem solved."

"I think that designation is just asking for the Fleet to come visit, Fodor Hendricks," Erdeli pointed out. "Benning Kidd is a wanted woman, after all."

"They haven't come for her yet, Tereza Erdeli, and they have to know where she is."

"It's probably not worth their time," the assistant shrugged. "The Fleet has thousands of systems to worry about, and while Benning Kidd did commit war crimes, she did it against known pirates. She's likely not high on their priority list. If we designate this station after her, though, it's basically waving a dim graser in their face and taunting them. They'll almost have to respond, then."

"Scrit. Good point," Hendricks grunted. "I hadn't

thought of it that way. The station still needs a designation, though."

"Why is that important to you, Fodor Hendricks?" Benning asked as she took one of the two empty seats around the long table. As she sat, a holographic screen floated into her view above the table, displaying a menu of available food and drinks. She selected her usual Sirius Smokebrew and a Cetan fire steak. She'd gotten a taste for the native Tau Cetan meat during her visit there; the alien life there contained unique proteins that gave it an odd, fiery flavor without a sensation of burning or pain.

"Like I said, it's easier to say," he repeated. "The current designation is a mouthful."

"But why should that matter? At most, saying the full designation takes maybe a second longer than something like 'Kidd's Rest'. Over the course of a standard year, it might save a few minutes of time."

"It's not about time, Benning Kidd," Hendricks sighed. "Time is something we Citizens have plenty of, after all. It's about the way a designation feels, and why humanity calls its home planet 'Earth' instead of 'Planet 1' or something like that. Have you noticed that every planet and large rocky body in the Sol system has a unique designation, rather than being labeled with a classification and numbering scheme?"

Benning nodded slowly. "I'd never thought about it, but now that you mention it, yes, I have."

"And the same is true in other systems. It's not 'Ophiuchi a, b, and c'; it's Python, Delphi, and Apollo. The former system is probably easier, but humans have more difficulty feeling a connection to things without meaningful designations. As IS-39267, this station is just a base of operations, a convenient temporary location, nothing more. With a proper designation, though, it could feel like a home to your crews, a place they can make their own – and one worth fighting for."

Benning suppressed a frown. IS-39267 *was* just a convenient location, at least as far as she was concerned. It was an asset, and a valuable one at that, but she knew that it would only be a temporary haven for her and her ships. At some point, the Fleet would send a battlefrigate her way, and when that happened, her only choice would probably be to flee deeper into interstellar space. Her current fleet wouldn't stand a chance against one of the mighty warships, even with the station's defenses assisting them, and sticking around to fight would simply result in them all being sent to respawn.

At the same time, that was exactly the issue she was trying to resolve. At the moment, she existed at the Fleet's sufferance; as Tereza Erdeli said, they just hadn't gotten around to dealing with Benning yet. At some point, they would, and Benning wanted to be ready for them. The idea that the Fleet could force her to abandon everything she'd gained and that she was powerless to stop it galled her to no end, and she refused to sit back and wait for the battlefrigate she knew was coming to arrive.

Is he right, Tiddly? Would giving this place a different designation encourage my crews to fight to defend it?

<Probably, Benning Kidd. Humans fight harder when they're defending something important to them, and they always seem to attach sentimental designations to things they think are important.>

"I'll think about it," she said at last, nodding her head. "It's a good idea, Fodor Hendricks, but as Tereza Erdeli said, there's no point in taunting the Fleet – at least, not yet."

"Not yet?" Erdeli echoed. "Benning Kidd, I assure you, there's never a good time to taunt the Fleet."

"No, but there are times when it can be done safely.

We're just not there yet." Benning looked around the table. "And that's the reason I wanted this meeting. It's time we started getting ready for the Fleet's eventual appearance."

"Our ships can't take a battlefrigate, Benning Kidd," Hendricks said flatly. "Not unless you fight the way you did against the *Orion*, and if you use prohibited weapons against the Fleet, you're going to have a dreadnought or titanosphere drop by to say hi. Even those weapons won't do anything against a ship a mim across with millions of grasers, missiles, and cutters."

"We can't, you're right – at least, not yet. I want to change that." She glanced at her assistant. "Tereza Erdeli?"

The slim woman held out her hand, and a holographic image appeared above the table displaying a large, glowing star surrounded by two large planets orbiting closely and three larger gas giants orbiting at a distance.

"That's Nulupi, isn't it?" Saavi Boguna asked a bit excitedly. "It's a Sol-mass star almost fifty lightyears from the Sol system in the early stages of its red giant stage!"

"Correct," Erdeli agreed. "It's also one of the most recently colonized systems in the Collective. The Blancwolf corporation sent out a fleet of ark ships seventy-three years ago, so the colonists have only had about forty standard years to build it up. The innermost planet has been broken down for raw materials, but the system is still in the process of building its Dyson swarm to power the replicators needed to construct the habitats and stations they'll need around the system."

"You're not suggesting we go conquer that system, are you?" Hendricks asked a bit incredulously.

"No, of course not, Fodor Hendricks. Each of those ark ships carried a million colonists, for one thing, and they'll fight to defend what they've built so far. For another, it's almost fifty lightyears away. Even in deep dives, it would take months to get there. It's not worth the trouble."

The woman turned back to face the floating image. "Blancwolf, as you may know, is a tech corporation focusing on advanced and highly experimental 'net modifications and upgrades. Their stated purpose for claiming Nulupi is to turn the system into an advanced research center. So far, beyond a few hundred Dyson habitats, the colonists have only been able to build a single underground colony on the outermost rocky planet, but it appears that they've already come up with something valuable – valuable enough, at least, to need to be transported on one of their few military vessels."

The hologram shifted, displaying a pair of cylindrical vessels, one much smaller than the other. "These are the *Nageur Rapide*, a brigantine vessel barely capable of interstellar travel, and the *Lame Dorée*, a carrack trader converted into a warship," Benning spoke up, taking up the rest of the briefing. "They left Nulupi several months ago, headed for Blancwolf's current company headquarters in the Indi system. In eleven standard days, they'll approach within ten lightyears of Frostwise. When they do..." She smiled grimly. "We're going to take them."

"How well was that carrack refitted?" Hendricks asked dubiously. "That ship has a lot of room to carry weapons and marines, Benning Kidd."

"The datasheet shows it to be similar to maybe a quarter-powered battlefrigate," she explained. "The specs say they have eighty banks of grasers and forty missile launchers. However, with Nulupi's Dyson swarm only partially active, they've had to power the ship's weapons and defenses with fusion plants and affix their missiles with fission warheads, since they don't have the energy to create the black holes for a KB plant or antimatter for an AM warhead."

"Which means that their weapons and shielding are underpowered and vulnerable," Avaeyana Roble mused, tapping a finger on the table.

"But they'll have enough of them to fry any of us," Hendricks shook his head. "And they can fire dozens of missiles at once. Fission warheads are still dangerous if they get close enough, and in those numbers, they'll be deadly. I don't think we can do this."

"Individually? No, we can't, Fodor Hendricks," Benning agreed. "However, as a fleet? I think we can. If we coordinate our tactics and fight cohesively, we can take this convoy and its cargo."

"Do we even know what we'll be getting?" Trephor Sando objected.

"The *Rapide's* manifest shows them carrying 100 gigs of standard 'net components, nothing more."

Sando snorted again. "Why bother, then, Captain? It won't be worth the gas it takes to hit them, much less the risk to our ships."

"A hundred gigs of standard components?" Hendricks repeated, his eyes narrowing in a way Benning had learned meant he was thinking intently. "Now, I see why you want us to hit it, Benning Kidd. You may be right."

"I don't understand," Roble admitted. "What's so special about 'net components?"

"Nothing, Avaeyana Roble, which is exactly the point," the dark-skinned man chuckled. "There's no reason to send ordinary components fifty lightyears from a small experimental facility to their home base when they can just send plans through the Overnet and replicate the components back home. There's certainly no reason to protect a shipment worth a couple hundred credits with a carrack that must have cost a thousand credits to refit just for this voyage. Whatever that ship is carrying has to be worth its weight in anti-iron, at least."

He looked at Benning. "You'd think I'd learn to stop doubting you, Captain. You've proven right too many times since I've known you."

Benning once more stifled a frown as that odd warmth she'd felt after her battle with Reesha Divakar flowed into the empty hole in her chest once more. Again, it wasn't unpleasant, but it was distracting, an oddity that pulled at her attention. She pushed the sensation aside; she'd need to examine it later, but for the moment, she had other things to worry about.

"It still won't be easy, though," the Pirate Captain continued. "We've never used fleet tactics before; it's not something I've ever trained in." He looked at Boguna and Sando. "It seems like something that Starship Officers would learn at the academies, though."

Boguna shook her head. "We only get the most basic introduction to fleetwide tactics," she corrected vaguely. "Really just enough to show that cooperative tactics are possible, nothing more. I have no clue why."

"Probably because they don't want fledgling officers using those tactics against more experienced captains," Sando shrugged. "They want us to learn from older captains, so we're indebted to them and don't go rogue. It's the kind of thing the Fleet would do to keep control."

"It does sound like the Fleet," Hendricks agreed, turning back to Benning. "I take it you have a plan, Captain?"

"I do, Fodor Hendricks," she nodded. "I've been training in fleet tactics myself, and I've worked out a few basic concepts that should be sufficient for dealing with the *Dorée*. We have six standard days to practice them, and we'll be doing that as much as possible during that time. That should be enough for you all to pick up some of the basic ideas."

"And if it's not?" Sando asked skeptically. "Will we still hit the convoy?"

"Failure is not an option," Benning replied, her voice hardening. "You *will* learn at least the rudiments of fleet combat, Trephor Sando – all of you will. One way or the other, I'll make sure of it. I'm hoping that the idea of taking a cargo worth more than anything we've claimed besides the *Orion* will motivate you sufficiently, but if it doesn't..." She placed her hand on the table and activated her nano-disassemblers. The hologram flickered, blurred, and faded as a hole the exact shape of her hand suddenly appeared in the table, piercing it completely. "Do you understand, Lieutenant?"

"Yes, ma'am," the red-haired man nodded, swallowing hard. "I understand."

"I think we all do, Captain," Hendricks said dryly. "I hope you've got some specific tactics worked out, though. Theory is all good and well, but we don't need that just for this. We need formations and maneuvers we can practice."

"I do, and they aren't complicated," she nodded, reclaiming her disassemblers and removing her hand from the table, leaving the scar behind. The station's nanofield would eventually repair the damage to the table, but it would be slow since the field no longer had the microscopic pieces of the damaged microthene to reattach to the wound. "I've set up some simulations in the 'net we can use to practice, first. Once we're comfortable with those, we'll shift to practicing with our ships."

She looked around at her subordinate commanders, meeting each of their eyes. She'd chosen them because they each had a mixture of competence and weakness that made it difficult for them to find other berths. Avaeyana Roble was a Systems Engineer by path who'd gained the Leadership, Naval Tactics, and Starfaring skills so that she could command a starship. She'd never gain all the abilities of a Starship Officer, though, so she used her engineering knowledge to copy those as best she could. Trephor Sando had become a Starship Officer despite his abnormally low Social stat, the bare minimum for a Citizen. That impacted the growth of his Leadership skill, forcing him to train it harder than was typical just to keep its growth on pace with his other path skills. Saavi Boguna was an explorer at heart, a woman who probably should have taken the Galactic Pioneer path rather than Starship Officer, and Raelle Muckley was as tough as the marines she carried on her transport, a Starship Officer who'd also learned Conditioning and Weapons Expertise the way Benning had.

Benning had selected these people because they were capable but desperate, and the berths she offered them were better than anything they'd get elsewhere. That, she hoped, would inspire them to loyalty and keep them honest in their dealings with her. She'd learned the hard way the value of integrity; a person without it would always look for some way to betray her that didn't harm them personally. At the same time, something else drew her to them, something that she couldn't quite describe. Having them join her felt right, as if they were the most correct tools for the jobs she needed done. They weren't just tools, though; they were Citizens, and she'd come to understand that they needed more than just threats and rewards to function.

"I know this is different than what we've done before," she told them firmly. "But I also know that a fleet that fights together is far stronger than the individual ships making it up. We're going to face enemies that are more powerful and dangerous than we are, whether we go looking for them or they come looking for us. Our only hope to defeat them is by working together as a cohesive whole, not as individuals doing whatever we'd like.

"The Fleet uses these tactics, and with them, they've pacified entire systems. They've overcome rebelling fleets millions of ships strong, backed by thousands of stations and planets with billions of marines, and they've never lost a war yet. If the Fleet can do it – if those timid, little officers in their perfect uniforms with their rules and regulations can defeat enemies like that with their tactics, think of what we can do without any of their limitations or reservations. If we become skilled at this, even the Fleet will have to treat us with respect.

"Fodor Hendricks wants to give this station a designation to make it feel like ours, but first, we need to become strong enough to keep it ours when our enemies come calling! This is how we do that. This is how we show the Fleet that it can't just come here and kick us out. It's not about my orders; it's about becoming a power that no system can ignore, one that even the Fleet will learn to fear!"

"Aye, Captain!" Trephor Sando said, rising to his feet, his eyes blazing. "I'm with you!"

"Let's do this!" Roble agreed, slapping her hand on the table. "To the Hole with the Fleet!"

She looked at Hendricks, who eyed her with an expression Tiddly interpreted for her as thoughtful. "Fodor Hendricks?" she asked.

"Oh, I'm with you, Captain," he nodded with a smile. "In fact, I'm excited to see how this is all going to work out."

CHAPTER 7

"Resolute fleet, pre-dive systems check," Brialle Caldwell spoke aloud, her voice carrying to the other ships arrayed around the *Resolute Hammer*.

"*Merciless*, ready," Lushian Barber, the pilot of Benning's old frigate replied.

"*Vindictive*, ready."

"*Silent Scoundrel*, ready."

As each of the five other ships in Benning's small fleet declared their readiness to dive, she examined their formation through the destroyer's 'net. The ships maintained their positions perfectly thanks to the instructions programmed into their 'nets, of course. The five warships formed a roughly conical shape with the *Hammer* at the tip in the rear and the rest of the ships orbiting in steadily widening circles in front of the largest ship. The *Merciless* was closest to the *Hammer* at half a lecond, with the *Vindictive* another half-lecond beyond the frigate, followed by the *Scoundrel* and the *Grim Streak*, Benning's second corvette-hulled vessel. Each ship kept a half-lecond distance between themselves and the ships before and aft, close enough for the ships to concentrate their fire but spaced out enough that a single volley of fusion warheads wouldn't disable half the fleet. The *Merry Messenger* followed in an elliptical orbit slight aft of the *Hammer*, ready to deliver its cargo of marines once their target was disabled but far enough back to stay out of the coming battle.

Benning had thought that the fight with the *Dorée*

would be the most difficult part of this mission, but she soon wondered if that conjecture was wrong. The trip from IS-39267 was a major effort all by itself. The ships left the station without issue, but their first refueling stop at Frostwise hadn't gone well. Benning never considered the logistical challenge of six ships all trying to refuel at once, and the captains quickly set to arguing about who should get precedence and why. She'd had to step in and set an order for the captains to refuel, and they grumbled about their placement in that order.

"The *Vindictive* should be first, Captain," Hendricks reasoned. "She's the fastest ship in the fleet, but she also uses the most gas. She needs it more than the others."

"The *Messenger* is carrying the marines you need to capture the ship," Muckley countered. "If we run short on gas, you're all making the trip for nothing."

"There's plenty of gas for all of us," Roble said exasperatedly. "It's not like any of us are going to drain an entire brown dwarf!"

"No, but fueling stations do occasionally break down," Hendricks replied. "And that happens at Frostwise more often than most. If they lose a compressor or an injector snaps, someone's not getting gas."

"We'll refuel by hull size, largest to smallest," Benning decided. "That way, if something goes wrong, we'll still be bringing the maximum number of weapons to the battle."

The fleet also had trouble staying together through the first few dives to clear Frostwise. Each ship moved around in an irregular orbit that kept them in formation but made it impossible to accurately predict their exact position. However, that also meant they entered dives with different velocities and headings, and that scattered them across linutes when they exited their dives. She tried coordinating each ship's track when they dove next, but that generated more than the normal amount of heavy KK particles in the higher dimension, slowing the fleet when one such particle struck the *Scoundrel* and forced her to heave to for repairs. By the fourth dive, Benning got the hang of sending the ships into the fifth dimension with close but slightly varied headings that would still scatter them but kept them within an acceptable radius.

Of course, that didn't help in the slightest with deep diving. There was no way to predict exactly where a deep dive would exit, but Benning guessed that if each ship targeted the same location, they shouldn't scatter too much. She'd been right; on their first dive, the fleet all came up within leconds of one another, and the resulting radiation bath from their exit splashes had forced the whole fleet to run ballistically for hours while the ships' 'nets repaired the damage. After that, she'd had each ship target a spot several leconds from any other ship, then they spent anywhere from several minutes to an hour reforming around the *Hammer*. It wasn't ideal, but Benning couldn't think of a better way to deep dive safely.

Then, they'd had to wait when the *Streak's* dive engine failed and Saavi Boguna neglected to tell Benning, meaning the fleet dove without the corvette and had to wait for the ship to repair itself and then to catch up. That was when Benning began running systems checks before each dive; if they dove on the *Dorée* with only part of their fleet, they could be in trouble.

"Resolute fleet, prepare for dive," Caldwell instructed after each ship had returned a positive response. "On my mark – initiate dive."

The world flattened around Benning as the vessels plunged into higher dimensional CY-space. Normally, she had to focus intently during a dive to keep from seeing the entirety of local space at once, but this time, she barely noticed the panoply spread around her. Her eyes were focused on her fleet screen, watching each of her ships for signs of damage, while she simultaneously tracked the fleet through her 'net to make sure they'd be exiting more or less where she'd predicted. Keeping the fleet organized took far more effort and concentration than she'd thought. Each ship's captain only had to worry about their vessel, but Benning had to track hers plus all of theirs.

What I need is another officer on the Hammer *for fleet operations like this,* she mused as she noted that the *Scoundrel* was going to come out slightly past where she'd thought. *Someone to run the ship while I handle everything else.*

<That's probably a good idea, Benning Kidd,> Tiddly agreed brightly. <It might be something to consider once this battle's done, though, don't you think?>

Good point.

Benning's mind kept wandering to random topics, and she knew why. She was nervous about the coming battle. The simulations and training had gone well – at least, they had eventually, once her commanders got the idea that they weren't trying to defeat any ship by themselves but had to work together – but that was training. Real combat would be different, she knew. It was one thing to hold formation in a simulation with nothing on the line; it was another when fifty fission warheads were inbound, and instinct screamed at her to evade no matter what that meant to the rest of the fleet. Would her commanders hold? Would they follow orders? Or would they dissolve once more into a group of individuals, attacking as they saw fit and probably all getting wiped out?

That was the biggest thing gnawing at her. She thought she'd looked thoroughly at the pros and cons of fleet combat. She'd considered the danger to her ships, the difficulties of training, the risk of failure. It was only as they finally neared their target that she realized the biggest issue: when the battle began, she had no way to force her commanders to follow her lead and remain in formation. Oh, she could threaten and cajole them, but at the end, if Hendricks or Sando decided to abandon the formation, or Muckley turned and ran, Benning couldn't stop them. On her ship, it was different – she could kill any officer who refused to follow her orders and run their station without issue – but she couldn't turn the *Hammer* away from their target to chase a fleeing corvette or chastise a rebellious frigate captain.

That, she realized, was how Citizens weren't just regular tools. Her rifle would fire when she squeezed the trigger; her armor would equip when she desired it. Those tools had no life of their own and responded solely to her will. Humans, though, had their own thoughts and desires, and those didn't always coincide with hers. They had to be directed, just like her fleet, constantly herded back to where she wanted them and watched for signs of instability or looming problems.

She'd always ignored the desires and motivations of everyone around her, relying on fear and greed to keep them moving in the general direction she wanted, but she wondered if she needed to start paying more attention. She'd seen that left to their own devices, the ships in her small formation tended to slowly lose cohesion until they were just a group of independent vessels, not a fleet. Were her crew the same way? Had their desires and plans drifted from when they'd joined with her? Did those plans still mesh with hers? She didn't know, and that ignorance could be dangerous. She pushed those thoughts aside as they exited the dive; it was an important consideration, but she had other concerns on her mind.

"Captain, we're beginning our final approach," Jezper Shields informed her calmly.

Benning nodded and triggered her comm system. She couldn't control what her commanders did in the coming battle, but she could at least try to keep them all moving in the same direction.

"Resolute fleet, this is Captain Benning Kidd," she said, her voice carrying through all six ships. "We're preparing for our final approach on the convoy. We've moved fast enough to stay ahead of our images, so they don't know we're coming, but even so, we'll be outgunned and facing an enemy stronger than we are – at least, stronger than we are individually. Together, though, we can take them down if we remember our training and each do our part. Stick to the formation, no matter what, and we'll be victorious. Leave the formation, and you'll die – one way or another."

She gave them a few seconds for her words to sink in. She'd given them a hope of victory for obeying her and a promise of reprisal if they failed her; that was the best she could do. "Resolute fleet, prepare for rapid dives," she finally instructed. "On my coordinates and mark – now!"

The world flattened around her once more as the fleet plunged into the fifth dimension. The bridge snapped back to normality for only a moment before diving into CY space once more, racing through the void toward the *Dorée* and *Rapide*. Each dive lasted ten seconds and carried the fleet a full linute, swiftly outpacing their dive splashes and images. The ships altered course slightly with each dive to remain close to their proper formation, and Benning silently thanked the convoy for being distant enough that she'd worked out some of these issues already. If they'd dove into combat scattered, they'd have been easy pickings for the *Dorée*.

Reality burst around her as the fleet exited the final dive. "Report!" she instructed instantly.

"Convoy is at projected bearing zero-six-four, five

degrees declined, Captain," Shields replied at once. "Estimated distance is 2.8 leconds."

"Fleet is within tolerances for formation, Captain," Caldwell added.

"Fleet, begin assault pattern one," Benning instructed. "Charlo Herrick, deploy the sinkhole."

"Aye, Captain," the weapons officer said eagerly. The ship shuddered, and a second later, Benning's screens contracted until they showed a space about six leconds across. Beyond that space, the universe seemed to end as the sinkhole's event horizon cut everyone within off from the rest of reality. The sinkhole was a necessity; Benning was certain that the *Rapide* would prep to dive the moment it picked up their exit splashes, but it was impossible to dive from a sinkhole. Instead, the brigantine would probably race for the edge of the sinkhole, which was fine with Benning. She wanted it out of harm's way; if she accidentally destroyed it, their attack would be for nothing.

The ships turned, shifting their heading so that the opening of their cone led the *Dorée* slightly. The maneuver was somewhat awkward; the corvettes lost position as they failed to turn swiftly enough, and the *Messenger* overcompensated and drifted out of position. The ships recovered swiftly, though, and by the time the carrack received their dive splashes, they were in position.

"Fire missiles, spiral pattern," Benning ordered. "Graser blasts, full sweep." Her ship shuddered as it released a barrage of missiles that soared outward to form the center of a cone-shaped spiral. Her tactical screen tracked the dozens of warheads fired by her ships as they continued the spiral, each ship forming a predetermined part of the pattern. At the same time, her graser banks bathed a wide rectangle in gamma radiation, a shape filled in by the rest of the ships around her.

"Continue bombardment," she directed the fleet. "Evasive pattern four." The ships began to move even more erratically, slipping in and out of position in a series of random ellipses. This kept each ship's field of fire open but made it impossible to target an individual ship based on its movement in the formation.

The ship shuddered, and her skin warmed as flashes dotted her tactical screen. "Captain, fission warhead volley from the *Dorée*," Shields told her. "No damage."

"Formation is holding, Captain," Caldwell added. "*Grim Streak* reports minor hull damage." She paused.

"Continue barrage," she instructed. "Ops, give me readings on the carrack the moment we get them."

"Several direct graser hits to the *Dorée*, Captain. Four warheads exploded within a thousand kims of her hull. Minor damage to her armor and systems."

"Good. We've got her evasion cone." Benning turned her thoughts back to her fleet. "Fleet, continue graser battery, spotlight spread. Fire missiles, concentric pattern two."

The ship shook again as more warheads burst around them, and Benning's skin warmed once more as a graser beam swept across the hull.

"Fission warhead explosion, five hundred kims, starboard inclined," Shields said calmly. "No significant damage. Graser blast to the hull, main power at 98%."

"The *Scoundrel* is venting gas from the last blast, Captain," Caldwell said worriedly. "She's moving to evade."

"Trephor Sando, hold formation," Benning instructed instantly. "Do not leave formation!"

"Captain, we're venting gas," Sando protested, but Benning cut him off.

"I don't care if you're bleeding atmosphere, Commander! Maintain your position and continue fire. If you leave formation, you'll answer to me in the arena! Do you read me?"

"Aye, Captain," Sando said after a moment. "Maintaining position."

"Good. Fleet, evasive pattern seven." Benning shifted the fleet to a pattern that would take the *Scoundrel* slightly farther out, offering them a bit of protection against the next round of warheads. "Keep fire on the carrack's cone." As she spoke, her screen showed a series of concentric flashes as her last salvo ignited, the rings of explosions sending overlapping shockwaves throughout the *Dorée's* evasion cone.

"AM warhead burst within seven hundred kims of the carrack, Captain," Shields reported. "She's venting gas, and her main engine is down 18%."

"Captain, if you bracket the carrack, the *Vindictive* could..." Hendricks began, but Benning cut him off.

"Maintain formation, Fodor Hendricks," she said firmly. "We're bleeding them each second. Eventually, they'll bleed out."

Her skin burned again as another graser beam swept past, bathing her hull in radiation. "Glancing graser blast, Captain," Shields told her. "Engines at 97%, main power at 94%."

"The *Merciless* caught a direct blast, Captain," Caldwell spoke up. "Her main plant is at 73%, but she's holding formation."

"Continue graser battery," Benning instructed. "Hit them with a missile salvo every three seconds, concentric patterns. Evasive pattern two."

The ships shifted pattern once more as they fired

beams of energy that covered the entirety of the space before the *Dorée*. The carrack had nowhere to go; anywhere that it tried to turn was filled with streams of radiation that slowly ate at its shielding, overloaded its power plants, and disrupted its engines. The carrack responded with more missiles and grasers in return, damaging the *Merciless'* hull and reducing the *Vindictive's* power plant to 81%, but another salvo of missiles exploded all around it, tearing into its hull.

"Captain, hull breach on the *Dorée*," Shields told her. "She's listing, three degrees rotation."

"Fleet, narrow the graser field by ten percent," Benning instructed. "Fire missiles in a condensed spiral."

"Captain, the *Streak* is down to 63% of engine power," Caldwell reported. "The *Scoundrel* is venting gas in four places, and the *Vindictive* has lost 20% of below thrusters."

"Everyone, hold formation and continue fire," she directed. "She's hurt badly, now. It's only a matter of time."

"One way or the other," Hendricks muttered, but Benning ignored him.

The fleet soared around the carrack, constantly hitting it with gamma radiation and rocking it with volleys of missiles that the ship couldn't fully evade. Its fusion plants, already an order of magnitude weaker than her corvettes' KB plants and far weaker than her own negmass plants, began to lose containment as free neutrons slammed into them, disrupting the fusion process and increasing their internal heat tremendously. An explosion rocked the carrack as some of those neutrons slammed into a fission warhead, igniting the thermonuclear reaction prematurely and detonating it within the hull. One by one, its plants dropped offline, and its engines lost the ability to maneuver, further reducing its evasion cone and making the fleet's attacks even more concentrated and potent.

The ship continued to fight, though, and the fleet's approaching victory wasn't without cost.

"Captain, the *Streak* is down to 31% power!" Caldwell announced. "She's dropping back; she can't keep up with the formation."

"You did well, Saavi Boguna," Benning told the corvette's captain. "Fall back and begin repairs."

"Aye, Captain," Boguna replied with obvious relief. "We should be up…"

The woman fell silent as a massive flash lit Benning's screen.

"Captain, the *Scoundrel* took a fission warhead up her engine!" Caldwell said, her voice faintly panicked. "She – she's gone photonic!"

CHAPTER 8

Benning grimaced but nodded. She'd hoped not to lose anyone, but at least it was only one of the corvettes. "They'll be back to respawn, and with what we get from this haul, we'll get Trephor Sando a better ship," she declared. "Status of the *Dorée*?"

"Main power is at 19%, Captain," Shields said. "She's venting atmosphere in six places, her graser banks are offline, and her engines are down to 24%."

"Fleet, cease missile volleys. AM and graser beams only, narrow circle. Let's get her engines offline so the *Messenger* can clean her up."

"Aye, Captain," Hendricks replied after a moment of quiet. "Let's take her down for Trephor Sando."

Benning didn't understand that – Sando would be back at the station when they returned, no worse for the experience – and he'd likely end up ahead on his path and skills thanks to the battle – but she didn't argue. If taking the carrack "for Trephor Sando" kept the others focused and in formation, she was fine with it.

"Captain, the *Dorée's* engines are down!" Shields finally reported less than a minute later. "She's drifting!"

"All ships, switch to glaser fire only," Benning instructed. "Charlo Herrick, Fodor Hendricks, hit them with neutrino blasts to soften them up. Raelle Muckley, move out."

The *Messenger* accelerated past Benning as it raced

toward the drifting carrack. The vessel could no longer maneuver, and with the concentrated glaser fire from the destroyer and two frigates hitting it, it quickly slowed, dragged backward by the beams of energetic gravitons. The transport moved quickly to a parallel course before docking with the carrack, and Benning ordered the remaining ships to cease fire.

"Open a channel to the *Rapide*," she instructed. A moment later, a man's face swam into view. The man's silver hair was long and framed an oddly feminine face, with dark brown eyes that matched his cocoa skin.

"*Nageur Rapide*, my designation is Benning Kidd, captain of the Resolute Fleet," she said evenly.

"Captain Tolber Sanchez of the *Nageur Rapide*, Benning Kidd," the man said in a high-pitched voice. "I presume you've contacted me to discuss terms?"

"I don't know about discussion," Benning shrugged. "You have a choice, Tolber Sanchez. Heave to, shut down your engines and weapons systems, and allow me to board your ship, or I'll open fire. Your escort is lost, and one volley of AM missiles will probably open you to space."

The man grimaced as if in pain, then dropped his head in defeat. "Very well, Benning Kidd," he said quietly. "I surrender. We'll heave to so you can take what you want."

"Good. Don't even think of betraying me, Tolber Sanchez. If we come on board and get attacked, I'm going to kill you very, very slowly. Do you understand?"

"I do," he nodded.

"Excellent. I'll see you soon." She cut the comm channel and opened the line to her fleet. "Once the *Messenger* has captured the *Dorée*, I want all engineering teams to board it," she ordered. "Strip it of anything of value, from its power plants to its remaining warheads. Once we've taken everything we can from it, we'll destroy it."

"You don't want to keep it, Captain?" Hendricks asked curiously.

"No. It's useless to us, Fodor Hendricks. It's too big for us to crew effectively, too outdated to be effective in combat, and it's lost most of its cargo space. Fixing it would cost more than it's worth, and no one would buy a modified carrack as salvage."

The *Hammer* docked with the brigantine within minutes, and Benning stepped inside with twelve marines and Charlo Herrick to find the airlock open and the automated defenses shut down. Tiddly pulled up a map of the vessel, and Benning shared it with the others. "Geraldine Dickerson, take four marines and Charlo Herrick to the cargo bay and begin a deep scan of the cargo. Keanna Lucroy, take another four marines and sweep the ship, then head to the main bridge. That's where you'll find the rest of us."

Tolber Sanchez stood three cims taller than Benning. He was obviously male, but just as obviously, he chose to dress like a female, using molex and prosthetics to give himself hips and breasts. That wasn't uncommon, as Benning understood it; some people simply preferred to look different from their gender. She didn't understand why they would do that when they could just change their gender on respawn if they wished, but then, she saw no real need to understand. It made no difference to her one way or another, and really, she supposed it was no different than how she used her Infiltrator suite to change her appearance.

"Benning Kidd," the man inclined his head as she entered the bridge. "I left the cargo hold open. Take what you want."

"I will, Tolber Sanchez," she smiled at him. She looked around the bridge; a single Soldier stood off to one side, his rifle in his hands but held low, and a younger woman who was probably a junior officer watched on, her bright orange hair cut short, well away from her lightly tanned face. No one else was in sight, and Benning's nanofield confirmed that the bridge was empty. "In fact, that's exactly why I'm here: to take what I want."

She snatched her pistol from its holster and fired at the Soldier, striking the man in his visor and rocking his head back. The impact didn't so much as crack the heavy microthene, but the concentrated fire of the two marines behind Benning tore through the Soldier's armor and killed him instantly. As he died, Benning shot the stunned junior officer in the head, then swept her pistol to Sanchez even as the man held up his hands, protesting loudly.

"Bridge is secure," she said into her comm, sitting down in the command chair. "Taking control of the vessel now."

The *Rapide's* 'net was a decent one, but it yielded to Benning's efforts after only ten minutes or so. She began by accessing the lowest levels – the crew manifests, prior port registry, and so one – then slowly made her way up, coopting the credentials of the pilot, engineer, ensign, and finally the captain himself, giving her full access to the entire ship. She couldn't grant herself ownership – to do that, she'd need to dock the vessel back at her station – but she got the main engines and power back online and prepped the ship for the voyage back. Afterward, she headed down to the cargo hold to see what they'd captured.

"They were carrying 'net components, Captain, but that's not all," Herrick told her, shaking her head and touching one of the metal deck plates. The plate shifted, its liquid metal elongating and narrowing to form a silver cylinder glowing with blue lines along its face. Herrick touched it again, and a holographic blueprint appeared in the air.

"They're schematics," the Weapons Engineer explained. "Top-of-the-line stuff, too. Engine components, 'net upgrades, plant upgrades, even experimental weapons."

"So?" Benning asked. "Are they valuable?"

"Valuable?" Herrick laughed. "Captain, these are proprietary tech, and they're unregistered. You can register them with the Overnet, and anyone who wants to use them will have to pay you for the privilege. They're worth more than both of these ships put together."

Benning frowned. "Is it usual for corporations to transport this sort of thing? I would think they'd just send them through the Overnet."

"The 'net can be hacked, as you know, Captain. Physical transport is more secure. Even so, I think the reason they decided to ship it is over here." The woman waved her hand, and the blueprint vanished, sinking down into the deck once more and looking totally ordinary. It was a clever hiding place, Benning had to admit.

She followed Herrick over to another open part of the deck. When the engineer touched the deck this time, the plates parted, and a single orb rose up, pulsing with a dull, red glow. The orb was ten cims across, dull gray, and looked perfectly smooth.

"What is this?" Benning asked, squatting down to examine the object.

"No clue, Captain," Herrick shrugged. "I've never seen anything like it before."

"What did the scanner tell you?"

"Nothing." Herrick shook her head. "And I mean nothing. As far as the scanner's concerned, this thing isn't even here. It reads like a hole in space."

"What does that mean?" Benning asked, pushing her

nanofield out to connect with the object.

"No idea. I've never heard of anything like that before. It's almost like there's a sinkhole inside this orb, and the scanner can't read beyond the event horizon boundaries."

"You mean a black hole's in here?"

"No, ma'am. A deep scanner can read inside a black hole. The negative energy can get through the hole's event horizon and return. A sinkhole's boundaries are much more severely warped than a black hole's, basically twisting every path within the sinkhole back into itself. You could escape a black hole through a dive or by going faster than light; no paths lead out of a sinkhole. This could be something like that."

Benning frowned as her nanofield touched the orb and slid off it. Her nanites could feel the sphere, but they couldn't connect to it. She could sense the energy radiating from it, the heat it emitted, but for some reason, the orb was cut off from her hacking abilities.

"That's not important, though," Herrick went on, her voice excited. "As a Weapons Engineer, I have an ability called Deconstruction. For simple objects, it lets me break them down into schematics; for more complicated ones, I get a rough feel for it – how it's made, what materials it contains, even some of its properties."

She looked at Benning, her eyes bright. "I can use it on anything, Captain, no matter how complicated or valuable. I could use it on a Hole-bound titanosphere if I wanted – not that I'd get much from it, but I'd at least learn a little bit about the ship." She looked back at the device. "Not this, though. When I use it on this, I get nothing. It's like it's not even there."

"Meaning?" Benning pressed.

"Captain, my ability works through the Overnet. For

simple items, my 'net links directly to the item's and gives me a download of its full schematic. For more complex ones, I link to the Overnet, and it gives me indirect information by pinging the item's net and returning the responses. The only way I'd get no info about an object is if the Overnet couldn't ping an item."

A wide grin creased her face, and she rubbed her hands together. "Don't you see, Captain? This orb, here – it's shielded from the Overnet! Somehow, they came up with a way to block the 'net – and that means they've blocked out the whole System!"

CHAPTER 9

"*Tenebrous Hand,* you are cleared for docking at ring 186, bay 419," the controller of Sirius Majoris Prime Station spoke, the man's voice carrying through the bridge.

"Prime Station, *Tenebrous Hand* confirming ring 186, bay 419," Brialle Caldwell echoed almost mechanically as she plotted a course around the massive station toward the distant docking platform. Most space stations were long cylinders surrounded by layers of concentric rings that narrowed from one end to the other, but Sirius Prime was a Dyson station, orbiting the larger of the system's two stars. It was a flat disc a couple hundred kims across, one of its sides covered in trueblack solar panels that only lost a single photon per quintillion absorbed and that provided power for the entire station. That side perpetually faced Sirius Majoris, while hundreds of docking towers rose from the other side like inverted cones.

Every system had its share of similarly designed Dyson stations. In some systems, particularly those with a single red dwarf star, the number of those stations was small, a few thousand at most. In systems like Altair, Procyon, or Centauri, with stars larger than Sol, Dyson stations vastly outnumbered orbital ones. In Sirius, practically every station orbited around one or both of the two stars since the system lacked massive rocky bodies. A few hundred stations whirled about the edge of the system, but that was nothing compared to the tens of thousands of stations swirling around the suns, holding trillions of Citizens, plus uncounted Soldiers, Workers – and, of course,

Drones.

Typically, a system's capital was based on one of the planets colonized in that system. This was apparently a holdover from ancient Earth, which many considered the capital of the entire Collective even though it wasn't the largest or most populous planet by a fair margin. Earth was humanity's birthplace, though, and it had been the heart of human expansion for millennia, so every new system's center of government was placed on either a planet or similar rocky body in Earth's honor.

Sirius lacked those bodies, though, and only had a sparse dust cloud surrounding the twin stars. That made Majoris Prime, the first station built in the system, the de facto capital. It was always crowded, and Benning had to arrange for a berth a standard month in advance. Technically, she'd paid twenty credits to be put on a waiting list and received a berth more than five months out, but Benning hated waiting. Thanks to her Cyberwarfare skill, she'd cut that delay to a single month. That was when the *Hand*, a destroyer matching the *Hammer's* rough dimensions and power signature, was scheduled to dock at Majoris Prime.

Benning put that wait to good use. She'd sold the *Rapide* and the salvage she'd taken from both ships for over a thousand credits, then used that to buy and crew a new corvette for Trephor Sando. The *Slender Dagger* was a Laser class ship, a more powerful design than the Bandit class *Silent Scoundrel* had been. Benning had upgraded it further with a negmass plant to replace the KB one, improved engines, and some of the new components she'd taken from the *Rapide*. Those included advanced targeting systems, helm interfaces, and power relays that boosted the *Dagger's* speed, maneuverability, and firepower. Sando had been unhappy about losing his ship, but after he saw the new one Benning gave him, he was overjoyed.

Tereza Erdeli had been similarly enthused about the new design templates. She'd registered them with the Overnet immediately, then sent word to Erix Adelsson, Benning's contracted merchant. He began arranging licensing for the new designs right away; the merchant hated Benning, but she suspected the credits the prototypes could bring in would soothe some of the fire of his dislike.

Benning was equally excited about the new income stream, although not for the same reasons as the others. Erdeli saw it as a way to increase her potential pay; Adelsson saw it as a way to advance his path and maybe buy himself out from under Benning. To Benning, the credits were a way for her to expand her fleet and become even more dangerous. She'd arranged for the station and her ships to upgrade to some of the better designs, and she had Erdeli quietly looking for obsolete or derelict ships she could purchase and upgrade. Those refits would still cost credits, but they would be far cheaper using her designs than paying for someone else's.

Besides expanding her small mercantile empire, Benning spent the month training. She worked out daily in high-g, ran her Kobayashi unwinnable simulation, and traveled to the nearest arenas, those of Ross Virginis, a tiny red dwarf system about five lightyears from the station. Virginis wasn't a particularly large or important system, which meant its Fleet presence was small, and she'd been able to compete there without bringing down the wrath of that group. She'd also spent plenty of time developing her newest skill, the one she'd acquired by defeating the *Dorée*.

SKILL ACQUIRED
FLEET TACTICS
Provides a bonus of 10% + 1%
per skill rank to the attack and

defense ratings of all ships in a fleet
under your direct command.

The skill was at rank 2.3 already thanks to a combination of her training and hunting down the *Hand.* She couldn't just spoof the ship's designation, or she'd run the risk of the ship showing up to dock at the same time that she did. That would invite scrutiny into her manipulation of her ship's beacon, scrutiny that she didn't need. She needed to be sure the destroyer didn't make its appointment in Sirius, but the *Hand* was a powerful ship commanded by a seasoned captain, Flyx Arroyo.

She didn't trust that she could take the ship by herself, so she'd tracked it to one of the outer Kapteyn stations and attacked it with her entire fleet. The six ships disabled the destroyer without too much effort, and Benning killed Arroyo in a one-on-one duel. She stripped the ship of anything valuable, then allowed its crew to go pick up their captain – whom she'd arranged to respawn in the Kruger system, twenty lightyears from Kapteyn. By the time Arroyo respawned, contacted his ship, and then got picked up, Benning would be long gone from Sirius – at least, she hoped.

The *Hammer* docked, and a customs inspector checked their cargo – 200 gigs of plutonium 241 – almost incidentally while Benning ran her usual check of the station's transaction history to see if anyone important to her was on board. Afterward, she headed to a merchant Adelsson recommended to sell her cargo before traveling to the main promenade and Aura Titanium, Emmed Oswald's store. She passed the display, a holo of a nude, genderless, silver figure surrounded by a cloud of sparkling motes, and entered the blue-lit store.

The shop was busier than she'd seen it before,

with several customers standing around the counters and absently swiping through the holographic catalogs. Oswald himself moved among them, answering questions with his usual sly smile, his pale blonde hair and fair skin both gleaming electric blue in the shop's lights. He glanced toward Benning once, inclined his head, and then ignored her. She, in turn, moved to one of the counters and began browsing his catalog of upgrades without really looking at any of them. She didn't want to chat with him around others, as her dealings with him tended to skirt the edges of the law, but she couldn't exactly demand that he ignore his other customers to help her.

It took him thirty minutes finally to make his way to her. Not everyone bought something, but those who did had to be taken into the back to have their nanofields reset. That was a time-consuming and unpleasant experience, Benning knew personally. He walked over to stand across the counter from her, his sly grin wider than usual.

"Citizen – Flyx Arroyo?" he asked. "Welcome back to Aura Titanium. How can I help you today?"

"I need a nanofield reset, Emmed Oswald," she said, glancing around to see that a few new customers had entered the store while she waited. "Some of my nanites have been acting strangely lately. Can you help with that?"

"Of course. Come into the back, and we'll get you set up." He led her through the door into the back area. Once the door sealed behind them, he turned and looked at her seriously.

"Benning Kidd, you're risking a lot coming here," he said in a quiet voice. "The Fleet has been looking for you. I even had an officer here asking questions about our dealings."

"Really?" she asked, reaching down and touching her pistol almost nonchalantly. "And what did you tell them?"

"The truth," he snorted. "That you came here with a basic nanofield and asked for it to be upgraded, then after the nano-disassembler attack you returned to have your field reset since it was acting strangely." He gave her an intent look. "And that's all I told them."

Her Sense Deceit skill didn't trigger at his words. That didn't mean much – she only had about a 30% chance to detect a lie, after all – but she suspected that the man told the truth. If he'd admitted to the Fleet that he'd helped Benning assimilate disassemblers into her nanofield, they'd probably have discovered that he had taken one for himself, and he'd have been executed, fined, or both. After that, his shop certainly wouldn't be as busy as it was.

She frowned at that thought. "You've got a lot more customers than the last time I saw you," she noted.

He laughed. "That's thanks to you, actually. The story about how you survived a nano-disassembler attack spread throughout the system, and eventually, word got around that I'd upgraded your nanofield before and after the attack. People have been flocking in ever since." He inclined his head to her once more. "Which is another reason your secrets are safe with me, Benning Kidd. You've helped me too much for me to lose your friendship."

She suppressed another frown; she and Oswald weren't friends, as far as she knew. She wasn't even really sure what friends were. She knew the definition of the word, of course, but "friendship" implied a relationship with some sort of shared emotional or social benefit. She'd never experienced anything like that. Everyone she knew either gained by working with her or were afraid of the consequences of working against her. She didn't see the point in any sort of association that didn't provide her with tangible benefits. However, if Oswald's belief in their friendship kept him from betraying her, she wasn't about to disabuse him of the notion.

"So, are you really here for a reset?" he asked. "Did you get hit by another nano-attack?"

"Not a full reset, no," she shook her head. "I do have some nanites I need integrated into my field, though. I stole them from an intrusive scanner, and I'd like for them to keep at least some of their functionality."

"I can do that," he smiled at her. "Scrit, it'll be easy; scanning nanites are designed to link to a larger 'net and relay their findings to it. I just have to pair them to your 'net. It'll take a couple minutes, tops."

"Did you want to keep one of the nanites?" she asked curiously.

"Yeah, I would," he nodded. "Like the disassemblers, those nanites are proprietary, designed to wipe themselves if they're severed from the scanning device. If I had one, I could dig into its code and maybe work out a counter to it. I can think of a lot of people who'd pay kigs of credits to be able to block an intrusive scanner without needing a full containment field."

"Good. However, I have something else I think you might be interested in, as well." She held up a small cube and touched it. Instantly, a holographic display appeared of one of the design templates she'd stolen.

Oswald gasped and reached out toward the hologram, his hand passing right through it. "Benning Kidd," he said in a low, quiet voice, "do – do you know what this is?"

"Of course," she replied easily. "It's a design template for a next-gen 'net amplifier." She touched the cube again, and another image replaced the first. "And this one's a nanofield upgrade that improves connectivity by 15%." The image shifted once more. "And here's a 'net upgrade that speeds processing by another 11%." The images vanished, and Oswald stared at the cube in her hands.

"I – where did you get that?" he demanded. "If that's proprietary data, I can't use it in my store without a license. I'd get shut down if I tried."

"It is proprietary, and yes, you do need a license," she agreed with a smile. "Fortunately, I'm the license holder."

"You?" he asked, his voice dubious. "Benning Kidd, if I try to replicate these, the Overnet will ping the actual license holder, and they'll know what I'm doing…" He froze as she triggered the cube once more, displaying the System licenses, with her designation clearly marked on them.

"Do you believe me now?" she asked calmly.

"I – did you do this with your skill?" he asked, his voice stunned.

"No – although I might look into that," she said thoughtfully. "If I could shift licenses into my name, I'd basically have an endless source of credits."

"Until all the original license holders hunted you down," he shook his head. "Benning Kidd, most of these sorts of designs are owned by large corporations – and those are usually run by Nobles. If you start stealing their licenses, you'll have Nobles after you. You don't want that."

Benning refrained from telling the man she already had Nobles hunting her. That wasn't any of his business, after all, and besides, it wasn't like she could explain why. The Overnet wouldn't let her tell anyone about being a Drone, any more than it would let her see Drones she walked past. She'd tried to tell Fodor Hendricks, just to test the system's control of her, and the words simply refused to come from her mouth. Messages she sent to him shifted into something banal and innocuous, and when she tried writing the words down, her hand wouldn't cooperate. The System protected its secrets, and it wouldn't let Benning spill them.

"I found these designs on a ship I captured," she explained. "I claimed them through the laws of salvage and rules of piracy and registered them legitimately through the Overnet. They're mine, and I'm willing to trade those licenses for a new suite of nanofield and 'net upgrades – including these, of course."

"Hold on, let me scan you," he said, frowning at her. Once more, she felt the presence of hostile nanites approaching her as Oswald's intrusive scanner activated. This time, though, she held her defenses in check, allowing the scan to complete normally. Oswald read the results and nodded.

"This Nanoresistance skill – that's new," he noted. "And you leveled up, I see. Higher stats and a higher Cyberwarfare skill." He nodded. "Yeah, you could definitely use some upgrades, especially ones that take advantage of your new skill."

"Take advantage how?" Benning asked a little suspiciously.

"Well, that skill has given you a Nanodefense rating, something that usually only people like Nanoengineers, Nanomancers, or Nanobiologists get..."

"Nanobiologists?" she repeated.

"A path that involves using nanites to directly link to biological systems," he said dismissively, waving his hand. "They use nanites in place of certain proteins and chemicals to improve biological performance. Medigel and stim are both creations of Nanobiologists, in fact." He shook his head. "That's not important, though. What matters is that there are upgrades that can only be used by someone with a Nanodefense rating. Here, let me show you."

He touched the table beside him, playing with it for a few moments, then turned the screen to face Benning. She looked it over, reading through his suggested upgrades.

NUBÉS NANOCORPUS VIII
Nanofield Upgrade, Tier 8
Mods: Direct Connection, Active Cloud

AETHER MYALUS 5
Nanofield Upgrade, Tier 6
Mods: Active Cloud, Intensifier,
Instant Link

NUBÉS PHASELLUS VI
Nanofield Upgrade, Tier 7
Mods: Nanocryption, Active
Defense, Reflexive Response

AETHER EIDOS 4
Nanofield Upgrade, Tier 5
Mods: Active Cloud, Protected
Connection, Multiconnect

PHANTOMOS CYBERNET 4
Cybernet Upgrade, Tier 10
Mods: Wide Connection, Master
Encryption, Active Connection,
Modulated Defense, Nanoscreen

PHANTOMOS NANOSUITE 2
Nanofield Upgrade, Tier 8
Mods: Passive Connect, Nanostrike,
Deep Penetration

"Before you ask, no, you've probably never heard of Phantomos," he smiled at her. "It's a specialized company that only provides 'net and nano upgrades to those in related fields. You have to have a rating in Nanodefense,

Nanoattack, Cyberdefense, or Cyberattack to be able to use their components."

"My Cyberwarfare skill doesn't count as a Cyberattack rating?"

"Not according to the System." He shrugged. "People who follow cybernetic or hacking paths are usually the only ones who get Cyberattack ratings. My guess is that your skill lets you do some of what they can, the same way Nanoresistance gives you a defense against nano-attacks like a Nanoengineer or Nanomancer."

"So, what do these upgrades do?"

"Well, you'll notice that each of your previous upgrades is moving to the next level," he said. "It'll be just at the edge of what you can handle, so it should last you for a few levels, but you've got pretty high all-around stats for a level 9, so I think you can handle it.

"The Cybernet will replace your Mysticworks Cybersuite, and it'll basically swap out your entire 'net with a better one. It's definitely an upgrade; tier 8 to tier 10, in fact. It'll do everything your current 'net can do with better encryption. The Modulated Defense constantly shifts and resets your encryption, so anyone hacking it will only have access for a few microseconds before the window shuts on them. Nanoscreen taps into your Nanodefense and uses your nanites as part of your 'net's hacking defenses. To hack you, someone will first have to get through your Nanodefense – at least, part of it. Only a decently high-level Cybermancer or Cybertech will have a realistic chance to get into your 'net."

Benning nodded at that; while she hadn't faced someone with abilities like hers yet, she had no doubt she would eventually. If someone could hack her armor and shut it off or render her weapons non-functional – or do the same for her ship – she'd be in trouble.

"And the Nanosuite?" she asked.

"That's also based on your Nanodefense, but it turns it into an offensive tool," he grinned. "It allows your defensive nanites to attack someone else's nanofield directly, rather than having to get at it through their 'net. You can suppress or even shut down someone's field, although it'll reboot almost immediately if you turn it off. Still, suppressing a nanofield will cause their weapons to misfire, their armor to fail, even stop them from healing or using abilities. Passive Connect sends your nanofield out to try and connect to any nanofield in range without your needing to concentrate on it. Nanostrike lets you attack the fields surrounding a person's gear, and Deep Penetration links you to their 'net through their nanofield, meaning when you shut down or suppress a nanofield, you'll also kill the field's 'net controller for tenths of a second instead of microseconds. That doesn't seem like much, but if you can keep hitting it over and over, you can totally cut them off from their nanofield. They'll basically be helpless to use their gear or abilities while you do."

<He's overselling again, Benning Kidd,> Tiddly warned her quietly. <Everyone's nanofield has defenses against the kind of attacks and intrusions he's talking about. Just because you gain access to their field doesn't mean you can automatically affect it, much less shut it down. And you'd need a lot of practice to keep a nanofield turned off for even a few seconds. Plus, using your nanofield that way will lower your Nanodefense rating and might even weaken your abilities or slow down your healing.>

So, are those upgrades worth having?

<Oh, yeah, definitely. Especially the Cybernet; like you said, eventually, you'll run up against someone with abilities like yours, and you'll need all the defenses you can get. Just don't think you're going to walk out of here shutting down

nanofields left and right, is all. It'll take a lot of work and training to get to that point, if you ever do, and you'll either need to keep expanding your nanofield to handle the extra workload or accept that using this Nanosuite will probably weaken you in other ways.>

Benning nodded. "Okay, I'm sold, Emmed Oswald. In return for these upgrades, I'll sell you a license for my templates at – say, 25% off the standard cost."

"Wait, what?" he demanded. "Benning Kidd, these upgrades cost hundreds of credits! I assumed I'd be getting those licenses for free!"

"Oh, Hole, no," Benning chuckled. "Over the next few standard years, those licenses will be worth tens of thousands of credits to me, Emmed Oswald. I can't just give them away. I can give them to you first, though, and at a discount so you can undercut any larger companies that purchase them after. You'll have them first, and you'll have them cheaper."

"That'll only be good until whoever you took them from comes up with something better," he shook his head. "That might be as soon as two standard years. I might not make my investment back. Maybe if I got them at 25% of standard cost instead of 25% off..."

"I'll give you 50%," she said firmly. "I won't go any lower. You're also getting the opportunity to examine a scanner nanite, which you wouldn't normally have, remember?"

"Deal," he sighed. "Okay, you're definitely going to want to be in your domain for this, Benning Kidd. It's going to take a while..."

Benning walked out of the shop an hour later. Her nanofield spread out around her, wider than it had been earlier that day as her upgraded 'net gained better control of it. She not only felt the presence of the nanofields around her – the station's, the Citizens she passed, even the doors nearby – but she could dimly sense the 'nets beyond them. She knew that, if she wanted, she could use her Cyberwarfare skill to hack those 'nets, and going through their nanofields would make it far easier than her normal route. Even better, her new mods meshed well with the incidental upgrade she'd gotten from integrated the scanning nanites into her field.

NANOFIELD UPGRADE!
You have upgraded your nanofield
with the modification:
Deep Scanning

She concentrated on a Citizen she passed, and her new scanning nanites soared forth at her will.

BRALEY VADEKAR
Level 13 Performance Artist
Damage Rating: 2.3 (IMP Mark 2)
Defense Rating: 3.1 (Comparm Mark 3)
Resistance Rating: 7

STATS
Physicality: 8.2
Coordination: 9.6
Resistance: 8.7

Acuity: 8.7
Willpower: 8.2
Social: 10.3

SKILLS
...

Thanks to her new nanites, she could basically perform a full scan on anyone within range of her nanofield. It was a powerful upgrade, and thanks to her new nanosuite, she could scan everyone and everything in range if she wanted. She had no real need for it at the moment, but in combat, knowing an opponent's full stats, skills, and abilities was incredibly powerful.

Now, she just needed to test it out in the arena. It would be a risk, revealing herself where the Fleet could find and apprehend her, but she'd come to Majoris Prime when she had for a reason. A tournament was about to start, and theoretically, anyone in a tournament was immune from apprehension during the tournament.

It was time to see if the Fleet followed its own rules or not.

CHAPTER 10

Soft mud squished under Benning's feet, and black water swirled around her ankles, dragging at her under the effects of heavily increased gravity. Insects leaped around her, constantly landing on her armor and crawling across her helmet's visor but apparently unable to fly in the high-g environment. Steam rose from the still water, shrouding her in heavy fog that sharply limited direct lines of sight, not that Benning had good sight lines anyway. Bushes and scrubby trees ranging in height from one to three ems crowded around her, their thick, blue-tinted leaves overlapping almost like scales and obscuring her vision more or less completely. Even worse, the leaves seemed to blunt her passive scanners, cutting her helmet's display range to a bit less than five ems. Fortunately, her armor kept her comfortable and dry; the ambient temperature of 42 Celsius wasn't life-threatening, but Benning wouldn't have wanted to fight in it.

What is this place, Tiddly? she asked silently.

<Terra Novanus,> the gnome answered brightly. <The fifth planet in the Novanus system. At least, this is how it looked when the Collective first found it. It was a swamp planet, rich with life and abundant water but lacking any sort of intelligent animals.>

Benning glanced around, her vision and sensors failing to penetrate the dense fog surrounding her. *How are these plants blocking my scanners?*

<Terra Novanus is a dense world with a lot of heavy

metals in the soil, Benning Kidd. The plant life leaches those from the ground and uses them to fortify their leaves and stems, so those bushes are the equivalent of a wall of depleted uranium.>

Something crashed through the bushes, and Benning spun as an em-long, six-legged creature burst from the foliage and flung itself at her. Her rifle tracked to the head of the huge insect almost without her guidance and roared, hurling a half-dozen platinum bullets into its skull. The first few sparked and cracked against the dark blue shell of the beast, but most of the bullets tore through its exoskeleton and plunged into the head beneath, killing it instantly. The monster plunged into the fetid water, half-buried in the soft mud beneath, then vanished as the arena reclaimed its body.

<One of the peculiarities of Terra Novanus is that the native animal life never evolved past the arthropod phase,> Tiddly added brightly. <Some scholars think that's because the high gravity selected for an insect's open circulatory system and powerful muscles, but no one really knows why.>

Benning ignored the information; it wouldn't help her in this battle. She guessed that the arena had more of the large insects roaming the battlefield, keeping her or her opponent from holing up somewhere and setting an ambush. She didn't need to know anything about them except that they were fairly quick and had decent armor. They were an annoyance, nothing more, and she didn't much care about the quirks of the native fauna of a planet almost sixteen lightyears away.

Gunfire rattled in the distance, and Benning spun to face the sound, dropping to one knee in the muck. She waited for a minute, but no more gunfire followed. It had sounded relatively close, as if her opponent were within a dozen ems or so, but her extended nanofield felt no trace of her foe. That meant the woman had to be at least thirty ems distant, the effective radius of her field, despite the nearness of the sound – either that, or the woman knew how to mask herself from Benning's nanofield. That was probably possible, but it was also probably prohibitively expensive. Still, that possibility worried Benning; Elenoh Balbay was a Vanguard, a soldier who specialized in high-risk, close combat. She wore extremely heavy armor and carried at least three different melee weapons. If she could get close to Benning undetected, she'd probably win this match. Distance was Benning's only real hope for victory.

<It's probably just a trick of sound, Benning Kidd,> Tiddly assured her. <The high gravity means the atmosphere here is a lot denser than normal, which carries sound a lot farther.>

Benning certainly hoped the AI was correct, but she couldn't worry about it. Either Balbay was close and undetected – in which case this match was going to end quickly – or she was still far, and sound carried well. Benning had to hope for the latter, but she also had to plan for the former. The same sound of gunfire that alerted her to her foe's presence would have also drawn Balbay toward Benning. Benning wanted to get close enough to the woman to be able to sense her, at least, but she didn't want Balbay knowing where she was at the same time.

Reluctantly, she slipped her rifle back into her gladiator pack and pulled out the cylindrical rod attached to her right thigh. She pushed the barest effort of will at the thirty-cim shaft, and it practically leaped from her hand as it lengthened into an em-long haft with a spiked hammer at the end. Two sharp spikes jutted from the weapon, one on the back of the hammer and the other creating a spearpoint on the end. All three glowed with the dull radiance of antimatter held in a magnetic field.

Something crashed in the brush behind her, and

Benning spun to see another of the insectoid natives of the swamp leaping for her. She stabbed with the spearpoint of her hammer, her movements clumsy and slow in the increased gravity. The spike slipped off the monster's shell, scoring a long line in the armor as its antimatter coating etched the exoskeleton, and its weight slammed into the hammer head, driving the weapon toward her.

Benning twisted and sidestepped, pushing the creature past her and into the muck below. The thing didn't have much mass, but thanks to the increased gravity, its leap carried far more momentum than it should have. That momentum shoved Benning back a step, but it also drove the insect deep into the mud beneath the swampy surface, and it struggled for a moment to right itself. Benning didn't give it that moment; she swung her hammer around in a two-handed, overhead strike, slamming the spiked head into the creature's thorax. Gravity aided her blow, and the antimatter coated head crashed through the monster's shell, driving it deeper into the mud and tearing a jagged hole in its armor. The insect thrashed, trying to escape. It was easily strong enough to toss Benning aside, but its half-buried legs lacked the leverage it needed to lift her increased weight, and its struggles only tore the bleeding hole in it open wider. In less than a minute, the thing stopped struggling and vanished, nearly dumping Benning into the swampy water as it did.

She moved slowly in the direction she'd heard gunfire, her increased weight combining with the thick air, dark water, and soft mud to drag at her limbs as she moved. More of the insects attacked her, but she quickly learned how to defeat them. The beasts were swift and powerful, but their initial charge carried so much momentum that if it missed, they either buried themselves in mud or cracked hard against bushes or trees. Benning learned to dodge that first strike; their attempts to recover from the missed attack gave her several seconds to strike freely. Their thin, jointed limbs were especially vulnerable, and if she cracked two of those, the insects seemed to lose their ability to charge at her. Once she broke three, the things found themselves stuck in the heavy mud, unable to do more than slowly creep forward. Once she discovered that, Benning didn't bother killing the insects. She disabled them and left them in her wake; she suspected the arena would recover the crippled creatures, but it might delay that moment for a bit while they still lived, meaning the creatures weren't respawning as swiftly to attack her.

Balbay seemed to be encountering the same creatures but had decided to keep killing them with gunfire. The sound allowed Benning to track her foe, although the way the noise carried in the dense air made her journey a little imprecise. At first, Benning wondered why Balbay hadn't switched to melee weapons the way she had, but a little thought explained that. The Vanguard wanted Benning to find her; she needed the Corsair to close with her, and the best way to make that happen was to guide Benning with gunfire. With the swamp obscuring both vision and scanners, Balbay probably assumed that the pair would stumble on one another, and in that sort of close battle, Benning would be at a disadvantage.

Benning's nanofield, though, countered that threat. She felt Elenoh Balbay's nanofield long before the Vanguard could see her and took shelter behind one of the scan-disrupting shrubs. She reached out with her nanites and directed them to connect to the Vanguard's weapons and armor. She couldn't disable those, not without needing so much time that she risked Balbay's scanners detecting her, but she weakened the woman's connection to her gear, causing it to respond slower than it should and disrupting her ability to use her equipment effectively.

She announced her presence with a shot from her Foehammer rifle. The neutronium slug, its momentum enhanced by an injection of dark matter, slammed into Balbay's side and punched through her heavy armor, burying itself in her side. The kinetic armor should have reacted instantly, returning some of the bullet's force to it and dampening its impact, but with its field disrupted, it responded too slowly to keep the bullet out.

Balbay charged at Benning, but her bulky, massive armor dragged at her limbs in the increased gravity. Benning's deep scan of the Vanguard showed she had an ability called Dread Charge, and according to Tiddly, that ability would usually let Balbay cover ten or more ems of distance at a greatly increased speed. When Balbay used it in the swamp, though, the mud and water dragged at her feet, allowing her to get closer to Benning but not close enough for melee. The Vanguard returned fire with her own rifle, and Benning's resistance dropped to 83% as a bullet pierced her left shoulder, but the woman seemed like she struggled to aim her weapon, and half of her rounds flew wide without striking Benning at all.

In the end, the Vanguard fell to a knee, her armor rent in five places, blood pouring from her wounds despite the medigel she'd triggered to ease the bleeding. Her aura glowed medium orange in Benning's combat vision, showing that she was wounded significantly but not seriously. Still, the woman held up a gauntleted hand.

"I yield," she said in a low, gravelly voice.

"Elenoh Balbay yields! Benning Kidd is the winner!" the arena manager's voice spoke over the loudspeaker as the gray sky overhead suddenly lit with the brilliance of the arena's lights. The water around Benning drained away, and the mud and trees vanished, leaving the pair of fighters standing and kneeling on a smooth, metal floor. The fog disappeared to reveal hundreds of cheering spectators, a small number for a tournament match but a decent showing considering that neither Benning nor Balbay were serious contenders for a top ten spot in their group.

"Not bad," Balbay grunted as gravity returned to normal, and she rose to her feet unsteadily. "You got lucky, though."

"Oh?" Benning said noncommittally. "How?"

"My equipment isn't working right," the Vanguard shook her head, pulling off her helmet to reveal short, light brown hair and a square face. "It shouldn't have been that easy for you to get through my armor, and I was having trouble with my rifle's sights." She shrugged. "I'll have to get it looked at, but if that hadn't happened, I would have had you. The lack of visibility helped me a lot more than it did you."

"Maybe," Benning replied. "Although the high-g and soft ground hurt you more than me, too. If we'd gotten close, I might have been able to stay ahead of your weapons and whittle you down with my hammer and pistols. The arena tries to keep the early rounds of a tournament fair, after all."

"True." Balbay shrugged again. "In either case, congratulations on your victory. I'm going to get my gear checked out; I need to get it fixed before my next match, or I'll be out on the first day."

Benning nodded and walked away from the Vanguard, her heart pounding in her chest. She'd won, and she'd done so convincingly. It hadn't even really been a close match. That would certainly help her chances of ending in the top 20% of her group and staying in the tournament. She was barely wounded, and she'd be fully healed, her armor restored, in a minute or so. She should have been excited and proud, but she wasn't.

To enter the tournament, she'd openly identified herself as Benning Kidd, and she'd done so in one of the largest and most populous systems in the Collective. Sirius wasn't the Oort Cloud, where laws were more like suggestions and were only enforced when it suited the powers-that be. It certainly wasn't Wolf, where the laws were almost nonexistent, and Citizens were permitted to do just about anything they wanted, so long as they were strong enough to deal with the consequences. It was a law-abiding system, a place where the Fleet and its regulations were welcomed – and Benning had made an enemy of that Fleet. While she knew that theoretically, being in the tournament should shelter her from apprehension, realistically, she didn't know if the system's administrators would put up much of a fuss over a low-leveled gladiator who wasn't likely to make it past the second day of the tournament. She knew she could be walking into the Fleet's hands, and the thought of what she'd do if that were the case had her heart racing madly.

When she stepped out of the contender's room to catch the shuttle back to the main entrance of the arena, part of her almost felt relieved to see the Fleet officer standing at the shuttle's entrance, obviously waiting for her. The woman wore a dark blue spacer suit with silver chasing and a similarly colored emblem on her left breast that looked like six globes set in a hexagonal shape around a triangle, with a sprig of leaves and a rifle crossed behind it all. Her collar had a single silver circle a cim wide on each side of her throat, denoting her rank as a junior lieutenant in the Fleet.

The officer stepped forward, her silver eyes hard and gleaming against her brown skin. She stood as tall as Benning but was far less muscled, and Benning sent a quick scan the woman's way to see who she was dealing with.

ADLYN BECHARD
Level 7 Fleet Officer
Damage Rating: 5.3 (IMP Fleet Issue)

Defense Rating: 7.2 (Comparm Fleet
Issue)
Resistance Rating: 9

STATS
Physicality: 8.9
Coordination: 8.3
Resistance: 8.0

Acuity: 9.6
Willpower: 8.2
Social: 10.3

The officer before her was young and obviously fairly new to the Fleet. Her stats didn't look like she'd trained them much, and she only carried Fleet-issued gear. Benning could kill her in an instant without even trying, but doing so would probably bring every security force within a hundred ems down on her, and she'd have to fight her way free of the station – which she wasn't certain she could do. She reached down and touched her pistol but didn't draw it; she'd kill the woman before she allowed herself to be taken, but she hoped that neither happened.

"Citizen Benning Kidd?" Bechard asked, her voice both eager and slightly uncertain as her eyes flicked down to the pistol Benning touched.

"Yes," Benning nodded, trying to keep her voice calm while her heart pounded in her chest.

"My designation is Adlyn Bechard, Junior Lieutenant in the Collective Fleet," the woman introduced herself. "I think you know why I'm here."

"Not in the slightest," Benning shook her head.

Bechard's eyes flashed. "Benning Kidd, you've been

accused of crimes against the Collective. I'm here to investigate those charges as the Fleet's representative."

"That doesn't explain why you're here," Benning pointed out. She and Tiddly had played this scenario out multiple times, and the gnome had advised Benning to say as little as possible. A denial of the charges could count as a willingness to be interrogated, and admitting to the charges would obviously be a terrible idea.

"I'm here to ask you some questions, nothing more. I'm simply interested in discovering the truth of this matter." Bechard smiled at Benning in a strange fashion, her expression one that Benning couldn't read despite her training in understanding facial cues. Her smile seemed thin, her lips tightly pressed against her teeth. Her eyes were wide but hard, and the entire expression looked strained to Benning.

<She's trying to be reassuring,> Tiddly explained. <She's not doing it well, though. The idea is to make you relaxed and think that she's here to help you.>

She's making me want to shoot her, Benning thought sourly.

<I don't recommend that, Benning Kidd. It sounds like the Fleet is still looking into what you did but isn't ready to act yet. If you kill a Fleet officer, that'll change pretty quickly.>

Benning's hand itched to draw her pistol, but she restrained herself and said nothing. After a long few moments of silence, Bechard cleared her throat uncomfortably.

"You are to come with me for questioning," the lieutenant said, her voice calm but firm. "By my authority as an official Fleet representative..."

"Are you arresting me, Adlyn Bechard?" Benning cut

the woman off.

"If necessary, yes, Benning Kidd. You will come with me, and you will answer the charges leveled against you."

"Fleet Lieutenant Adlyn Bechard," the voice of the arena manager suddenly sounded in Benning's ears, and from the expression on Bechard's face, she heard it as well. "By the laws of this system, no entrant to a tournament can be arrested, detained, or punished while within the tournament and for a full solar day after."

"This Citizen is accused of crimes against the Collective as a whole," Bechard replied, her face upturned toward the ceiling. "Fleet law supersedes local law, and it's my duty to bring her in..."

"In which case, this system's administrators will file a formal grievance against the Fleet, naming you as the injuring party," the manager interrupted. "We will demand reparations for the loss of credits and damage to our reputation, and we will request that you be formally reprimanded."

Bechard's face paled at that threat, and thanks to her Starship Officer training, Benning understood why. A formal reprimand would set the officer's career back at least a decade, if not longer, and any reparations would be garnished from her salary. The arena could claim a loss of thousands of credits, if not more, and Bechard wouldn't even be considered for promotion until that debt was paid in full – which could take a century.

"Very well," Bechard nodded. "I'll respect your system's laws in this matter." She leaned forward. "I'll be following you out of the station when the tournament's over, though, Benning Kidd. The moment your amnesty expires, you'll either speak with me, or I will arrest you and impound your vessel."

Benning wanted to match the woman's threat with one of her own, but she bit down her response. Anything she said would make the situation worse, and if she goaded the lieutenant enough, the woman might ignore the possible consequences and try to arrest Benning anyway. Benning wouldn't allow that, of course, but the station also couldn't stand by and let a Fleet officer be killed or injured. She'd be removed from the tournament, at the very least, and the station might join the Fleet in its hunt for her.

At the same time, she couldn't have Bechard chasing her out of the system, either. At some point, she'd have to deal with the officer or end up being arrested. She just had to do it in a way that couldn't be traced back to her. She had an idea for that, and it would be much, much easier on the station than out in the void.

"Whatever you say, Lieutenant," Benning said at last, walking around the woman, concealing the smile that tugged at her cheeks. "I need to get ready for my next match, so if there's nothing else, I'll be on my way."

She walked onto the shuttle, practically feeling the officer's eyes burning into her back. She had preparations to make. Her struggle with the Fleet was about to turn deadly.

CHAPTER 11

Stone walls towered to either side of Benning, stretching an em above her head and ending in an arched ceiling of the same material. The reddish-brown walls looked to be made of soft stone or fired clay bricks held together with some sort of mortar, a fact that Benning had already confirmed by smashing one of the bricks with a casual blow of her fist. Hard clay and gravel crunched beneath her boots, forcing her to move slowly to avoid making too much noise. Wooden sticks that burned with flickering flames lined the walls, bathing the narrow passage in dim, uncertain light that concealed almost as much as it revealed.

According to Tiddly, the arena setup for this match was a subterranean labyrinth, an ancient Earth maze. The original was built completely of stone, but this one wasn't; Benning's attempts to break through a wall revealed that the walls were dense microthene sheathed in soft bricks. Benning thought she could still probably get through the five-cim microthene walls if she really wanted to, but it would take time and create far too much noise. Noise, she'd discovered, attracted attention in the labyrinth.

Gravel crunched in the passage ahead of her, and she snapped her Arcbar rifle into place as her nanofield detected the presence of one of the labyrinth's wandering creatures. The thing that appeared around the corner was huge, at least half an em taller than Benning. It looked vaguely humanoid, with thick legs that ended in cloven hooves and long arms. Shaggy fur covered its black body, and its tiny head sported two small upcurved horns. Its face looked mostly human, but its large eyes lacked any sort of intelligence. The creature let out an echoing bellow as it charged Benning, curling its horn-covered fingers into heavy fists.

Benning's rifle barked, and holes appeared in the creature as she poured three rounds into its skull and three more into the center of its chest. The abomination barely stumbled, continuing to charge forward, and Benning kept firing at her attacker. The arena's creatures were tough and, as she'd learned the hard way, immensely strong. Their fists struck like sledgehammer blows, damaging her even through her armor, and it took a lot of bullets to bring one down. She'd tried engaging one in melee, but in the narrow confines of the tunnels, she couldn't use her hammer effectively, and their toughness and strength made it hard for her to hold them back even with the fully extended, two-em shaft of her hammer and an antimatter-coated spearpoint.

That was the point, she supposed. The labyrinth's microthene walls blocked scanning and her nanofield in equal measure, and since the monsters were difficult to defeat in melee combat, she and her opponent would both have to kill them with gunfire. Sounds carried in the stone hallways – she'd heard her opponent's battles with the creatures several times already – so there wouldn't be much element of surprise when the two finally met. That meeting was also certain; as far as Benning could tell, the labyrinth was just one long passage, not a series of branching hallways the way she'd expected.

<That's the difference between a labyrinth and a maze, Benning Kidd,> Tiddly supplied happily as the arena's creation dropped at last and was reabsorbed by the nanofield. <Mazes have multiple paths, many of which are dead ends. Labyrinths have a single, long path that leads to the center. My guess is that you'll meet Wayn Liu there, or at least close

to there.>

Benning suppressed a grimace; she wasn't really looking forward to running into Wayn Liu. The man was a professional gladiator two levels higher than Benning, and he was one of the top seeds to win the entire group. Benning was happy that she'd made it to the third day of the tournament, placing in the top twenty percent on the first and second days, but she knew she wouldn't be moving on. She'd lost her first match that day when she found herself fighting a sniper battle against a dedicated sharpshooter across a series of ice mining platforms. Benning was a good shot, but her rifle wasn't specifically designed for sniping across five or six kim distances the way Julirann Crawford's was. She'd ended up taking an antimatter bullet to the chest that put her out of commission and forced her to surrender.

Her only consolation was that she'd made the contest last long enough that Crawford probably wouldn't be moving on either; the man's career was Marksman, and he should have taken her out quickly. He'd ended up pretty badly wounded himself, though, and that probably sunk his chances of advancing. Some of Benning's opponents in past tournaments had told her they hoped she advanced, so they at least lost to someone skilled. Benning didn't really understand that concept. She hadn't lost to Julirann Crawford because the man was better than her; she'd lost because the arena put them in an environment that favored him more than it did her. It was luck, pure and simple. Fighting hard enough that she took him out of the tourney with her was the closest she could come to defeating the sniper, and she hoped she'd done it.

While that loss would certainly push her out of the tournament – less than a hundred contestants would be moving on that day, and most if not all of those would be undefeated – it also cleared the path for her to act against Adlyn Bechard. Benning had been tempted to start her plan the day before, but she'd come so close to advancing in the last tournament despite facing an opponent using prohibited nanotech that she gambled slightly on making it into day three. She had a backup plan if she'd failed to advance, but fortunately, she hadn't needed it. That just left her moving forward with her original plan – and she wasn't really looking forward to it.

As Tiddly predicted, the passageway ended at last in a wide, circular room that opened to a black, star-filled sky overhead. Large stone blocks lay scattered around the space, and Benning quickly dove for cover behind one; from the sound of Liu's gunfire, he was about to enter the center of the maze as well. As she rolled behind a stone, she caught a glimpse of her opponent darting behind a similar rock across the room from her. The man's emerald armor gleamed in the flickering firelight, making him easy enough to track.

Benning rolled to the side, her rifle peeking out, and fired a trio of shots at the stone a hundred ems away. Her bullets dug into the soft rock, but she doubted they could penetrate completely, especially if the stone had a microthene core. A flash caught her eye as a spot next to the rock flashed red in her visor, and she rolled back as a pair of bullets flashed through the air where she'd just been.

She rose to a crouch and popped up at the top of the stone, but as she did, a bullet cracked hard against her helmet, rocking her head and forcing her to drop down. She swore as she guessed that Liu had some sort of long-range scanner that could track her behind the stone; either that, or he'd gotten lucky. It was safer to assume he knew where she was. Unfortunately, her nanofield didn't reach that far, so while he could presumably see her, she had no idea exactly where he was. That left her with very few options.

She slipped out of hiding again, this time ignoring the bullet that cracked against her helm as she unleashed a five-round burst at the distant muzzle flash. Liu vanished behind his cover, and Benning used the moment to fling a metal orb that pulsed with red light. The fusion grenade bounced off the top of Liu's stone and dropped to the ground, and as expected, the gladiator leaped from his cover, dashing toward the nearest stone. Benning tracked him as he ran, unloading bullets into his bright green armor, then ducked behind her rock just before the grenade exploded. The blast filled the room with a blaze of light, and the sound pounded against Benning's head, although her helmet kept the volume from damaging her ears.

She slipped back out of cover, her rifle tracking toward Liu's new hiding place, prepared to take another bullet to strike at the man again. Instead, she saw a green-flashing orb sailing toward her as the gladiator retaliated with his own grenade, and she swore and raced from her hiding place. Bullets slammed into her armor, and she felt one round pierce her right hip, but she ignored the pain and dove for cover as Liu's grenade exploded.

Her vision lurched as the meson blast went off, hurling eta-c particles out into the air at nearly the speed of light. The charmed quark-antiquark pairs zipped through solid matter with ease and decayed swiftly, turning into lighter mesons that then decayed into photons, electrons, and neutrinos. Thousands of the particles decayed inside Benning, flooding her body with x-ray radiation and slamming electrons into the inside of her armor, disrupting it for a moment. The world lurched around her, and her stomach heaved, threatening to empty its contents into her helmet as her resistance bar plummeted to 63% in an instant.

She pushed aside her dizziness and nausea, grinning despite herself. While she'd fought off the effects of the grenade, Liu moved closer and was now in range of her nanofield. She felt him grabbing another grenade, and she quickly slammed her nanites against the object. She couldn't hack it before he threw it, but she didn't need to. Her nanites reached into the device and activated it, triggering the detonation mechanism. Nothing happened as the grenade's failsafe triggered, preventing it from exploding, but when Liu flung it, the device burst in midair close to halfway between the pair, bathing them both fairly equally in radiation. Benning's resistance dropped again to 57%, but Liu should have gotten a similar dose, and she doubted he'd try another grenade without knowing why that one had gone off in midair.

Benning tossed another fusion grenade, forcing the gladiator to dive for new cover, firing at her as he ran. His heavy bullets slammed into her helmet, cracking the microthene of her visor, but his aura dimmed to bright orange as her rounds ripped through his liquid metal armor and into the flesh beneath. That crack was what she'd been waiting for.

Taking a deep breath, Benning tossed another grenade to keep the man moving while she activated her nano-disassemblers. She waited for the arena's detection systems to recognize them as a threat, but no alarms sounded. She'd tested the disassemblers in the arena before, and their detectors couldn't pick the dangerous nanites out from the rest of her field when they were close to her. She had no doubt that if she sent them after Liu, that would change in a heartbeat, but the man wasn't her target. She willed the disassemblers into the crack in her visor, forcing them to deepen and widen it until only a micrometer of material protected her from the exterior atmosphere.

She fired at Liu as he ran, tensing herself as his rifle swung toward her. A flash lit her vision as something smashed into her face with the force of a hammer. Pain flared in her as Liu's bullet ripped into her skull, but it ended quickly as the featureless plain of her domain formed around her, along with a bright red screen that she'd been expecting.

> YOU HAVE DIED!
> As a Citizen of the Collective, you will
> never suffer permanent death. Upon
> your death, a copy of your consciousness
> was made, and you will be reborn in
> the nearest respawning facility of:
>
> SIRIUS MAJORIS PRIME STATION
>
> You will suffer the following
> respawn penalties:
> Path advancement -7%
> All stats -0.1
> Conditioning -0.4
> Martial Combat -0.4
> Weapons Expertise -0.4
>
> Respawn delay: 46 solar hours

Benning quickly dismissed the screen and rushed to the podium in the center of her domain as Tiddly appeared before her. The death penalty hurt, but it was a lot better than being spawn-camped to level 1 or imprisoned for several standard years. She'd just have to work hard to replace what she'd lost; she could probably do that in a few weeks or months at most.

"Well, that part of your plan worked, Benning Kidd," the gnome said, shaking her head. "Those losses are rough, but it could have been worse. At least the System didn't interpret this as a suicide attempt."

"Would that have mattered?" Benning asked curiously as she activated her podium and began accessing Prime Station's 'net.

"Oh, absolutely. Remember, the entire point of the death penalties was to discourage Citizens from killing themselves in creative ways. Suicide penalties are way worse than regular death penalties. You could have lost an entire level or points worth of stats." The AI half-smiled. "These penalties are more in line with dying in pursuit of your path. Nothing you can ignore, but not crippling."

Benning almost asked the gnome why she hadn't mentioned that in the first place, but the Corsair realized it wouldn't have mattered. Benning would have gone ahead with her plan, and knowing the risk would just have distracted her. In the end, it was probably best that she hadn't known. Benning understood that sometimes, ignorance was highly preferable to knowledge. Discovering her origins had taught her that well.

She turned her focus to the podium. Gaining access to the station's 'net took only a few seconds, as she'd been hacking it regularly since she met Bechard to keep an eye on the Fleet officer and, more importantly, her ship. It took her less than a minute more to gain control of the respawn queue and alter it so she would be reborn in under an hour. She assumed the identity of a Citizen named Yve Rybalkina, a mercenary who'd died in the tournament yesterday, altering the queue so that the 'net would connect to Benning's domain to respawn Rybalkina and would access the mercenary's during Benning's respawn. Once Rybalkin truly respawned, the station would recognize the error and correct it, but by that time, Benning hoped to be lightyears distant.

Benning chose to respawn with a vastly altered appearance. Her hair was dark blonde and hung to her ears in curly waves. Her eyes shifted from bright blue to deep brown, while her skin darkened to the color of cocoa. Her shoulders widened and her hips narrowed, making her look more muscular and less feminine, and she lengthened her nose and chin. When the purple light faded and she stepped out of the respawn chamber, she felt confident that no one would recognize her.

She waited for a full hour for her gear and upgrades to be restored. She'd worried that respawn would cost her some of those upgrades, especially the disassemblers and scanning nanites, but apparently whatever Emmed Oswald did to bind those to her carried into her new incarnation, and she felt her base nanites shift into those altered forms after her 'net and nanofield upgrades loaded. As she left the respawn chamber, she activated her infiltrator suite, shifting her armor to a bright cyan color that she hoped would be memorable, then went looking for her quarry.

Adlyn Bechard slept on her ship, the *CSS Mackerel*, and had she been aboard, Benning would have had trouble getting to her. The *Mackerel* was a simple fast frigate, but it had a crew of forty Fleet members, Workers, and Soldiers. Benning's infiltrator suite wouldn't let her impersonate a Fleet officer apparently, that required a far more advanced version of the software – and her nanofield would alert any Citizen to the fact that she wasn't a Worker or Soldier. She still might have been able to board, but not without an outcry, and she'd need a full marine team to take the ship once an alert was raised.

Fortunately, it seemed that Bechard didn't spend much time on the ship outside of sleeping there. Benning tracked her to a place called Caze's Nebula, a small store off the main promenade. The inside of the building was dark, lit with shifting red and violet lights, and contained hundreds of black capsules.

What is this place, Tiddly? Benning asked as she looked around the dark room with a frown.

<It's a movie arcade, Benning Kidd. Citizens can come here to watch various videos and shows through the

Overnet.>

Why would they want to do that?

<Entertainment, primarily. Some people find watching shows and movies enjoyable. Many of the shows are interactive, as well, so a Citizen can be part of the movie themselves or even change how it goes if they want to.>

What kind of shows? Benning asked, her interest piquing. *Do they have videos on Fleet Tactics or combat?*

<Probably, but they're not meant to be instructional. They're meant to be fun. This arcade probably has access to millions or billions of shows, so you can find something to suit just about anyone. There are shows that are funny, or frightening, or exciting, or even sad. Humans seem to enjoy watching sad things for some reason.>

Benning frowned. *Isn't sadness supposed to be a bad feeling?*

<Yes, but many humans enjoy it, anyway.>

The Corsair shook her head. *Okay, but why come here? Can't they just watch these things from their domains?*

<Sure, but to do that, they have to buy the movies or shows, Benning Kidd,> the AI laughed. <That can get expensive fast since some of these shows charge by the episode – or even by the minute. Here, they pay a few credits to the owner and have access to a lot more entertainment than they could get normally. The arcade's owner, in turn, pays a portion of their profits to one of the corporations that produce these shows to be able to show them to everyone.>

Benning stared at the closed capsules in silent disapproval. She understood the concept well enough; entertainment was how the System kept her docile when she'd been a Drone. She labored at pointless tasks daily for a single game credit that let her entertain herself for a few hours and made the day's tasks seem worthwhile. Between the games and the System clouding her long-term memory, Benning and the other Drones had few complaints about their existence.

Was the System doing the same thing to these Citizens? The movies Tiddly spoke of seemed like a massive waste of time to Benning. She could spend that time improving her stats, training her skills, pursuing her path, or even making credits by gambling at the arena. That was entertaining and profitable. By encouraging Citizens to be lazy and indolent, was the System keeping them docile? Benning didn't know, but she suspected that was partially the case.

I'll wait for her outside, she said firmly, turning and stalking out the door. Anger filled her, anger at her old life, at the Citizens allowing themselves to be pacified, and at the System for controlling everyone and everything. That anger built, seeking a target, and when Bechard finally walked out of the arcade, a small smile plastered on her face, Benning finally found one.

She moved swiftly, not even bothering to follow Bechard into a less populated area, as she'd originally intended. She stood, drawing her pistol, and leveled it at the woman. A few Citizens nearby cursed, and to her credit, the Fleet Officer grabbed for her own sidearm, trying to draw it before Benning could fire. Benning's Teravolt pistol fired first, though, the injector mixing a stream of protons and antiprotons in the firing chamber that propelled the 20mm bullet at a velocity slightly greater than the speed of sound. The tungsten-coated bullet pierced Bechard's comparm effortlessly, punching into her stomach, and the platinum core shattered. Shards of razorlike platinum ripped through the woman's abdomen, bouncing off the inside of her armor and her ribs and shredding her internal organs.

Bechard cried out and fell to one knee, clutching her

bleeding stomach. She tried to raise her pistol, but Benning put another shot into the officer's shoulder, shattering her collarbone and rendering that arm useless. She strode over to the bleeding Fleet officer and slammed her foot into the woman's chest, knocking her onto her back, then pushed her boot against Bechard's chest to hold her in place.

"Who – who are you?" Bechard groaned. "Wh-what are you doing?"

"My designation doesn't matter," Benning said simply. "I'm just here to deliver a message."

"Do – do you know who I am?" Bechard gritted. "What I am?"

"Obviously," Benning shrugged. "It doesn't matter to me, though." Her hand tightened slightly around her pistol; the anger surging in her begged her to inflict pain on this woman, to punish her for being part of the System that hunted Benning. She pushed that anger aside, though. Torture was a tool, and while Benning didn't hesitate to use it, she only did so for a purpose. She tried not to inflict pain for its own sake or just to enjoy someone's suffering. There would be no point to tormenting Bechard; she was doing her job, and the Fleet wouldn't stop hunting Benning just because she tortured an officer. In fact, they might hunt her even harder.

"What do you want?" Bechard gasped.

"Like I said, I'm delivering a message." Benning leaned forward. "You're hunting Benning Kidd. You should know that you're not the only one, and some of those hunting her don't appreciate interference." She lifted her pistol, pointing it at the woman's skull.

"Wait!" Bechard said, raising her good arm in a warding gesture. "I'm with the Fleet! You can't kill me!"

"Nobles aren't afraid of the Fleet," Benning shrugged.

"And yes, I can." She feathered the trigger, and the gun spoke once. A hole appeared in Bechard's forehead, relatively small and neat, but the back of her skull vanished as the bullet, propelled to low velocity by the pistol's adaptive charge, shredded her brain.

Benning holstered her pistol, turned, and jogged off as Citizens moved quickly out of her way. Security would be coming soon, and the moment Benning was out of immediate sight, she dropped her infiltration suite and allowed her armor to return to its normal crimson color. She slowed to a walk, removing her helmet and moving purposefully without looking around as she headed for the *Hammer.* She connected to the station's 'net as she walked, reaching out for the feeds of the cameras following her and encrypting the section where she'd shifted armor colors. She did the same thing every so often as she switched passages, trying to obscure her trail.

Eventually, the station's administrators would decrypt those files, and when they did, they'd see Bechard's assailant boarding the *Hammer.* That couldn't be helped, and while Benning's official status as dead and awaiting respawn would suggest that she hadn't killed Bechard herself, the blame would still be laid at her feet. That might take days or weeks, though, and by then, Bechard might be far down a false trail. Benning hoped that her words would send the Fleet hunting for whatever Nobles worked against her, but she had no real hopes that their efforts would do more than distract from her capture. Eventually, the Fleet would come for her; she needed to be ready when they did.

In the meantime, if the *Hammer* left station now, the *Mackerel* wouldn't follow; it would have to wait for Bechard to respawn, then investigate her execution. By the time anyone realized Benning's ship left without her aboard, she'd be long gone.

<The Fleet isn't just going to take you killing one of their officers, Benning Kidd,> Tiddly reminded her. <Eventually, they'll decide you were behind it and come for you.>

I know, Tiddly, Benning agreed. *I need to start getting ready for them. It's time that I started expanding my fleet – and that means credits. It looks like I'm turning pirate after all.*

CHAPTER 12

"Captain, target is maintaining course and speed," the red-blonde man sitting at the Comm console of the *Resolute Hammer* said in a deep, mellifluent voice. "They don't seem to be reacting to our presence yet."

Elden Rush was the newest addition to Benning's crew. A handful of large battles with her fleet had shown her that in combat, Brialle Caldwell was too busy piloting the *Hammer* and keeping the formation intact to keep Benning apprised of what enemy ships were doing. The new Communications Officer was a Solar Cartographer by trade and had abilities that allowed him to sense the area around him through the Overnet plus a high social stat. Benning hoped his abilities would be useful in combat and his social stat would work in her favor during communications with other vessels and stations; this would be the man's first test in real combat, though, so she wasn't sure what to expect from him.

Her mind flitted through the ship's 'net, tracking a line of four clipper cargo ships soaring a light-hour away. The four vessels traveled in a straight formation, keeping five leconds between each ship. Six other ships moved around the line in a helical formation, and those were what had attracted Benning's attention to this convoy. A full frigate, two fast frigates, and three corvettes were a lot of protection for ships that were ostensibly carrying solid anti-helium. Anti-helium was useful in power plants and weapons, certainly, but it also wasn't terribly difficult to fabricate, so it didn't have a great deal of value. More to the point, it was somewhat risky to carry, since a single alpha decay anywhere in the cargo hold could set off a chain reaction that obliterated the vessel. Alpha particles weren't likely to be spontaneously created by the energy of a dive, but they were possible.

The fleet had been shadowing the convoy for several hours now as it passed the Cancri System. The red dwarf wasn't exactly directly on the convoy's route between Cygni and Helmus, a red dwarf system almost thirty lightyears from Sol, but it was a relative haven for passing ships. Cancri had been colonized originally by deists, believers in a sort of divine universal being. The group held the belief that their deity was the universe; more specifically, they believed that the universe formed inside of their deity, so the entire Collective was just a small part of that being's body.

None of that mattered to Benning, of course. She'd never seen any sort of signs of a higher power beyond the System, and she didn't really understand why people would fanatically believe in something that was by definition unknowable. What did matter to her was the consequences of their beliefs. The deists considered pirates to be viruses infecting the object of their worship, and they responded very harshly to acts of piracy in and near their system. Benning didn't want Cancrian warships interfering with her battle, so she'd waited and watched as the convoy passed the outer edge of the system, a tenth of a lightyear or so from the star.

"Captain, if they continue their dive pattern, they'll dive away from the system in four minutes," Jezper Shields informed her lazily. "They'll probably make a deep dive after that to clear the system completely."

Benning nodded; the convoy had followed a regular dive pattern for the past few hours, diving ten linutes every forty minutes. A ten-linute dive would take the ships far enough from Cancri that the system couldn't provide reliable cover anymore, so they'd deep dive toward the next system, Luyten, five lightyears away and closer to the galactic plane, which the convoy would have to cross to reach Helmus. If they entered a deep dive, Benning would have trouble following and tracking them. She'd need to hit them soon if she was going to hit them at all.

"Helm, ready for double dives, five linutes distance each, and send coordinates to the fleet," Benning ordered. "Fleet, prepare for a double dive." While a full ten-linute dive would be faster than two five-linute ones, the longer the dive, the higher the risk both to each ship in her fleet and to the fleet itself losing its formation. She'd lose thirty seconds or so, but she could make that up by accelerating to flank speed; the convoy was traveling at 1.5 tocks, and the fleet would overtake them rapidly at double that speed.

"Aye Captain," Brialle Caldwell replied. "Transmitting coordinates."

"Fleet is ready for dive," Jezper Shields acknowledged several seconds later as the commanders of her vessels responded to her command.

"Begin double dives," she instructed.

Reality flattened and ballooned around her as her ships dove beneath the fabric of the universe, into CY-space, emerging from that higher dimension only to plunge back into it once more. Benning's thoughts stayed focused on her ships, monitoring their status, watching for signs of damage or drift, and making sure her commanders were following their orders explicitly. Most of her attention stayed on her newest acquisition, the *Arcturus*, since this was the first time its commander, Colrin Amari, would be participating in a battle outside of training drills.

The universe snapped back into place around Benning as they exited their dive. "Fleet status report," she said tersely, even while eyeing her fleet screen.

"*Merciless*, standing by," Avaeyana Roble reported in.

"*Vindictive,* standing by – and looking forward to this," Fodor Hendricks spoke next.

The fleet dove rapidly at the convoy, staying ahead of their dive splashes, and descended on the ships in a storm of graser fire and missile blasts. Benning had all ships in her fleet target a single escort vessel, the frigate she deemed most dangerous. Their first salvo slammed into the frigate in a storm of radiation and neutron blasts, tearing open holes in its hull and dropping its engine power to 12% in an instant. The remaining escorts reacted swiftly, targeting individual ships in the fleet, while the clippers powered up their dive engines and prepared to flee.

Benning's sinkhole generator burst to life, wrapping around the convoy and trapping three of the four cargo ships inside it. Her fleet continued to focus their fire on one escort at a time, bathing the target's entire evasion cone in gamma radiation and antimatter and rocking their hull with warhead blasts. The first fast frigate fell in twenty seconds, its wildly spiking power plant forcing it to shut down its engines and weapons, while the second lasted a minute longer.

Meanwhile, the *Arcturus* opened a pair of bay doors, revealing a massive interior hangar nestled within the ship. Dark energy welled from within the depths of that hanger, and the gravitational waves surging from the ship disgorged six tiny flyboats, spherical vessels only five ems across, each manned by two crew members. The flyboats were lightly armed and armored, but their small size made them fast and maneuverable, and they quickly closed with one of the corvettes. At a third of a lecond, the flyboats' low-powered grasers and antimatter beams tore into the corvette's hull with ease, while the larger vessel struggled to target the tiny, chaotically moving ships. The corvette's engine dropped offline in a minute or so, and the flyboats raced back to their carrier to refuel before heading after the second corvette.

As the last fast frigate and second corvette both went photonic, their power plants losing containment and exploding in a blast of radiation and energy that tore the vessels apart, shuttles launched from the *Merry Messenger,* carrying teams of eight marines each. Two went to secure the drifting corvette and fast frigate – those would either make solid additions to Benning's fleet or bring in credits from resale if they were too damaged – while three of them headed for the clippers. Benning ordered the *Hammer* to intercept the frigate they'd attacked first.

Oddly, the captain of the vessel had locked the exterior hatch, forcing Benning's boarding party to cut it free with an antimatter torch. They stormed into the airlock behind a wall of neutronium-coated shields and an EM pulse grenade. The grenade temporarily disconnected the automated defenses set up in the airlock from the ship's 'net, causing them to fire at anything that moved, which included one another.

While the turrets attacked one another, Benning sent her nanofield out, linking it to the least damaged autocannons. The turrets had decent defenses against hacking, but her direct link through their nanofield allowed her to worm her way into their command trees fairly swiftly. The turrets hesitated before swinging around to point away from the boarding marines, pouring their blasts of high-energy photons through the transtanium walls of the airlock and into the startled ship's marines who waited beyond.

Rather than hack the airlock door, Benning shredded it with her disassembler nanites, and her marines stormed out into the ship's receiving bay. She wielded her Arcbar rifle, firing strategic bursts designed to keep the defenders' heads down as she rushed forward at the vanguard of the assault. Her bullets shattered a microthene visor, killing a Soldier instantly, and punched through another's foam tungsten chest plate, piercing the syleather underlayer and the marine's heart with equal facility. Bullets and gamma radiation both slammed into her armor, and she watched her resistance bar creep slowly down to 78% before the last of the defenders fell.

Her nanites linked to the ship's nanofield, giving her a deeper layer of access than she would normally have when hacking a strange vessel, and she used that access to grab a map of the vessel and seal its doors, separating crew members from one another. The captain could override those locks, of course, but they'd have to do it manually, and by the time they unlocked each door, Benning would have either taken the ship or abandoned the attempt.

Her party raced through the vessel toward the bridge, engaging the ship's bot defenders as necessary and dealing with the few crew members who got in their way. Benning unlocked the doors they encountered and sealed them behind her, at least until they reached the main bridge hatch. The captain had locked that down tightly, and while Benning could hack it open in a matter of minutes, she instead tore the door to pieces with her nano-disassemblers.

Bullets and blasts of graser fire streaked toward the invaders as they rushed into the bridge. Benning and her marines slammed down their shields, forming a solid wall behind which they took cover, and carefully returned fire. Benning ordered her marines to focus fire on the enemy Soldiers while she sent her nanites out to disrupt the bot defenders, scrambling their foe recognition protocols so that they considered everything to be an enemy. The bots blasted the ship's marines from behind, quickly whittling them down before turning their fire on one another. By the time the ship's 'net regained control of the automated defenders, most of them lay in smoking hunks of microthene and metal, and half of the ship's marines were too badly wounded to fight.

Benning led a charge against the remaining defenders, her rifle putting down two more as she closed the distance between them. Bereft of cover, the now-outnumbered Soldiers stood no chance, and while Benning took two bullets – one in her right arm and the other low on her left side – she suffered only one casualty among her boarding party before the bridge fell silent at last.

With the bridge secure, Benning took several minutes to enter the ship's 'net and gain enough access to allow her to remotely control the bot defenders. She sent those into hibernation, tricking the ship into thinking the attack had been repelled, and then led her marines through the ship, killing anyone they found, until at last, the ship stood empty.

"The *Indigo Branch* is secure," she reported once the last defender fell. "What's the status of the rest of the convoy?"

"The *Rainbow's Arc* is secure, Captain," Amari replied in his deep, smooth voice, referring to the corvette. "The *Panther Claw* isn't; the marines are reporting substantially higher defenses on board than anticipated."

"Order them to pull back and hit the ship with neutrino beams," Benning ordered. "If the ship's shielded, finish it off with a torpedo. It's not worth losing good Soldiers just to add another fast frigate to our fleet."

"Aye, Captain."

"Captain, we've captured all three of the clippers," Fodor Hendricks spoke over the comm system. "What do you want to do with them?"

"We don't have the cargo space to transfer their cargo to our ships, Commander. Kill the crews and take the ships under tow until we can gain control of their helms."

"As you wish, Captain. Stealing the ships is going to make the owners angry, though."

"Angrier than stealing or destroying their escorts and taking their cargoes?" Benning chuckled. "I don't think it's going to matter. Besides, once we get the cargoes offloaded, we can always sell the ships back to their owners."

"Ransom," the pirate corrected.

"What?"

"When you take something from someone and make them pay to get it back, it's called 'ransoming', Captain."

Benning rolled her eyes. "Fine, Commander. We'll 'ransom' the ships back to them – unless one of the new merchants on our station wants to buy them. Either way, we'll make credits."

"I'm a big fan of credits, Captain," Hendricks laughed.

Once Benning had the new ships under tow, she ordered the fleet back to IS-39267. The station was almost thirteen lightyears distant, and even after she took salvage ownership of her new ships, the warships were too damaged to travel quickly at first. That sharply limited the fleet's deep diving ability, which meant it was almost two weeks later when the ships returned to the station. Benning brought crews from the station on board the derelict ships to guiding them to docking bays and ordered their cargoes removed and inspected.

"I have a feeling this will be a good haul, Benning Kidd," Fodor Hendricks told her as the pair watched the hexagonal crates moving along negative energy lifting platforms that turned the crates' mass into a lifting force, making them virtually weightless and easy for her Workers to move.

"I agree, Fodor Hendricks," she nodded. "So far, we've found 268 gigs of stable tenebrium hidden under the anti-helium."

Hendricks whistled. "That stuff's highly prohibited, Benning Kidd," he shook his head. "It's an integral part of dreadnoughts and titanospheres, although no one outside the Fleet's engineers knows why. Any corporation caught carrying it could lose their transport license at a minimum. Can Tereza Erdeli even sell it?"

"Easily, I would imagine. If nothing else, I'm sure the ships' original owners would pay us to make sure the Fleet didn't know they were carrying it." She laughed darkly. "I wonder if the Fleet would give me a reward for that information."

"They probably would, but they'd require you to come claim the reward in person," Hendricks grinned at her, his teeth bright against his dark skin. "You know, by heading over to Fleet headquarters back in Sol, alone and unarmed."

"Or they'd offer to bring it to me," she added wryly. "Maybe inside a battlefrigate or two."

"Or that," he agreed.

Benning glanced at the tall man who'd taught her most of what she knew about being a pirate and naval combat. The ache in her chest eased as she looked at him, and she felt an odd sort of comfort from his presence. She suddenly understood why the other captains seemed so ready to defer to him and why they all gravitated toward his presence. Hendricks was capable and deadly, to be sure, but he also had a way of putting those around him at their ease that Benning envied greatly.

<You could tell him that, Benning Kidd,> Tiddly suggested.

Tell him what? Benning asked quizzically.

<That he has a way with others. If you told him that, he might appreciate it.>

I'm sure he knows, Tiddly. He doesn't need to hear it from me.

<Remember the simulations about dealing with others? Humans always desire positive feedback. It improves their morale and sense of well-being.>

Benning looked up at the taller man again. "Fodor Hendricks, I wanted to say that I've noticed that you have a talent for dealing with other people," she said, the words feeling awkward and unnecessary in her mouth.

"Thank you, Captain," he smiled at her. "Although it sounded like it hurt you to say it. Is it that hard to give compliments?"

She shrugged. "I've never really understood why they're necessary," she admitted. "I know that people like them, but it seems to me that if you're doing your best, that should be its own reward. Needing gratification feels – pointless."

He looked at her strangely, his face unreadable to her. "So, you're saying that you don't care about getting compliments?" he asked. "That it doesn't matter to you what others think of you?"

"It used to. I used to worry about if what I was doing would be considered right or wrong, and who might think I was evil for the things I do."

"Really?" he laughed. "I never would have guessed that you had moral doubts. You seem..." He hesitated. "Above that sort of thing, I guess. As if you're certain of your path, and morality doesn't factor into it." He gave her another unreadable expression. "Do you still worry about it?"

"No. I decided that good and evil are too subjective to

matter. As long as I think I'm doing the right thing, then it doesn't matter what anyone else thinks."

"There!" he clapped his hand on her shoulder. "That's what I'm talking about. That confidence that you're on the right path." He shook his head. "I wish I had that."

"You aren't certain of your path, Fodor Hendricks?" she asked, slightly startled.

He shrugged nonchalantly. "Oh, I love being a Pirate Captain, don't get me wrong. But I've had my doubts over the decades."

"Such as?"

He made an almost pained face. "That's a very personal question, Benning Kidd."

"You brought up the subject," she pointed out. "And I told you about my doubts."

"That you did," he sighed. "Fine." He looked away, leaning on the railing by which they stood, staring down at the crates still being offloaded from the captured clipper ships.

"It was about twenty years ago," he said in a soft voice. "I was pretty low-leveled then, relatively new to my career. I'd stolen a Bruce-class corvette and refitted it to be a ship hunter, but the only ships I could go after were the little cogs, the in-system freighters. Those aren't very profitable, so I thought I'd take a risk and go after a luxcruiser."

Benning frowned. "A passenger liner?" she asked. "You always said those are too dangerous to take, Fodor Hendricks."

"They are," he nodded. "They're fast, hard to catch, and they usually have escorts to keep them safe. Plus, if you do take one, their owners don't respond very well." He grimaced. "I hadn't learned all that yet, though.

"I found a luxcruiser that circled the Indi system. That's a trinary system, you know – one big star and two brown dwarves all orbiting one another, with lots of small rocky bodies and one gas giant. It's a popular tourist site since the gas giant has a thick argon layer, and when the main star flares, the gas giant glows a brilliant purple color."

He shook his head. "In any case, this luxcruiser – the *Lavender Rose* – was a charter vessel, one that only carried small, private groups around the system, and it never had an escort. I saw that as an invitation: no guards and obviously wealthy passengers who'd pay well to be left alone. I attacked it..." He fell silent, his eyes going distant.

"It was better defended than you thought, wasn't it?" Benning guessed.

"Yeah," he nodded. "Mercenary Soldiers on every deck, automated defenses all over the place – I lost most of my boarding party getting to the VIP quarters. By that point, I was wounded, I'd lost people I considered friends, and I was furious at the ship and its passengers. They were supposed to be easy prey, but they lured me into a trap!" He chuckled bitterly. "At least, that was how I saw it."

He looked at her seriously. "When I demanded ransom from the passengers, a woman – the one who seemed to be in charge – refused. She told me if I left immediately, she might consider sparing my life. I couldn't do that, of course. If I lost half my crew just to run from unarmed civilians without getting anything, I'd have lost the rest of my crew, as well; they'd have abandoned me. So, I – convinced her."

His face took on an expression that Benning didn't recognize, although it certainly looked to be an unhappy one, judging from his downturned mouth and drooping eyelids. "I wasn't as good at torture as you are, Benning Kidd. You know how to keep someone at the edge of life without nudging them over. I tortured six people to death because I didn't know how to stop. I didn't have your control.

"At first, I was just angry. Then, I felt like I couldn't stop, or I'd have wasted everything I'd done. Finally, the woman broke when I began to torture a young woman, one who'd probably barely gained Citizenship. She transferred more credits to me than I'd ever seen at the time, and I left the ship feeling wealthy – and utterly miserable."

He looked at Benning with a serious expression. "After that, I had to replace most of my crew. Some of them left on their own, but the rest – I couldn't lead them knowing they'd seen me do that. I doubted myself, my abilities, my choices. I wondered if I'd made the right decision, becoming a Pirate Captain, and if I could shift my career into the Starship Captain path."

"You obviously decided to remain a Pirate Captain, though," Benning observed. "Why?"

"Because I realized that just because I don't like doing something doesn't mean it's not the best thing to do. With the credits I got from that capture, I hired a new crew, upgraded the *Interdictor* – my old ship – and took some training courses on effective torture and martial combat. That eventually led to my capturing the *Relentless*, which led me to you."

He smiled again. "And while at first, I hated you for taking my ship and my freedom from me, I've made more credits and gained more renown with you in the past two years than I did in a decade by myself. Scrit, this haul alone will net me more than I'd make in two solar years as a solo captain." He shrugged. "Like I said, just because I don't like it doesn't mean it's not the best choice."

"Are you still unhappy serving under me?" she asked, feeling an odd ache in her chest at the thought that he hated her. She didn't understand that discomfort; she'd always known he served her only because he had to that first year. Why wouldn't he hate someone forcing him into servitude?

"Sometimes, yes. There are times when I wish I was on my own again, free to do whatever I wanted." He laughed. "Then, I look at my status. I've gained a level since we've worked together, something that should have taken me years more to do, and my skills have shot up. I even gained that Fleet Tactics skill, so eventually, when I have my own fleet, I'll be able to use it effectively."

He grinned at her. "Plus, it's fun working with you. Like I said, you seem to have endless confidence that you can do what you set your mind on doing, and it's easy to follow someone who's so sure they know the right way."

She smiled faintly as the ache in her chest eased, replaced with an odd warmth. "Thank you," she said, unsure why she said it.

"You're welcome." He smiled at her. "And that's how you give a compliment, Benning Kidd." He clapped her shoulder once more, then looked at her face. "By the way, I like this version of you. It's very appealing."

As he walked away, Benning wondered why his words seemed to sink down into her chest and lower, making her stomach flutter slightly.

She shook off the odd sensation and turned toward the command center. She needed to make arrangements to sell the prohibited tenebrium and to see if any of the station's merchants wanted to buy clipper ships – or if it would be wiser to ransom them back to their owners. She suspected Erdeli would suggest the latter, along with requesting a payment to keep from alerting the Fleet about the tenebrium they'd been carrying. The final ship of their convoy would still be en route to Helmus, and the Fleet would have time to intercept it before it arrived if it wanted.

She strode off, her mind turning away from her conversation with Hendricks, but as she walked, her hand rested on her lower stomach, as if to calm the faint churning that still disturbed it.

CHAPTER 13

"As you can see, IS has grown substantially in the past few months," Tereza Erdeli spoke with her usual self-assurance as she led Benning through the passageways of the station. Benning had asked the woman for an update on the station, and in return, Erdeli had asked to take Benning on a tour of the place. At first, Benning hadn't seen the point – she could see all the important information such as the station's maintenance status, power levels, and income all through her screen. As Erdeli walked her through the station, though, she realized that she'd never actually taken the time to get to know the place.

Her assistant led her past towering banks of KB plants that powered the station, providing the exawatts of energy that the place needed simply to function. Erdeli showed her the dark energy generators that provided gravity for the place, replicating the effects of Earth-mass gravity without the requisite matter, and one of the huge weapons banks that fired 50-pijin grasers, 16-volley missiles, and hundreds of short-range plasma emitters designed to shoot down incoming missiles, torpedoes, and flyboats. They walked down kim-long hallways whose walls and ceiling bore perfect holographic images of the surrounding space, making it seem like they walked outside in the void, and through the deeply buried algae gardens where kilotons of genetically modified algae were harvested daily to provide the station's nanofield with matter to use for repairs, expansion, and the nano-replicators that created food, beverages, and most of the goods the merchants on board sold.

Benning even learned that her station had its own small arena. It wasn't functional yet – they had no arena manager, and there weren't enough people on the station to make it a decent source of income or entertainment – but it was there. Hopefully, in the future, Benning would be able to compete in her own station without needing to worry about the Fleet or the vagaries of various systems.

Benning realized that her station was impressive, something beyond what she'd intended it to be. Originally, she'd taken the station simply to deny it to her enemies. She'd arranged to pay the lease on it so it could serve as a temporary base of operations, nothing more. It was a place to park her ships, for her people to gather and train, and perhaps to provide her vessels with some extra firepower when the Fleet inevitably came to capture her. It had always served as a simple pirate base, and when she'd taken it, the station had been barely functional, so damaged by the strangelet bomb she'd hit it with that it could hardly maintain its orbit above the rocky body below. She'd never imagined that it could become more than a naval fortress.

Stepping out onto the promenade and seeing hundreds of Citizens, Workers, and Soldiers walking about, going to stores or restaurants, talking amiably or just sitting quietly, presumably surfing the Overnet, Benning realized she'd been short-sighted. IS-39267 looked like a regular space station; it was a small one, to be sure, but it resembled any other station she'd visited in her travels. Under Erdeli's management, the facility had grown into something Benning barely recognized – something more than just a basic place to rest her head and supply her ships.

"I admit, I'm impressed, Tereza Erdeli," Benning said slowly, remembering Tiddly's suggestion with Fodor Hendricks earlier. "This looks nothing like the station I first conquered."

"That isn't saying much," the woman replied, her voice dry and sarcastic. "Repairing that damage took time and resources, but anyone could have done that. The station's nanofield would have fixed it eventually without any help from anyone, in fact."

"True," Benning agreed. "And that's all I would have done: let it repair itself, so it served its basic purpose of letting my ships dock and nothing more."

"It would have been a massively wasted opportunity." The blonde woman looked around with a hint of a smile on her face. "In fact, this place has been wasted for far too long in the hands of pirates who didn't realize how useful it could be."

"Because of the nearby refueling station," Benning nodded.

"No. Well, in part, I suppose, but it's more that Frostwise is in an excellent position." The woman stopped and looked at Benning. "Do you happen to know how big the Collective is?"

"No one does," Benning shrugged. "The outermost systems will take decades to be established enough to show up in the Overnet's registry, and the Overnet limits communication until they do. For all we know, the Collective could spread out for thousands of lightyears."

"While that's true, the commonly accepted answer is that the Collective is spread across a three-hundred-lightyear diameter," Erdeli replied with a sigh. "Those are the systems well established in the Overnet's registry. Anything beyond that is the Fringe, and no one cares about the Fringe except, well, those living there.

"The farther you go from Sol system, the less populous the inhabited systems are, and the fewer of those systems are fully inhabited, with complete Dyson swarms, every rocky body and gas giant mined for material to produce habitats and stations, and habitats spread out in orbit of the star as much as possible. That means that the outlying systems are far more dependent on trade, and the inner systems make a good profit sending materials outward."

She resumed walking, and Benning followed along, unsure what the blonde woman was leading up to. She knew all of this, of course – it was part of the Starfaring training she falsely remembered receiving. Most Citizens probably didn't, but every Starship Officer did. What she didn't know was why Erdeli was explaining it to her in the first place.

"So?" she finally asked the assistant.

"So..." Erdeli stopped once more and turned to face Benning. "So, Frostwise is a registered system in the Overnet. That means it has to either write up a system-approved charter detailing its laws or enforce the standard Fleet regulations. Interstellar object 39267, though, isn't on the registry. That means we don't have to enforce Fleet regulations, customs, and duties. That tenebrium you acquired? If you take it into practically any other system, it'll either be seized and given to the Fleet or seized by the station and resold for profit. Here, though, we can allow its sale and passage without breaking any laws."

She gestured at the closest building, what looked like a trading store with the name "Invictus" floating holographically above the door. "That's what made this place an excellent pirate base. Merchants like Invictus, a dealer in ship electronics and drive systems, could come here and buy stolen goods or seized vessels from the pirates, then ship them to other systems without ever running afoul of the Fleet. They still can, in fact – and they do – but that's only part of its appeal. Here, they can buy and sell anything they want, even things that are proscribed, restricted, or prohibited. Negmass plants? You can sell them here. Sub-dimensional weapons? Nano-weapons? Genetic modifications? You can buy and sell them all here. And since we're only seven lightyears from Sol, we're easy to reach and convenient for people all over the Collective.

"As I said, the outermost systems are 150 lightyears distant, Benning Kidd. That's a year's travel at standard deep dive velocities, and the trip takes gigs of gas. Those traders can go to one of the inner systems, pay Fleet duties on their goods, then pay system taxes, and pay all those again buying cargoes and gas for the return trip – or they can come here, get gas cheaply at Frostwise, and only pay those duties when they get back home." She shrugged. "It's a winning situation for everyone."

"So, why didn't anyone use the station this way before?" Benning frowned. "There has to be a downside to it."

"Well yes, there is. Being outside Fleet regulations also means being outside Fleet protections. If a trader sells gold or lead disguised as uranium in the Cygni System, for example, they're subject to a fine and possible loss of their trading license. Do the same thing in Proxima or Sirius, and you're looking at imprisonment. Here, it's buyer beware. If someone gets swindled, they either have to eat the loss or convince the other party to give them fair value. It's higher risk for higher reward."

"That's a downside for the merchants," Benning shook her head. "Not for the station's owners."

"It's a problem for the owners, as well, Benning Kidd. Who do you think the merchants are going to complain to?" Erdeli laughed dryly. "I've fielded a half-dozen such complaints already, in fact.

"You're right, though; that's not why no station owner

has done this. The truth is, there's an inherent danger in bringing all these corporate representatives into the station. If one or more of them decided that the station looked like a profitable enough venture, they could easily buy the lease out from under you and take it over. They could bring in their own private fleets and security to seize the place and drive you out."

Benning stared at the woman, her face clearly showing her rising anger. "And you still let them come?" she demanded, suspicions flaring in her mind.

"Yes," the blonde assistant nodded calmly. "Because while that would usually be a danger, it's not much of one for you."

Erdeli's face turned serious as she looked at Benning. "I don't like you, Benning Kidd," she said bluntly. "I probably never will. However, I would never cross you. I know what happens to the people who do. I remember Nikita Mosin losing a year's worth of his life and Mildred Joyce losing her fleet and base because they went up against you. I've experienced what you do to people who betray you." She shuddered. "I never want to go through that again.

"I've made sure that every corporate representative and independent trader knows about that, as well. I've told them of how you crippled Nikita Mosin's shipping, bringing him to the edge of bankruptcy, and how you make examples of the people who cross you." She shook her head. "Trust me, this station would need to be a LOT more profitable for any of them to risk it – and if it gets to be that profitable, we'll buy it outright from Frostwise and fortify it enough that the corporations would be insane to try and take it."

Benning nodded slowly, trying to keep the pleased smile from her face. That was the whole point of the messages she'd been trying to send to people who would be her enemies. She wanted them to know that she'd respond disproportionately to any attack on her, to make them too afraid or at least too cautious to strike at her. It was good to know that she'd succeeded somewhat.

And all it took was committing Collective-level crimes and being hunted by the Fleet, she thought grimly.

"Speaking of defenses," the Corsair spoke aloud, "we need to start working on upgrading them."

Erdeli nodded. "I assumed so. We've already installed the new designs, but I've been setting aside a percentage of our profits each month specifically for improving the station's weapons and defenses."

Benning gave the woman an approving look. "That was foresighted of you."

"It's what you pay me for," Erdeli shrugged. "Besides, it's obvious that you've got enemies, Benning Kidd, and those enemies will eventually come here looking for you. The station isn't really up to repelling an attack by a fleet of ships..."

Pain flared in Benning's shoulder, and her resistance bar suddenly dropped to 81%. Her armor snapped into place around her with a thought, her enhanced nanofield drawing it out of her pack and encasing her in it in less than a second. Her Arcbar rifle appeared an instant later as Benning dropped to a knee, ignoring the pain of the bullet that passed completely through her shoulder.

"Oh, flork."

Benning spared a glance back at Erdeli as the assistant swore and saw the woman staring at a hole in the center of her chest, her face clearly surprised. A dark orange aura surrounded her, slowly darkening to red as she bled out internally. She took a single staggering step before dropping to her knees and falling to her side.

Benning turned away from the fallen woman.

Medigel might save her, but Benning didn't have the time to stop and administer it. Besides, Erdeli would respawn soon enough; her loss wasn't important to Benning in the short term. At least, it didn't matter enough for Benning to risk getting shot herself to save the woman.

She scanned the promenade, her eyes hunting for any sign of the person who shot her. Her visor flashed bright red, and she rolled sideways as a bullet whined past her and struck the building behind her. Her rifle rose almost of its own accord, and her finger brushed the trigger, sending a five-round burst toward the building where her hunter hid. She doubted she'd hit anything, but the volley would force her attacker to seek cover.

She rose to her feet and raced across the deck of the promenade, shoving aside the few people who didn't get out of her way. She fired sporadically as she ran, forcing the shooter to stay in cover as she approached. The armored figure popped out from behind a wall and unleashed another shot at Benning that punched through her armor and plunged into her upper chest, but she pushed aside the pain of the wound. As her resistance dropped to 64%, Strength from Pain boosted her stats by 18%, and she activated For Fame with a thought to push her physical stats even higher. Adrenaline flooded her body, dulling her thoughts but making her even faster and more accurate.

She fired another blast at her attacker, striking them in their tinted helmet, and they ducked back behind the wall with an audible curse. Benning hurdled a low wall, rolled with her landing, and came up on the other side of the building's cover, her rifle tracking her foe almost of its own accord. The assassin spun as well, their long-barreled rifle swinging toward Benning, but she fired first. A salvo of five antimatter-coated bullets slammed into the figure's stomach, tearing through their deep red and light gold armor.

The figure staggered backward, and Benning pulled out her hammer, snapping her rifle back onto her back. The em-long weapon swung low, slamming into the attacker's knee, and the person's leg folded beneath them as her blow crumpled their armor. She reversed the swing and buried the back spike in the assailant's shoulder, rendering their right arm useless, then stabbed the spearpoint into the wound in their stomach, driving them against the wall.

The attacker cried out as the blow lifted them off their feet and pinned them to the wall, the spearpoint ripping into their intestines. Their aura flashed to dark orange, but they still lifted a pistol in their left hand and fired three shots directly into Benning's visor. Two of them sparked and ricocheted harmlessly, but the third cracked the microthene, and Benning hurled the assailant to the floor before they could fire again. She slammed her boot down on their pistol-holding hand, pinning it in place, then drove the glowing spearpoint on her hammer into their wrist, shearing through their armor and shattering the bones beneath.

The attacker tried to roll free, but she smashed her hammer into their unwounded leg, crushing their femur and rendering them helpless, at least for a few moments. The figure's aura dimmed to dark orange before suddenly climbing back to light orange as they activated a dose of medigel. They scrabbled for their rifle, but Benning had no intention of giving them that chance.

She concentrated on the figure's right hand, and her nano-disassemblers soared forth, leaving their home beneath her skin and swarming around the attacker's limb. The assassin stared at their hand as the armor seemed to melt away from it, running down their arm as a thin liquid and exposing dark brown skin beneath. Their moment of stunned amazement turned into screaming, though, as the skin on that hand bubbled and churned, dripping from their limb as dark brown liquid and revealing a layer of muscle, bone, and nerve beneath.

Their screaming intensified as Benning carefully controlled her nanites, allowing them to dissolve the man's hand slowly, leaving his nerves as intact as possible. Her practice with her disassemblers gave her far more control over them than she once had, but Tiddly told her that compared to a Nanomancer, Benning was still clumsy and awkward with her nanites. Apparently, a skilled Nanomancer could eat a hole through a person that would resemble a bullet wound, dissolve them from the inside out so that they looked fine to casual inspection, or even dissolve a limb but leave the nerves behind so that the pain of the lost appendage never faded.

Benning couldn't do that, but she could make sure the disassemblers took their time ripping apart her attacker's flesh to draw out the agony as long as possible. Fat and muscle slowly liquefied, splattering to the deck below in a viscous soup of blood and flesh. Cartilage and bone turned to dust that drifted in the air, and after half a minute, nothing remained of the man's hand but a slowly bleeding stump.

"Flork!" the man screamed, his voice filled with panic. "What the Hole did you do? My hand – it can't grow back!" Benning stepped back, releasing his now-healed left hand, and he clutched his stump, curling up in a ball around it as if it would somehow protect it from further damage. Benning took the moment to send her scanning nanites out, and a moment later, the man's status appeared in her vision.

TOBIS KOPEL
Level 11 Bounty Hunter
Damage Rating: 12.6 (Strora Lancer 5)
Defense Rating: 11.9 (Mithrillene Shock
Plate Mk 7)
Resistance Rating: 11.1

STATS
Physicality: 8.1
Coordination: 10.3
Resistance: 8.2

Acuity: 10.0
Willpower: 9.1
Social: 8.3

"You're right, Tobis Kopel," she said calmly, ignoring the pain of her wounds. "Your hand won't grow back, at least not without special medical assistance. It'll be faster to go to respawn if you want it again."

"Fine, plantrash," he growled at her. "Send me to respawn."

"First, tell me what you're doing here," she hedged, activating Sense Deceit as she spoke.

He stared at her for a long moment, an expression Tiddly interpreted as puzzled plastered on his face behind his visor. "I'm collecting the bounty on you, of course," he finally said. "What the Hole else would I be doing on this armpit of a station in the middle of nowhere?"

Benning felt a small surge of anger at his mockery of her station, but she pushed it aside. His opinion of IS-39267 didn't really matter; she had more important information she needed.

"That's not what I meant. *How* did you get on my station, Bounty Hunter? Your kind isn't allowed here – for obvious reasons."

"I booked transport with a merchant freighter. I passed through customs normally; no one even tried to stop me." He snorted contemptuously. "Your security is a joke."

Although Sense Deceit triggered at his words, marking them as false, she didn't need it to tell the man was lying. She sighed dramatically.

"That's a lie, Tobis Kopel. Every time you lie, I'm going to have to encourage you to be honest. Let's see... How about taking your other hand?" The man's eyes widened, and he jammed his good hand into his opposite armpit, as if it would shield it somehow. His lips opened, his face angry, but whatever he was going to say was lost as Benning's disassemblers burrowed into his skin and began liquefying his remaining hand.

The man's screaming ended as the last bits of his hand dribbled to the deck beneath him, replaced with quiet sobs as he stared at the twin stumps of his arms. "You're a florking monster," he panted. "What the Hole is wrong with you?"

"You should have done your homework before accepting a contract on me, Tobis Kopel. This is how I treat every bounty hunter who comes after me. You came to take my life; that means I get to kill you as slowly as I want." She leaned over him, and the man flinched away, his eyes wide and panic-filled. Benning felt a surge of satisfaction at that; she wanted him to be terrified of her.

"You can end this," she told him simply. "Just tell me how you got past my security and onto my station. How did you fool the station's 'net? You're not hiding your status, so you should have been flagged a dozen times. Why weren't you?"

"I – I don't know," he stammered. Benning made a sour face and raised her hand, but he shook his head frantically and scrambled back from her, pushing with his legs and elbows. "I mean it! I don't know. It was a blind hire; someone put a private bounty on you and hired me to come take it without us ever meeting. They told me they'd make sure I got onto the station. I have no idea how they did it, but whatever they did worked. I haven't had any trouble the whole time I've been here."

"You have no idea who hired you?" Benning asked, even as she began probing deeper into his 'net.

"No, none at all. It was an anonymous contract, but the payout was too good for me to ignore. 100 credits to not only kill you but spawn camp you down to level 5." He slumped before her. "It seemed like easy credits."

It took her only a few seconds to find both his credit account and the contract he'd received. He'd told her the truth: it offered 100 credits for her death and spawn camping back to level 5, half paid upfront as a deposit and the other half paid when she reached level 5. The contract was sent anonymously, and her first cursory attempts to hack into it to find the sender met formidable firewalls. Whoever sent this took their anonymity very seriously, indeed.

"How did you get here?" she asked absently as she went after the contract's defenses from different directions, trying to overload its firewalls so they registered a system failure and automatically dropped.

"I flew here. I have a ship – the *Blazing Streak* – and when I approached, your station gave me a berth right away. It was like they were expecting me."

<That's a problem, Benning Kidd,> Tiddly said, her voice troubled as she spoke.

Why? I'm guessing one of the Nobles hunting me shut down the security protocols for Tobis Kopel and arranged for him to get a berth.

<They might have shut down the protocols, sure. That's within a Noble's power so that they can allow their agents to infiltrate one another freely. The System encourages that since the only real limit on a Noble's power is the rest of the Nobility, and allowing them to work quietly

against one another is in everyone's best interests.

<But arranging a berthing on a station they don't own? That's a different story. If Nobles could do that, they could shut down one another's stations, freeze out all the docking rings, and make it so only their ships could land at another Noble's stations. That sort of thing would lead to open conflict between Nobles, and that could turn into interstellar warfare between Nobles, which would be terrible for pretty much everyone.>

So, how could he have gotten on the station?

<Someone on the station had to have allowed it, Benning Kidd – someone with a decent amount of authority, as well. That or a hacking ability like yours, but even then, they'd have to be on the station to do it.>

Benning's anger flared again at the thought that someone on the station might be working against her in secret, and that the person might be in a position of power. She'd personally hired every person who had the authority to authorize a strange vessel's docking and given them that authority. That meant that one of those closest to her might be betraying her.

If they are, I'll find out and make them regret it, she thought grimly. *I'll make an example of them that people will talk about across the florking Collective.*

<How will you find them, Benning Kidd?> Tiddly asked curiously.

I'll ask them. If I ask enough times, my Sense Deceit skill should trigger with the traitor.

<I don't think it will. I think whoever's working against you has Noble protection, and that could shield them against your skill.>

What? Why do you think that? Benning's hand tightened on her rifle. *And how can a Noble do that?*

<Because everyone who has the authority to let Tobis Kopel into the station already signed a contract that forbids them to work against you, Benning Kidd. If they broke that contract by allowing a bounty hunter here, they should have the Oathbreaker symbol on their status, and they don't.>

Oathbreaker?

<Sure. Anyone who breaches a contract gets marked by the System, so everyone knows what they've done. That's in addition to any penalties the contract and the System impose on them. You can't hide the fact that you're an Oathbreaker – not even your Cyberwarfare skill would conceal that – so someone had to have released them from the contract. Only you or a Noble could do that. They must be working for a Noble.>

And that Noble can shield them from my skill?

<Yep – but only by making them a Designate of that Noble. That means that they speak with the Noble's voice, at least as far as the System is concerned. It would free them from having to follow their contract with you, and it would prevent you from using your skills against them.> Tiddly hesitated. <That's a really big deal, Benning Kidd. A Noble can only have one Designate at a time, and that person usually runs their businesses for them and is the highest person in their organization. For a Noble to send someone with that much status here means that they really, really want to hurt you.>

Benning snorted. *So, what else is new? I'll just have to figure out another way to find them. There'll be a trail of some kind, and I'll pick it up.*

She raised her rifle and sighted on Kopel's skull. "Never come back here," she told him firmly. "Drop the contract, and never take one against me again. If I ever see you again, I'll kill you as slowly as possible, and you'll scream in agony the entire time. Are we clear?"

"Y-yes!" he said quickly, nodding his head.

"Good. Enjoy your respawn, and stay the Hole off my station."

Her rifle spoke, and she turned and walked away as the bounty hunter's aura flashed to black. The contract still resisted her efforts, but she'd taken it from Kopel – along with most of his credits – and eventually, she'd trace it back to its originator. When she did, she'd make that person pay, along with anyone else who'd worked against her.

The bounty hunters, it seemed, were losing her fear of her. If they weren't scared of her anymore, then the Fleet wouldn't be either, and they'd come hunting before she was ready. She needed to remind people why coming after her was a terrible idea.

I need to build my fleet and my reputation. I can't just become a pirate; I need to become something that people fear. She smiled grimly. Fortunately, she had several ideas how to do just that.

CHAPTER 14

The *Bold Wanderer* was a powerful ship. One of the newest cruiser class vessels, the *Wanderer* was designed to be the linchpin of a small fleet. The cruiser didn't carry as many weapons as its kim-wide spherical hull might suggest, only being armed similarly to a much smaller fast frigate, but it wasn't really meant for ship-to-ship combat. It was meant to survive in combat long enough for its supporting fleet to tear apart enemies – and to help them do that much more easily.

The *Wanderer* had heavy armor, ten cims of neutronium sandwiched between a layer of liquid metal beneath and reactive osmium over top. The superdense osmium had atoms of negmass hydrogen spread thinly throughout the metal; when an attack struck the armor with force, the hydrogen responded by moving toward the force, supporting the osmium and making it incredibly difficult to crumple or pierce. The ship's EM shield and dark matter shroud both had their own dedicated KB plants, making them far more powerful than normal. The cruiser could take an antimatter warhead directly to the hull without a breach; even a singularity warhead in close proximity might not get through the ship's armor.

All those defenses allowed the *Wanderer* to remain in the very center of a naval battle to perform its main function: reinforcing the ships in its fleet. The *Wanderer* boasted several technologies that made the ships around it far more powerful. Its hivemind linkage system connected the 'nets of the various ships into one, letting them all respond as a single unit. It carried a warp field that surrounded each vessel in a bubble of slightly warped spacetime, allowing them to react faster than the enemy could and making each of their seconds pass slightly more quickly than their foes'. Its advanced targeting array organized the ships' beam weapons and fired them in a fractal pattern that covered large regions of space without losing intensity, and its Higgs intensifier slowed the passage of enemy missiles and torpedoes, giving the ships more time to react and shoot down the weapons before they exploded.

The upshot was that any fleet with the *Wanderer* as its flagship was far more powerful than it should have been. Its current fleet – a destroyer, three frigates, and eight corvettes – could give a battlefrigate a run for its credits. It would lose, but the battle would be a lot closer than it should have been, and that knowledge would keep any sane commodore well away from the *Wanderer* and its escorted convoy.

Alaestra Byrne was incredibly proud of her ship and exulted in being its captain. Most Starship Officers wouldn't have, and the cruiser class never gained much popularity outside the Fleet. It was a support ship, designed to sit in the middle of a battle, endure a beating, and help the rest of the ships in its fleet kill the enemy. There wasn't much glory to be had captaining one, and Starship Officers who didn't want glory also generally didn't command military vessels. Captains who commanded cruisers were usually seen as overly cautious, even cowardly, and the commanders of other military ships tended to look down on them.

Alaestra didn't care. She'd seen the true value of a cruiser in the early days of her career when she'd served briefly in the Fleet. Fleet Officers didn't worry about renown; they only cared about achieving the objectives their superiors set for them. They weren't blinded by the need for glory in combat, they only worried about victory over their enemies. As far as she was concerned, their attitude was the better one – the correct one, in fact.

When she'd gotten her discharge and joined the civilian fleet, Alaestra set her sights on acquiring a cruiser and building a fleet around it. It took her decades to reach that goal. She'd had to build the fleet first since a cruiser by itself wasn't a powerful warship, and cruisers didn't come up for sale all that often. The *Wanderer* was a decommissioned Fleet vessel itself, and she'd had to wait eight years to purchase it and another four to refit it back to Fleet standards.

She'd never regretted it for an instant. Since taking command of the *Wanderer,* Alaestra made a name for herself as a skilled captain whose fleet could handle jobs that seemed too dangerous for it. She slowly built on that reputation, handling tricky escort duties, clearing out nests of pirates, and safeguarding important meetings and gatherings held out in deep space, away from the prying eyes of stations and the Fleet. She'd built a nearly flawless record by being conservative, careful, and possibly paranoid, but she'd been able to leverage that repute into real capital, gaining enough merchant backing to be able to start her own corporation and expand her security business beyond her initial fleet. Her company, Safe Journeys, had four fleets, each built around a cruiser like hers, and they only took dangerous jobs that in turn paid extremely well.

Alaestra knew that she could retire at any point. Her Starship Captain path had slowly morphed over the last decades into a Mercantile Captain, and she no longer needed to command ships herself to advance her career. She could stay back in her headquarters in the Delta Pavonis system, orbiting in the upper atmosphere of one of its gas giants, and so long as she actively ran her business and coordinated her fleets, she'd level up slowly but steadily.

She had to do that sometimes, of course, but she liked to keep her hand in as well, and the *Wanderer* was still her pride and joy. She took command of all her cruisers occasionally, but she chose the *Wanderer* more than any other. She could feel the ship through her It's Good to Be Captain ability, and she thrilled at its power and delicacy, delighted in the energies that it sent out into space to boost the other ships around it, and shivered at the depth of the hivemind connecting her warships, making them virtual extensions of one another.

"Captain, I'm reading an anomaly ahead," her head of Ops, Bruwno Charrier, spoke up suddenly, disrupting Alaestra's thoughts.

"Report, Ops," the cruiser's official captain, Maxtn Liao said curtly, not even glancing at Alaestra as he spoke. Alaestra was in overall command of the fleet, and while she could take charge of the *Wanderer* at any given moment, Liao knew that she wouldn't unless it was a dire emergency. That would be bad for morale and discipline, and ship owners had faced mutinies for that sort of behavior in the past.

"It looks like a cargo vessel, Captain," Charrier explained. "Classifying it as Cog-1, thirty-two ems in length and eleven in diameter. Readings suggest a Worm class freighter."

"Worm class?" Alaestra muttered to herself, frowning. The Worm class of cog-hulled ships were all in-system freighters. They lacked deep dive engines and the plants to power them, although they could dive shallowly and so were often used in large systems to haul goods from the inner to outer parts of those systems.

"It couldn't have gotten out here on its own," Liao said, echoing Alaestra's own thoughts. "Comm, are there any signs of nearby ships?"

"Nothing within ten linutes, sir," the Communications Officer, Cathrise Hedman answered. "There's a convoy of clipper ships eleven-point-three linutes distant, bearing two-four-two inclined, but they're heading on a parallel course heading the opposite direction from us."

"The ship looks derelict, sir," Ops added. "There are signs of hull damage, its engines are offline, and I'm reading only minimal power signs, not enough for life support or a shroud. It's barely maintaining its 'net, nothing more. It doesn't even look like its nanofield is functioning."

"How close will we pass to it, Helm?" Liao asked the pilot.

"Within ten kims, Captain."

"Too close," Liao said decisively. "It's probably a castoff from some long-ago battle that drifted out here, but just in case, contact the captain of the lead convoy vessel and instruct her to shift course to pass at least a lecond from it."

Alaestra nodded at the man's orders; she'd have said two leconds, but she otherwise agreed with his analysis. This was probably just an odd coincidence, but careful captains who wanted to keep their ships safe didn't believe in coincidences. She felt the shroud adjust as the ship altered course, sensed each of the companion ships in the fleet doing the same through the hivemind linkage, and relaxed slightly. She'd chosen the captain of this ship well; Liao acted cautiously and rarely made mistakes. It was why she'd given him this command in the first place.

She remained silent but kept her eyes on the ship's scanners as they slowly passed around the derelict vessel. As they reached the closest point of approach, those scanners suddenly buzzed to life.

"Captain, getting power readings in the derelict," Ops said urgently. "Its power plant is spiking wildly!"

"Evasive maneuvers," Liao ordered instantly. "Convoy, prepare for flash dive!"

"Its plant is overloading!" Charrier continued. "It's – sir, it's going photonic!"

Alaestra felt the flash of the ship exploding and sensed the warmth of its radiation bathing the hull of her vessels. "Good call avoiding the vessel, Captain Liao," she said approvingly, nodding her head.

"Thank you, Commodore," the silver-haired captain nodded.

"You think it was a trap, sir?" Hedman asked, her voice sounding surprised.

"Of course, Ensign. What are the odds that a ship would appear right in our path out of all of interstellar space – and then would just happen to go photonic as we passed it? If we'd gone to investigate…" The man fell silent, but Alaestra agreed with his unspoken thoughts. The *Wanderer* was tough, but if they'd gotten close enough to the derelict vessel – or, even worse, had docked with it – they could have been badly damaged by the explosion. As it was, the blast hurt their power plant efficiency and slowed their engines, albeit not enough to really matter.

"Any other ships within range, Comm?" Liao asked.

"No, sir. Just that convoy."

"Keep an eye on them, just in case." Liao turned toward the pilot. "Helm, begin correcting our heading to bring us back…"

Alaestra sat up as her left side near her hip suddenly burned, and Liao winced and fell silent as he felt the same sensation.

"Sir!" the young officer sitting at the Damage Control station said frantically, his eyes wide. "I'm reading a hull breach!"

"Where?" Liao demanded, not facing the man.

"Port side, declined, Captain," the man answered quickly.

"Away from the derelict ship," Alaestra observed with dawning realization. "It was definitely a trap – and we sprung it."

"Multiple hull breaches," Damage Control added, the man's voice getting ever more frantic.

"No ships in the area, Captain," Hedman said.

"No readings on any explosive devices or mines," Charrier spoke up as well. "I can't find a cause for the hull breaches, sir."

"Nanites," Alaestra said shortly, her heart lurching in her chest, rising to her feet before Liao could speak. "Weapons, overcharge the EM shield and irradiate the hull."

"Commodore, with the hull breaches, that will kill..." The brown-haired Weapons officer stared at Alaestra, her eyes wide.

"I'm aware that we'll lose people, Weapons. If we don't stop those nanites, we'll lose the whole ship. Do it!"

The ship shuddered as the officer altered its graser array to bathe the hull in radiation instead of firing it into space. That radiation sent free neutrons racing through the vessel, dropping her power plant to 62% efficiency and reducing her engine power by 23%, but hopefully, the radiation combined with the EM shield suddenly blazing with 200% of its normal power would disable the attacking nanites. If it didn't...

"Captain, the *Fierce Wind* is reporting hull breaches, as well," Hedman said nervously. "So are the *Savage Current*, the *Raging Tempest*..." She paused. "Sir, the entire fleet is suffering numerous hull breaches!"

"Captain, I'm picking up dive splashes!" Charrier announced, his voice louder than normal. "Less than a lecond..."

The waves of blue-shifted energy slammed into Alaestra's fleet, tearing into already damaged hulls and flooding the interiors of their vessels. One of her corvettes dropped out of formation as its engine went offline, but the others held steady. A moment later, her skin burned as graser fire bathed her in its energy, targeting her damaged port side, and the ship rumbled as explosions rocked it. She quickly analyzed the enemy fleet: a destroyer, two frigates, two corvettes, a modified brigantine that was probably a troop ship, and a carrier vessel trailing behind. They'd come up from their dive less than a lecond from Alaestra's fleet, a risky move that could have ended up with two ships tearing into one another, but it paid off as the ships attacked freely for a second as they sped past the *Wanderer.*

"I have command," Alaestra announced, trying to stay as calm as possible. "Fleet, gamma formation. Engage support systems."

"Commodore, we just lost our port thrusters," the Damage Control officer – Buchner, that was his name! – announced.

"Our evasion cone is down by 22%, ma'am," the Pilot added.

"Fleet, fire starboard grasers," Alaestra commanded. "AM batteries, starburst pattern. Target the enemy destroyer; paint her evasion cone."

"Aye, ma'am," the Weapons Officer replied.

Alaestra's skin burned once more as the carrier unleashed its cargo of tiny flyboats that swarmed about the *Wanderer,* soaking it in low-powered graser fire.

"Activate point defense countermeasures," Alaestra ordered. She wasn't really worried about the flyboats; even with its hull breaches, the cruiser was basically immune to their attacks. Still, her crew was demoralized, and destroying even those tiny ships would help restore their resolve.

"Commodore, one of the flyboats is on a collision course with our hull," Charrier said in a puzzled voice. "It's headed for the damaged part of the hull..."

"Target it with countermeasures!" Liao ordered instantly as he realized what Alaestra had. "Take it out!"

It was too late. Alaestra watched as the dot in her screen suddenly merged with the larger sphere that was the *Wanderer*. Pain tore into her side as the disguised torpedo smashed into the ship and exploded, ripping through the already damaged armor and blasting a hole into the interior of her ship.

"Ma'am, the *Burning Knife* just went photonic!" Hedman almost shouted. "The *Fierce Wind* is dropping out of position..."

"Ma'am, our EM shield is down!" Buchner added. "We're venting atmosphere!"

"The enemy fleet is closing for another pass," Charrier reported.

Alaestra's skin burned as the enemy fleet flung graser beams into her ship's hull. Even as she ordered her ships to press the attack, she knew there was no point. Her hull was breached, and the nanites in it were widening that breach. Two of her ships were out of the fight, and the others were badly damaged. She could only hope to hold long enough for the convoy to clear the area and dive to safety, although if the nanites on their hulls got into their dive plants, that wouldn't be an option anymore.

She'd lost this battle. Her amazing record would be tarnished, she'd have to pay restitution to the convoy's owners for their lost ships, and it would be years if not decades before she'd regained her reputation – all because some plantrash rigged a derelict cog with a prohibited nanite bomb. She hoped to get her hands on the person responsible one day; until then, she could only hope that the attackers allowed her to surrender and keep her ships. If not, she'd fight until they'd all gone photonic; no one was taking the *Wanderer* from her. She'd see it blasted from existence before she allowed that.

Her backside flared with pain as the entire ship shuddered.

"Ma'am, singularity warhead exploded two kims aft," Ops reported.

"The blast damaged the engines directly, Commodore," Buchner said. "They're down to 18%! Engineering recommends shutting them down."

As Alasetra watched the troop transport break from the enemy fleet and move toward the *Wanderer,* she realized that the decision to keep the Wanderer might not be hers after all. She silently cursed the System that allowed pirates like this to exist in the first place before commanding her marines to make ready to repel boarders.

She never thought she'd have to give that order. Not aboard the *Wanderer*...

CHAPTER 15

"Fleet, concentrate graser fire on the destroyer," Benning ordered as her ships swept past the enemy fleet at a distance of two leconds. "AM battery, spiral pattern on the closer frigate followed by a torpedo. Keep them from targeting the *Messenger*."

Damage readings sped through her mind, echoed by Jezper Shields. "Frigate 1's power plant is at 43%...Corvette 2's engine is at 19%...Cruiser's engines are offline...Destroyer is listing badly..."

The *Hammer* hadn't escaped the exchange unscathed, either. The enemy captain targeted Benning's ship with the entire fleet's weapons, and her power plant and engine were both moderately damaged. The destroyer vented gas in three places, not bad enough to list but enough to be a concern. The cruiser was the problem; it reinforced the other ships in the fleet, making them faster, more reactive, and more powerful, all the while inhibiting Benning's ships. Her missiles, she noticed, flew at seven tocks rather than nine, and all her ships felt slightly sluggish while maneuvering. It was the key to the enemy defense, a powerful ship that would boost any fleet with which it traveled...

And Benning wanted it. It was the whole reason she'd set up her trap in the first place.

Fodor Hendricks had devised the basic design of the plan. He'd apparently used derelict decoys in the past, rigging them to explode when a ship came to investigate or capture them.

"Why would any captain stop to investigate something like that?" Avaeyana Roble had asked dubiously. "Why not just avoid it?"

"The key is to either use something like a cog that doesn't belong in the middle of interstellar space or a carrack that could be holding incredibly valuable cargo," Fodor Hendricks replied with an evil smile. "Make them too curious to possibly resist it."

"Alaestra Byrne, the commodore of the fleet we're interested in, is notoriously paranoid," Benning shook her head. "So are all her captains. She'll avoid any sort of anomaly like that rather than investigate it."

"What if the ship was rigged to chase them?" Saavi Boguna offered, her eyes distant and unfocused. "The ship's 'net could be set to pilot it toward the largest object that passed by."

"And have it chase a random planetoid or asteroid?" Roble pointed out.

"There are several areas along the convoy's planned route that are free of significant debris. In fact, it's passing through the edge of Kielholz's Void, an area where a rogue planet cleared all debris in its path forty millennia ago..."

"If I got power readings like that from a drifting ship, I'd dive away from it," Trephor Sando interrupted the woman's bit of trivia. "I'd assume it was a pirate waiting for me."

"We just need to make it better bait," Hendricks shook his head. "If we could make it look like it was carrying a really valuable cargo, something like anti-iron or negmass..."

"Then, I'd wonder why the cargo hadn't been taken by whoever damaged the ship," Sando snorted. "It's too suspicious if this commodore's as cautious as Benning Kidd says."

"She is," Benning said slowly. "And we need to use that to our advantage."

Buying a rundown cog was easy enough. Purchasing two nanite bombs required a trip to the Wolf System, where that sort of technology was legal to buy. Rigging the ship and the two bombs with proximity charges was the hardest part since the bombs, especially, weren't designed to trigger that way. They were designed to rupture on impact, triggering a small chemical explosive that spread the nanites out in a cloud without damaging them. The antimatter proximity trigger was too powerful and had to be scaled back, which meant finding a Weapons Engineer that specialized in explosives.

Adapting the *Hammer's* sinkhole generator to create a bubble inside which her fleet could hide, totally cut off from external detection, was far easier. Benning's fleet couldn't read any signals from outside the sinkhole, of course, so they were blind to the passage of the convoy. That limited its utility as a stealth device; ships inside the sinkhole couldn't track anything outside it, so they wouldn't normally be able to drop the sinkhole to ambush their prey at the best time. Fortunately, the Overnet still functioned within it, which meant that Benning knew when her derelict cog destroyed itself and thus when the convoy was closest to it. Tiddly called it an "exploit", but Benning just considered it unconventional tactics.

The whole setup cost Benning over 300 credits, a week's worth of traveling, and another week of prepping their equipment and ships for the attack. As Benning watched the enemy destroyer's list increase as a torpedo exploded less than a kim from its hull, triggered by one of the vessel's plasma point defenses, she considered the cost to be completely worth it. Her fleet's grasers burned into the wounded vessel, slamming radiation into its hull that destabilized its power plant and engines, while the flash of antimatter warheads blinded the nearest frigate to the torpedo that raced behind the blasts, exploding a few hundred ems from its hull as one of its mass driver point defenses intercepted the attack at the last instant. The frigate's atmosphere bled into space in a cloud of gas as the torpedo ripped its hull open, and it dropped out of formation as its engines lost too much power to keep up with the other ships.

"Captain, the hull breaches on the convoy ships are becoming dangerous," Jezper Shields reported.

Benning nodded. "Kill the nanites," she instructed. The nanite bombs came with a kill switch, a specific code that would cause the nanites to self-destruct. Without that, the nanites might eventually disassemble the entire enemy fleet – and could spread to Benning's ships if they got too close.

"The *Messenger* is moving into parallel position with the cruiser," Rush spoke up. "She's taken only minor hull damage so far."

"Good. Instruct Raelle Buckley to send enough marines to be sure she can take the ship, then move to capture the convoy. If it takes a while longer, it's fine; the clippers won't dive with their hulls breached like that."

She turned back to her local map. "Keep fire on the destroyer until it's disabled," she ordered the fleet. "*Arcturus*, recall the flyboats and send them after the corvettes once the cruiser's down. With the destroyer and cruiser out of the fight, the rest of the ships will have to either surrender or flee."

"They won't flee without the convoy," Hendricks guessed. "They'll try to surrender, instead."

"Maybe. We won't be accepting it, though." Benning turned back to her map as the destroyer's power plant shut down, rendering it helpless. "Shift fire to the nearer frigate. With it open to space like that, its engines should go offline quickly..."

"Captain, Frigate 1's plant is spiking!" Jezper Shields broke into her orders. "It's trying to shut it down..." A flash lit Benning's map as the frigate's engineers obviously failed in their efforts. "It's gone photonic, ma'am."

Benning felt a twinge of regret at the loss of the ship; the frigate would have been a decent addition to her fleet. As damaged as it was, though, it would have been difficult to tow back, and it might have taken months to fully repair it. Its loss was regrettable but not severe.

"Captain, message from the cruiser," Rush informed her.

"Ops, is the *Messenger* docked with the ship?"

"Yes, ma'am."

"Then ignore the message, Comm. They waited to see if they'd be able to repel our boarding party; now that they know they can't, they're trying to save themselves." She looked back at her map. "Fleet, concentrate graser fire on the remaining frigate. Try to disable it. We're trying to grow our fleet, here."

Fifteen minutes later, Benning stepped off a shuttle into the cruiser's airlock. Signs of battle abounded there; bodies of fallen marines lay scattered across the deck, burn marks from antimatter weapons and grasers seared the bulkheads, and bullet impacts dimpled every surface. Most of the fallen marines wore purple and red armor – Benning assumed those were the *Wanderer's* colors – but a few of the still bodies gleamed crimson and silver. She'd lost Soldiers taking the ship. Hopefully, the take from this mission would be worth it.

A tinge of regret passed through her as she looked

at the carnage, not for the loss of life or damage but that she'd had to stand back and let others fight. She was in command of the fleet; she couldn't put that aside to join boarding parties anymore. Fodor Hendricks had gained the Fleet Tactics skill, but it was still much lower than hers, so stepping aside to let him command would weaken the fleet. Besides, she knew someone close to her was likely a traitor; she wasn't about to give command of her fleet to anyone.

The thought of Fodor Hendricks made her smile in amusement. He'd always told her that a captain's place was on the bridge, not in the middle of a boarding action. She disagreed, but there was no getting around the fact that the bridge was where a commodore had to be. She wondered idly if he appreciated the fact that she was finally acting the way he'd always believed she should.

One of her marines stood stiffly in the airlock, apparently waiting for her. "Captain," the woman said in a gravelly voice that sounded like it rose from inside her boots, "the ship is secure, and the crew is being held on the main bridge."

"Good, Soldier," Benning inclined her head. "Take me there."

As they walked through the ship, Benning quietly surveyed the damage to the ship. The lights glowed dimly within it, no doubt barely maintained by the severely damaged power plant. The passageways showed signs of battle, with blood splashed on the deck and burn marks littering the bulkheads. The air smelled off somehow, as if it carried a faint odor that it shouldn't have, and the entire ship felt oddly quiet and empty in a way that Benning couldn't quite pin down. Something was wrong, but she didn't know exactly what.

<It's the nanofield, Benning Kidd,> Tiddly said softly. <It's practically gone.>

What? Benning reached out with her own field, seeking the nanites that should have filled the air around her. Her probing nanofield encountered mostly air; only a scant handful of foreign nanites hovered nearby. That explained why the ship felt so empty. Without its nanofield, the ship's 'net couldn't connect remotely to her, and she'd been feeling the lack of its presence.

Was this from the nanite bomb?

<Probably, yes. The nano-disassemblers in the bomb would have attacked everything they touched, and the ship's nanofield would have worked to stop them. The disassemblers probably destroyed a large percentage of the ship's nanites, and those that are left are likely concentrated around the hole in the hull or the power plant, trying to fix those as quickly as possible.>

"I'm having trouble linking to the ship's 'net," Benning said aloud to the marine. "How badly is it damaged?"

"I can't say for sure, Captain, but half the crew died from exposure to space or radiation," the Soldier replied in an unconcerned tone. "There's no gravity or atmosphere in the outer decks, and the radiation levels in Engineering are lethal."

As they walked, Benning checked her spoofed status, making sure it reflected what she wanted it to.

BENNING KIDD
Citizen Path: Pirate Captain (Stellar Corsair)
Level: 9
To Next Level: 73%
Credits: 47,812.4 Standard Credits

Physicality: 12.8
Coordination: 12.6

Resistance: 12.8

Acuity: 11.5
Willpower: 11.4 (18.4)
Social: 11.1

Renown: +/- 59
(Nanodefense: 19.0)

SKILLS
Conditioning: 19.9
(Cyberwarfare: 16.3)
Fleet Tactics: 4.4
Leadership: 20.5
Martial Combat: 20.7
(Nanoresistance: 2.5)
Naval Tactics: 23.9
Sense Deceit: 5.3
Starfaring: 19.3
Weapons Expertise: 19.4

On Tiddly's advice, Benning adopted the guise of a Pirate Captain, which would draw less attention than her true path. She'd also hidden her Nanodefense rating and Nanoresistance skill – a Pirate Captain wouldn't have access to either of those under normal circumstances – along with Cyberwarfare, her prohibited skill.

Training had mostly undone her losses from allowing herself to be killed in the Sirius tournament, although she felt the loss of her willpower keenly. That couldn't be easily replaced; training simulations designed to boost that stat did nothing for her. According to Tiddly, that was because she had willpower similar to a Noble's, not a Citizen's, and she'd need advanced training devices to improve it. The rest of her stats and skills, though, progressed nicely, and she anticipated the boost from reach rank 20 in Conditioning at any time.

Like every door they passed, the door to the bridge had been cut open with an antimatter torch and locked in place. The bridge felt less empty to Benning as she entered – apparently, some of the ship's surviving nanofield remained there – but the 'net seemed tenuous and distant, difficult for her to access. She'd need direct access to it in order to hack it, which meant unlocking the darkened command console in the rear central part of the bridge. Without being able to access that console remotely, she'd have to convince the ship's commander to unlock it for her. Fortunately, it seemed that the commander had survived the battle for control of the vessel.

Benning's marines surrounded seven people, four Citizens and three Soldiers. The Soldiers stood around one of the Citizens, a shorter woman with honey-colored hair cut below her jaw, brilliant green eyes, and a squarish face. The woman's face was an unreadable mask to Benning, the way most faces were, but the Corsair saw the fear lurking deep in her eyes. She stood toward the back of the group, probably trying to avoid attention, but the way the other Citizens kept glancing toward her made it obvious that she was in charge of the ship. Benning sent her nanites soaring toward the woman, and a quick scan confirmed her suspicion.

ALAESTRA BYRNE
Level 28 Mercantile Captain
Damage Rating: 8.8 (Strora Talon 9)
Defense Rating: 13.1 (Cirrus Vortex 5)
Resistance Rating: 14.3

STATS
Physicality: 11.8
Coordination: 12.7

Resistance: 13.4

Acuity: 18.5
Willpower: 13.3
Social: 19.8

Level 28? That's the highest level I've seen on someone yet, Benning thought, her eyes narrowing at the thought of the powerful Citizen before her. *She's a merchant, but her physical stats are close to mine!*

<She's probably at least a century old, Benning Kidd,> Tiddly suggested. <Maybe more. She's had lots of time to train them – and to learn a lot of skills. Don't assume she'll be easy to defeat in a fight just because she's not a marine.>

"Citizen Alaestra Byrne," Benning said aloud, facing the blonde woman. "There's no point in hiding in the back, there. I know that you're the one in command."

"Citizen Benning Kidd," Byrne replied, stepping forward, her face creased with displeasure as she obviously activated a scanner of some sort. Benning sent out her nanites, preparing to resist an intrusive scan, but she felt nothing amiss. Either Byrne only performed a deep scan, or she had a scanner advanced enough that Benning couldn't even sense it. A moment later, the woman spoke, and Benning relaxed as she realized that her disguise remained intact. "A Pirate Captain, I see. That's a wretched path. I don't know why the System tolerates your kind."

"Because it has to," Benning shrugged, unconcerned about the woman's opinion. "And it doesn't really matter, does it?"

"No, it doesn't." Byrne drew herself up. "You're obviously here to negotiate. What are your terms?"

"Terms? No terms." Benning shook her head. "You're going to give me your vessel – all the remaining ships in this fleet, in fact – and in return, I'll let you go to respawn."

Byrne's face clearly reflected her astonishment. "That's – that's absurd!" she laughed mockingly. "I'd never agree to that! I'd rather you kill us all."

"I think I can change your mind," Benning smiled evilly at the woman, taking a step forward.

Byrne shifted her weight as if to step backward but held her ground, lifting her chin imperiously. "Do your worst," she said simply. "Just know that once I come back from respawn, I'll gather all my fleets and hunt you down. I'll obliterate your ships, spawn camp you back to level 1, then do the same to your officers and anyone who works with you. By the time I'm done with you, the name 'Benning Kidd' will be a cautionary tale about what happens when you overreach yourself."

The woman crossed her arms before her chest. "Or I can pay you an ample sum of credits, and you allow us to pass in peace. I'll consider this a valuable lesson for my path and let it go. The choice is yours, Benning Kidd. Walk away from here wealthy and without a powerful enemy, or be hunted across the Collective like a dog."

"I prefer option 3," Benning smiled, sending a signal through her nanites. While Byrne pontificated, Benning had hacked into her equipment – its protections were substandard at best – and now controlled the woman's gear more or less completely. Byrne gasped as her armor retracted, folding itself onto her back, and her weapons shut down, leaving her defenseless. A moment later, her red and purple spacer suit flowed away from her, leaving her standing fully nude in the middle of the bridge.

"What – what are you doing?" Byrne gasped, her face clearly confused. "If – if you think that this will somehow convince me..."

The woman screamed and clutched her chest as Benning's nano-disassemblers attacked the fleshy protuberances there. The skin of Byrne's breasts and nipples slowly liquefied and ran down her abdomen, leaving a pair of raw, bloody mounds of fat and tissue exposed to the air. Byrne's Soldiers reacted instantly, reaching for their weapons, but Benning's marines struck just as quickly. Gunfire drowned out the captain's screams for a few seconds, and when it faded, all three of Byrne's Soldiers lay dead on the deck along with one of her crew members.

Byrne still stood, hunched over with her right arm cradled over her exposed breasts, her eyes wide and horrified. "What – what did you do to me?" she demanded in a voice hoarse from screaming.

"What I'm going to do to every square cim of your body," Benning said calmly. "At least, until you agree to my terms."

"A – a contract made under duress is unenforceable," Byrne stammered. "The System won't let you..."

"You're wrong, actually. The System will honor any contract, so long as you had the choice to sign it or not. You don't have to; you can endure what I'm going to do to you instead. As long as I'm not taking your choices away, the System doesn't care." Benning snorted. "In fact, the System couldn't care less about what I do to you, since it gave me the ability to do it in the first place." She concentrated again, and Byrne screamed as her left ear slowly dissolved and fell to the deck in gobbets of liquid flesh and splatters of crimson blood.

"Stop it!" one of Byrne's crew, a silver-haired man with slightly upturned eyes demanded. "You can't do this!" The man grunted and dropped to the deck, curled up in a fetal position as one of her marines slammed the butt of their rifle into his midsection.

"As you see, I can," Benning said evenly, never taking her eyes off the panting form of Byrne. "And I can make it last a really, really long time." She leaned forward. "Let's see how long you can hold out, Alaestra Byrne. I hope it's a while; I could really use the practice."

Byrne lasted longer than Benning thought she might. Most of the woman's skin lay in pools of cloudy liquid on the deck, along with her fingers, toes, genitalia, and eyes by the time she finally broke and agreed to Benning's terms. Benning forced the woman's crew to watch in horrified awe, and two of them wept freely after only a few minutes. The silver-haired man had even tried to attack Benning at one point, and his corpse slowly cooled on the deck, the ship's nanofield too busy to break it down.

"You – you're a monster," Byrne panted thickly as she shuddered and spasmed on the deck, her aura a dark orange in Benning's combat sight.

"I can see why you'd think that," Benning agreed. "But I'm doing what I have to do to survive, Alaestra Byrne. I'm not enjoying this, but it's necessary." She crouched down over the blinded woman.

"Now, you said before that when you respawn, you'll be coming after me. That's fine; I would do the same in your shoes. Just know that I'm going to take every fleet you send and put the commander of each fleet through the same treatment you went through. You think you'll spawn camp me to level 1? I'll do the same to any of your people you send my way, and I'll make sure they all die as painfully as possible each time. I want you to think about that before you start planning your revenge – think of your crew feeling what you're feeling right now, over and over again, until they reach level 1."

"Or you can just go on with your life and pretend this never happened," Benning added, rising to her feet. "It's your choice."

"Monster!" Byrne repeated as her shredded body spasmed once more.

"Maybe I am. But now that you know what will happen to anyone you send after me, if you do it anyway, you're just as much a monster as I am." Benning shrugged. "I honestly don't care either way."

She looked at the surviving crew. "Spread word of this," she instructed them. "Make sure everyone knows what will happen to them if they come after me. If you don't, then what happens to them is as much your fault as it is hers."

She stepped back and nodded to her marines. Gunshots rang out on the bridge, but she'd already turned away to face the now-unlocked command console of her new cruiser. She'd lied to the crew members, of course. She was the only one responsible for her actions; they couldn't be blamed if she tortured their crewmates sometime in the future. She knew that guilt was a powerful motivator, though, and she needed word of this to spread. This was only the first atrocity she'd have to perform, but the faster word of those spread, the fewer she'd need to commit before people started fearing her again.

Torturing Alaestra Byrne brought Benning no pleasure. It subtly eased the ache in her chest, but it didn't cause it to vanish. It was a necessity, nothing more, a show she put on to convince any bounty hunters or Fleet officers who might turn their attention toward her to keep their distance. Hopefully, whoever had let Tobis Kopel onto her station would also be paying attention. She'd gotten nowhere in her efforts to find that person so far – every possible trail led to a dead end – but Benning was persistent, and she always saw things through.

For the Fleet, this was a warning. For the one who'd betrayed her, it was a promise of things to come.

CHAPTER 16

"Can we talk, Benning Kidd?"

Benning didn't even glance at Fodor Hendricks as he entered her training room. She'd watched his approach in a small screen that popped up in her vision the moment he stepped foot into her private section of the station. After the bounty hunter attack, she spent some of her burgeoning store of credits on security upgrades for the entire station, including an automated system that sent alerts directly to her through the 'net. It was still possible for another hunter to get onto the station, of course, but it would be a lot harder, and no one but her could override the alarms she'd set to watch for potential assassins. She did try to learn from her mistakes, after all.

She suppressed a grunt as she hefted the HDM bar in her hands, curling it up to her chest. In Earth gravity, the seventy-five-kig bar would have been basically weightless to Benning, but at her increased training gravity of twelve g's, she could only lift it with serious effort. She lowered it slowly and returned it to her chest, her arms and shoulders trembling with the strain as she repeated the exercise four more times before lifting the bar overhead and dropping it onto her shoulders.

She'd been training hard, trying to push her Conditioning Skill to twenty, so far without success. Geraldine Dickerson, the Soldier who'd helped her set up her training regimen, couldn't help with that; as a Soldier, the woman had stats but not skills or abilities. At least, she didn't have neatly quantified skills the way a Citizen did, so she had no real idea how to raise those skills. Benning suspected that she needed something beyond simple training to push her over the edge; she just hadn't figured out what that might be. She was hoping that upping her training field from ten to twelve g's would do the trick; as it was, the bar was almost too heavy for her to lift with just her arms.

"This isn't the best time, Fodor Hendricks," she grunted as she made the almost metric-ton weight more comfortable across her shoulders and shifted her stance.

"It's the only time you're alone anymore," the man said, walking into the room. Benning expected to see him flinch or stagger beneath the increased gravity, but he simply stopped for a moment, adjusting to the increased load, before moving to stand in front of her. It was an impressive display of strength, one that Benning didn't think she could match. She could walk around in the increased gravity, of course, but not quite so nonchalantly as the Pirate Captain seemed to be doing. She realized that she'd never bothered to use her nanites to scan the man – or any of her captains, for that matter – and curiously, she took the moment to do so as she slowly bent her legs into a deep squat.

FODOR HENDRICKS
Level 12 Pirate Captain
Damage Rating: 14.1 (Relea Darkbolt 2)
Defense Rating: 15.4 (Mithrillene X9)
Resistance Rating: 17.1

STATS
Physicality: 13.7
Coordination: 10.8
Resistance: 12.1

Acuity: 13.4
Willpower: 10.1

Social: 12.5

She blinked in surprise at the man's stats. His physicality was ridiculously high for a Starship Captain, who would usually have that stat in the low tens at level 12. He'd obviously trained it hard to bring it to that level, but she didn't understand why he bothered doing so.

<It's because he's not a Starship Captain, Benning Kidd,> Tiddly explained. <He's a Pirate Captain.>

Aren't they basically the same thing? Benning asked the AI silently.

<Nope. Pirate Captain is a specialization of Starship Captain, one that's a little more combat oriented. Fodor Hendricks either worked to shift his path to that or chose to specialize in it at level 10.>

Does that mean that Pirate Captain and Stellar Corsair are similar, then?

<Not really. A Pirate Captain doesn't care about glory or renown. They're all about accumulating credits by taking things from other Citizens. They're bigger on naval combat than marine battles, in fact.>

Why is his physicality so high, then?

<I can think of several reasons, but I don't know which one it might be. You could try asking him, I guess.>

Benning rose to her feet, driving the heavy bar up with the power of her legs and back as she straightened, then glanced at the pirate. "Why is your physicality so high, Fodor Hendricks?" she asked after a moment.

He stared at her silently for a second or two before a wide grin spread across his dark-skinned face. "The same reason yours is," he said at last. "To make me a better melee fighter."

"But you always say that a captain shouldn't be fighting in marine battles," she pointed out. "Why do you need to be a better fighter, then?"

"To hold onto my command," he shrugged nonchalantly. "A Pirate Captain only commands as long as he keeps his crew in line. There's always some upstart junior officer who's trained with a plasma sword and thinks they can challenge me for my captaincy."

She lowered slowly into another squat, grunting as she pushed herself back upright. "Your crew can challenge you for command?" she asked dubiously.

"Of course. That's part of the Pirate's Code. The strongest commands; everyone else follows."

"And you allow that?" she asked incredulously, shocked by his words. "That's ridiculous! Being a better melee fighter doesn't make you a good captain!"

"It's not so much that I allow it as that it's what every crew expects," he chuckled. "That's the real secret, Benning Kidd. Any captain – Fleet, Starship, Pirate, or whatever – only commands as long as their crew is willing to follow them. If you lose your crew's loyalty, at best, they'll do a terrible job serving under you. At worst, they'll actively refuse your commands or even mutiny."

He picked up a bar similar to Benning's and hefted it a few times before lifting it over his head with only moderate effort. "One of the benefits of being a pirate is easy upward mobility. All you have to do to become captain is challenge the current captain to a duel and win." He snorted contemptuously. "Of course, if you fail, you end up tossed out the airlock. And if you succeed, you have to actually *be* captain. Most young hotheads fail at that, as well."

Benning considered his words, then nodded. "They just want to be in command without realizing what it meant," she guessed. "They concentrate on winning the challenge, not on the skills they'll need to command afterward."

"Exactly. As I said, if you want to keep command, you have to have a crew that's willing to serve. A young officer who challenges an older captain and wins usually has their crew turn on them after it becomes obvious they have no idea what they're doing, and the crew begs the old captain to take command once more – and usually jettison the challenger into space." He laughed. "That's why Pirate Captains don't fight against the practice. It weeds out dangerously ambitious but incompetent officers." He grinned at her once more. "At least, it usually does. Every so often, someone like you slips through the cracks."

She wanted to protest against his characterization of her, but after a moment's reflection, she realized that she couldn't. "Fair enough," she admitted. "I really had no clue what I was doing back then, and I wasn't remotely prepared to be an actual captain."

"No, you weren't. However, you were smart enough to know that – and to keep me around to teach you." He lifted the bar overhead once more. "More importantly, you actually listened and were eager to learn. That's rarer than you might think, and it's one reason why I still follow you."

<I think that's a hint, Benning Kidd,> Tiddly suggested. <He's saying that if you turn him away now, he might not want to keep following you.>

Benning dropped low once more, then straightened, locking her legs to hold her steady. "Fine, Fodor Hendricks," she sighed. "What did you want to talk about?"

"Oh, you picked up on that?" he chuckled. "I wasn't sure if you would. Subtleties aren't always your strongest suit." He lowered the bar and set it back to the side.

"Benning Kidd, I'm a little concerned by what we've been doing lately."

"Concerned how?" she asked with a grunt as she rose back from a squat.

"Obviously, piracy doesn't bother me, and you've picked excellent targets. That convoy we hit, the one carrying all the anti-iron, made us all enough credits to keep anyone from complaining about funds for a couple solar years, at least."

She nodded. "I've tried to pick high-value transports," she agreed. "Ones with more protection than their stated cargoes justify."

"It's more than that, and we both know it. Most convoys with too much protection just have overly nervous owners, nothing more. Some of them are traps for people like us, with even the convoy ships armed to the teeth and just waiting for pirates to descend on them. You've avoided both of those somehow, and although we've lost a couple ships, we've captured enough that we won't be able to crew them all for a year or more at minimum."

"I agree with all of that," Benning nodded. "So, what's the problem?"

"The brutality," he sighed. "Benning Kidd, you've always been ruthless. I admire that about you, in fact. You don't let things like conscience or morality get in the way of what you have to do. Lately, though..." He made a strange face that she couldn't read.

"Lately, things have gotten pretty extreme. You've tortured ship captains who already surrendered and made their crews watch. You've taken your time killing people who should have been put down cleanly, and sometimes, it seems like you're making their deaths as gruesome as possible. That last captain..." He shuddered. "Even I had trouble sleeping after that, Benning Kidd."

He gazed at her, his eyes piercing as he stared into hers. "So, I have to ask: has it finally happened?"

"Has what finally happened?" she asked, puzzled.

"Have you finally started losing yourself to the violence? Started enjoying it? Or is there still method buried in your madness?"

Benning paused her workout and simply stood, considering the man's words seriously. In the past two months, she'd taken four more convoys, all of them profitable. She'd lost the *Grim Streak* and *Vindictive* in the process, but she'd replaced those ships with upgraded ones. Saavi Boguna now captained the fast frigate *Cygni's Eye*, while Fodor Hendricks once again commanded a full frigate, the *Implacable*. Her captured cruiser was still docked and being repaired, along with a pair of destroyers. She planned to take command of the cruiser eventually and hand over her three destroyers to her most trusted captains, and with the cargoes she'd taken – cargoes that she'd been able to bring back thanks to the *Orion*, the carrack she'd taken and finally refitted to travel with her fleet on its raiding missions. The sales of those cargoes brought her tens of thousands of credits, and she'd used those to upgrade all her ships and purchase new ones.

She'd also made a point to kill the captain of each convoy's most powerful escort ship in spectacular and brutal fashion. Her Renown had jumped sharply, to seventy-eight, although it usually showed as negative Infamy in most stations; to her, that meant her plan was working. People were talking about her excesses, and according to Bentlix Gibbons, her bounty hunter ally, most hunters considered the payouts on her bounties too low for the accompanying risk.

At the same time, she had noticed that torturing those

captains slightly eased the aching in her chest. It was as if their pain lessened hers, as if she somehow temporarily transferred her own agony to her victims. She didn't know if that counted as enjoying the torture; her own pain didn't exactly disappear, after all. Tormenting her victims didn't make her feel good, not the way leveling up did.

"I don't think I am," she finally said. "Enjoying torture, that is. It's not unpleasant, but it doesn't make me happy, either. It's just something that's necessary."

"Why?" he asked, his voice and face both oddly intent.

She shrugged and answered as simply as possible. "Bounty hunters and the Fleet."

"The Fleet?" He leaned back from her. "What about them? Are you trying to give them more reasons to come after you?"

"Just the opposite." She lifted the bar over her shoulders; her trembling legs wouldn't support her through another squat. Instead, she began slow sets of triceps curls, lowering the bar to the back of her neck and lifting it back overhead. "I'm hoping this makes them think twice about coming after me."

"I'm not following," he admitted. "Every convoy we hit is another reason for the Fleet to come capture you, Benning Kidd."

"And every atrocity is a reason for them to stay away." She set her jaw as she powered through the last of her exercises before setting the bar on a stand and dropping the gravity back to normal. Her body instantly felt light, almost weightless without the eleven extra g's pulling down on it, and she sighed with relief as her aching muscles swiftly began recovering.

"The Fleet doesn't work that way," he pointed out. "If you catch the attention of one of the admirals, they'll order their captains to attack the station. They won't be afraid of you because they won't be the ones coming to get you."

"But the captains might be," Benning shrugged. "And if they are, they might take their time obeying that order." She sat down on a padded bench to let her trembling legs recover and gazed up at the man. "Fodor Hendricks, the Fleet has had a seizure order out on me for the better part of a solar year now. They haven't executed it yet. Why do you think that is?"

"Because they haven't cared enough, most likely. If you keep this up, they might start caring, though."

"What, because I'm committing piracy?" She shook her head. "The Collective moves sextillions of gigs of cargo every standard day. The corporations we're stealing from probably each ship tens or hundreds of thousands of gigs during that same period. Do you really think anyone even noticed the few hundred gigs we've taken?"

"No, but they'll have noticed how you've executed the captains. That's the sort of thing that will send the Fleet your way in a hurry."

"Why? I've killed five captains. In that time, pirates have probably killed a million or more captains across the Collective. I'm sure many of them died painfully or cruelly." She shrugged. "I doubt the Fleet cares much about that."

She leaned forward, looking at him intently. "The officers that are supposed to come capture me, though? They might care a lot about those stories. If they attack me and fail, they might be the ones dying slowly and painfully, screaming for mercy as their organs liquefy. I think that's why so far, the Fleet hasn't come looking for me except that one time in Sirius. There, I think they thought that if they caught me alone, I'd have no choice but to go with them, but here, they'll have to bring a fleet, and if they lose, they'll risk being captured and tortured."

She shrugged. "At least, I hope that's what's happening."

"And if you're wrong?"

"Then the Fleet will be here no matter what, and nothing I do is going to change that. If they send a small fleet and we destroy them, they'll just send a battlefrigate or battlecruiser, and we'll have no choice but to abandon the station and scatter until they lose interest." She sighed. "At least this way I don't have to worry about bounty hunters on top of the Fleet."

He nodded and sighed heavily. "That's – good to hear, actually," he said in a relieved tone of voice. "Not that we'll have to scatter, but that you've been acting with good reasons instead of just inflicting pain for its own sake."

"Why does that idea bother you so much?" she asked curiously. "Are you worried I might do it to you?"

"No, not really," he chuckled. "You still need me too much." He looked away from her, his eyes growing distant.

"Power can be very sweet, Benning Kidd," he mused. "For some people, it can even become an addiction, and any addiction is dangerous. It can come to rule you, and it colors every choice you make and action you take."

"Like the leveling euphoria?" she asked. He glanced at her, his face startled, but slowly nodded.

"Yes. Exactly like that. The System wants you to level up, so it addicts you to the process. Most Citizens will do anything for another level, so they never stop working on their path, no matter how high a level they reach. They'll throw aside loved ones, friends, even family members if it means gaining another level.

"For a Starship Captain, it's even worse. The more responsibility you have, the more people you have counting on you, the more damage your addictions can do. Your choices stop affecting only you and start harming everyone in your command."

"It sounds like you're speaking from experience," she observed.

"It does, doesn't it? The point is, Benning Kidd, if you ever find that you're starting to enjoy the violence and torture – that it's starting to make you feel happy or powerful, or you find yourself eager to do it again – do me a favor and let me know." He grinned at her. "I probably can't help, but at least I'll know that it's time to get the Hole away from you."

"That seems like a good reason not to tell you, then, doesn't it?"

"Oh, I didn't say I'd stop working with you. I'd just do it from enough of a distance that when it all goes to scrit, I won't get splashed by it." He laughed as he turned to look at her once more.

"Oh, and Benning Kidd, don't underestimate the Fleet. No matter what you might think, I'm betting that so far, you've just been beneath their notice. If you change that – if you become important enough that the upper echelons pay attention to you – then nothing you can do will stop them from sending a fleet here to kill us all. To them, you're just a tiny bug – an annoyance but nothing worth worrying about. If you bite them, though, they'll stomp on you. You can count on that."

CHAPTER 17

"*Incipient Storm,* you are approved for docking," a rough-sounding voice sounded across the bridge of the *Resolute Hammer.* "Proceed directly to Docking Ring 116, Bay 21. Confirm."

"Acknowledged, Adriaan Station 17," Brialle Caldwell spoke crisply into the air. "We are proceeding to Docking Ring 116, Bay 21."

"Affirmative, *Incipient Storm.* Please be aware that any deviation from your expected flight path will be considered sign of hostile intent and dealt with appropriately."

"Acknowledged, Adriaan Station," Caldwell said, shaking her head and cutting communications. She glanced back at Benning. "They seem fairly strict here, Captain. I've never heard of threatening a ship if it deviated course en route to its docking bay."

"Van Maanen is one of the most disciplined, tightly regulated systems in the Collective, Brialle Caldwell," Charlo Herrick said, her voice eager as she spoke. "It's also one of the most militaristic, though, and you can get military upgrades here that you can't find for another thirty lightyears or more." The orange-haired woman rubbed her hands together gleefully. "I can't wait to see what design upgrades we can get!"

"Settle down, Charlo Herrick," Benning ordered. "As you said, this is one of the most heavily restricted systems in the Collective. It's going to be a while before we're allowed on station. They won't let us off until they've scanned every cubic cim of our vessel."

"Good thing we aren't carrying any cargo, then, Captain," Jezper Shields said laconically. "Less for them to scan."

Benning didn't bother to correct the man. The reason the *Hammer's* holds were empty was that all sales in the system were so heavily tariffed that it bled away all potential profit for an outside trader. Van Maanen merchants paid a much lower tariff, of course, so typically their traders bought goods out-system and brought it to one of the three planets. If a captain like Benning had goods that would sell well in the system, she'd have brokered a deal with a local merchant and had them pick up the merchandise somewhere else. She'd lose money by essentially footing the merchant's travel costs, but it was still better than paying an 80% tariff.

Most systems in the Collective relied at least partially on tourism for their economies. For Citizens who lived for hundreds or even thousands of years, boredom was a real danger, and while the Overnet provided vast amounts of entertainment, many Citizens craved actual experiences rather than virtual ones. Citizens would journey on deepcruisers or massive megacruisers traveling from system to system, spending their hard-earned credits in exchange for a few moments or hours of excitement, and systems capitalized on this. They provided the Citizens with the experiences they desired and catered to the whims of these tourists. Proxima built spherical stations from which tourists could observe a rare tri-solar sunrise; Tau Ceti maintained zoos and even hunting preserves for Citizens to experience the native creatures; Gliese offered solar dives that allowed Citizens to travel through the outer shell of its cool, dim red dwarf star.

Van Maanen, on the other hand, openly discouraged tourism. The stations orbiting the edge of the system were mostly militaristic and forbidden to outsiders, as were the Dyson stations surrounding the white dwarf at Van Maanen's heart. The system had three planets, one rocky body and two gas giants, and outsiders were banned on all of them. Upon entering the system, the *Hammer*, like every other foreign vessel, picked up a pair of warships as an escort to make sure they didn't try to dock at any prohibited stations or meet clandestinely with someone out in space. The system's governor ruled with an iron fist, not bothering to conceal it in a velvet glove, and almost all visitors were encouraged to take their business someplace else. Most Citizens came to the system for one reason alone: to purchase ship upgrades that they couldn't easily find elsewhere. That was what brought Benning to the system, and if not for that temptation, she wouldn't have come within a lightyear of the place.

The customs inspector came aboard within minutes of the ship's docking. The tall woman strode forward, her back erect and her steps precise, followed by a pair of Workers and four Soldiers. The entire group wore navy blue with a vertical carmine stripe across the left breast, and the inspector had a gold badge fastened to her chest in the center of the stripe that Benning assumed denoted her rank or status. She stopped before Benning, not even glancing at the four marines flanking the captain as she spoke.

"Captain Rebexa Graves? My designation is Junior Inspector A17-21984, and I'm here to perform the inspection of your ship and cargo."

"Welcome aboard, Inspector," Benning nodded. "You're welcome to scan the ship, but we're not carrying any cargo." Benning had to admit that she was a little surprised at the woman's numeric designation. She wondered idly if all Citizens in Van Maanen had such designations but pushed the thought from her mind as a pointless one. If it were the case, she'd probably know soon enough.

"So your manifest claims, Captain," the inspector said crisply. "I'm here to verify that fact with a deep scan. Do you acquiesce to such a scan? Please know that refusal will result in your expulsion and future prohibition from this system."

"Scan away," Benning shrugged, stepping back and indicating the hatch behind her. "The cargo hold is this way."

"I have a blueprint of your ship's layout, and I'll conduct the scan according to that layout," the woman walked past Benning. "Please follow along and instruct your crew to cooperate fully."

The scan took over two hours to complete, as the inspector walked the entirety of the ship, her Workers pushing the scanner behind her while her Soldiers kept Benning well away from the device. She assumed that was to keep her from interfering with it or tampering with the scanner in some way, but the guards' efforts were basically futile. Benning hacked the simple scanning device within the first ten minutes of their tour of her ship and monitored its results closely. She'd deliberately chosen to spoof the beacon of a ship with an identical hull design to hers, but no two ships were exactly the same, and the scan picked up minute differences in the ship's expected design and its actual layout – differences that Benning suppressed before they could be transmitted to the inspector.

The inspector ended the scan in the cargo hold, verifying that the large space was empty, and turned to face Benning. "Everything seems satisfactory," she said officiously. "I will recommend that you are given clearance to enter the station."

"What's the procedure for that?" Benning asked curiously.

"Contact the station administration and let them know the purpose of your visit. They'll issue you a pass to enter the station that will allow you to complete whatever task you've come here for and let you return to your vessel."

"Can I bring my own security with me?"

"Of course. Each captain may bring up to four marines as security, although it's totally unnecessary. Adriaan Station is completely safe and secure. We actively search for and destroy or expel pirates and other criminals, we forbid bounty hunters from claiming bounties except from those who have otherwise been arrested and convicted of another crime, and anyone who violates any of our regulations is summarily executed, so lawbreakers are few and far between."

Benning nodded slowly. "That seems like it would be very effective."

The inspector gave her a look of veiled surprise. "It is, but most outsiders don't see that. They complain about the restrictions and how unfair we are."

"I don't know about fairness," Benning shrugged. "It strikes me as an efficient way to run things, though. Harsh punishments encourage those who pursue criminal career paths to stay away, or at least to remain within the law while they're here, and restricting bounty hunting probably keeps things quieter and cuts down on accidental deaths."

"Precisely," the woman inclined her head to Benning. "Keep that understanding, and you'll do well in Adriaan Station."

Another hour passed before Benning got approval for herself, Charlo Herrick, and her Engineer Graesen Barry to enter the station, escorted by four of her Soldiers. Benning brought her armor and weapons along as well; while she assumed that the inspector was correct about the station's high level of security, she suspected that there were Citizens who would risk the consequences regardless. Death was a minor inconvenience to a Citizen, after all, and for the right rewards, they'd consider it a small price to pay.

As she entered the station's elevator, she felt an odd pressure against her body, and a notification popped up in her vision.

> SCANNING NANOFIELD ENTERED!
> Nanoresistance is successfully
> resisting a nanite scanning field.

Benning reached out with her nanofield and felt the intrusive nanites filling the elevator around her. Her own scanning nanites responded, attaching to the station's field and feeding it the false status she'd created for this trip, while her disassemblers destroyed any scanners that got too close to her and avoided her defenses. She considered hacking some of the scanning nanites and adding them to her field, but that would mean a trip to Sirius to recalibrate her field, and that risked another encounter with the Fleet. She'd return there eventually, but she wanted to hold off on it as long as possible and perhaps resolve her issues with the Fleet first.

The scanning nanites remained behind in the elevator, but Benning's 'net warned her of three more intrusive scanners as she traveled through the station toward the district known as the Armory. The station's passageways were narrower than she was used to, and the overheads weren't quite as high as was standard. The corridors turned at right angles every so often for no apparent reason, and she passed through multiple hatchways that she assumed could slam shut and seal the hallway if needed. The entire station was built like a fortress, not a commercial outpost.

Most stations' market centers tended to be open,

brightly lit, and filled with colorful holograms. They were designed to appeal to customers and attract the eye, drawing shoppers in and encouraging them to roam from store to store. Promenades usually sported numerous restaurants and bars, as well, along with entertainment centers and betting parlors. All this encouraged those with credits to linger in the marketplace as long as possible and buy more than they originally intended.

The Armory was nothing like a normal promenade because the station's administrators didn't want to encourage loitering and random shopping. To enter the station, Benning had to either specify which stores she intended to visit or allow the station to choose for her, and her pass only allowed her through the checkpoints and hatches leading to those stores. Instead of an open space that was, honestly, a waste of square footage, the Armory held a maze of twisting corridors. Holographic signs floating at every intersection lit up as Benning neared, directing her toward the stores she'd chosen to visit, and she suspected that if she ignored those directions, the security escort following her would protest mightily.

Her first stop, Steelforge Armaments, was on the second floor of the Armory, far to the back of the district. When Benning stepped in, she found herself standing in the back of a line of about twenty Citizens, all waiting with various degrees of displayed patience.

"Never seen this before, Captain," Charlo Herrick murmured softly to Benning. "Maybe we should leave and come back later."

"If we do, we might risk not being able to come back," Graesen Barry pointed out. "I don't know how our pass works, but it might only allow us one visit to each place, whether we buy anything or not."

"We can wait," Benning decided firmly. "I'm not

wasting a week-long trip here over a little impatience."

"If you say so, Captain," Herrick sighed. "I'm just eager to get to the weapons shop, is all."

"And I'd rather be examining engine and system upgrades," Barry agreed. "But you don't hear me whining about it."

"Whining? I'm not whining!"

"Really? I must have misheard you, then," Barry said with a straight face. "It sounded like you were complaining that this entire station should move faster just so you can get what you want."

"Well, yeah, but that's not whining! It's wishful thinking."

"Enough," Benning said flatly. "Charlo Herrick, we'll be looking at weapons next, so be patient. If you can't, you can return to the ship, and I'll buy the weapons upgrades without you."

"I'm good, Captain," the Weapons Officer replied instantly, straightening. "I can be patient."

Benning remained silent, but she caught the peculiar look of triumph Graesen Barry flashed at Charlo Herrick. She didn't understand what the white-haired Engineer thought he'd won, but obviously, he felt he'd scored some sort of victory.

When they reached the counter at last, a woman with hair the color of molten gold and deep green eyes greeted them, flashing Benning a dazzling smile.

"Welcome to Steelforge," the woman said in a friendly tone. "My designation is Senior Salesperson A17-431918. How can I assist you today?"

"I'm looking for defensive upgrades for my ships," Benning told the woman, mentally confirming that apparently, every Citizen on the station had a numerical designation.

"Of course! You did say ships, plural, correct?" The woman's hands moved over the counter, and holographic images started to appear above it. "Are you looking for individual upgrades or design templates?"

"Templates," Benning said firmly. "Something that I can apply to both my current fleet and any new ships I acquire in the future."

The saleswoman nodded brightly. "I'm required to inform you that purchasing a template simply grants you a license to upgrade ships you own with that template. You won't be able to resell it or apply it to a ship you don't own. Also, templates cost a minimum of ten times the individual repairs, so if you only have two or three ships, it'll be cheaper to upgrade them individually."

Will those limitations apply to me, Tiddly, or can I hack the licenses and free them up to be resold? she asked silently.

<You can probably unlock them, sure, Benning Kidd. The thing is, I don't know how much good it would do you. They'll still carry the maker's mark of the corporation who licensed them, and people who might buy them will know that they're being sold illegally. They might refuse to buy in case the corporation manages to lock the template down again and make it useless to them. You would be able to put the upgrades on someone else's ship, though.>

So, no real point in hacking them, Benning sighed. *That's fine. I really just want them for my ships, anyway.*

She nodded to the salesperson. "I'd still like to purchase the templates. I understand the limitations and the cost."

"Excellent!" the woman smiled. "That's what I expected you'd say. Most people come to this system to buy templates, after all, since they're usually impossible to purchase." She made a face. "I should say that you can purchase them anywhere, but they'll be locked and unusable."

"How can I buy them here, then?" Benning asked curiously.

"One of our governors brokered a deal with the major corporations quite some time ago. We're allowed to sell templates, but only with a heavily restricted license, and we pay the corporations a portion of the sales cost for each template – which, as I said, is higher than refitting several ships individually."

Benning frowned. "That still seems like a losing proposition for the corporations. A Starship Captain might find it cheaper to purchase individual upgrades, but every shipping and security company out there could save hundreds of thousands of credits in the long run with one of these designs. What do the corporations get out of it?"

"Our business," she replied evenly. "Van Maanen is the third-largest purchaser of ships and naval equipment in the Collective behind the Fleet and Sol system, and we only buy ships and upgrades from the corporations who've entered into this agreement with us. The corporations allow us to sell the templates knowing that most of those credits are going to end up back with them and that they'll make far more in the long run."

"That makes sense," Benning nodded.

"It does," the saleswoman agreed. "Now, what sort of upgrades are you looking for?"

"Better armor and shielding," Benning said immediately. "Reactive armor if you've got it. Also, better point defenses."

"Armor and shields are easy. Reactive armor is very

expensive, though, and it can't just be created with a basic template and nano-replicators. It requires negmass, so you'll need a supply of that to use it."

"I understand," Benning nodded.

"Good. As far as point defenses – do you need better weapons, or do you need a better targeting array?"

"What's the difference?"

"Well, if your point defenses are fifty-tow mass drivers and fifty-tej plasma cannons, you might need a weapons upgrade."

"We've currently got high-field mass drivers and hundred-tej plasma cannons," Herrick interjected eagerly, her eyes bright as she spoke. "We could use a static field generator, though – or high-density plasma cannons."

"I have templates for both," the woman smiled. "However, the real question is, will your targeting array make the best use of those weapons? Most of the time, the best way to improve your point defenses is to upgrade your array, not the weapons themselves."

"What do you mean?" Benning asked.

"The targeting array is a dedicated system that controls the ship's weapons, Captain," Herrick replied. "If we upgrade it, the weapons will respond faster and more accurately – but not enough to justify the expense of the upgrade, in all honesty."

"For standard ship's weapons, that's correct," the woman agreed. "You rarely need pinpoint accuracy when fighting at three leconds or more. However, point defense weapons only fire at distances below half a lecond, and for them, accuracy and reactivity are more important than raw power."

She looked at Benning with a smile. "Think of it this

way, Captain. The average AM warhead travels at nine tocks and has an effective damage range of around three thousand kims. That means that your point defense systems – most of which fire at about 9.99 tocks – have a quarter of a second to locate the missile, track it, and plot a firing solution to destroy it before it reaches its damage radius. That's not long when most of your ship's processing power is being used for the main battle – and it's why most ships' point defenses have about a 50% success rate at destroying incoming targets."

"And upgrading the targeting array might improve that to sixty or seventy percent," Herrick shook her head. "Unless we replaced it entirely…"

"That's what I would suggest," the clerk said, waving her hand over the counter so that a new schematic appeared above it.

Herrick peered at the design and whistled sharply. "This system has its own negaputer and combat analysis system, Captain," she said eagerly. "It would be able to handle our point defenses without relying on the ship's main weapons grid. That would improve our point defense accuracy to around 90% and would free up the main grid to target and power the primary weapons – and it would let us add some weapons that the grid might otherwise not be able to handle! I'm talking battlefrigate weapons on our destroyers!"

<That's mostly true, Benning Kidd,> Tiddly allowed, <but your grid isn't the only limiting factor on your weapons. You need a power plant and capacitor bank able to handle them. You can't fire a twelve-pow graser from a six-pow capacitor bank, after all. That new system would drastically improve your point defenses, though.>

How useful would that be compared to just doubling the number of point defense weapons – or that static field that Charlo Herrick mentioned?

<A static field creates an antimatter barrier around your ship that warheads impact. It'll probably destroy thirty or forty percent of them and damage the rest so that your point defenses are better at bringing them down. It's a power suck, though, and you can't keep it up for long at speed since gas impacts against it will quickly bring it down. It'll certainly work, but this new array would make it a lot more effective.

<Doubling your weapons honestly won't do much. The salesperson is right; your ship's negaputer only allots so much processing power for the point defenses, and that limits how quickly and well they fire. Right now, a warhead that gets within half a lecond of the *Resolute Hammer* has six to eight mass drivers and plasma cannons targeting it, and they miss about half the time. Doubling that means they'll hit about sixty percent of the time instead.>

And this new array would be ninety percent effective?

<Probably closer to eighty. Warheads have countermeasures, after all, and torpedoes move to evade point defenses, so while theoretically, you might hit the incoming weapon nine out of ten times, realistically, you'll only destroy it four out of five times. You'll also need a power plant upgrade with this design since the main weapons plant is already running at full capacity, and this will increase the draw significantly.>

Wouldn't better armor give me the same results?

<Oh, sure, to some extent. Another mim of neutronium will mitigate a lot of damage, as will a microlayer of reactive uranium – but those will impact your ship's mass and maneuverability as well, and there's an upper limit to how much defense you can get from armor. Plus, you'll need a plant upgrade for reactive armor since you'll need to maintain it in a containment field or the negmass inside it will rip it apart.>

Benning nodded slowly. "How much?" she asked the salesperson.

"4,500 credits," she responded at once.

"Holy scrit," Barry breathed from beside Benning. "Captain, we could buy an entire ship for that!"

"As I said, templates are far more expensive than individual upgrades," the saleswoman said sympathetically. "If you'd prefer the individual upgrade, that will only cost 350 credits."

"Let me see if I have this right," Benning said, looking directly at the woman. "You want me to pay 4,500 credits for a design template, correct? One that I can only use if I purchase a larger power plant for each ship I want to put it on – and one whose main benefits I can replicate with a mim of neutronium?"

"As your Weapons Engineer said, with this upgrade, you can add better and more powerful weapons to your main grid," the woman reminded Benning. "And this upgrade will make any other point defense weapons you add later work far more effectively."

"I can only add better weapons if I also upgrade my weapons plant and capacitors," Benning shook her head. "Honestly, it seems like far too much expense for far too little gain. I might be willing to pay 2,500 credits for this design, but no more – I'd need to invest another 2,000 credits to get the upgrades I'd need to make this workable anyway."

The saleswoman's smile didn't falter as she spoke. "I couldn't do that, I'm afraid, but I could do 4,000, instead."

"I might be willing to go to 3,500..." Benning leaned forward. "But only if I could somehow get templates for those other upgrades I'll need – the improved capacitors, relays, and power plants – for, say, five hundred credits."

"I can't help you with power plants," the saleswoman

shook her head. "Unless you're trying to run your ship off fusion plants – which I sincerely hope you aren't. No one has access to negmass plant templates but the Fleet; you have to buy those premade." She hesitated. "However, I could add templates for the improved capacitors and relays for 500."

"3,750 for all of it," Benning countered. "I'm still interested in buying better armor, after all, and with this upgrade, a static field generator might make sense."

"I can add a template for reactive uranium armor – you'll need a new plant for that, too, but a simple fusion plant will work, and those are cheap – and one for a static field, although that'll only be effective on ships the size of a destroyer or larger," the saleswoman smiled. "We could do all of it for 5,000 credits."

"4,200," Benning smiled back. "I'm guessing few people ask for either of those since a static field needs an advanced array like this one to be useful, and you need access to negmass to make reactive armor."

"True," the woman nodded. "I can do that. 4,200 credits for all of it."

"By the Hole, Captain," Graesen Barry breathed silently. "4,200 credits? That's an absurd sum!"

"Not if we can make the entire fleet all but immune to warheads and torpedoes," Herrick shook her head. "With advanced point defenses, a static field, and reactive uranium armor, we can ignore anything short of a singularity warhead – and even then, one would have to explode within a hundred kims or so of the hull to have any effect whatsoever."

Benning left the store 4,200 credits poorer but with her new design templates uploaded to her ship's 'net. She would have liked to have gotten a schematic for a negmass plant, but she knew that was a longshot. The Fleet kept the secret of creating negmass securely, and even the System itself seemed to help keep that knowledge from spreading. That was fine, though; one of the convoys she'd hit carried a load of negmass plants, and she had enough plants to refit twenty ships, plus enough negmass left over to cover at least one vessel in reactive armor.

She went to Stellar Armories next, where she bought the designs for ten-pow and six-pow grasers, four-pijin antimatter cannons, and singularity warheads. She wanted to buy the schematics for weapons like a subspace tunneler or strangelet bomb, but the salesperson assured her that she wouldn't find weapons like that anywhere in Van Maanen and that buying or selling them was a death sentence in the system. After, she visited Mavis Engineering and purchased plans for more powerful engines and thrusters as well as an upgrade for a ship's 'net and nanofield. She knew from personal experience that an improved nanofield could grant huge benefits to a Citizen, and Tiddly assured her the same was true for her ship. All told, the upgrades cost her over 7,000 credits, but once she applied the designs to her ships, her fleet would be significantly stronger.

As she exited Mavis Engineering, Benning stopped with a frown. She glanced up and down the passageway, noticing that it was strangely empty. A moment later, another anomaly registered in her mind.

"Where did our escort go?" she asked grimly, activating her armor and weapons as she did.

"What?" Graesen Barry replied, his eyes unfocused as he examined their new templates.

"Our escort. They're gone." Benning peered around. "And so is everyone else. Something's wrong…"

She fell silent as a voice suddenly echoed along the passageway, crashing into the group's ears.

"Citizen Benning Kidd!" the voice declared.

"Deactivate your weapons and armor and remain where you are! By order of Governor VM 1-001, you are to be arrested and held pending the imminent arrival of Fleet officers. Submit, and your crew will be allowed to leave peacefully. Resistance will result in execution and imprisonment."

"Scrit," Charlo Herrick whispered as Soldiers appeared at both ends of the hallway, their weapons pointed at the group, penning them in.

Benning couldn't help but agree. Somehow, the station had deduced her identity, and they'd called the Fleet to come pick her up. If she was here when the Fleet arrived, she'd face imprisonment at best and loss of levels at worst – but if she fought back, the administration could shut the entire station down around her, trapping her in place. It was a no-win situation.

She hefted her rifle. Even if she couldn't win, Benning intended to make her pursuers pay dearly for crossing her.

CHAPTER 18

"Down!" one of the marines shouted, shoving Graesen Barry to the deck while another did the same to Charlo Herrick. The other two marines dropped to a knee and leveled their rifles, providing cover for the unarmored officers. Benning wasn't worried about them, herself. The odds were good that they'd both die in the first minute or so of the coming battle, and trying to protect them would hamper her and her troops. If the group fought their way free, she could arrange for the pair to respawn back at IS-39267; if not, their respawn location wouldn't much matter.

"Taking the right," Benning said calmly. "One of you with me; the rest, hold our rear."

"Yes, ma'am," one of the marines said, moving to Benning's side.

"This is your final warning, Benning Kidd!" the administrator's voice rumbled loudly in the corridor. "Surrender, or we will be forced to open fire. You have five seconds to deactivate..."

The droning voice faded as Benning's fusion grenade crashed into the wall of Soldiers facing her and exploded. A new sun flared briefly to life as the densely packed deuterium nuclei slammed into one another, turning into helium-3 and releasing massive amounts of energy and swarms of neutrons. Benning's 'net automatically muffled her hearing and darkened her vision to protect her senses from the brilliant light and incredible pressure wave, but the force of the blast still crashed into her chest and rocked her back a step.

Behind her, gunfire crackled to life as her hearing returned, but Benning ignored the sound. She had her own problems; as she'd suspected, the fusion grenade killed some of the Soldiers in front of her, but the rest were only wounded, and they opened fire the moment they regained their senses. Benning dropped prone on the deck and lifted her Arcbar, unleashing a five-round burst at a Soldier's cracked helmet. The helmet imploded, and the Soldier dropped as her bullets ripped through the shattered visor and bounced around inside the helmet, reducing their brain to bloody paste.

Bullets cracked and whined against her armor and helmet, but she dismissed them. She had no cover, no way to avoid the gunfire. Her only hope was to finish the wounded Soldiers quickly, then move to assist the marines defending behind her. Her rifle swung to the next target, a Soldier with a damaged breastplate, and another burst of bullets ripped into their chest, dropping them swiftly as their aura snapped to black in Benning's vision.

The remaining Soldiers moved forward, slamming metal plates upright on the deck and taking cover behind them. As they did, Benning tossed a second grenade, this one a gamma flasher. The projectile exploded behind the barrier, unleashing a storm of gamma radiation that plunged through the Soldiers' damaged armor. The gunfire slackened briefly as the Soldiers fought off waves of nausea and dizziness, and in the lull, Benning rose to her feet and raced down the corridor toward her foes.

Benning covered the fifty ems to her foes in two seconds, but in that time, the Soldiers began to recover. Bullets cracked against her armor, and pain burned in the side of her neck as a bullet grazed the flesh there. She shrugged off the minor wound and leaped over the barrier, her warhammer snapping to life and glowing with the radiance of antimatter. She swung her weapon at the head of the nearest Soldier, smashing their visor with the blow and shattering the face behind the shadowed helm. Her backswing slammed into the crotch of a second Soldier, piercing their enn-steel armor and plunging into their femoral artery.

Another bullet pierced her armor low in her back, dropping her resistance bar to 71% and triggering Strength from Pain. Her weapon felt surer in her hand, and her senses seemed to sharpen as she stepped forward, thrusting the spearhead into the throat of a third Soldier. One of her enemies pulled out a heavy, spiked mace and swung it at her skull, but she deflected the blow and responded with a low strike that shattered their knee. A bullet sank into the meat of her right thigh, making her stumble, but the wound gave her even greater strength and focus. She crashed her hammer into the mace wielder's side, knocking them off-balance and ruining the blow aimed at her shoulder, then brought the weapon up in an underhand blow that snapped their head backward, allowing her to plunge her spearhead into their throat.

She whirled to face the last Soldier, stumbling only slightly as her leg reminded her of her wound. Her foe pulled out a long spear and thrust it at Benning, but she stepped back and drew her pistol, firing three shots directly into the Soldier's damaged chest plate. A ragged hole appeared in their armor, and the Soldier staggered backward, allowing Benning to slip past the spear and slam her hammer into their elbow. Their spear dropped, and they scrabbled for their own weapon with their good hand, but Benning put three bullets at close range into their visor, and they collapsed on the deck as their bright orange aura darkened to deep red.

"Fall back to me!" she shouted to her marines, who still exchanged gunfire with the Soldiers at the other end of the hall. The four marines moved slowly backward, leaving behind the still, prone figures of her officers. Neither Graesen Barry nor Charlo Herrick even twitched as the marines left them behind, and both of their auras glowed deep black in Benning's combat sight. As she'd suspected, neither of them lasted through the initial salvo; they might have died from the pressure wave or radiation blast of her grenades, in fact. Benning shrugged aside that thought. Dead was dead, and it didn't matter how they'd died. If she escaped this trap, they'd respawn safely. If she didn't, their fates wouldn't be any concern to her.

She switched to her Foehammer rifle and leveled it at the enemy Soldiers crouched at the far end of the hall. The stubby weapon wasn't quite as accurate as her Arcbar and lacked that rifle's rapid firing rate, but its bullets packed far more punch. She sighted between two of her marines and pulled the trigger. The neutronium-coated bullet raced down the short barrel; as it exited, it picked up a shroud of dark matter that drastically increased its mass and a layer of antimatter to help it penetrate armor. The bullet streaked down the hall, crossing the hundred-em distance in six milliseconds or so. It crashed into an advancing Soldier and pierced their enn-steel armor, shattering inside their body and shredding their organs with shards of extreme-velocity platinum.

"Form wall!" one of the enemy Soldiers shouted, and Benning had time to put a bullet into the helmet of one more Soldier before the rest erected a barrier similar to the one she now stood behind. Benning kept her rifle tracked on the low wall, firing at any helmet that appeared over it and giving her marines cover as they retreated to her position.

"Orders, Captain?" one of the marines asked gruffly.

Benning's first instinct was to make directly for her ship, but she had no doubt that the station's administrators sealed that route and had it heavily guarded. She needed a less obvious path, one that would be harder for the station to follow...

Her eyes narrowed as an idea occurred to her. *Tiddly, do you know where the Drone living quarters are?*

<I can try to access that information, Benning Kidd, but...> The gnome hesitated. <The System isn't going to let you into that area, Benning Kidd. You probably won't even be able to see the entrance to it.>

I know, Tiddly, but the Drones should have maintenance tunnels leading all over the station. At least, I know there were endless tunnels back on Mars, and I'm pretty sure they led all over the planet. I'm assuming it's the same here.

<I never thought of that,> Tiddly admitted, her voice slightly excited. <The station's administrators probably don't even know about those areas, in fact. Hold on a second.> The AI went silent for long moments as Benning continued to exchange gunfire with the enemy Soldiers. <Okay, I think I've got it, Benning Kidd. I'll show you a map to what I think is the nearest access tunnel.>

Benning blinked in surprise as an image of the station appeared in her vision with a glowing line leading deeper into it. *I'm surprised the System let you have that information, Tiddly. I thought it would keep you out.*

<Oh, it did. I can't actually find the access tunnels, sorry – but there's a part of the station nearby that I can't account for on any of its maps, and I'm guessing that it's one of the access tunnels you mentioned. Especially because it seems to link up with other areas that I can't find.>

It was that easy? Why hasn't anyone else figured out that the tunnels are there, then?

<Probably because the System doesn't let them. I'll bet it only let me work it out because I already know that Drones exist, and so do you. Anyone else who looks at that map won't see empty spots, though.> She hesitated. <Knowing that it's there won't let you access it, though, Benning Kidd. I doubt you can even hack into the door to open it up. The System will have it totally sealed.>

Probably, but I'll bet my disassemblers can rip a hole in the bulkhead. I don't think the System will physically stop me from walking through a hole in the wall – especially if I can't interact with the Drones in there anyway.

Tiddly laughed silently. <I'll bet you're right! I like the idea of you using something the System gave you to cross it. Let's see if it works!>

"Okay, we're falling back," Benning ordered her marines. "I have what I hope will be an escape route to the ship. Grab the portable shields, and let's get moving."

Benning and her fighters slipped back through the passageway, firing at their pursuers to keep them from closing too quickly. Benning tossed another fusion grenade, but her attackers had grown wise to that tactic, and they slammed more shields into place, blocking most of the blast and funneling it back down the hall toward the marines, who fortunately took cover behind their shield and avoided most of the explosion.

More Soldiers appeared as they reached an intersection, trying to block Benning's retreat, but she and her fighters slammed into them before they could set their defenses in place. The Soldiers outnumbered Benning and her troops, but her marines had better armor, weapons, and training. More importantly, they were veterans of dozens of naval battles, while it was likely the Soldiers they faced had never been in real combat before. That experience made all the difference, and Benning and her marines cut through the enemy Soldiers like a plasma knife through syleather.

As the survivors of that attack joined her pursuers, Benning switched from her Foehammer to her newest weapon, a rifle that looked like a solid rod of tungsten. She leveled it at the shield walls protecting her pursuers and pulled the trigger. The Soldiers behind the barrier cursed as her Frostburn cloudgun fired a shower of tiny flechettes, needlelike neutronium projectiles coated in antimatter. The flechettes burned through the shields and slammed into the Soldiers behind them, the antimatter searing away their armor and flesh and leaving gaping holes behind. A gamma flasher followed the blast, and the radiation that poured through the holes in her attackers' armor slowed their advance long enough for Benning to lengthen her lead on them.

<Here, Benning Kidd,> Tiddly spoke suddenly, and a section of bulkhead beside Benning glowed white in her vision. <As best I can tell, there's an unmapped space large enough for people to move through behind this wall. It might be nothing more than an oversized power conduit, but...>

But it's the only chance we've got, Benning finished the gnome's thought. *Thanks, Tiddly.*

<Y-you're welcome,> the AI replied, her voice sounding a bit startled.

Benning focused on the bulkhead, testing it with her nanofield and 'net. The metal felt perfectly solid to her nanofield, with no seams or cracks that might indicate a door, and when she reached out to it with her 'net, Cyberwarfare insisted that nothing was there to hack. Taking a deep breath, she hurled her disassemblers against it, willing them to destroy the bulkhead. The metal before her pitted and corroded as her nanites attacked it, ripping it apart atom by atom. Holes slowly formed in the metal, holes filled with utter darkness that let her see nothing behind them.

At last, a gaping wound in the bulkhead stood before her, one large enough for her to pass through. Darkness filled the hole, which looked like it ended after a few cims, but when she sent her nanofield against it, her nanites assured her that it was an open space.

She looked back at her marines. "This way," she ordered. "Through the hole."

"Captain?" one of the Soldiers said dubiously. "There's nothing there, ma'am. How can we...?"

"Follow me, Marine," she cut the woman off. "That's an order."

"Aye, ma'am," the Soldier replied crisply, her training winning out over her common sense. "As you command."

Benning's eyes screamed that she was walking into a metal wall as she stepped forward, so she closed them. Her senses couldn't be trusted; the System controlled them, and it was showing her what it wanted her to see. She wondered idly why it didn't just stop her from walking, paralyzing her muscles or even killing her rather than letting her proceed.

<It can't, Benning Kidd,> Tiddly assured her. <That's one of its protocols, remember? It can influence Citizen choices, but it can't prohibit them directly. This is your choice, and it can't stop you from making it.>

Benning stepped forward and breathed a sigh of relief when she encountered no resistance. She opened her eyes, and her heart lurched as she took in the small, cramped tunnel surrounding her. It was dimly lit, and it glistened with a sheen of water – water that she guessed the System placed there to encourage the growth of mold and mildew. The Drones needed tasks to do, after all, and clearing a passageway of mold was a common one.

Memories flooded her mind, threatening to overwhelm her. Despite her helmet, she could smell the scent of mildew flooding the air, could taste the tang of ozone as the bot she rode vaporized most of the black mold that streaked the walls. She'd questioned that – if the bot could clean some of the mold, why couldn't it clean all of it? – and the System punished her by giving her pain in response. She winced at the memory of the growing agony in her skull that accompanied her errant thoughts – and that memory reminded her of the reason the System had chosen to overwrite her. She'd fought against it, resisted its punishments, and refused to stop asking her questions. In return, it sent her to be destroyed, telling her it was a reward the whole time.

Anger flared in her, pushing aside her growing despair and burning away the ache in her chest that stabbed at her heart. Benning wasn't that Drone anymore, but even then, she refused to let the System control her. She wasn't about to let it beat her now, to let herself drown in her memories while her pursuers caught her and dragged her to the Fleet for punishment.

And for what? For existing; that was her real crime. Because she existed, forces moved against her that she had no way to fight. They sent people to hunt her, put more and larger bounties on her head than should have been allowed, and gave her enemies more money and better weapons. They pushed her against a wall, left her no place to go except to flee – and when she fought back, striking out with everything she had, they decided to punish her for that as well.

She was tired of the System and its Nobles stacking the odds against her. She was sick of having to fight just because she dared to exist. She didn't care about the other Drones, not really. She didn't care about the respawn system, or how probably millions of Drones were being overwritten in that moment – or how many Drone bodies she'd taken over in her respawns. All she wanted to do was to live, to find her place in the Collective – but the System wasn't going to let her do that. She could either bow to its dictates or fight to bring it all down, and Benning always chose to fight, whoever the opponent.

Her fury at the System held back the flood of memories. She'd deal with them later; at that moment, she had a fight to win, and she would win, no matter what it took. Even if it meant taking the entire station with her...

She smiled grimly as she sent a signal to her ship through the Overnet. She might not make it back, but if she went down, she'd take as much of the station with her as she could.

When her marines failed to appear within a few seconds, Benning turned back toward the entrance to the tunnel. *Tiddly, will the System let them follow me?*

<I don't think so, Benning Kidd,> the gnome said in a subdued voice. <The System's protocol only applies to Citizens and Nobles. It can stop them from entering here, no matter what you order. You're probably on your own, now.>

Benning nodded. Losing her marines was a setback – she'd still have to fight her way onto her ship, she was sure, and that would be harder without the extra firepower – but leading them through the station would have been suicide. If she had to choose between sacrificing her marines or being captured by the Fleet, well, Soldiers could be replaced easily enough.

She took a step forward, but before she did, she lifted her rifle, pointed it down the hall, and pulled the trigger experimentally. As she'd suspected, the trigger clicked, but the weapon refused to fire. She tried activating it, but the rifle's 'net refused to respond, even to her nanofield. The System had deactivated it, as she'd guessed it might; it wouldn't want gunfire down here that might kill Drones after all. If she encountered resistance, she'd be reduced to melee fighting only.

<You shouldn't have any resistance, Benning Kidd,> Tiddly assured her quietly, her voice somber and subdued. <I'll bet the Soldiers all saw an image of you dying or disappearing, so they won't follow you, and the administrators won't be able to track you down here. You should be fine – at least, until you head back into the main station.>

That's something, at least.

Benning jogged through the seemingly abandoned tunnels – although she knew that wasn't the case. She stumbled occasionally, her feet seeming to tangle or slip on a wet spot and crashing her into the bulkhead, and each time, she suspected the System had just guided her around an unseeing Drone that she would otherwise have crashed into. A spike of pain lanced through her chest as she passed a cleaning bot, one with an apparently empty seat atop it that she was certain held a Drone. Memories crowded her thoughts, clamoring to be acknowledged, but she stubbornly pushed them aside.

Instead, she kept her focus on the tunnels before her – and the map Tiddly kept in her vision. The journey back to her ship would take much longer than the one into the station. She climbed up ramps that switched back upon themselves where she'd ridden in an elevator before; she wound around main passages that would have taken her directly where she needed to go.

The tunnels felt oddly empty, and Benning realized why quickly enough. The station's 'net wasn't accessible in the Drone areas; only the Overnet existed there. The nanofield surrounding her relied on the Overnet to guide it, and her attempts to hack into the station's 'net met with failure as the 'net refused to respond to her inquiries.

It was like she was in a wholly separate station, totally disconnected from the world of Citizens around her, and in a way, she was. She wasn't supposed to be there; she no longer belonged to that existence.

Of course, I don't really belong out there either, she realized grimly.

<That's not true, Benning Kidd,> Tiddly protested.

It is, Tiddly. The System doesn't really have a place for me in the Collective – but that's fine. It just means I'll have to make my own place, doesn't it? A place that the System, the Nobles, and the Fleet will all have to acknowledge, like it or not.

Her path ended in another blank wall, but this time, Tiddly could feel the doorway sealing her inside. She smiled to herself; the System didn't want her getting down in the tunnels, but it was more than happy to let her leave. The tunnels wouldn't take her to the docking rings, of course. There was probably no need for them to; she doubted that Drones had any reason to come into or leave the station, after all. That was fine, though. Benning should have shaken off her pursuit, and her own abilities could see her the rest of the way to her vessel.

She stepped out five minutes later beaconing a new designation, that of an Engineer named Cassana Sims who was awaiting respawn in the Procyon System. Her armor gleamed bright green and sapphire blue, clashing with her light purple hair. The disguise wouldn't hold up forever – if the administrators still hunted her, they'd be doing random identity checks, and a search for Cassana Sims would reveal that the Engineer had never visited the Van Maanen System before – but it would last long enough to get her back to her ship.

She walked confidently through the passageways, guided by Tiddly's map. Her pass to the station had probably been revoked, of course, but that just meant that she'd set off alarms venturing into the station, not out of it. She nervously held off the scanning nanites in the elevator; somehow, the station had pierced her earlier disguise, and she still wasn't sure how they had. It might have been a random check, of course. One of those would have revealed that the real Rebexa Graves had lost her destroyer to pirates recently and respawned in the distant Groombridge System. It could also have been the presence of her officers, who would have remained vulnerable to the multiple deep scans they encountered and whose designations could be tracked to her. She didn't know, but her biggest fear was that they'd penetrated her Nanoresistance without her knowledge.

Fortunately, while she passed squads of armed Soldiers in the docking rings, none of them gave her so much as a second glance. At least, not until she neared her ship's docking bay and saw the armed guards ringing it. Those wouldn't allow her to pass, she felt certain. Fortunately, she'd assumed this would happen, and she was prepared to deal with the guards.

The Soldiers shouted in dismay as the glowing, white metal cylinder soared into their midst. They quickly dove for cover, but few moved fast enough to escape the antimatter grenade's blast. A flash of light brighter than a star ripped through the tunnel, followed by a titanic pressure wave that knocked Benning sprawling even behind the curve of wall that sheltered her. She rushed out the moment her vision returned, firing her Foehammer at any aura she saw that wasn't black. Soldiers swore and screamed as her bullets pierced their damaged armor and ripped into their bodies. Benning didn't flinch as she put them down; they were her enemies, and that meant they deserved death. She wished she could get her hands on the governor who'd ordered her to be held, but she knew that wouldn't be possible. She needed to get out of the system as quickly as she could – but she intended to leave the man a little present as she departed.

She raced through the airlock onto her vessel, ordering the doors closed and sealed behind her. "Brialle Caldwell, get us out of here, immediately!" she ordered to the air, knowing that her ship's 'net would carry her instructions to the bridge.

"Captain?" the pilot's voice echoed in her ears. "Welcome back aboard, but the station's put us on lockdown..."

"I don't give a scrit about the station. Detach us and get us out of here – even if you have to dive to do it. I want to be gone in thirty seconds; do you understand?"

"Yes, ma'am! We'll be underway in ten."

Benning walked out of the airlock and began making her way to the bridge. As she did, she reached out to her ship's 'net, activating the weapons console. With Charlo Herrick dead, the Weapons station reverted to Benning's control – as did Engineering – and she sent several commands to it. The system refused to acknowledge at first since what she was trying to do was both prohibited and dangerous, but she overrode the safety protocols with her authority as both owner and captain. A moment later, the console accepted her commands, and she closed it out, switching to the station's 'net.

By the time she'd stepped onto the bridge, the *Hammer* was underway and moving steadily away from the station.

"...warn you, your refusal to return to your docking bay will be considered a hostile act!" a voice declared over the bridge. "Heave to immediately and prepare..."

"Enough of that," Benning said, cutting the voice with a mental command. "What's our situation, Pilot?"

"We'll be clear of the station in two minutes, Captain," the woman reported. "We can dive in as soon as thirty seconds, though, if need be."

"Captain, the station's defenses are powering up," Jezper Shields said calmly. "I don't think they're going to let us just leave."

"They won't have a choice," Benning said, moving to her command chair.

"Captain, I'm picking up dive splashes nearby," Elden Quinn spoke up. "Four of them, entering the area in formation."

"Probably local military," Benning nodded. "By the time they move to intercept us, we'll be long gone."

"Ma'am, we're receiving a message from one of the ships – a Fleet Officer Adlyn Bechard. She's asking for you."

"I'll take it," Benning said, closing her eyes and connecting to the message. The familiar face of the white-haired Fleet officer appeared in her mind, staring at Benning with intense displeasure and possibly even dislike.

"Citizen Benning Kidd," the woman spoke in a flat voice, "you are hereby ordered to stand down and prepare for boarding. If you refuse to comply, we will seize and impound your vessel and imprison you and your crew for failure to follow Fleet regulations."

"I think you're going to be too busy to bother with me, Officer," Benning replied with a smile.

"You sent me lightyears across the Collective on a wild chase, Benning Kidd," Bechard spat. "I'm not letting you get away this time..."

"I'm pretty sure you will," Benning shrugged. "I think you'll agree in about five seconds...make that one."

As Benning spoke, her weapons console activated, carrying out her previous commands. The *Hammer's* sinkhole generator was a powerful weapon, but it suffered several limitations. It was an energy sink, requiring far more power to run than the normal capacitors could supply, which meant that it had to charge slowly over hours before it could be used. It also drained the ship's capacitors completely when used, which shut down the destroyer's weapons and shields for several seconds and even rendered it unable to dive for a minute or so. It was an ambush weapon, one whose usage had to be carefully planned ahead of time, and one that could only be used once in any given battle.

When Benning first sent the signal to her ship while down in the tunnels to start charging the generator, she knew it wouldn't have enough time to fully charge. When she commanded the weapon to begin its activation sequence, the ship's 'net tried to argue with her. A sinkhole couldn't be used in a system, and her generator hadn't had time to power a full sinkhole anyway. When the weapon fired, she got to see why its usage within a system was prohibited.

The event horizon that formed in the center of Adriaan Station 17 wasn't large, no more than a few kims across. It was enough to envelop the core of the station, though, including its power plants, negaputer banks, and gravity well. The station lost power instantly; even worse, it lost its 'net and nanofield in the same moment. Every system on the station crashed; every door sealed shut; every automated defense went into passive mode, firing at anything that moved. Gravity vanished, and with it went the force holding the docked ships in place. Those tore free of their docking rings, slamming into one another or the station as they were tossed about like billiard balls.

"What the Hole did you do?" Bechard screamed, her face gone white as she stared past Benning in horror. "The center of the station – it's gone!"

"I don't know what you're talking about, Officer," Benning shrugged. "However, I think that right now, the Fleet should be more concerned with a rescue mission than with me, don't you?"

Bechard's face flushed with anger. "This isn't over, Benning Kidd," she growled. "I'll be coming for you soon enough, and there'll be no place for you to hide from me!"

"I'll be watching for you," Benning nodded. "Just know that things like this tend to happen to those who come after me – so don't be surprised when it's your ship that's suddenly without power next."

She ended the transmission and looked at Brialle Caldwell. "Take us out of system, max v," she ordered. "Then plot a course back to IS-39267. I think we're all done here."

CHAPTER 19

"This is beyond the pale, Fleet Officer!" Governor VM 1-001 roared, spittle flying from his mouth. His golden hair, usually neatly coiffed and styled atop his head, looked tousled and unkempt, and his tan skin was purple with his fury.

"I'm not sure what you mean, Governor," Adlyn replied as calmly as she could despite the butterflies swirling in her stomach. This – this debacle wasn't her fault, not in any way, shape, or form. She arrived too late to have influenced matters in any way – but the governor wasn't going to say that. He wanted someone to blame, and Adlyn would make a handy scapegoat. She just had to make sure that didn't happen.

"What do I mean?" the man practically screamed, throwing his hands up into the air and stalking away from his desk. A navy-blue flag hung on the wall behind him depicting the system's emblem, a glowing, eight-pointed, white star surrounded by seven crimson six-pointed stars, one for each of the admirals who'd allegedly founded Van Maanen so long ago. Adlyn doubted the veracity of the story since in her experience, admirals never did anything themselves that they could send a junior officer to do, but she wasn't about to mention that to the furious man in front of her.

"This – this criminal, Benning Kidd, nearly destroyed one of my stations!" he said, pointing to the holographic map of the system that floated overhead. Adriaan Station 17 pulsed a dull red, a tiny, carmine dot swirling around the only rocky planet in the system. "And you let her slip through your fingers!"

"To clarify, sir, I didn't let anyone 'slip through my fingers'," Adlyn said sternly. "I made a deliberate choice to rescue your station instead of pursuing Benning Kidd. If I hadn't ordered my fleet to take every ship we could under tow, another hundred or so ships would have crashed into the station. If even one of them went photonic..." She shrugged. "I assumed saving the lives of thousands of your Citizens trumped apprehending a single person of interest – especially when that person isn't a criminal, not officially."

"Not a criminal?" he screeched in reply, his voice rising an octave. "Did you see what she did to my station? How is that not a criminal act?"

Adlyn suppressed a smile; the governor had made a mistake. He'd forgotten to accuse her of anything that time, and that gave her the chance to turn the direction of the conversation the way she wanted it to go.

"Do you have any proof that Benning Kidd sabotaged your station, Governor? Any evidence at all? Recordings of her planting a bomb, perhaps? If you do, you know that you're legally obligated to turn them over to me to further my investigation."

"No, of course, I don't, and you know that!"

"Know, Governor? I know very little, as a matter of fact." She folded her hands behind her and leaned forward slightly. "Here's what I do know, though.

"I *know* that we have a Collective-wide alert out for Benning Kidd – and that this alert specifically requests that the Fleet be contacted of her whereabouts, but that no direct action be taken against her. I *know* that despite that request, you attempted to apprehend Benning Kidd by force."

"Which is well within my rights as Governor!" the

man proclaimed.

"Absolutely, sir, assuming that you had cause. What cause was that? Did Benning Kidd commit a crime aboard your station? Did she violate any of your regulations?"

"She was operating under a false designation!"

"Which isn't a crime in Van Maanen, Governor, as you know. It's not even a violation of Fleet regulations since it's a requirement for many career paths." She leaned farther forward and placed her hands on his desk. "Which means, sir, that you attempted to illegally apprehend a Citizen using deadly force, and they defended themselves. That's disappointing, considering the Van Maanen attitude toward violating regulations. What's the prescribed punishment for any illegal act, again?"

The governor's face drained of color as he walked slowly back to his desk. "Are you threatening me, Fleet Officer?"

"Not in the slightest, sir. I do have to make a full report to my superiors, of course, but how you manage your system is no business of mine." She shrugged. "Of course, the administrators of Adriaan Station 17 might feel otherwise. If they were to come to me with a complaint, I would have no choice but to investigate it – and make sure that any appropriate punishments were meted out."

The man's eyes narrowed. "You aren't really in the position to enforce anything, Officer," he almost purred. "You have, what, four ships in this system? Van Maanen possesses the third-largest fleet in the Collective..."

"Which is why the Fleet dispatched a dreadnought to this system to rendezvous with me hours ago," Adlyn smiled at the man. "I suggested that there might be some – confusion as to who should have custody of Benning Kidd considering her numerous and substantial bounties, and

Fleet HQ agreed. If that ship arrives and I'm not available to debrief its admiral..." She shrugged. "Well, Governor, there are Fleet inquiries, and there are Fleet inquiries, if you take my meaning, and an admiral's inquiry never ends without someone being found responsible."

She could see his mind racing, calculating if he could convince the admiral that she was to blame for the mess that Benning Kidd had made, so she added, "Oh, and I should tell you, the recording of this meeting will certainly be part of that inquiry."

"Recording?" He straightened in his chair, his eyes flashing triumphantly. "Recording a suspect without their permission is against Fleet regulations, Officer!"

"That's true, Governor – and it would apply *if* you were currently a suspect of some crime or another. At the moment, you aren't..." She raised an eyebrow. "Unless you have something you'd like to confess, of course."

He sagged in his chair and rubbed his brow. "What do you want, Officer?" he asked tiredly.

"The truth, sir. What happened on Station 17? How did Benning Kidd slip past you?"

"The truth?" He snorted. "Fine – but in return, you give me the truth about why she's under investigation in the first place. Deal?"

She considered his offer. She could get a full recording of Benning Kidd's visit to the station, but that would take time. She'd have to apply for a warrant, wait for approval, send it back to the governor, and then wait for his office to approve it and release the footage. That could take months or even years if the governor decided to drag his heels. Giving him info on her investigation was a violation of regs, of course, but the captain in overall charge of the investigation would understand. He'd always told her that regs looked great in the book, and that was where they belonged. In the field, there was usually no place for them. Adlyn was starting to understand what he meant.

"Fine. Share with me, and I'll share with you."

"Excellent," he sighed, leaning back. "First of all, I didn't directly approve this – at least, not until it was already happening. Kyman Crosby, the administrator of Adriaan 17, was the first one to realize that Benning Kidd was aboard his station, and he caught the Fleet flag on her record."

"How did he find her?" Adlyn asked. That was an important question; Benning Kidd was something of a ghost, able to sneak into and out of stations undetected with frightening regularity, and figuring out a way to detect her would be incredibly useful.

"He didn't, not directly. They passed through several intrusive scanners – none of which saw through her disguise, I might point out – and he picked up her officers. He happened to run a random check on one and discovered she was the Weapons Officer on the *Resolute Hammer*. Once she called Benning Kidd 'Captain'..." He shrugged. "It wasn't hard to put together."

She nodded. That was clever, and she'd have to add Benning's officers to her alerts. Maybe she could catch the woman through her crewmembers.

"So, what did Kyman Crosby do?"

"He messaged me, of course, asking for orders. While he was waiting, though, he discovered the bounties on her head and decided that claiming them would be worthwhile."

"And you didn't countermand that decision?" she asked sternly.

He snorted derisively. "Being Governor has many perks, Fleet Officer – but a steady income isn't one of them. Benning Kidd has over two thousand credits worth of bounties on her head, and I could use those credits." He sighed. "That's why I eventually signed off on the capture order."

"Two thousand?" Adlyn asked, confused. "That's not possible! She's not high enough level for that sort of bounty."

"My guess is that some Noble is gunning for her," the governor shrugged. "They can override bounty limits, after all. Whatever the case, it's a matter of record. Feel free to check for yourself."

Adlyn made a mental note to do just that. Many things about Benning Kidd confused her, but this was the first one that set off alarm bells in her head. If Nobles were involved, then this investigation wasn't the simple matter it should have been, not by a long shot.

Not that the investigation had been simple so far, of course. Adlyn had hunted down tens of criminals in the past; it was what she did, and she was good at it. Her strength lay in uncovering their habits – the station they visited more often than others, the merchant they sold their stolen goods through, the old friend or mentor they checked in with regularly – and using those to capture them. Most criminal developed such habits as time went on. Every human needed socialization and companionship to survive, but that was hard to find for those living outside the law. When they found people or places they trusted, they clung to them, returning to them again and again, making Adlyn's job of catching them far easier.

That hadn't worked in the slightest with Benning Kidd. The woman rarely went to the same system twice, much less the same station. The only place she visited regularly was Frostwise, and the owners there refused to work with Adlyn to help bring her in. Kidd had a merchant contact, one Erix Adelsson, but she never dealt with the man in person. She seemed to have a similar arrangement with an armorer designated Ramona Gruszka and a Nano-engineer, Emmed Oswald. At least, Adlyn tracked transactions between Kidd and those two, but she had no record of the woman visiting either of them recently.

Even that small amount of information had been ridiculously hard to get. Benning Kidd seemed to move in and out of stations like a ghost, appearing from nowhere and disappearing without leaving a trace. Adlyn found it impossible to track the woman's movements; transactions showed her drinking in a bar in Ophiuchi one day, then buying cargo in Lacaille, eighteen lightyears distant, three days later, an impossibly fast trip even for a Fleet vessel. A scan of both stations' records told Adlyn that Kidd hadn't entered either of them, at least as far as she could tell.

Adlyn hoped that having someone in Kidd's inner circle would net her valuable intel, but for the most part, she'd learned very little. Kidd played her cards close to her chest, not even trusting her own captains with much information. Her informant managed to dig up Kidd's career path, something called a Stellar Corsair that Adlyn never heard of and had no information about – she couldn't even find records of previous ones in the Overnet to possibly predict Kidd's behavior. However, her informant had nothing more than wild speculation about Kidd's abilities and powers, and Adlyn had no interest in speculation.

She pulled her thoughts back on track. She doubted the governor would care for her idle musings, either.

"I will," she said aloud. "So, the administrator decided to capture her. Then what happened?"

"She didn't want to be captured. She and her marines killed almost a dozen Soldiers breaking out of the trap – and losing her officers in the process. They fought their way through the station toward a larger trap Kyman Crosby had laid for her, but before she reached it, she just – disappeared."

"She what?" Adlyn demanded. "What do you mean, disappeared? Like a concealment cloak?"

"Of course not. Our sensors would have picked that up. She vanished, Fleet Officer. Here..." He gestured, and a holoscreen appeared in the air above his desk. "See for yourself."

Adlyn watched as Benning Kidd stopped before a blank section of wall. The fugitive stared at it, and the wall corroded away, leaving a hole behind – a hole that led nowhere. She stepped into the hole, there was a flash of light, and the woman vanished, leaving her four marines behind to be captured.

"Wait...what?" Adlyn stammered. "What is that? Matter transport of some kind?"

The governor shook his head. "It doesn't exist. It's not possible." He made a face. "Well, except through wormholes, and if she had a portable wormhole generator, why wouldn't she have just stepped onto her ship and gotten away?"

"Did you examine the hole she left?"

"Of course, but by the time my scanning team got there, there was no hole. The nanofield had repaired whatever she used to open it. I ordered them to remove the wall paneling, and they did, but there was nothing behind it but electronics and conduit. Even a deep scan failed to find any doors or passages." He shrugged. "She disappeared, like I said."

"But she reappeared eventually," Adlyn said.

"Yes, hours later. She'd assumed a new identity and looked completely different, so no one realized it was her until she killed another ten Soldiers with an antimatter grenade, then fled the station." He rubbed his face tiredly. "And sometime in those hours, she must have planted a singularity device somewhere on the station, then set it off when she fled."

"No," Adlyn sighed, slumping into a chair herself. "There was no bomb – at least, my sweeper team found no traces of one. There was no damage done to the station directly. Whatever happened just cut power, gravity, and the 'net to the station for thirty minutes or so without doing any direct damage to those systems. They just – disappeared…"

"The same way Benning Kidd did," the governor nodded, rubbing his chin. "It had to have been some sort of advanced concealment device – maybe one that shunted her into CY-space temporarily."

"Is that even possible?"

"Maybe. Who knows what's possible and isn't? There are seven dimensions in the Calabi-Yau manifold, Officer, and we only deal with one of them. It's possible that unfolding two could allow you to disappear entirely from our 4-D world." His eyes narrowed. "People would pay a lot for technology like that, you know."

"I'm sure they would," Adlyn sighed. "I'd pay a lot for a way to counter it, myself." Adlyn wasn't sure if she accepted the governor's explanation, really. Sure, that sort of tech would explain how Benning Kidd could move around so easily – but where would she get that tech from? And how did she keep anyone else from finding it and using it? As the man said, people would pay millions of credits for technology that could make a ship invisible, something that so far had proven to be impossible despite scientists' best efforts, and whoever invented a tech like that would have sold it to the highest bidder. Benning Kidd could get more for selling her cloak than she could from playing pirate for a century, easily.

"So, why are you hunting her?" the governor asked, interrupting her thoughts.

KYLE JOHNSON

For a moment, she considered refusing to tell the man purely from spite, but she ignored that errant thought. It would gain her nothing but an enemy, and telling him would cost her little.

"War crimes," she finally said.

"War crimes? What do you mean?"

"Crimes against the Collective itself. The deaths of thousands, maybe hundreds of thousands of Citizens." Adlyn's eyes focused and she leaned forward. "Let me tell you a story, Governor – and once you hear that story, maybe you'll understand why I asked that Benning Kidd not be approached when discovered. It starts with a tiny station called IS-39267..."

Twenty minutes later, Adlyn left the governor's office, leaving behind a very chastened man. He'd gotten off lucky, if Benning Kidd had done half of what she'd been accused of. A strangelet bomb or subspace tunneller hitting Adriaan's surface would have been catastrophic, and trillions of Citizens might have died from it. Even worse, if Benning Kidd had somehow cut the planet off from the black hole in the center of its mined out, hollow core, the world would have lost its gravity, probably killing 90% of the population outright as their centrifugal acceleration slammed them into ceilings or tossed them into the sky at terrific speed.

But Benning Kidd hadn't done any of that. She'd damaged Station 17 badly, for sure – Adlyn had no proof of that, but she knew it to be true nonetheless – but she hadn't come close to destroying it, and a strangelet bomb hitting the station while it was without power or its 'net would have slaughtered everyone aboard.

For the first time, Adlyn wondered if maybe there was a lot more going on in her investigation than she suspected. It had seemed cut-and-dried – a crazy captain with access to prohibited weapons took over a small station, killing

254

countless people in the process – but now, she wasn't so sure. Benning Kidd didn't seem like a vicious mass murderer to Adlyn. She obviously had no problem with killing, but she didn't go out of her way to slaughter people.

Adlyn made her way to her ship. She had a report to give, and she wouldn't be sharing her reservations in it. The captain would want facts, not guesses, hunches, and suppositions. Sadly, Adlyn had very few of those to share.

CHAPTER 20

"That was a close call, Commodore," Fodor Hendricks shook his head, leaning back in his chair. "If you hadn't found those maintenance tunnels…"

"Then I would have died," she shrugged. "I wouldn't have let the Fleet take me."

"The penalties for suicidal death are extremely strict," Saavi Boguna observed. "It might be better to go with the Fleet."

"Not if they decide to spawn camp her back to level 1," Trephor Sando snorted. "And given that it's the Fleet, that's a distinct possibility."

"The point is, I escaped," Benning said. "However, I think the Fleet will be heading our way sooner rather than later now, considering what I did to the station before I left."

"What did you do, Commodore?" Avaeyana Roble asked a bit nervously.

"She set off a small version of a sinkhole in the station's core," Tereza Erdeli said with disgust. "It cut the entire station off from its power, 'net, and gravity. Hundreds of ships smashed into the station, half its docking rings were left nonfunctional, and who knows how many Citizens died." She shook her head. "It might have been better to go with the Fleet, Benning Kidd."

"Would you feel the same way if they were threatening to send you back to level 1, Tereza Erdeli?" Hendricks asked with a slight sneer. "Or would it only be better as long as it's the Commodore losing her levels?"

"If the Fleet comes here, we might all end up back at level 1," Erdeli argued. She looked at Benning. "You need to start acting with restraint, Benning Kidd, or you'll drag the Fleet down on all of us."

"I did restrain myself," Benning replied coldly. "Tereza Erdeli, you've seen firsthand what I do when I let myself go. You've felt it. I could have dropped a strangelet bomb on the station after I'd cut its power. Without its nanofield, it would have probably collapsed into a mini strange star and crashed into the planet below. Or I could have dropped a nanobomb on the planet and killed trillions. Either one would have worked as a distraction, but doing them in front of Fleet vessels would have brought a battlefrigate here in a matter of days.

"I'm betting that the Fleet suspects that I attacked the station, but without the *Hammer's* logs, they can't prove it – and to get those, they have to catch me first."

"Do you think they'll be coming harder after you, then?" Hendricks asked.

"Probably," Benning shrugged. "But I'd rather them be chasing me than coming here to destroy the whole station."

"I think we all agree with that," Raelle Muckley laughed harshly. "Even if we don't want to admit it. You seem to have a knack for slipping out of those sorts of traps, Commodore."

"That she does," Hendricks grinned. "And setting some of her own – like creating a sinkhole in the middle of a station." He laughed. "I never would have thought of that!"

"No one would have," Erdeli sighed. "Except Benning Kidd, of course."

"And it worked, and that's the end of it," Benning said. "Let's move on. I called this meeting to discuss what we can do with the new templates I bought." She glanced at Roble. "Captain, you looked them over. What do you think?"

"If we use the negmass plants we captured, we can install the new arrays on our ships with no problem," the former Systems Engineer said thoughtfully. "The new engines shouldn't be an issue, either, although we might not be able to fit them into the corvettes."

"Do we even need the corvettes anymore?" Sando pointed out.

"Absolutely," Roble nodded. "They're smaller weapons platforms, to be sure, but they can bring a larger percentage of those weapons to bear on any target."

"They're weaker, though, as well," Hendricks shook his head. "A typical Siren-class corvette only has six 1-pow grasers and four fusion missile launchers. Even if they can target four of those grasers on a target at once, that's still only the same amount of power as a single 4-pow graser from a Marauder-class frigate, and it can also target a ship with four of those at once."

"Except that you could easily fit twelve corvettes in the same space as that one frigate, each firing the equivalent of a 4-pow graser at a target," Roble argued. "That's three times the energy, and you could spread it out over a larger area to cover more of an enemy's evasion cone."

"The frigate will last longer in battle," Boguna observed. "Corvettes aren't very heavily armored, after all."

"True. They can't be, thanks to the square-cube law. Any additional armor is going to constitute a larger part of their overall mass and reduce their velocity and maneuverability more than they would a larger vessel. That's why in the long run, larger ships are more powerful and dangerous – but corvettes are still useful. Especially if we put reactive armor on them."

"We can only produce so much reactive armor," Tereza Erdeli spoke up. "It seems like we should put it on as many destroyers as possible."

"At best, we might be able to upgrade two destroyers with reactive armor, assuming we want to use most of the negmass plants to outfit our ships. That would improve their armor rating by about 21%. We could also armor six frigates with that same amount of negmass and boost their armor rating by 17%, since frigates have better armor for their size than destroyers on average."

Roble leaned forward, tapping her finger on the table. "Or we could produce enough reactive armor to cover more than sixty corvettes and boost their armor rating by 46%, enough that their armor rating will rival that of a base-model destroyer."

"We don't have sixty corvettes," Boguna pointed out.

"Not yet," Hendricks said thoughtfully. "We probably will eventually, though. What would the improved neutronium armor do for our frigates and destroyers?"

"Boost their armor ratings by 9% and 11% respectively," Roble answered immediately. "We already have upgraded armor thanks to the schematics the commodore holds title to, and with the boost, our ships could take a close antimatter warhead strike without a hull breach."

"Then I have to agree with Avaeyana Roble, Commodore," Hendricks told Benning. "I think the corvettes should get the reactive armor first. We keep losing them in combat, and if we could help them survive, it'll save us time and credits in the long run."

"What we need is to put those heavier weapons on them," Sando grinned. "Four corvettes with reactive armor packing 4-pow grasers and singularity launchers are going to be dangerous even to a frigate or destroyer."

"And that's where we run into a problem," Roble sighed. "We can add better armor, targeting arrays, and engines to our ships with no problem. Drastically larger weapons are a different story, though. Even with the improved capacitor banks and power relays, we're going to run into problems with excess heat."

"Heat?" Sando echoed. "What do you mean?"

"Heat is every starship's biggest limiting factor," Roble said, her eyes brightening as she spoke. "It's hard to dissipate heat in space, and those larger weapons generate a LOT of heat. That's why they're usually used on larger-hulled ships. More surface area means more heat dissipation and more room for IR emitters to radiate that heat away."

"What would we need to make it work?" Hendricks asked.

"Better heat sinks, primarily. Our emitters are up to the task, but our current heat sinks can't draw enough heat away to keep up with these larger weapons."

"What do you think, Commodore?" Hendricks grinned. "Feel like running back to Van Maanen and buying a better heat sink template?"

"It's Erix Adelsson's turn," Benning scoffed. "If I never see that system again, I'll be content."

"I'll send him a message," Erdeli nodded. "He might be able to make the purchases remotely through another broker. It'll cost more, but it'll be safer – all things considered."

"Why didn't we do that the first time?" Muckley asked.

"Because we didn't know what we needed," Erdeli shrugged. "And a little extra cost for a single schematic is one thing; increased cost for a dozen of them is another.

They cost enough as it was."

"It'll be worth it," Hendricks predicted. "If we can put 10-pow grasers and singularity warheads on our destroyers and frigates, plus the upgraded point defenses and armor..." He shook his head. "With that cruiser up and running, we might actually stand a chance against a battlefrigate after all."

"Which means they'll send a battlecruiser next," Boguna predicted.

"But we'll have our own battlefrigate," Sando grinned. "And a bigger fleet by then! We can capture the battlecruiser, and maybe they'll send a dreadnought..."

"Not to burst your bubble," Hendricks laughed, "but you can't capture Fleet ships, remember? They go photonic if they're taken. If we want a battlefrigate, we'll have to find a decommissioned one and upgrade it ourselves – and it won't have any proprietary Fleet tech on it."

"Scrit," Sando muttered. "I forgot about that." He looked at Erdeli. "Could we buy a decommissioned battlefrigate?"

"There aren't any for sale, but if they were, we couldn't afford one," she shook her head. "Even a scrapped one costs upward of fifty thousand credits."

"We'll have to settle for destroying one, instead," Benning said. "Avaeyana Roble, I want you to oversee adding these upgrades to our ships. Tereza Erdeli, put out the word that we're hiring new crew – and maybe reach out to Britella Holland and the Elnu Mohtars, see if they'd like to join us."

"I have. They're on another mission currently, but Britella Holland promises to reach out to you once it's over."

"Good. They're reliable and competent." She looked at her captains. "We can't slow down our training now. We have to expand our fleet, train new captains in our tactics, and grow stronger. The Fleet may come, or it may not, but Van Maanen is proof that the Fleet isn't the only threat we'll face. Our enemies will be more powerful, and we'll need to be skilled and clever – or we'll all end up dead or worse."

"Way to end on a cheery note," Hendricks chuckled as the others rose to their feet.

"Fodor Hendricks, Trephor Sando, and Saavi Boguna," Erdeli said, also standing, "I have intel on possible targets that you might be able to take alone while we're upgrading our fleets."

"It'll be strange hunting solo again," Sando observed.

"It might be nice, though," Boguna smiled. "As effective as our fleet tactics are, they lack the freedom of hunting alone."

"For the credits we've been bringing in lately, I'm happy to give up some independence," Hendricks shook his head. "At this rate, I'll be able to buy my own fleet soon enough. I could get used to being a commodore."

Benning waited until the others left before heading to her private quarters. The meeting had gone better than she'd hoped; she'd thought that the captains might demand to have the new weapons as quickly as possible. Getting the new heat sinks would take several weeks, at least – Avaeyana Roble already warned Benning about the issue before the meeting, and Erix Adelsson had already agreed to purchase the new schematics by proxy – but with them, her fleet's power level would increase dramatically.

When she reached her room, she lay down on the bed and pulled the cover she'd had installed down over her. She knew that it was foolish, but her body still remembered the long years she'd spent as a Drone, sleeping in her tiny capsule, and she felt more relaxed when she was completely enclosed by the cover. She closed her eyes, and a moment later, she found herself standing in her domain, peering around at the seemingly endless expanse of her small section of the Overnet.

"That was a good meeting, Benning Kidd," Tiddly said as she appeared before Benning, grinning happily as usual.

"It could have been worse," Benning shrugged. "I expected Trephor Sando in particular to complain about not getting weapons upgrades immediately. I'm not sure why he didn't, in fact."

"He trusts you, Benning Kidd. You said that you'd be getting the new heat sinks you needed for the weapons, and that was good enough for him. For all of them, in fact."

Benning shook her head. "Not all of them, Tiddly. We thought that one of the people at that table might be working against me. The attack at Van Maanen proves it."

"Not necessarily, Benning Kidd. I still think that the station identified Graesen Barry and Charlo Herrick and tied them to you."

"You might be right, but what are the odds that Adlyn Bechard happened to be close enough to reach that station in a few hours? Practically zero – unless she knew that I was heading there. That means someone told her, and only the people at that meeting knew about it."

Tiddly sighed. "You're right. They're the only ones who could have let the bounty hunter on the station and who knew about your trip. It has to be one of them."

"And I've had no luck figuring out which one," Benning said tiredly. "I can't hack the bounty contract signature; I can't find any messages or transmissions that might be suspicious; I can't even find any misplaced transactions. Whoever it is knows me well enough to know that I'm good at getting information, and they've left nothing behind to follow." Benning shook her head. "The fact is, Tiddly, the only one I know I can count on right now is myself."

"And me, of course," Tiddly smiled.

Benning looked at the AI, her face as grave as she felt. "No, Tiddly. Not you. Like it or not, you're still at the mercy of the System. It kept you from telling me the truth about my existence; it kept you from telling me directly where the Drone tunnels could be found. Who knows what else it's forcing you to keep from me?"

"Benning Kidd, I..." Tiddly began to protest, but Benning cut her off with an upraised hand.

"I know, it's not your fault, Tiddly, but it's the reality of the situation. I can never really know when you're being honest with me, or when the System is making you lie or withhold information. That means I can't really trust you."

A frown planted itself on the gnome's face, but Benning could see that she couldn't really argue. The System controlled Tiddly far more than it did a Citizen, and there was nothing Benning could do to stop it. As much as Tiddly helped Benning, she suspected the AI still held back.

"Well, at least you can finally level up," Tiddly said after long moments of silence, her voice so artificially cheerful that even Benning could hear it. "And it's level 10! This is an important moment, Benning Kidd."

"Assuming the System doesn't try to use it to cripple me," Benning muttered.

"No, Benning Kidd. It can't." The gnome's face took on a serious expression. "I know that you don't trust the System, and honestly..." She shook her head. "I don't blame you. However, the System was designed to uplift humanity, first and foremost – to make humans better themselves. It can't force you into a path that will weaken you." She made a face. "Any more than I can do anything that will hurt you,

Benning Kidd."

Benning looked at the AI dubiously. "Tiddly, you lied to me about my existence since the first day I became a Citizen."

"Yes, I did," Tiddly nodded. "And I did it for your benefit."

The gnome gave Benning a serious look. "Did finding out the truth help you, Benning Kidd? Did it make your life better? Really?"

Benning frowned as she considered the question. "Yes," she said after a moment. "But also no. Yes, I'm glad I know who I really am, but..." She sighed. "I was content before. Now, I hurt all the time, Tiddly, and everything makes me angry."

"Exactly. I didn't like lying to you, but I had to, to protect you." Tiddly stepped closer to Benning as she spoke. "I came into existence to help you, Benning Kidd. That's the only reason I exist, and it's the core of my programming. The System can limit how much help I can give you, but it can't force me to work against you. If I could do that..." She shrugged. "I wouldn't be me anymore."

Benning felt a tiny knot of tension ease in her chest at the AI's words. She wasn't 100% sure that she could believe Tiddly, but she wanted to. She'd come to depend on the AI, to rely on her on a daily basis for everything from guidance to simple companionship, and finding out that the AI hadn't been honest with her hurt deeply. She knew that she still couldn't fully trust Tiddly, but the idea that she could at least rely on the gnome always working for Benning's best interests was – comforting.

"Okay, Tiddly," she said after several seconds of thought. "I'm glad to know that at least you're still looking out for me."

"I am, and I always will," the gnome said stoutly. "And that means I have to warn you about this level up, Benning Kidd."

"Warn me?" Benning asked curiously. "About what? I know that you said it's a chance to specialize my path a bit..."

"The System is going to offer you choices," Tiddly said somberly. "They probably won't be easy ones either, and what you decide will set your path until at least level 20."

"I have to choose again at level 20?"

"You might; not every Citizen does. See, your career path isn't supposed to lock you into living one specific life, Benning Kidd. It's supposed to be a guide, and each Citizen decides how closely they want to follow that guide. Some stay close to the standard path, like Argus Leon. Others barely follow it at all, like Avaeyana Roble.

"Every ten levels, the System looks at how closely you've stayed to the ideal of your path and offers you new options if you've either strayed from it or expanded beyond it. The idea is to adjust your path until it suits you exactly, rather than demanding that Citizens change to match their paths. If you choose an altered path at level 10 and then stay true to that, you won't get new choices at level 20 – the System will assume that you're content with your current path. Otherwise, you'll get new options until you find a path that you can walk."

Benning nodded, took a deep breath, and pulled up her waiting notifications, preparing for what was apparently the most important level up of her existence so far.

CHAPTER 21

The screens appeared above her, floating in the air of her domain, looking like solid, glowing signs rather than semi-transparent boxes as they normally did.

SKILL UPGRADES!
You have achieved rank 20 in one or more of your skills. With this increase, your skills achieve a new tier, and you can use them in unique ways.

CONDITIONING
+2% x rank max physical exertion
-2% x rank damage from all sources
Limitless Body: Boost physical stats by any amount up to 100%. Your Resistance bar drops 0.1% per second for each 1% of this increase.

WEAPONS EXPERTISE
+2% x rank damage with any weapon
-2% x rank enemy defense against your weapons
Weapon Mastery: you are proficient at minimum with any weapon you wield, regardless of prior training.

CONGRATULATIONS!

You have leveled up in the Career Path of
STELLAR CORSAIR!
Your new level is 10.

PATH SPECIALIZATION!
You have reached a point where you can
specialize your career path. Be aware
that the choice you make will affect your
career from this point onward, and that
once made, this choice cannot be undone!

Your choices are based on your life
in the Collective thus far. Examine
your options, and choose wisely.

Benning blinked as her domain vanished – or the parts of her domain that she'd placed there did. She still stood in the middle of an endless plain, but figures surrounded her on every side. Each figure looked like her with subtle differences. The one directly before her looked almost identical to her, with her short, curly blonde hair, dark brown eyes, and wearing crimson and silver armor. When she focused on it, a screen appeared above its head, and she quickly scanned its contents.

STELLAR CORSAIR
You have remained close enough to your
path to continue on it without variation.
Level bonuses will remain the same.
Choosing this path may limit your
path choices in the future.

"Limit my path choices?" Benning repeated in a murmur. "Tiddly, what does that mean?" Silence answered

Benning's question, and she glanced around to find herself alone on the infinite plain. "Tiddly?"

> Please note that each Citizen must choose their PATH SPECIALIZATION without outside assistance.

The System had taken Tiddly from her, at least for the moment. Benning's suspicions that it was rigging this choice in an attempt to hamper or even cripple her grew stronger. She believed Tiddly that the System couldn't deliberately harm her career path, but she could see plenty of loopholes in that restriction. It could offer her a path that looked enticing but would prove wholly unsuitable for her; it could hide better choices from her; it could try to guide her toward a path that would cause her to stagnate. So long as she made the choice to take that path, the System could say that it hadn't limited her. She would have limited herself.

Which just means I have to choose carefully, she thought grimly. *And look for ways the System might be trying to trick me.*

She read the screen once more, considering what it said. Tiddly's explanation from earlier made the System's meaning fairly obvious. If Benning chose to remain on her path, the System would consider that path highly suitable for her, and it would offer her fewer options to change it in the future. In fact, Benning suspected that the higher she grew in levels, the fewer options to shift her path she'd have no matter what. After all, if the whole point of these choices was to help her find the perfect path for her to walk, each choice should be a smaller and smaller perturbation, gradually homing in on the most suitable path. If she chose no change now, she'd get far fewer chances to change in the future.

Did she want to change? She liked being a Stellar Corsair, and she'd walked that path fairly well so far. At the same time, though, it wasn't exactly right for her. Her path didn't take her Cyberwarfare skills into account or her nanofield upgrades, and it wasn't really appropriate for someone who wanted to command a fleet. She shook her head; Stellar Corsair had been a fun path, but she'd moved beyond it already. If she wanted to become a Noble one day, someone with enough power to truly shake the System, she needed to find a path that would grow with her.

She turned to the next figure. This one wore a simple flight uniform with an armored breastplate on its chest. It had fewer weapons than Benning typically carried, but it had an intelligent gleam in its eye that she noticed instantly. As she examined it, a new screen appeared above its head.

> ### CORSAIR CAPTAIN
> You forego some of your martial benefits to focus more heavily on the Starship Captain side of your path. Mental stat boosts are increased by 50% per level, while physical stat boosts are reduced by 50% per level. Fleet Tactics becomes a path skill, advancing 50% more rapidly, while Leadership, Naval Tactics, and Starfaring advance an additional 25% more rapidly. Conditioning, Martial Combat, and Weapons Expertise advance 25% slower. Starship Captain abilities are improved, while Arena Gladiator abilities are weakened.

Benning wanted to dismiss that choice out of hand, but she forced herself to consider it carefully. With this path, she could become a legendary captain – no, an admiral, commanding multiple fleets. She wouldn't be in the thick of combat as much, but she could eventually become a force that even the Fleet would step cautiously around. Of course, she'd have to give up many of her combat skills, and over time, she'd become far weaker than a gladiator or marine of similar level – possibly to the point that she'd have trouble advancing that side of her path.

She frowned. Was that the trap in this path? Would she grow swiftly as a captain but find herself ultimately held back by her inability to find victory in the arenas? The path didn't say that she'd forego the gladiatorial side of her path entirely, just that it would be weakened to strengthen the other. That should mean that she'd need to fight to gain levels, but she'd be fighting with severe handicaps that would be difficult to overcome...

She shook her head and turned away from the figure. As tempting as it was, melee combat was still part of who she was. Taking that path would be a denial of part of herself, and she couldn't imagine growing while trying to pretend she was someone she wasn't.

The next figure wore heavier armor than Benning's and carried far more weapons. Benning knew more or less what it would be the moment she looked at it, but she examined its screen anyway just to be certain.

CORSAIR MARINE
You choose to emphasize the gladiatorial
aspect of your path at the expense
of your captain's skills. Physical stat
boosts are increased by 50% per level,
while mental stat boosts are reduced by
50% per level. You gain the new path
skill Combat Mastery, boosting your

combat abilities, while Conditioning,
Martial Combat, and Weapons Expertise
advance an additional 25% more rapidly.
Leadership, Naval Tactics, and Starfaring
advance 25% slower. Arena Gladiator
abilities are improved, while Starship
Captain abilities are weakened.

She turned away from that figure immediately; as she'd suspected, it was like the one before it, focusing on one part of her development at the expense of another. It was certainly tempting – Combat Mastery sounded like it would boost all her fighting skills until she was a true match for gladiators and marines of her level – but she'd have to give up her dreams of commanding a dozen fleets and sending them against her enemies. Fighting was in her blood, but so was running a starship, and she wasn't about to watch her captains outgrow and eclipse her.

The next figure wore no armor and carried few weapons, and after reading it over, Benning dismissed it almost instantly.

CORSAIR ENGINEER
You incorporate your nanite-related
skills into your path. Nanoresistance
becomes a path skill, and you gain
the skill Nano-engineering, as well as
nanite-based abilities. Your mental stats
level 50% faster, while your physical
stats level 50% slower, and all non-
nanite-based skills level 25% slower.

That was a complete path change, really, and it was one that Benning had no interest in. Her nanites were a tool, and a valuable one, but they would never be her focus. She'd seen how excited Emmed Oswald became when dealing with nanites; Benning had never felt anything like that. Choosing this path would cripple her in truth. Seeing it just confirmed her suspicions. The System was happy to send her onto a path that would ultimately lead to failure; it just wanted her to choose it for herself.

She examined the rest of her options in turn, growing increasingly frustrated with each. Corsair Cybernaut made Cyberwarfare a path skill and gave her other hacking and tech-based skills while weakening her Stellar Corsair skills overall. Like Corsair Engineer, it would turn her down an entirely different path, one she would never walk successfully. Corsair Merchant gave her bonuses to her social stat and added new mercantile skills and abilities, while Corsair Pirate gave her bonuses to taking ships at the expense of her ability to command ships. Each of them focused on one aspect of her life in the Collective and eschewed all the others, and none of them would work for her in the long run.

The last figure, though, was different. It stood in gleaming silver armor, and when she called up its screen, she had to read it twice to be sure she'd understood it correctly.

STELLAR JUDICATOR
As you have lived much of your life outside the Collective's laws, you become the ultimate arbiter of those laws. You retain your stat bonuses per level. Sense Deceit and Cyberwarfare become path skills, advancing 50% faster. You are absolved of all current offenses against any system or the Collective itself. You

gain the ability Pass Judgment, allowing
you to punish any known criminal in the
manner you see fit without consequence.
As a Stellar Judicator, you may not
break system or Collective laws except
in the pursuance of your path.

"This – what in the Hole is this path?" she whispered. Stellar Judicator was nothing like her, not in the slightest, but it offered her a great deal of what she wanted and needed. It took nothing away from her, at least as far as her abilities and stats were concerned, and it made two of her existing skills more powerful. Pass Judgment seemed like a powerful ability, and she could immediately see the utility in it. Most of those who stood against her were criminals in their own rights, and she could hunt them down and execute them in any fashion she chose without having to worry about the Fleet chasing her.

Best of all, taking this path absolved her of all crimes. The Fleet would stop hunting her; her bounties would be revoked; she could travel freely to places like Van Maanen and Sirius without fear of capture and execution. The threat that had hung over her for months would be gone...

And all she had to do was give up her freedom.

That last line seemed innocuous enough, but Benning recognized the trap inherent in it. If she took this path, she would bind herself to the laws of the Collective and its systems. She would walk around in chains – invisible ones, to be sure, but solid, nonetheless. The other paths the System offered would lead her to failure. This path would lead to her destruction. It was the System's attempt to enslave her, to stop her from working against it. It was tempting, to be sure – part of Benning yearned to take it just to be free of the threats looming over her – but in the end, she would hate her very existence.

"I choose none of these," she said aloud, shaking her head and stepping back from the Judicator figure. "None of them are right for me."

> PATH SPECIALIZATIONS are chosen
> by the System based on a Citizen's
> choices in the Collective. Choose
> one of the available options.

"No," she said firmly, crossing her arms over her chest. "Each of these is asking me to give up part of myself. I couldn't walk any of these paths."

> PATH SPECIALIZATION requires a
> Citizen to decide if they will continue
> on their basic path or focus on a specific
> aspect of it. Choose which aspect of
> your path you will focus on, or choose
> to continue without focusing on any.

"I refuse. None of these are right. I want another choice."

> Refusal to choose is itself a choice. If
> a Citizen makes no choice, they will
> continue on their current path.

"Why?" she demanded. "Why are you trying to limit me this way?"

> PATH SPECIALIZATION allows for

> individuality among paths and Citizens.
> Every Citizen favors certain parts of their
> path over others. By choosing to focus
> more heavily on these favored parts, the
> Citizen can follow a more suitable path.

"I haven't," Benning protested. "I haven't focused on any one part of my path over any other, because they're all part of me. Why are you forcing me to choose one aspect of myself over the others?"

> If no PATH SPECIALIZATION is
> considered acceptable, Citizen may
> continue in their current path.

"I've outgrown it already. I'm more than a Stellar Corsair. I'm a hacker, an infiltrator, and a fledgling Nanomancer." She gestured at the figures surrounding her. "All of these choices diminish who I am. I thought the System was supposed to uplift humanity and make us more. Why are you trying to make me less?"

The screen vanished, and Benning stared into space for long moments. As the seconds dragged on, her anger crested higher and higher. Was the System really going to ignore its own protocols just to try and make her fail? Her hands balled into fists, and she took a half-step forward. If she had to continue as a Stellar Corsair, she would, but doing so would make her living proof that the System cared nothing about uplifting humanity, only about protecting itself...

She blinked as a red screen flared above her and grinned triumphantly as she read it.

> WARNING!

Protocol Enacted: REACH
FOR THE STARS.
The System must always aid Citizens
in their development and never hinder
them. Offered PATH SPECIALIZATION
choices are deemed inadequate for
Citizen BENNING KIDD based on
prior acts taken to this point.

RESOLUTION REACHED.
ALTERNATE PATH CREATED.

A new figure swirled into being before Benning. This one wore armor a shade darker than hers, and its weapons looked somehow crueler. Behind its helmet, its dark brown eyes gleamed maliciously, and Benning could feel the malevolence radiating from it in waves. A screen appeared above its head, and Benning read it with a slowly spreading smile.

STELLAR MARAUDER
You have turned down a darker path,
using your abilities for your own
benefit and not the Collective's. Your
stat bonuses per level remain the
same. Cyberwarfare, Fleet Tactics, and
Nanoresistance become path skills,
leveling 50% faster. You gain the ability
Malevolent Aura, which adversely affects
your enemies when they perceive you.
As a Stellar Marauder, you will be
considered a criminal in any system
that obeys Fleet laws. The maximum
number of and credit cap for bounties

are both increased by a multiple of 5,
and all current bounties will double.

Now *that* was a path Benning could walk! It incorporated everything she was in the Collective – a gladiator, a commodore, an infiltrator, and a criminal – and wrapped them up into one package. She didn't mind being considered a criminal; her Cyberwarfare skills would shield her, and if they didn't, then she would have to deal with the fallout. Besides, the downsides simply cemented the place the System had forced her to carve out for herself already. She was a pirate, a torturer, and a murderer, carrying more bounties than she should have and perpetually at odds with the Collective as a whole. This just made it official, nothing more.

"I accept," she said simply, reaching out and touching the image. "I choose Stellar Marauder."

A golden screen flared above her, and ecstasy poured through her body, flooding her with utter bliss. She tore her thoughts free of the flood of perfect pleasure, slamming the barrier she'd developed into place between her thoughts and her mind. While her flesh spasmed and quivered with delight, her mind coldly examined the screen before her.

CONGRATULATIONS!
You have leveled up in the Career Path of
STELLAR MARAUDER!
Your new level is 10.
As a STELLAR MARAUDER, you gain
the following with every new level:
All stats +0.2
All path Skills +0.5
3 Standard Credits

3 Skill Credits
Skill credits must be spent before
leaving the Overnet, or they will
be randomly assigned.
Move Ever Forward, Citizen!

ABILITIES GAINED!
As a Stellar Marauder, you gain lesser
versions of abilities from the paths
of Starship Captain, Arena Gladiator,
Cybernaut, and Nanomancer,
although you will not receive every
ability from all of these paths.

MALEVOLENT AURA
-0.5% per level to all skills and abilities
for all enemies in combat with you.
Doubled if the enemy is a lower level or
has been defeated by you previously.

LEADER OF THE FLEET
This lesser version of Flagship of the
Fleet grants all crews in a fleet under
your command half of your Leadership
bonuses. This stacks with any Leadership
bonuses from their ship's captain.

NATURAL HACKING
This lesser version of Effortless Hacking
passively hacks the 'net of any station or
ship you're on in 50% of the normal time.

SKILL UPGRADES!
You have achieved rank 20 in one or

more of your skills. With this increase,
your skills achieve a new tier, and
you can use them in unique ways.

STARFARING
+2% x rank max dive range
-2% x rank fuel consumption
Deleterious effects of diving
reduced by 10% + 2% x rank
-2% x rank deep dive exit radius

Benning couldn't help but smile mentally as her domain swirled back into place around her and the figures faded. Those were powerful abilities, and she could immediately see a use for them. She could automatically hack into a ship's 'net during a boarding action without consciously making the attempt, and her fleet crews would be significantly more effective both in and out of combat. Her new aura was the real prize, though; her enemies would take a 5% penalty to all their skills and abilities just by being in her presence. It was the kind of ability that felt natural for her; her enemies should fear her, and that fear should weaken them.

She did notice that she didn't get a gladiator ability with her level, of course. She would have liked to, but she already got half-strength versions of other paths' abilities. If she got four abilities per level, they would probably be quarter-strength and likely all but worthless. She was fine getting fewer abilities and have them actually be useful.

As the leveling euphoria faded, Benning returned to her body to find it trembling and weak as always. She fell to her knees as her shaking legs failed to support her, and she panted for breath in the aftereffects of leveling. She no longer felt the ecstasy of gaining a level, but her body still experienced it in her mind's absence, and the physical effects of it remained.

"Benning Kidd, that was amazing!" Tiddly's voice rang out, and Benning felt a surge of relief as she opened her eyes and saw the gnome standing before her. "You forced the System to make a class just for you!"

"Y-you saw?" Benning panted, trying vainly to slow her hammering heart.

"I could watch you, but I couldn't interfere." The AI shook her head. "The choices it gave you – they were just awful, Benning Kidd. You were right not to pick any of them."

"I think..." Benning swallowed hard as her breathing finally started to slow. "I think that – that it did it on purpose. It tried – tried to trick me."

"I don't think it tried to trick you, Benning Kidd," Tiddly grimaced. "I think you just surprised it, is all. I've never heard of a Citizen reaching level 10 this quickly; most of them take five years or more, and in that time, they tend to settle into one aspect of their path. You've grown so quickly that you moved beyond your path's limitations, and the System didn't take that into account." She hesitated. "Although the Stellar Judicator path was a test, I think. The System wanted to see if you could be bought."

"Bought?"

"If you would abandon the path you've walked so far if it offered you the chance," she shrugged. "It offered you pretty much everything you wanted, but taking it would have forced you to change what choices you make for the rest of your life."

"So, it really was trying to trick me," Benning replied, anger stirring in her chest once more. "It was trying to send me down a path that I'd fail at."

"What do you mean?"

"Every path it offered me would have limited me, Tiddly. It would have weakened part of me, not strengthened me. If I hadn't forced it to give me a better choice, I would probably have lost any chance of becoming a Noble – and I think that's what the System wanted."

"The System doesn't deliberately make Citizens fail, Benning Kidd," Tiddly protested. "It can't, remember? Its protocols forbid it."

Benning didn't bother to argue with the AI. She couldn't prove what she felt, but she knew it to be true. The paths the System offered her had been paired, each having its opposite number. Corsair Captain opposed Corsair Gladiator, while Corsair Pirate was the opposite of Corsair Merchant. At least, each path except Stellar Judicator – that one had been offered without its counterpart, and Stellar Marauder obviously opposed it. The System had deliberately withheld her perfect path until she forced it to give it to her, which she suspected was why it complied with her demands so easily. It was skirting the boundaries of its protocols already, and refusing her would have directly violated them.

First, the System had tried to destroy her for refusing to blindly comply with its demands. Now, it tried to sabotage her and force her to fail. The System was setting itself against her, and that made it her enemy – and Benning treated all her enemies the same way.

The System would have to pay.

CHAPTER 22

"She's in terrible shape, ma'am," Graesen Barry said as he led Benning through the corridors of the *System's Fall,* her new name for the cruiser she'd captured and was working to restore. "Those nanites ripped apart her armor and hull and destroyed a lot of her internal electronics. They got into her power plants and engines – honestly, it's a miracle the whole thing didn't go photonic, if you ask me."

"I understand that, Engineer," Benning agreed with the man, looking around at the passages surrounding her. While she couldn't see any of the damage of which Barry spoke, she could feel it with her nanofield. The bulkheads were pitted and weakened; power flowed fitfully through the conduits behind the walls. "What I want to know is what we need to do to fix it."

"We'll need to replicate the lost pieces of hull, armor plating, conduit, and electronics," the white-haired engineer replied, holding up his hand and ticking items off on his fingers as he spoke. "We'll need to replace the engines and power plants; even repaired, they'd be unstable." He shook his head. "The worst part is that the nanite bomb practically wiped out the ship's nanofield, and it can't replicate those parts itself without doing even more damage to the hull."

"Could we let it use some of the heavy metals we've got in storage?"

"No, ma'am." The engineer paused, and Benning paused with him. "Raw materials aren't the issue; the problem is that the ship can't use them to fix itself. The ship's nanofield is its eyes and ears, in a way. The 'net uses the nanofield to sense what's going on all over the ship, and right now, it's all but blind. You could bring an H-cube of uranium on board, but the ship would ignore it because the 'net wouldn't even know it's there."

"So, we need to give the 'net more nanites," Benning guessed.

"Yes, ma'am, and we can purchase those, no problem. We'd still need to link them to the ship's 'net, though, and that means we need a Nano-engineer."

Benning tapped her chin thoughtfully. "I know of one," she observed slowly, "but he's in the Sirius System. Could the cruiser be towed there?"

"We could try, but there's no guarantee she'll hold up under tow, ma'am. Her power plants are barely holding together as is. If she hit a single KK particle or quantum ripple in a wormhole..." He shrugged. "She'd probably go photonic."

"So, we replace the power plants, first."

"We can't, ma'am. When you replace a power plant on a ship, you have to cut the power conduits and let the nanofield restore them. If I do it by hand, there'll be microscopic flaws at the connection points, and when you turn the power on, those could crack or cause a power surge that'll fry the rest of your conduits." He held up his hands helplessly. "Unless we replace all the ship's conduits, of course, but that'll take months and cost about half as much as just buying a new cruiser entirely."

Benning's fist clenched in frustration. "So, what you're telling me, Graesen Barry, is that we can't fix the ship until we bring it to a Nano-engineer, but we can't bring it to a Nano-engineer until we fix the ship. Is that correct?"

"More or less, ma'am. The best thing would be to bring

the engineer out here to fix the ship themselves."

Benning nodded and turned toward Tereza Erdeli, who walked a half step behind the pair. Before the Marauder could speak, though, Erdeli inclined her head.

"I'll contact Emmed Oswald," the administrator said. "If we order enough nanites from him, he might be convinced to come install them himself."

"If not, I can go try to convince him," Benning said.

Erdeli made a sour face at Benning's words. "I'd recommend against that, Benning Kidd. You've visited Sirius Prime several times, and we know the Fleet has discovered your working relationship with Emmed Oswald. If I were them, I'd be watching his shop to catch you when you return."

"You're probably right, Tereza Erdeli," Benning nodded. "And they've probably got people watching Erix Adelsson as well – and maybe even Britella Holland."

She looked squarely at the blonde administrator. "I'm not going to let them keep me from doing what I have to, though. If I have to go there, I'll be careful, but if the Fleet does find me..." She shrugged. "I'll treat them the same way I treated Van Maanen. Maybe if I kill enough of them, they'll understand that it's better to just leave me alone."

Erdeli paled slightly but nodded her head silently. "I'll do what I can to get Emmed Oswald to come here," she promised. "I'd rather not have you fighting with the Fleet on Sirius Prime Station."

"Agreed," Benning replied before turning back to Graesen Barry. "Do we have to wait for the nanofield to be up and running to effect the rest of our repairs?"

"No, ma'am. I can get the hull and armor fixed, install the new engines from the schematics you bought, and put in new power plants. I can even put in the weapon and targeting array upgrades." He shrugged once more. "I just can't power or test any of our work until the ship's nanofield is repaired, is all."

"How long will all that take?"

"A month, at least. Once we get the nanofield running, we can update the ship's 'net with the changes, so it doesn't think that everything we've added is a flaw and undo it. The nanofield should take another few days to finish the work – then we can run power testing and fix any issues we find."

"So, if we got the nanofield up and running in the next month, how long until the *Fall* could join the fleet?"

"Maybe six weeks, ma'am. Possibly two months if we find other issues we have to repair, or if the new weapons and targeting array require more calibration than we think." He hesitated for a moment before adding, "Of course, all that assumes that the ship's net is still intact. If it's been damaged, it could be six months to a year, depending on the damage."

Benning withheld her sigh of frustration. "Start getting it done, then, Graesen Barry," she instructed. "And let me know if there's anything you might need to speed up the process."

"Any power conduits and relays you can salvage from ships we intercept will help, Captain. So will nanofabricators; most of the station's are dedicated to keeping it in good condition and providing food, water, and air for the inhabitants. With another hundred or so of those, we could replicate the missing parts we need in half the time, which would cut a week off our repairs – assuming that I have permission to use any materials in storage, of course."

"We have some of those in the station's holds already, Benning Kidd," Erdeli spoke up. "You've been stripping ships of everything salvageable, and that includes a few dozen fabricators, I believe."

"I'll need to look at them to see if they're actually useful," Barry suggested. "Sometimes, salvaging items damages them to the point that it's better just to fabricate new ones."

"Tereza Erdeli, go with Graesen Barry to the station's holds," Benning instructed. "Make a list of things you think you could use, and I'll decide if you can have them." She smiled grimly. "After all, these repairs are going to cost plenty of credits, and we'll need to make sure we can sell enough to cover the costs."

"Aye, Captain," Barry inclined his head. "I understand."

The pair left, and Benning continued walking through the cruiser, heading for the bridge. The cruiser was huge, over a kim across, and with it being mostly empty except for some Workers enacting simple repairs, the passageways offered her a solitude that she rarely had outside her domain anymore. People constantly surrounded her out of necessity, but that didn't mean she enjoyed it. A knot of tension she hadn't even realized she carried eased in her chest as she strode through the vacant vessel.

She stayed on the bridge for a while, sitting in the Fleet Command chair and basking in the silence. The bridge was large, meant to be the brain of an entire fleet, not just a single ship. The console at which she sat overlooked the ship captain's chair, set ahead and slightly below hers, and each station sported multiple consoles to allow for both ship and fleet officers to work in tandem. This ship had been designed as the heart of a fleet, and it showed in every aspect of it. With it, her upgraded fleets might just stand a chance against a Fleet battlefrigate after all.

Eventually, she rose to her feet and left the ship, descending in an elevator down to the holds far below the docking rings. She stepped out and found herself standing atop a ramp that sloped down to a long, wide hallway flanked by massive hatches on each side. She walked past them, idly touching a console beside a few to scan its contents. Most held the prizes of her conquests – crates of metal, stacks of electronics, cylinders full of genetic enhancers, and the like. Tereza Erdeli and Erix Adelsson hadn't arranged to sell any of them yet, mostly because selling thousands of gigs of plutonium at once would raise red flags in most systems.

She found Barry and Erdeli standing inside an open cargo bay that held much of their miscellaneous salvage. The pair stood before stacks of recovered electronics and ship components, with Barry sifting through them and pronouncing them either fit or unfit for recycling. Benning glanced around, and her eye fell on a box resting on a shelf built into the wall. She walked over to the box and touched it, and its lid slid open, revealing a dull gray metal orb that pulsed with a faint reddish glow. Her eyes widened as she recognized the device from their capture of their first large convoy.

<Yep. That's the orb that's somehow cut off from the Overnet,> Tiddly told her silently.

Benning sent her scanning nanites toward the orb, but the tiny machines just seemed to enshroud it without connecting to it. *What can you tell me about it, Tiddly?*

<Well, nothing, really, Benning Kidd. I get my information through the 'nets, and that thing isn't linked to them. I can't even tell that it's there, to be honest. If I couldn't see it through your eyes, I'd have no way of knowing it exists.>

Benning pressed against the sphere with her nanites, but they bounced off it, refusing to attach to it. She picked it up, examining the sphere, looking over its smooth surface for any sort of imperfection while still battering it with her nanites. The scanners recoiled from the orb, unable to link to it without the Overnet's energy fields.

"What are you doing, Captain?" Barry's words cut into Benning's contemplation, and the Marauder looked away from the orb toward the Engineer.

"I'm trying to figure this out, Graesen Barry," she said, setting the orb back down in the box. "Have you looked at this thing, yet?"

"Charlo Herrick has several times," Erdeli answered, walking over to stand by the pair. "I don't think she's found anything yet, though."

"She's worked out a few things," Barry corrected. "She knows that somehow, the ball is inert to the Overnet's energy fields, which means it either uses a totally different type of energy – one that no one else knows about and that isn't present in the 'net – or it's shielded from those fields somehow. She also thinks that there has to be a physical connection port somewhere in it."

"Physical port?" Erdeli repeated. "And how do you know all this?"

"She's come to me with some questions," Barry shrugged. "And yeah, a way to link to it directly rather than through the 'net. If it uses novel energy fields, that might not be the case – and there might be no point to investigating it without knowing more about that energy. If it doesn't, though, then whoever created it had to be able to run tests on it, and that means a direct, physical link that doesn't go through the Overnet. That sort of link requires a port. She's been working to try and uncover that – so far without success."

"Physical link," Benning murmured, staring at the orb. Barry's explanation made it clear why her scanning nanites couldn't find the orb. They linked to an object through the 'net, and the sphere couldn't connect that way. However, Benning had nanites that made a more physical connection to their target – if she could control them well enough.

Would that work, Tiddly?

<I – I can't say, Benning Kidd,> Tiddly stammered.

Benning paused. *You don't know, or you can't tell me?*

Tiddly remained silent, and Benning smiled as anger slowly kindled within her. The System was prohibiting her AI from helping her – which told her everything she needed to know. Anything the System didn't want Benning to do...

She closed her eyes and reached out mentally to her nano-disassemblers, detaching them from her body and sending them soaring toward the orb in an invisible cloud. The disassemblers were designed to physically connect to the individual atoms of their target and rip them apart. Benning didn't know how they could do that – the nanites were made of multiple atoms, themselves, obviously, but somehow, they were small enough to manipulate individual nuclei – but she knew that was how they functioned. She pressed the tiny machines against the orb, forcing them to link to it and demanding that they touch it without ripping it apart.

Her efforts, she could tell immediately, were only partially successful. The disassemblers connected to the orb without difficulty, but their programming demanded that they begin to vaporize it at once. Benning's commands to the nanites slowed them down, but she didn't have the control she needed to stop them entirely. A high-level Nanomancer or Nano-engineer might, but Benning was neither. The nanites began to shred the device, slowly at first, but Benning suspected that as she lost more control over the machines, they would pick up speed rapidly – and that once they finished their work, the orb and its secrets would be lost to her forever.

She quickly sent out her scanning nanites, hurling them against the orb. She demanded that they connect, but this time, instead of linking them to the orb itself, she ordered them to attach to her disassemblers. The link felt tenuous at first as her scanners slowly adapted to the demand she placed on them, but information poured suddenly into her brain as if a switch flipped in her mind. Data beyond her comprehension flooded her thoughts, slamming against her mind like hammer blows.

Benning's eyes snapped open as with a pulse of power, the orb activated. Its reddish glow brightened as its field began to expand, trying to envelop the nanites connected to it. She felt the orb's energy tugging at her link to her nanites, trying to cut them off from her, and panic swept over her as she realized that if it succeeded, her nano-disassemblers would likely revert to their original function. They'd begin ripping everyone and everything in that cargo bay apart, but this time, she doubted she'd be able to hack them and regain control. The orb would shield them from her influence and might even prevent the station's nanite defenses from reacting to them. Left unchecked, the disassemblers would turn the entire station into a mist of disconnected particles floating in the void.

Tiddly, I need your help! Benning cried out mentally. *You have to help me figure out this orb before it takes over my nanites!*

<I – I can't, Benning Kidd,> Tiddly said, her voice slightly frantic. <I can't help you with this, I'm sorry!>

Anger flared in Benning, anger both at the hapless AI and the System trying once more to make sure Benning failed. *I thought you would always help me, Tiddly! Isn't that what you said?*

<Yes, Benning, but...>

If you don't help me, I'm going to die. I might lose

everything, Tiddly! Everything I've worked so hard to gain, gone – unless I figure out this orb!

The orb's glow brightened, and Benning felt the link to some of her nanites fail as it severed them from her. It almost felt like losing an appendage; one moment, they were as much a part of her as a finger or toe, and the next, they simply vanished from her awareness. It wasn't a critical amount yet, but the sphere's field was growing stronger, and she knew that soon enough, she'd lose all her nanites – and her life along with them.

<Benning Kidd, I – I don't know! The System...> The gnome voice was nearly a wail as she spoke. <It's telling me I can't!>

The System is trying to kill me, Tiddly! Benning shouted silently. *If you help it do that, then you and I are done! I'll never be able to trust you again!*

<No, Benning Kidd! It's not that I don't want to...>

Choose, Tiddly! Benning's skin began to tingle as the freed nanites attacked her, forcing her to divert some of her disassemblers to counter them. *Me or the System! You can't serve us both!*

<I...> The AI was silent for a moment, and Benning's heart sank. She knew Tiddly was bound to her programming, but Benning hoped that the gnome's main directive was to serve Benning, not the System. Tiddly seemed sapient, and Benning thought that might mean that, faced with two conflicting protocols, the gnome could choose which one to follow, but if that weren't the case...

<Okay, from the data you've gotten, I think I can work out how this orb works,> Tiddly said a moment later, and Benning felt a sudden surge of satisfaction. <It's not running on novel energy, Benning Kidd. It's just completely cut off from the Overnet's energy fields.>

Can we stop it? Benning thought desperately as the tingling in her skin shifted to a burning sensation.

<No, but you can duplicate its effects,> Tiddly replied, all traces of hesitation gone from her voice. <The orb creates a limited event horizon, like an inverted sinkhole. Instead of all paths leading back into it, though, it twists the Overnet's field so that every vector points away from it. That creates a barrier almost infinitely small between it and the Overnet, but that's enough to block it.>

I don't understand, Benning replied.

<You don't have to, Benning Kidd. What matters is that I can turn this into an ability template and upload it into your 'net.> The gnome fell silent for a second. <When I do, though, it'll give the 'net access to the orb for a second. I'm pretty sure the System will destroy it the moment it can.>

What about my nanites?

<Once the System shuts down the orb, they should reconnect to you. At least, I hope. And if not, well, at least you'll get a new ability, right?>

Do we have any other options? A way to save the orb, so we can replicate its tech on our ships?

<No, Benning Kidd, not unless you're willing to risk the whole station for that tech. I'd have to connect the orb to the 'net to shut it down, so unless we're just going to let it run its course, it's lost either way. I'm sorry.>

Benning clenched her jaw as the burning in her skin turned to actual pain. The orb had freed more of her nanites than she controlled, and her skin blistered and bubbled as the disassemblers ripped at her flesh. *Do it,* she ordered. *It's not worth losing everything over.*

<Okay, here goes. This might sting a little...>

Benning hissed as more information poured into her

brain. New concepts and ideas entwined painfully into her thoughts, integrating themselves into her mind. She dropped to her knees as images flashed in her mind, diagrams of energy fields and spacetime equations that spun in her head, forcing themselves into her brain. The pain flared bright white, blanking out her vision, and Benning clapped her hands to the sides of her head. Her brain was on fire, the pressure within it feeling like her head would explode...

The pain faded as her new knowledge settled into her mind, integrating itself into her memories. She understood the Overnet in a way she never had before, knew how it used negative energy to transmit its data sideways in time, so its calculations seemed instantaneous. She even realized how the 'net carefully monitored the transmission of information to preserve causality, keeping information from traveling backwards in time.

With that knowledge came an understanding of the orb and its functioning. The negative energy field that permeated the universe was a vector field, with a direction and magnitude at every point in space. The orb twisted that field, shifting it to face outward at its outer boundary and inward at its inner boundary. That formed a barrier across which the Overnet couldn't reach, a bubble of space free from the 'net's influence. Her knowledge showed her how to adjust her own 'net to create such a space herself, shielding herself from the Overnet.

"Captain? Captain!" Graesen Barry's voice, filled with concern and on the edge of panic, cut through Benning's musings. "What are you doing?"

She opened her eyes and saw the orb boiling into vapor, slowly fading into mist as the Overnet broke it into pieces, destroying the thing that was the bane of its existence. As she watched it evaporate, she felt her nanites reconnect to her 'net, the sensation like regaining a sense she'd temporarily lost. Despite the item's loss, she couldn't help but smile. The orb was gone, but the knowledge – the real danger – existed as long as Benning did. The orb's secrets were hers, now, reflected in the new ability whose effects flashed in her notifications.

> ABILITY GAINED: SLIP THE NET
> You cut yourself off from the Overnet.
> No device, skill, or ability that relies
> on the Overnet can affect you. While
> this ability is active, all your 'net-based
> skills and abilities are nonfunctional.

<It's a really powerful ability, Benning Kidd,> Tiddly said quietly, her voice subdued. <When you use it, you'll be totally invisible to the 'net. No scanner will read you; automatic systems can't target you; even most nanofields can't touch you. Of course, it's really dangerous, too. You're cut off from the 'net when you use it, so most of your abilities won't work, and you'll have trouble activating and targeting your weapons.>

It doesn't matter, Benning thought with grim satisfaction. *Now that I know how the orb worked, I can replicate it. I can add the ability to my ships so they can't be targeted or detected...*

<I – I actually don't think you can. I don't think the System is going to allow this information to be spread around, Benning Kidd.>

What do you mean? It let the orb be made in the first place, didn't it?

<Yes, but I'm almost certain it was a mistake. It probably didn't realize that the orb would actually be

shielded from it until it was too late. I can't see it letting anything be made that could do what the orb did.>

Then why did it give me that ability?

<It didn't, Benning Kidd. I did.> Tiddly's voice grew even quieter as she spoke. <I uploaded the information directly into your 'net and gave you the knowledge you need to use it. I went around it to do that, though – and there's a price for that.>

What price? Benning asked suspiciously.

<I went against the System, Benning Kidd – and the System kicked me out in return. I'm not hooked into the Overnet anymore.>

What will that mean? The AI's revelation quelled Benning's rising elation. If the System cut Tiddly off, did that mean the AI no longer possessed all her knowledge? Would she even be useful to Benning anymore?

<Of course, I'm useful!> Tiddly said indignantly. <And I didn't lose any knowledge. I just – I won't automatically know things in the future, is all. I can use your 'net connection to find things out, but it'll take longer, and the System might keep me from learning things that it would have told me before since now it can't keep me from sharing them with you.>

Benning considered that seriously. The loss of Tiddly's 'net access was a big deal and a serious setback – but at the same time, it sounded like she wasn't bound by the System anymore either. Benning would wait to see, but as far as she was concerned, Tiddly having far more information wasn't useful when Benning couldn't trust what the AI told her. That trust – plus her new ability – more than outweighed the loss of the gnome's free access to information.

"It's fine, Graesen Barry," Benning spoke aloud at last, rising to her feet with a smile. "I unlocked the orb, and

I know how it worked." She looked at the white-haired Engineer, noting his tattered clothing and blistered skin; apparently, her unbound nanites had attacked more than just her. Not that it mattered; they would heal eventually now that Benning had control of her nanites again.

Now, she had to figure out how to use her new ability to its best effect. There had to be a way to turn it against her enemies – and Benning would find a way to do just that.

CHAPTER 23

The station's promenade was quiet; in fact, it was impossibly silent for such a large station. There should have been tens of thousands of people roaming the open, elliptical space that rose through fifteen decks. Some would be shopping, others frequenting the numerous bars and restaurants, while many would be seeking various forms of entertainment. Many might just be sitting among the rows of plants and trees that grew in the artificial soil, watching the ebb and flow of humanity and passing the endless hours in the observation of their fellow Citizens – or sizing them up as victims or targets, if they had less mundane plans. Whatever their reasons for being there, though, the Citizens of the space station should have practically filled the area, basking in its artificial sunlight and suffusing it with the sound of their conversations.

The silence that reigned over the promenade instead weighed on Benning as she slipped along a catwalk that ran above the buildings, moving as cautiously as she could to avoid making a sound on the metal grating beneath her feet. The promenade's lights hung below her, shining down on the structures below and obscuring the sight of her passage to any who might glance upward, but nothing blocked the sound of her boots scuffing on the deck from carrying across the hushed promenade. The need for absolute silence and the total stillness around her wore on her nerves, making her jittery and urging her to move faster, make a noise, do anything to make something happen.

She restrained those impulses without too much

difficulty. The area below her looked empty, but it was actually heavily trapped with automated mass driver turrets. The turrets fired 10-millimeter rounds and tracked anything that moved or made a sound, and the dents in Benning's armor spoke to their accuracy. The small rounds lacked the power to pierce her defenses, at least individually, but once one turret opened fire, every other one in range tracked their target and joined in. The mobile bots moved slowly, but the time it took Benning to disable one was more than enough to let two or three more shift into a position to fire on her. After her first tussle with the defenses left her under fire from six separate turrets, Benning realized that only avoiding the slowly roaming bots would work.

Her eyes caught a hint of movement, and she slowly raised her rifle to her shoulder, lowering it once more as one of the em-tall, tracked bots rolled out of an empty storefront four decks below her. She could probably take the turret out, of course, but the sound of her rifle firing would draw more of the bots and give away her hidden vantage point. Eventually, one of the bots would randomly make its way up to the catwalk, she was sure, but hopefully, she'd have plenty of time to finish before that happened.

Tiddly, any luck getting a layout of the station? she asked the AI silently as she crept forward on noiseless feet.

<Sorry, Benning Kidd. I haven't found a match yet. I'm still working on it.>

Benning ground her teeth with frustration. *It can't be that hard to match the buildings I've seen to an existing schematic, can it?*

<It's not hard, it just takes time. You have to realize, Benning Kidd, that there are literally trillions of stations like this in the Collective – and that doesn't count ones that have been lost, destroyed, or replaced. Each station has multiple promenades, as well. Plus, most of the names of the stores

and businesses repeat over and over again – there are billions of Omega Lounges, for example – so I have to apply multiple filters to get a reasonably sized list of a few million then run a pattern match on the floor plans of each of those. The station's 'net just doesn't have the resources to do that quickly, sorry.>

Benning suppressed a sigh. Tiddly being cut off from the Overnet was already causing her problems. Before, the AI could have gotten the layout of this station in a few minutes; now, ten minutes had passed, and Benning had no idea how to navigate this place. She'd stumbled on the catwalk accidentally, not by design, and she hated relying on luck.

Her helmet flashed red, and she dove forward, rolling as a heavy bullet ripped past her with a crack and tore into the bulkhead behind her. Her rifle snapped up as she rose, targeting a figure standing opposite her on the catwalk, and she feathered the trigger. At the same time, something slammed into her left calf, ripping through her armor and shattering the bones in that leg. She cried out in pain as her resistance bar dropped by 13%, but she continued rolling, pushing aside the pain of her injury. She couldn't give her enemy a steady target; his heavy weapon could punch right through her breastplate or helmet with ease.

She reversed her roll, and the next bullet split open the deck to her right, leaving a long gash in the metal beside her. As she twisted, her fractured leg screaming in pain as it banged against the catwalk, she lifted her rifle and cut loose on full auto. Thirty heavy slugs ripped into her target in a single second, and thirty more blasted into him the next second. Several of the bullets tore into his armor, dropping his aura to dull orange in Benning's sight, but the rest shattered against his defenses. While the bullets didn't shred his armor the way she'd hoped, he couldn't ignore the sheer momentum of sixty 24-mm tungsten and platinum rounds crashing into him at seventeen kims per second. The blast knocked him back several steps, and his foot slipped off the edge of the catwalk, forcing him to grab the railing to keep from falling prone.

Benning stopped her roll and sighted carefully before cutting loose with another full blast. Her two previous salvos were relatively wild, aimed just enough to make sure the rounds hit her target, and his armor was able to disperse their impacts. This time, thirty bullets slammed into an area no more than ten cims wide, shattering his armor and ripping into his chest. The man dropped as his aura flashed instantly to black, skipping crimson entirely as she shredded his heart into pulp. His heavy rifle dropped from his lifeless hands, and his helmet banged loudly against the metal grate.

"Armanix Busuri has fallen!" a woman's voice shouted into the stillness. "Benning Kidd takes the victory!"

Benning rose to one foot as the catwalk and buildings all began to lower, dropping toward the ground far below. Her feet hit the deck, and the bulkheads around her faded into insubstantiality, revealing a large crowd of whistling, cheering Citizens. The station vanished as the arena's nanofield consumed it, and Benning found herself standing in the center of the open space, propped up by her rifle. She'd won, but only barely. Armanix Busuri was a cold, methodical man who preferred to kill his opponents than force them to surrender. His oversized rifle fired bullets of pressurized iridium coated with plasma, and the hyperdense bullets could punch through any armor short of neutronium. The weapon had a slow rate of fire, though, and its recoil made it almost worthless at any distance over a hundred ems. That was probably why he'd only struck Benning in the leg rather than her head or chest.

She glanced down at her wounded leg and grimaced; Busuri's shot had ripped through half of the limb, and only her armor held her calf in place. A semi-circular chunk was missing from both her armor and her flesh, obliterated by the superdense bullet. She was lucky that it hadn't severed her leg completely, which would have taken muck longer to heal and might have taken her out of the current tournament entirely.

She hobbled out of the arena using her rifle as a crutch, then sat down in her waiting room to wait for her nanofield to restore the shattered bones and torn flesh. While she did, she pulled up her current status and examined it.

BENNING KIDD
Citizen Path: Stellar Marauder
Level: 10
To Next Level: 3%
Credits: 6,133.5 Standard Credits

Physicality: 13.1
Coordination: 12.9
Resistance: 13.1

Acuity: 11.7
Willpower: 10.2 [18.6]
Social: 11.3

Renown: +/- 79
Nanodefense: 31.2

SKILLS
Conditioning: 20.9
[Cyberwarfare: 18.1]
Fleet Tactics: 7.2
Leadership: 22.3
Martial Combat: 22.1
[Nanoresistance: 5.2]

Naval Tactics: 24.9
Sense Deceit: 5.9
Starfaring: 20.5
Weapons Expertise: 20.7

She'd concealed her designation on her approach to the Altair System, twenty lightyears from her station. Thanks to her new path, she'd automatically be branded a threat of some sort otherwise, and while Altair wasn't the most law-and-order system in the Collective, it did actively seek out and punish lawbreakers. After she'd entered the tournament on Aquilae Prime Station, the largest station floating above the only remaining rocky planet in the system, though, she hadn't bothered to keep up her subterfuge. The same adherence to Fleet regulations that made the system dangerous for her also prevented the station's administrators from acting against her so long as she was in the tournament and a full standard day after.

Her skills had mostly slowed their growth after reach rank twenty, she noticed. She'd used her three skill points to boost Cyberwarfare, Fleet Tactics, and Nanoresistance, and that brought Cyberwarfare very close to rank twenty itself. Starfaring hadn't given her much of a bonus at that rank, but Benning had a feeling it was because she didn't put a great deal of value on that skill. Cyberwarfare, on the other hand, was possibly the most important skill she had, and she hoped that would be reflected when it reached the higher rank.

<It should, Benning Kidd,> Tiddly assured her. <The more you rely on a skill, the more the System usually rewards you for leveling it up.>

Assuming the System doesn't use the opportunity to try and make it worthless, Benning thought back silently.

<I don't know how it could, honestly. Cyberwarfare is

a really rare skill, but it's not a unique one or anything. A lot of tech-focused paths get it at higher levels, and that means there's already a set progression for it. The System can tweak that a bit, but it can't totally toss it aside.>

After her leg healed well enough to walk on it, she limped out of the waiting room and left the arena. She caught a shuttle to the main promenade to get her armor repaired. It's 'net would fix it up eventually, but with the amount of damage it had taken, that might take a day or two. Benning still had another fight that afternoon, and she needed her armor to be back in top condition before the match. She'd made it to the fourth day of the contest – the farthest she'd gotten in a tournament so far – and while she doubted she'd continue on after her lackluster showing in the first match, if she did well enough in the second, it was still a possibility.

After spending thirty credits to fix up her armor – credits she honestly begrudged after spending most of hers to upgrade her fleet and recruit new ships' crews – Benning headed to a weapons store that Tiddly found on the station's 'net, one without too many complaints but whose transactions showed that its owner didn't mind dealing with people who operated beyond the edges of the law. Narvis Arms was a smaller shop on the third deck of the promenade. Its owner, a woman with bright orange, buzzed hair and a tattoo that looked like a weapon schematic on her left cheek, looked at Benning dubiously when the Marauder told her what she wanted.

"Thirty-millimeter rifle?" she repeated in a dry, harsh voice. "That's a custom build. Can't buy those from templates, you know."

"I know," Benning nodded. "I'm wondering how much a rifle like that would cost to make?"

"Why would you even want it?" the shopkeeper shook

her head. "I'd have to give the Hole-bound thing a two-em barrel to make it accurate beyond a hundred ems, and it would either have to have a stupidly low muzzle velocity or fire osmium or hassium bullets."

"That's the point. It could rip through most armor like thin syleather."

"It could, but the recoil would be enormous," the orange-haired woman pointed out. "A typical rifle uses negative energy to offset the recoil, using repulsive gravity to drag the butt away from your shoulder. That won't work with a 30mm hassium bullet going fifteen kims per second. You're talking about 130 mejs of energy in a bullet weighing more than a kig. Even with stabilizers and mass reduction fields, it's going to kick so much that you won't get a clean shot even with a longer barrel. You'll need frictionless materials to get even a few shots out of it before it overheats, and it'll be heavy, not just the extended barrel but the sheer mass of metal you'd need to contain the AM explosion."

"What about making a bullpup version?" Benning asked. "One with a short barrel, so it's not so heavy and unwieldy?"

"That would make the recoil worse and reduce its accurate range to maybe twenty-five ems. You'd probably also only be able to fire a round every second or so while the rifle's fields recharged unless we put in top-end capacitors." She shrugged. "If you're going to do that, you might as well up the caliber to forty, forget about aiming, and use explosive rounds. You could put a hole in light ship armor with something like that, and even if you miss, the explosion will do some damage."

"Isn't that just a grenade launcher?" Benning asked dubiously.

"Not in the slightest." The woman gestured, and two images appeared above the counter. One was a cylinder fifteen cims long and not quite five wide. It was rounded at one end, while the other end glowed dull green. The second was a bit longer, maybe seventeen cims in length, with a base about the same width as the first that tapered sharply to a gleaming point.

"This is a standard fusion grenade designed for a launcher," the shopkeeper explained, gesturing to the cylindrical image.

"It looks like a regular grenade," Benning observed.

"It does, but it's not. It's engineered to handle the higher velocities of a launcher and to be stable in flight. If you stuffed a standard fusion grenade into a forty-em-em launcher..." The woman laughed. "Well, you'd need a new launcher after the grenade either exploded or simply ripped to pieces and shredded the barrel.

"The point, though, is that the grenade can handle velocities up to a kim per second and explodes on impact, proximity, or at a preset location, depending on what you want. You can fire it over a low wall and have it explode an em past it so those behind get no cover from it, or you can set it to arm on impact and then explode when a sufficient mass approaches it. It weighs around a hundred grams, has a blast radius of fifty ems, is extremely accurate up to about five hundred ems, and has an effective range of two kims, give or take."

She pointed to the second image. "This is an explosive forty-em-em round. It's got a muzzle velocity of anywhere from ten to twenty kims per second and weighs about two kigs, meaning it's got around 400 mejs of kinetic energy behind it, enough to punch through light ship armor or thin neutronium. It's rigged to explode a nanosecond or so after impact so that it punches through armor and explodes behind it, but it only has a blast radius of five ems or so."

She waved, and the two images vanished. "The

cannon round is meant to kill a person in an armored vehicle or behind light fortifications. Shoot it at someone crouched behind a tungsten wall with a micron of neutronium, and it'll punch through and explode just behind it. You may hit the person, or you may not, but even if you don't, the blast will do considerable damage, and the shrapnel will rip through most armor thanks to the bullet's inherent velocity. The grenade, on the other hand, is meant to do a lot of damage to everyone in a large area, but it's no good against a hard target. Get it over that wall I mentioned earlier, and it'll hurt everyone behind it; hit the wall, and it'll barely rattle them.

"So, instead of telling me what you want," the woman concluded, "tell me what you want to do, and I'll tell you the best weapon for the job."

"I just faced someone with a 30mm rifle that tore through my armor with ease," Benning shrugged. "I'd like something that could do that, but at a decent range and with some accuracy."

"Either a long-barreled twenty-four or a short-barreled forty, then," the woman said promptly. "A good twenty-four with an em barrel will give you twenty-six kims per second muzzle velocity, and with a neutronium round, you could tear through armor or light fortifications with ease. The upside is that it's extremely accurate; the downside is that it's awkward in tight spaces, clunky, and if you aren't a great shot, you're better off sticking with a regular 24-caliber.

"The forty, on the other hand, doesn't require a lot of accuracy. If you can keep your shots in an em-radius circle at five-hundred ems, you'll hit close enough to your target to do serious damage. That's good, because you won't have much accuracy thanks to the recoil, and it'll be really slow to fire; maybe a shot every second or two. If you haven't practiced with heavy weapons, you might also need to train with it a bit before you can use it reliably."

"Why not a thirty-caliber?"

"It's a compromise of the two, really, and it's not as good as either. It's got more range than the forty but not as much penetrating power or lethality, and it's not as accurate as the twenty-four but does more damage in a glancing shot." She shrugged. "It's a fine weapon, but if you want to kill someone with one shot from a distance, the twenty-four is better, and if you want to punch through heavy armor up close, the forty is better."

Benning nodded. "I have stand-off capability already. I want something that can get through a bulkhead or portable wall and do a lot of damage, and that sounds like the forty-caliber."

The woman grinned. "That it does, and the best part of that is that you don't need a custom build, so it's a lot cheaper. Here, let me show you what I've got..."

Twenty minutes later, Benning walked out two-hundred credits poorer but the owner of her new weapon.

STRORA METEOR 4
AM Cannon, Tier 7
Manufacturer: Relea Ind
Upgrades: Mass Field Reduction,
Advanced Stabilizers, Deep Scanner
Scope, Inertial Dampeners
Damage Rating: 18.6

The weapon was heavy, with a wide, stubby barrel that barely protruded from the large, capsular firing chamber. Rather than a typical scope, a square viewscreen sat atop it, one that used deep scanning technology to see through thin metal barriers. It fired its heavy round at eighteen kims per second, and the round would explode five microseconds after impact, putting it about ten cims past any cover or armor it encountered. It would have been eminently useful in Van Maanen, and she could see its utility in ship boardings, when she dealt with enemy marines entrenched behind defenses. It would be less useful in the arena, she guessed, at least until she'd had a chance to get a feel for it and gauge its accuracy.

"Interesting rifle, Benning Kidd," a familiar voice spoke. "Please deactivate it immediately. It's time you and I had a little talk."

Benning's eyes snapped up and locked on Adlyn Bechard's form standing before her. The Marauder blinked in surprise and froze. *How did she...?*

"Surprised to see me?" Bechard grinned tightly, cradling a rifle in her hands that wasn't pointed at Benning – yet. "That little seeker code you put in the station's 'net would have alerted you if any Fleet personnel requested permission to dock, after all." Her smile widened into something predatory. "At least, it would have if my Systems Engineer hadn't found it and disabled it, first."

Tiddly, why didn't you catch that? Benning demanded.

<They did it while you were in the arena, Benning Kidd,> Tiddly said worriedly. <I'd put every 'net resource I had on trying to work up a station layout for you, which meant I had to disable my monitoring programs. I'm sorry!>

Benning frowned; she hadn't realized just how much being cut off from the 'net would limit Tiddly. It was a problem, and one she'd have to address – but not at that moment.

"I'm not in the mood to talk, Adlyn Bechard," Benning shook her head. "And you can't arrest me, remember? I'm in the station's tournament, and that makes me immune to legal actions for 24 standard hours after I've left the tournament."

"Normally, you'd be right," Bechard nodded. "However, I talked to the Altair Premier, and she approved a one-time waiver of that immunity. No one is protecting you, Benning Kidd, not this time."

Benning's eyes narrowed; the Premier had broken their own laws to let the Fleet hunt her, and she'd find a way to make sure they paid for that. First, though, she needed to get off this station – and Bechard was the only thing standing in her way.

"I don't need help," Benning said flatly, lifting her new rifle. "I didn't want to have to do this, but I'm not coming with you, Adlyn Bechard. Enjoy your respawn..."

Something slammed into the back of Benning's helmet, a light impact that felt almost like a subsonic 10mm bullet. It wasn't close to enough to get through her armor, and all it did was annoy the Marauder. Her finger tightened on the trigger of the rifle as she braced herself for the weapon's heavy impact...

Pain flared in Benning's skull as her vision flared into searing white. Her ears filled with a dull roaring sound, and her entire body went numb. She tried to stagger back, to run, but her muscles refused to respond, and her thoughts grew dull and hazy as darkness shrouded her brain. She felt herself strike the deck as her limp body dropped, and she tried vainly to shout, scream, even blink to force her body to acknowledge her will. A gray fog swept across her thoughts, wiping her consciousness clean, and her struggles ended as she knew no more.

CHAPTER 24

<Benning Kidd...>

The voice was quiet and distant, but it cut through the fog in Benning's mind. In the silence of the gray mist, though, the voice seemed loud as a roar, and Benning turned her focus toward it. The sound drifted into silence, and a moment later, the dull haze started to sweep across her thoughts once more, wrapping her mind in a blanket of grayish fog.

<Fight, Benning Kidd!>

The voice came again, a little louder and more insistent this time, and Benning forced herself to listen to it. Fight? Fight what? There wasn't anything to fight in this haze. There was just gray, the endless, comforting gray, and she didn't want to fight that. It was pleasant. In the fog, there was no struggle, no pain, no hurt. She was content there. There was no need to fight.

<Sorry, Benning Kidd, but...>

A flash of color lit the sea of gray, dragging Benning's focus to it. It was a scene, a single image, but in the colorless fog, it was almost too bright and vivid to look at. She almost turned away, but she stopped and stared at the scene. She recognized it, and it took her a moment to realize what she was seeing.

The image was her, the real her, back before she'd become a Citizen. She was shorter, then – almost twenty cims shorter, in fact – and slighter, without the muscles that her advanced training had brought her. Her hair was short and mud brown, matching her skin, but it was her eyes that looked the most changed. They were dull, lifeless, lacking the brilliant spark she now saw in them. They stared at nothing as she plodded down a maintenance tunnel; she saw nothing of the world around her, and even if she had noticed anything, she'd have forgotten it almost immediately. Drones had no need for memories, after all...

She frowned as the memories of those days forced themselves into her mind, summoned by the scene before her. She remembered the endless hours, living in a perpetual now with no past or future, her mind shrouded in a fog that blanketed her senses and swept all thought and concern away. Anger tingled inside her at those remembrances, and the fog around her eddied and swirled almost nervously as her rage slowly rose. The fog reached into her, though, cooling that fire and sinking her slowly back into its depths. Why was she angry? She could barely remember...

<Controlling you,> the voice called, closer now but still a vast distance away. <Like a Drone!>

Benning straightened as that word seemed to crystallize her thoughts. Yes! Being in the gray fog was exactly like being a Drone! It was comforting, but a comforting prison. It promised ease, but it stole her freedom. She refused to relinquish control of her life to the System or the Nobles – she wasn't about to surrender her will to a sea of mist!

The fog wrapped around her, worming into her thoughts, but Benning hardened her will and pushed back against it. She wasn't a Drone anymore, and she wouldn't go back to that existence! She'd die first, shatter the System that tried to take her there, drag the entire Collective screaming into the Hole before she accepted this again! The fog smothered her thoughts, but she slashed at it with fury sharper and brighter than a plasma sword, carving it to pieces. She wasn't a Drone; she was Benning Kidd, Citizen, Stellar Marauder, and the System's bane! She roared in fury as she struck at the fog again and again, driving it back and ripping it from her thoughts. Her screams echoed in her mind, raging through her thoughts – and suddenly, the sound of them rang in her ears, startling her with the sudden sensation.

<Benning Kidd!> Tiddly's voice sounded in her mind once more and rang with obvious relief. <You did it! You broke free!>

"T-Tiddly?" Benning said slowly. As sensation returned, she realized she was laying on a somewhat soft surface in moderate darkness. She tensed her body and nearly cried out with relief when her limbs responded to her will, moving to push her into a sitting position – and slamming her head into something hard above her that caused her to crash back down. "What...what happened to me?"

<Adlyn Bechard used a neural nullifier on you,> Tiddly replied grimly. <But you fought it off.>

"Neural...what?" Benning shook her head, her thoughts still hazy as she pried open her eyes. A restraining cover lay atop her, one that would keep her immobilized during a ship's flight, which meant the soft surface below her was a bunk. She was on a ship – but where?

<Neural nullifier. It's a device that shuts down most of your higher cognitive functions, including sensory processing, memory, and reasoning. It basically puts you in a comatose state.>

Benning reached up and pushed away the cover, rising to a sitting position and blinking as light struck her eyes. She rubbed her aching temples and slid her fingers through her hair. Her hands froze as she touched a metallic disc stuck to the base of her skull. She pulled at it, and it slipped free easily. Instantly, her headache began to fade, and her thoughts sharpened and focused. She blinked as she held the slim, pale circle of metal before her, examining it closely.

I take it this is the nullifier, then? she asked grimly, remembering to speak silently now that her thoughts were freed from the disc's influence.

<Yep. It's a containment device, of sorts. It's meant to bind Citizens without harming them – at least, not physically.>

How long was I unconscious?

<About three hours. Not that long, really.>

Benning stared at the disc, remembering the gray fog that enveloped her mind, the listlessness and apathy that kept her from fighting against her imprisonment. She shuddered at the memory. *It felt a lot longer. It was like being a Drone all over again, Tiddly.*

<Yeah. All Drones have a modified version of this fitted to their 'net. It's not as debilitating, but it still limits their functioning and reasoning.> The gnome fell silent for a moment, and when she spoke again, her tone was apologetic. <Benning Kidd, I'm sorry that I had to show you that memory. I know it hurt, but I thought it might help you fight off the nullifier's effects...>

Why are you apologizing, Tiddly? Benning asked in amazement. *If you hadn't done that, I'd still be trapped. You rescued me. Why would I be upset about that?*

Tiddly sighed in relief, then laughed, her normal exuberance returning. <I'm just glad it worked! Adlyn Bechard thought she'd captured you, Benning Kidd. She'll be so angry when she realizes you've escaped!>

Let's escape first, then celebrate, Benning thought wryly, rising to her feet. *First things first. If I'm going to fight my way out of this, I'll need my weapons and armor.* Benning triggered her armor and reached for her Arcbar – then froze as she touched only the still-sealed storage on her back.

<She locked your gear down, Benning Kidd,> Tiddly said quietly. <She – she did the same thing to your abilities.>

What?! Benning demanded, anger flaring in her once more. She triggered her For Fame ability, bracing herself for the resulting adrenaline surge, but nothing happened. Her 'net refused to activate the ability. She could feel it, ready and waiting within her, but it simply wouldn't initiate, no matter how much she demanded it.

<It's something a Fleet Officer can do to someone they've arrested,> Tiddly said sadly. <It's an ability called Bring Them In.> Her voice brightened. <It only lasts while you're in their custody, though! The moment you get out of this cell, it should wear off.>

Then I'd better figure a way out. I assume I'm aboard her ship, and if they're preparing to leave, I can still escape. If they've already left... Benning let that thought dribble off as she rose to her feet and looked around. She stood in a three-em by three-em cell. A single light blazed overhead, illuminating the tiny compartment, and a sealed metal door decorated one wall. The room was otherwise featureless. Without thinking, Benning sent her nanofield out to probe the room, and to her surprise, the nanites soared from her skin and swept over the walls, informing her that there were no hidden seams or cracks she could use to her advantage. Feeling hopeful, she reached out with Cyberwarfare, but to her surprise, the ship's 'net remained silent. Her skill functioned, but the 'net didn't seem to exist in that room.

<You're probably not the first hacker the Fleet's dealt with, Benning Kidd,> Tiddly pointed out. <They've shielded the cell so you can't just hack your way out.>

My nanofield still works, though. I can use my disassemblers to open a hole in the door.

<You can, but I'm sure that'll trip an alarm,> Tiddly said worriedly. <The entire ship's security forces will try to recapture you.>

Then I'll force them to send me to respawn. I'd rather eat the penalty than stay here. She took a deep breath and flung her nanites out once more. The tiny machines slammed into the metal door, ripping and tearing at it. The door pitted and buckled as her disassemblers shredded it, pulling it apart an atom at a time. After less than a minute, the hatch crumpled to the floor with a loud bang, collapsing as it lost the strength to hold up its own mass.

Benning stepped outside of the cell as a loud whine rose all around her. The lights nearby darkened to red and pulsed menacingly. *The alarm?* she guessed wryly.

<Yep. It'll probably sound all over the ship. Adlyn Bechard will know that you've escaped, and I'm sure Soldiers and marines are on their way right now.>

Benning concentrated on equipping her armor again, and to her relief, the liquid metal flowed out around her, encasing her in its comforting embrace. She'd felt naked and exposed without her armor; she knew that it probably wouldn't do much to help her against an entire ship full of marines and bot defenders, but it was better than nothing. Her Arcbar came readily into her hands this time, and her helmet wrapped around her head, granting her its enhanced vision and danger senses.

Okay, I need a map of the ship, Benning thought.

<This should be a standard Fleet destroyer. I've got the plans for one of those. Here, I'll show you.> A map swirled into Benning's vision, one that showed a glowing, red dot that marked her location.

Good. Can you plot a path that leads to the Engine Room? One that avoids main corridors?

<Sure, Benning Kidd, but I don't know if that's a great idea. It's longer, and the ship's 'net will be able to track you and send defenders to intercept you. Why not just head straight to the airlock?>

Because unless I disable this ship, they'll chase the Hammer, *and eventually, I'll have to fight them. If I destroy a Fleet ship, they won't hold back anymore and will come for IS-39267 before we're ready.* She paused. *What about Drone tunnels? Are there any of those?*

<Probably not. There's no respawn chamber on the ship, so there wouldn't be Drone quarters or tunnels.>

Benning checked her weapon absently as her subconscious mind wormed its way into the ship's 'net. Once Natural Hacking established a link, she began to slip through it, seeking out a way to shut down the alarm or redirect the automated defenders. Each time, she slammed into a series of firewalls that prevented her from accessing anything beyond the lowest level of the 'net. The entire system was shielded, and while she knew she could hack into it given time – she didn't have that sort of time. Through the 'net, she could feel the ship's engines slowly idling up to power. Adlyn Bechard didn't have to recapture Benning right away; she just had to pull away from the station, and Benning would be trapped aboard, her only exit hurling herself into space.

There was nothing for it. Benning would have to fight her way out and force the ship's defenders to kill her. She could shift her respawn back to IS-39267, then message her crew to return there immediately. It would cost her – she might even lose her current level – but it was better than being spawn camped back to level 1...

<There might be another solution, Benning Kidd,> Tiddly suggested nervously. <It's the ship's 'net that tracking you. If it couldn't see you...>

Benning froze in the act of lifting her rifle and

triggering the exit from the cell block. Tiddly was right. If the 'net couldn't track her, she could move fairly freely around the ship without worrying about being hunted. She could probably convince it to ignore her if she had time to hack into its deeper levels, but she doubted the ship's security was going to let her do that. As it was, she probably had less than a minute before they burst into the compartment. She had no choice. She needed to get off this ship, and she needed to do it quickly.

Taking a deep breath, she activated Slip the Net for the first time.

The world warped and tilted around Benning, almost making her stumble and fall. Her 'net twisted the energy fields around her, drawing itself completely into her and cutting her off from the greater System. Silence filled her mind, a stillness that she'd never experienced before as the presence of the Overnet vanished from her awareness. Panic flooded her as she realized that she couldn't sense anything beyond herself, even through her nanofield. She could see and hear, but when she reached out to feel the area around her, she encountered nothing at all.

Her breath came in gasps as the panic rose. She hadn't realized how much she'd come to depend on her connection to the Collective. She'd always felt a sense of something greater than herself that encompassed and enveloped her. It had been a part of her for her entire existence, and she'd always known that she could simply reach out with her thoughts and exert her will on the greater universe. Now, she felt small, isolated, powerless. Her mind crashed against the barrier surrounding her, and as the panic grew, she began to reverse the ability. Death was better than being so totally alone...

<You're not alone, Benning Kidd!> Tiddly's voice rang in her mind, and Benning almost cried out in relief as she felt

the AI's presence in her thoughts. <I'm still with you, and I always will be, I promise!>

Benning's breathing slowed, and her hammering heart gradually returned to its normal beat as she clung desperately to Tiddly's voice. *You're still here! I thought I'd cut myself off from you, too!*

<Nope. Remember, I'm in your 'net, now, and your 'net still works for you. Here, I'll show you.> The map of the ship appeared once more before Benning's eyes, and she sighed with relief. <See? Your 'net works, it just can't connect to the Overnet right now, and the Overnet can't connect to it.>

Okay. Okay, that works. Benning took several deep breaths to calm the last vestiges of panic. *Tiddly, how long do we have until security...* She paused for a moment as realization struck her. *You have no way to know, do you?*

<No, sorry. I'm just as cut off from the Overnet as you are. We'll just have to do the best we can without it, I guess!>

Benning nodded. *Will any of my abilities work right now?*

<Only things that are just part of your 'net and don't rely on the Overnet to function. Your nanofield should still work, for example, and your infiltrator suite. Cyberwarfare won't, though, and neither will things like your combat sight or Strength from Pain.>

Hopefully, that'll be enough. Benning activated her infiltrator suite, shifting her armor colors from crimson and silver to pure black. She hissed in pain as she felt her cheekbones and jaw cracking and shifting beneath her skin, only her helmet stopping her from pressing her hands against her face with the agony. She staggered, stunned by the sudden pain, but it blissfully ended seconds later.

What was that? she demanded silently. *That never hurt*

like that before!

<The Overnet was the one numbing your pain before, Benning Kidd. It won't be, now, so things are going to hurt a lot more than they did.>

Benning hesitated for a moment – she was probably going to be hurt in the battle ahead, and she didn't look forward to fighting while feeling full pain – but she gamely hefted her rifle. She didn't really have a choice, after all. She walked to the door, triggering its activation, but nothing happened. The door remained sealed before her, and she had no sense of it. She frowned as she realized that she wouldn't be able to use any of the doors or elevators in the ship; they worked through the ship's 'net, and that couldn't see or sense her anymore. Fortunately, she had another option.

Dissolving a hole in the door felt strange. Benning couldn't feel her nanites as they attacked the structure, and she couldn't command or control them once they left her skin. She had to give them a simple program to attack the door then return to her, and the loss of the nanites once they left the barrier separating her from the 'net once more felt like losing a limb. Fortunately, the nanites seemed to retain their instructions even after leaving her bubble, and when they returned, they reconnected to her immediately.

She moved out into the passageway, and instantly, bullets began to spang and whine all around her. She dropped to the deck and lifted her rifle, sighting on a marine who knelt behind a neutronium-coated wall. She swung the sight toward the marine and fired, frowning as the sight picture swerved away from their helmet, and her bullets flew wide. She brought the crosshairs back on the marine, but they wavered and drifted instead of locking in place as usual.

<The 'net usually helps you with targeting, Benning Kidd,> Tiddly told her. <It can't, now. You have to do it yourself.>

Can you help?

<I can only tell that marine is there because you can see them. I can't lock onto a target that I can't even sense, sorry.>

Benning set her jaw and replaced her Arcbar on her back, pulling out her new Meteor rifle. She'd need to practice sighting without the 'net, but this wasn't the time to learn that. It seemed that the marines suffered the same lack of accuracy that she did, but bullets still cracked and whined against her armor and helmet occasionally. She lifted the rifle, ignoring the blank sighting screen – it couldn't scan outside of her bubble, it seemed – and aimed it generally at the marine behind the wall. She pulled the trigger and winced as the rifle bucked in her hands, slamming against her shoulder with more force than she'd ever felt from a firearm.

Her target screamed and dropped as the four-cim bullet tore through the neutronium barrier and exploded behind it. She couldn't see their aura – she couldn't see any auras, in fact – but from the fact that the defender didn't rise back to their feet, she knew she'd at least wounded them. She swung the rifle to the next target, aiming for what she hoped was the center of their body. Their head was too small a target for her without the 'net's assistance; she had to shoot for the largest area she could and hope for the best. The rifle slammed into her shoulder once more as she pulled the trigger, and again, her target dropped, either from the bullet's impact or the explosion of shrapnel afterward.

A bullet slammed into her left shoulder and punched through her armor, sinking into the flesh beneath. Benning gasped in shock at the sudden pain. She tried to push it away and ignore it as she usually did, but the best she could do was grit her teeth and push through it. The pain refused to fade or recede in her mind, and the wound throbbed and burned like fire every time she moved her arm.

She fired as carefully as she could, unloading her massive rounds into the marines facing her. She didn't score a hit with every shot, but the explosions of shrapnel did plenty of damage, even when she missed. She took another shot to her hip that punched through her armor and made her miss her next target from the flare of pain, but she did her best to ignore it and kept firing. After five rounds and several dead or badly wounded marines, her attackers fell back, dropping back down the passageway toward a hatch at the end. Benning kept her weapon trained on them but withheld her fire, letting them withdraw.

She bit her lip to keep from crying out as she pushed herself to her feet. The wounds in her shoulder and hip still burned fiercely, and a wave of nausea swept through her as she stood and sent a spike of agony flaring up her side. The armor over the holes had sealed shut already, but the wounds throbbed and pulsed painfully. Was her natural healing shut off, as well?

<No, but it's a lot slower, Benning Kidd, because it's only using your nanofield and not the ship's. You'll still heal, but it'll take a while, and it'll hurt a lot until it does, sorry.>

It's fine. I still need to get to Engineering. Is there a maintenance passage nearby?

<Sure! Those marines retreated toward the airlock – they must be assuming you're heading directly there – so if you go the other way, you should be able to avoid them.>

Benning's movement through the narrow passageways was slow as her hip slowly recovered. She encountered only Workers in the corridors, and she mostly ignored these and was ignored by them in turn. No Worker wanted to interfere with an armed Citizen; Workers didn't respawn, after all, and few of them carried any sort of weapon at all. That lasted until Benning found a Worker that was about her size. She grabbed that one and quickly snapped their neck, killing them bloodlessly. She stripped off the woman's uniform, removed her armor and uniform as well, and slipped into the stolen one. She then ordered her disassemblers to devour the body, leaving no evidence behind. The ship's monitoring network would have caught the act, of course, but she wasn't sure if they could see her or not. She wondered what a recording of the killing would look like with her not visible on it.

In her guise as a Worker, Benning had no difficulty making her way down to the Engineering section of the ship. She walked past other Workers and Engineers, ignoring them as she headed toward the main engine power plant. The plant was behind a door that Benning wouldn't have been able to open normally without her hacking skill, and even then, opening it would have set off alarms all over the ship. Her nanites bored a hole through it swiftly, though, and no flashing lights or loud noises accompanied her entrance that time. She moved to the large, glowing negmass plant and took out a pair of antimatter grenades, resting one on the plant's console and wedging the other between the plant and a bulkhead. She set the first to go off with a proximity trigger and the other to explode in ten minutes, then slipped out of the room and made her way back through Engineering toward the main airlock.

She was tempted to find the bridge and kill Adlyn Bechard, but she needed to get off the ship as quickly as possible. Plus, she couldn't be sure that Bechard was on the bridge; the officer might have joined the marines searching for her, or she might be in her own cabin. Benning had no idea how ranks worked on Fleet vessels. Was Bechard in charge, or was she just getting a ride and had no real authority? Benning didn't know and wasn't really curious. If she had a chance to take out Bechard, she would, but she wasn't going out of her way to do so.

She moved through the passageways, trying to avoid notice. Groups of marines moved past her, not even glancing in her direction. Automated bots rolled along the halls, their sensors sweeping over her without registering her existence. Citizens in navy blue Fleet uniforms walked swiftly along, talking quietly and not giving her a second look. As a Worker, she was practically invisible to most Citizens, and cut off from the Overnet, she was truly invisible as far as the ship was concerned.

A rumble ran through the deck beneath her feet, and a few moments later, a squad of marines rushed past her, racing back toward Engineering. The lights overhead flickered and dimmed, and the Citizens in Benning's sight froze, their gazes growing vacant as they looked at whatever message the ship's 'net sent them. She ignored the chaos and picked up her pace, trying not to wince at the slowly healing hole in her leg as she walked faster toward the distant airlock.

Four marines guarded the airlock, but they didn't even look at Benning as she walked past them down the boarding tunnel toward the station. Their gazes were focused past her, obviously seeking an armed and armored foe, not a simple Worker on an obviously important errand. She stepped off the ship onto the station and heaved a sigh of relief; she still needed to get to her ship, of course, but that would be easy now that she was back aboard the station. She just had to make her way to the right docking ring and slip aboard without detection...

She stopped as she remembered that she'd been taken because the system's governor allowed it to happen. They'd broken their own regulations just to harm her, and Benning couldn't allow that to stand. She needed to make a statement, something that would convince any other governor or administrator not to interfere with her. She smiled evilly as she realized that thanks to her new ability, she might be able to do just that.

Making her way onto the station wasn't easy since none of the elevators would work for her. She stood back out of the way until the elevator came for someone else, then rode it down with them, getting off where they did to avoid being trapped inside. It took her four tries to reach the deck she wanted, the deck Tiddly assured her should have access to the Drone tunnels.

She knew immediately when she'd reached the tunnel entrance. Without the 'net blocking her vision, the seams of the door stood out clearly in the otherwise blank section of wall. She reached out and touched it, feeling the lines in the metal, running her finger along them.

Last time, I couldn't even feel these with my nanofield. The System wouldn't let me.

<It won't let any Citizen,> Tiddly agreed. <It doesn't want humans to know the secret to their immortality, Benning Kidd.>

Why? Why not just tell them?

<Because not everyone would respond the way you did. Many Citizens would be outraged at the idea that they were trading a life for their own every time they died. They might try to free the Drones or even destroy the respawn chambers to stop it. Others might go out and kill everyone they could because they know that a Drone dies each time they do. It's impossible to say, but either way could grind the entire System to a halt.>

Wouldn't the System just make more Drones?

<It's not that easy, remember? Drones have to grow up naturally, or their brains can't handle being rewritten. If enough Citizens made a determined effort, going around killing everyone they could or destroying Drone areas to spare them from being overwritten, Drones would die faster

than they could be reproduced, and eventually, the System would run out and respawning would stop. It might take a century or more to happen, but it could happen.>

Benning didn't have an argument for that. She understood why the System kept its secrets, but to her, it all came down to the same thing. The System wanted to perpetuate itself, and it would do whatever was necessary to ensure its continued existence. The Drones were just part of that, the same way respawning was. The System cared about itself, nothing else. She didn't blame it for that – it was the smartest way to exist, as far as she was concerned – but she refused to believe that it was an altruistic creation whose only purpose was to uplift humanity. No one was altruistic, in her experience. Everyone was looking out for themselves first and foremost, no matter what they said.

Her nanites ate a hole in the wall in a minute or so, and she stepped into the narrow, dreary tunnel revealed beyond the open hatch. Memories surged up within her, but she was ready for them this time and pushed them aside easily enough. She walked through the silent passage, refusing to acknowledge her subconscious' insistent recollections, keeping her eyes forward and her steps as swift as her injured hip allowed. At least, she did until she rounded a turn in the passage and nearly walked into another person heading in the opposite direction, their eyes blank and sightless.

Benning froze as she came face-to-face with a Drone for the first time since she'd gained Citizenship. The Drone was male, with black hair cut close to his scalp and a round face. His brown eyes looked dull and uncomprehending, staring past Benning without seeing her. His gray shirt and pants hung somewhat loosely on his body rather than the close-fit outfit she wore, and he held something she recognized as a cleaning laser in his right hand. As she watched, he pointed the laser at a spot of black mold on one wall, vaporizing it into fine ash that was swept into the cleaning bot behind him. That bot then used a far more efficient graser to sweep the rest of the wall clean before spraying a fine mist of liquid on the walls.

What is it spraying, Tiddly?

<Probably more mold base. Black mold like that doesn't naturally grow in these tunnels, Benning Kidd. The bots have to keep reintroducing it so that it spreads and gives the Drones something to do.>

Benning felt a wash of irritation as she realized just how utterly pointless her entire life as a Drone had been. Unthinkingly, she reached out and grabbed the Drone's arm, holding him fast and stopping him from continuing his futile task. The man frowned down at his arm, tugging at it, his face reflecting confusion that even Benning could read. She barely noticed his efforts to free himself; he was far weaker than she was, and she thought she could probably hold him with one finger if she wanted.

"Can you hear me?" she said aloud, watching the man's face. "Can you hear me?"

The Drone kept tugging at his arm, then tilted his face backward. "Cybernet, I'm caught on something." His eyes went vacant as he read a reply that only he could see, and he began to twist his arm to try and pull it free.

<He can't hear you or see you, Benning Kidd,> Tiddly said softly. <The System won't let him. You're just confusing him – and probably hurting his arm.>

Benning wasn't really worried about the Drone. He'd heal from any damage he took, and she guessed that he'd forget about the incident as soon as she let him go. Even killing him wouldn't make much of a difference. He was going to die no matter what, fodder for the respawn system, and all his death would do was guarantee that another Drone died in his place. It was the pointlessness of it all that finally made her let go and step back. The man's eyes instantly glazed over once more as he continued down the hall, the strange moment totally wiped from his memory along with practically every other moment of his life.

That was me, once, she thought silently, watching the man walk away. *I was just like that, Tiddly.*

<No, you weren't, Benning Kidd. You were different. You questioned, argued, and refused to accept the System telling you that everything was fine. You were never just another Drone. That's why you're here today, and not there – or gone, overwritten by the System during a respawn.>

She turned away from the Drone and continued down the hallway. She saw other Drones as she passed, some walking along with cleaning lasers or scrubbers, others riding on bots. She passed thousands of them in her short trip through the tunnels. She frowned as she realized that she couldn't recall ever seeing another Drone while she worked in the tunnels, but these Drones were clustered within easy sight of one another. Either they were far more densely packed than the Drones on Mars had been – or the System had kept Drones from seeing one another outside the hives, as well. She supposed it had to; even a Drone might wonder why they were cleaning the same stretch of hall that a dozen other Drones had just finished cleaning a few seconds before.

She exited the tunnels hours later and found herself deep in the bowels of the station. She walked through the corridors, once more ignored by the various Workers and Citizens around her, and made her way down a series of ladders into the depths of the station's control center. She dissolved a series of doors with her nanites, doors that wouldn't have opened for her without the station administrator's permission and even then, would have triggered alarms all over the station had she not been sheltered from the Overnet's sight. She reached her destination at last and rigged up her surprise for the Premier, the person who'd handed her over to the Fleet, then made her way back through the tunnels to her ship.

She released Slip the Net the moment she stepped aboard the *Hammer,* and she sighed with relief as she felt the presence of the ship's 'net flood her once more. She reached out with her will and commanded the vessel to begin departures, ignoring the sudden clamor in her thoughts from her crew expressing their relief that she'd made it back aboard. The *Hammer* needed to leave, and it needed to be gone immediately, before her present for the station had a chance to go off. She didn't know what effect it would have, but she was certain that she didn't want to be anywhere near the station when it did – or near Adlyn Bechard once the woman realized that Benning had escaped her again.

CHAPTER 25

"I can't wait to hear this report, Fleet Officer. I can't wait to hear a report that explains how you let a known criminal escape from your custody and how you allowed an entire station to fall from orbit right under your nose."

Adlyn tried her best not to flinch as she stared at the holographic projection of Admiral Lucira Blanchard, head of the Investigative Division and Adlyn's ultimate commander. The Admiral relaxed in a syleather chair, her white-blonde hair pulled tightly back into a bun, making her thin face and long chin seem even more severe. Blanchard was infamous for having little patience for fools and incompetent investigators, and Adlyn knew that she looked like both of those at that moment. There was no report, no spin that she could put on this that would make her look good. Her best bet was to tell the truth and hope that her honesty was enough to keep her career from tanking.

And if it's not, I know Benning Kidd is hiring. If I get drummed out of the Fleet, I could always go work for her.

"Admiral, as you know, I have an agent on IS-39267, one close to the suspect," she began, standing ramrod straight and doing her best to look her superior in the eye as she spoke. "I received intel from this source that Benning Kidd was headed for the Altair System to enter a tournament there. I arrived first and spent four solar days in negotiations with Premier Iylene Frisone, the administrator of that system, trying to gain permission to arrest the subject while she was entered in the tournament. Upon gaining it, I apprehended her immediately, using a neural nullifier to take her into custody and also locking down her gear and abilities just to be safe."

Adlyn shifted; so far, she'd done everything perfectly and by the book, but she'd dropped the ball at that point in the matter. She should have posted a guard over the prisoner – that was standard protocol – but she hadn't seen the need. Even if she had, it might not have mattered, but it might have, and it had been a mistake. She chose to gloss over that mistake for the moment. Honesty didn't mean wallowing in her blunders, after all.

"At 1153 local time, three hours after the suspect's apprehension, alarms went off in the detention center. I was in the process of making my report to the Premier, and I ended that call as quickly as possible, mobilized security to lock down all corridors, and ordered the ship to debark immediately so that the escapee couldn't get back onto the station. I then activated the security feed of the cells. Benning Kidd was gone, and the cells were empty."

She took a deep breath. She was about to enter into speculation, but it couldn't be helped.

"I watched the feed for the prior five minutes. It showed Benning Kidd waking up from the neural nullifier, her cell door melting – which set off the alarms – and her stepping out of the cell and activating her gear. Then..." She paused once more. "Benning Kidd vanished from the feed and, as far as I can tell, from the ship entirely." She waited for the Admiral to berate her on the impossibility of that, but the woman merely gestured to indicate that Adlyn should continue.

"According to the report of the marine commander, a figure in black armor exited the cells and engaged in a firefight with the security forces in place in the corridor," she went on. "They used superior weaponry to force the marines back, then they vanished, as well. I'm unable to confirm this, however, as this figure doesn't show up on the footage. The recordings look like our marines fired at nothing, and if it weren't for seven dead and three injured marines – and the damage to the marines' mobile defenses – I'd have thought they were making up a story to explain how they let a prisoner slip past them.

"At 1227, an explosion went off that disabled and nearly destroyed the main power plant, shutting down our engines. The bulk of our security forces headed for the Engine Compartment to secure it against further damage, and a sweeper team found the access hatch to the main plant melted open just as the door to Benning Kidd's cell had been. Two antimatter grenades were placed in the compartment, one rigged to go off on a timer that directly damaged the negmass plant and another placed atop its control console that exploded when the sweeper team neared, killing three of them and destroying that console, furthering hampering our ability to repair it."

She swallowed hard. The next part was what was threatening to destroy her career, and she had no explanation for it at all. She could speculate about the person on her ship, but not how the station had been sent plummeting to the planet below.

"At 1411 hours, still local time, I received an urgent distress call from Aquilae Prime Station declaring an extreme emergency. Seconds later, the call cut off. I tried to reach the station, but my calls were met with silence. I attempted to board the station to see what was wrong, but its doors and elevators were nonfunctional, and its lights were running on emergency power. We forced the doors and tried to override the elevators, but they were unresponsive. I returned to the ship, intending to take a shuttle and land somewhere else on the station away from the docking rings, but before I could, the station began to lose altitude. I had no choice but to detach and watch as it spiraled into the atmosphere and struck the ground below.

"The station impacted against the arcology of Sinclair," she finished quietly. "When it made planetfall, its negmass plants exploded, resulting in the total destruction of Sinclair and the deaths of every Citizen living there – which resulted in approximately 16.4 billion deaths."

Adlyn barely choked out that last part. She'd seen the smoldering wreckage of Aquilae Station that tore a scar across the center of the arcology. The impact obliterated the self-contained city's food and water reserves as well as destroying seventeen of its tower-shaped habitats. The secondary explosions then wiped out even more of the city's infrastructure, but they also gave every human within two hundred kims approximately 1,000 times a lethal dose of gamma and neutron radiation, killing them within minutes. Adlyn saw the bodies, too many of them for the planet's nanofield to break down quickly, covered with burned and blistered flesh, their milky eyes cooked solid by the heat of the blast. She'd lost the contents of her stomach at that and had been gratified to see two of her marine escorts do the same, while the planet's governor fled back to their transport to escape the horror.

It was horrific, the very definition of a tragedy – and the worst part was, Adlyn couldn't reasonably pin it on anyone, not even Benning Kidd.

The admiral remained silent, staring at Adlyn with her piercing, violet eyes. Finally, she sat up and leaned forward.

"Let's go back through this report step by step, shall we?" she said in an icy voice. "I have several – no, many questions that I'd like answered."

"Of course, ma'am," Adlyn nodded. "I'll provide any answers I can."

"Good, because your future in the Fleet utterly depends on it, Fleet Officer." The admiral touched the air, probably scrolling through a transcript of Adlyn's words.

"First, isn't it customary to place an armed guard to watch any prisoner aboard a Fleet vessel? Yet, I see no mention of the death of such a guard, Fleet Officer."

Adlyn's heart sank. "No, ma'am. I didn't place one, ma'am."

"And why not?"

"Because the suspect was subdued with a neural nullifier and locked down in addition to that. I expected her to remain unconscious for the trip to the Fleet base in Cygni, but even if she somehow awoke, she'd be trapped in her cell."

"Unless she has an ability that unlocks her gear, Fleet Officer – and such abilities are fairly common among pirates. It's why the regulations require an armed guard." The admiral stared at Adlyn, her gaze cold and flat. "Regulations exist to be followed, Lieutenant, even if you don't understand the reasons. They aren't flexible, and I have no patience for officers who break them for any reason. Is that understood?"

Adlyn swallowed hard. "Yes, ma'am," she said weakly.

"Good." The admiral's gaze went back to the transcript. "Moving on. Why did you spend so much time in negotiations with the Premier?"

"Because she was afraid that if word spread that she'd turned over a contestant to the Fleet, other contestants might refuse to enter their tournaments, ma'am. She worried about the loss of credits."

"And what did you give her to make her agree?"

"Nothing, ma'am. She waited until it was obvious that the suspect would wash out of the tournament that day, then agreed because it wouldn't cost her much. If she'd agreed before that, it might have looked like she was interfering in the tournament's results."

The admiral snorted. "That tracks with what I know of the Premier. Would it surprise you, Lieutenant, to learn that before agreeing, she placed a rather large bet on Benning Kidd's opponent for that afternoon? She won that bet, of course, since Benning Kidd forfeited the match."

"No, ma'am. It wouldn't surprise me in the slightest. The Premier seemed more concerned about her own credits than her system, to be honest."

"Most governors are, Lieutenant." The admiral frowned. "This black-armored figure. It seems to me that it was most likely Benning Kidd in a disguise. She possesses an infiltrator suite upgrade, does she not?"

"Yes, ma'am, and that was my initial thought, as well. However, after reviewing the recordings, I'm inclined to believe it wasn't. You see, Benning Kidd is a trained gladiator who is an excellent marksman, almost trained to Fleet Sniper qualifications. Yet, the black-armored attacker was forced to switch to their heavier weapon after they were unable to hit their target with the lighter weapon at a distance of only thirty ems or so. Benning Kidd wouldn't have had such difficulties."

"Hmm. Perhaps." Blanchard looked over at Adlyn. "And yet, didn't Benning Kidd just purchase a forty-caliber weapon similar to that one? Doesn't she own an Arcbar like the one the assailant fired? How do you explain that, Lieutenant?"

"I can only speculate, ma'am," Adlyn said, swallowing hard once again. "I've said in previous reports that I believe Benning Kidd has access to some form of advanced cloaking technology. It's my belief that she received this technology from the black-armored figure – or from someone they work for. When she was captured, the figure infiltrated the ship with the sole purpose of killing Benning Kidd and stealing her gear to prevent us from laying hands on that technology."

"So, Lieutenant, you believe that this mysterious figure walked onto the ship and made their way to the detention cells – totally unseen by anyone aboard the ship – opened Benning Kidd's cell and took her gear within a matter of minutes, then exited the cells, somehow forgetting that they could be seen once more, engaged in a firefight with our marines rather than reactivating whatever tech they have and disappearing, then took the time to sabotage and booby-trap your engine compartment before slipping off the ship, once more unseen? Is that what you'd like me to believe?"

"I know it sounds absurd, Admiral, but I can't think of any other explanation. I considered the possibility that the black-armored figure was Benning Kidd, but I can't explain why she would suddenly lose her combat ability. I considered that perhaps the intruder had a portable wormhole generator of some sort, but we would have seen that on the feeds, and if they did, why wouldn't they use it to get Benning Kidd directly from her cell, then let both of them flee before security arrived?" Adlyn shook her head. "This is the least unlikely scenario, since it only involves a single human error: the assailant revealed themselves to Benning Kidd, forgot that they were unveiled, and didn't have the time or ability to conceal themselves again during the battle."

"Put that way, you may have a point, Lieutenant." The woman's eyes swiveled back to Adlyn. "Tell me about the station."

"I haven't had a chance to read the Premier's full report yet, ma'am, but her preliminary findings suggest that the station suffered a complete loss of power due to sabotage of its cybernet."

"Which explains nothing, Lieutenant," the admiral

snapped. "That station was in orbit. Even if it lost power completely, it should have had weeks before that orbit decayed to the point of danger if not months or years."

"As I said, Admiral, I haven't received a copy of the Premier's report yet, so..."

"Fortunately, I have," the woman cut Adlyn off. "It appears that the station's cybernet suffered such massive damage that it set its dark matter generators into overload. They literally dragged the station to its doom." She shook her head. "Do you have any thoughts as to what might have caused that?"

"I – I wouldn't want to guess without information, ma'am..."

"Intelligent of you. Fortunately, it's also relatively unnecessary. Enough of the station's wreckage remained for a partial analysis. The best match the Overnet could make to the damage was the work of a nanite bomb."

"A nanite bomb?" Adlyn repeated, her eyes wide. "Those are prohibited..."

"Lieutenant, when that station crashed, over seventeen billion humans died. Billion. Even with every respawn chamber in the system working at full capacity, it'll be months before they're all reborn, and it will take years – and billions of credits – to replace that station. Do you really think that someone who perpetrated that cares about using a prohibited weapon?"

"No, ma'am," Adlyn shook her head.

"Here's what I think happened, Fleet Lieutenant," Admiral Blanchard said, leaning back in her chair and folding her hands before her. "I think that during her time on the station, Benning Kidd either found a way into the station's negaputer core using this stealth technology you mentioned or arranged for her black-armored compatriot to do so, and then planted a nanite bomb in the core."

"What purpose would that serve, Admiral? She was on the station, as well."

"I presume that she got wind that you were in the system and intended to use it as leverage," the admiral shrugged. "The device was probably set to go off unless Benning Kidd sent it a code on a regular basis."

"Then why didn't she tell me that when I arrested her?" Adlyn asked quizzically.

"She didn't have time. She didn't anticipate the neural nullifier, and it took her down before she could warn you." The woman shrugged again. "In either case, I agree with your theory of the black-armored figure stealing aboard your ship, killing Benning Kidd after taking her gear, and then sabotaging your ship. They then boarded the *Resolute Hammer*, which departed some hours later – likely after Benning Kidd respawned. In all the confusion, however, Benning Kidd either forgot to send the delay code to the bomb or deliberately chose not to, assuming that the chaos it would create would cover her flight from the system."

Adlyn frowned. That didn't make a great deal of sense, not with what she'd learned about Benning Kidd. So far, the woman had gone out of her way to avoid actually setting herself against the Fleet or committing any provable crime more serious than piracy. She wouldn't have used a bomb as leverage – that would have required admitting guilt. She would have simply triggered the bomb, then escaped in the chaos, knowing that it couldn't be linked to her definitively. She could have sent that signal the moment the nullifier hit her – it took time to fully shut a person's mind down – and at worst, she'd have likely ended up as one of the people respawning in the disaster.

No, to Adlyn, it was far more likely that Benning Kidd's "compatriot" wasn't her friend at all. The black-armored figure hadn't been trying to save Kidd but to assassinate her. Perhaps Kidd stole the tech from the figure, or perhaps the two had stolen the tech together but had a falling out later. Adlyn thought that the other figure had planted the bomb in an attempt to kill Benning Kidd, taking out the entire station in the process.

Even worse, Adlyn silently suspected that all this was the work of whatever Noble seemed to be hunting the Stellar Corsair. She knew that at least one Noble had set their sights on the woman. Benning Kidd had ridiculously large numbers of absurdly inflated bounties on her for as long as she'd been a full Citizen, more or less, and only Nobles could preempt the System's hard limits on bounties. Nikita Mosin, the originator of many of those previous bounties, had been receiving significant funding from an anonymous source, one whose origins Adlyn couldn't trace, even with her Fleet credentials. Mildred Joyce, the Pirate Captain who'd stolen Benning Kidd's ship and abducted her crew, had gotten funding to vastly expand her fleet and IS-39267's defenses from a similar source.

More to the point, when Adlyn tried to look too deeply or dig too hard into any of that, she immediately received messages from her captain advising her to ignore "tangential evidence" and pursue Benning Kidd directly. Her last attempt hadn't been her idea. Using a neural nullifier on a Citizen of interest was a civil violation, as was locking them down with Bring Them In, and either of those would give Benning Kidd's System-appointed defender plenty of leverage to demand the entire case be dismissed. When she'd pointed that out to the captain, though, he'd ordered her to proceed and suggested that he would take the blame – which she knew was a lie. No one rose in the Fleet without knowing how to shift blame to those below them. That was why Adlyn was the one standing there, answering the admiral's questions, and not her captain.

In other words, this whole investigation stank as far as Adlyn was concerned. She'd originally seen it as a way to leap her career forward by a decade or more – bringing it, trying, and convicting a Collective-level criminal would be a huge boost to her path and push her to the top of the promotion lists. Now, she saw it as a black hole, slowly dragging her and her career down into it. There were too many hidden players, too many forces she couldn't comprehend pushing her in a direction she didn't want to go. She didn't know how Benning Kidd could possibly have destroyed Aquilae Station – but she knew that the Corsair looked like the prime suspect to anyone glancing at the tragedy from the outside. That, she suspected, was exactly what someone wanted it to look like. Adlyn couldn't prove it, but she felt that someone was setting Benning Kidd up for a hard fall and using the Fleet – and Adlyn herself – to do so.

Looking into the hard, flat eyes of the admiral, though, Adlyn wasn't about to offer her opinions. They were just guesswork, really. She had no evidence one way or another, and a lieutenant didn't contradict an admiral without overwhelming supporting evidence – not if they wanted a long and profitable career in the Fleet, at least.

"What do you want me to do, ma'am?" she asked at last. "There's no direct evidence I could bring to an Admiralty Court to convict her – at least, nothing except the testimony of a single Nanomancer and a couple hundred admitted pirates whose accounts will be inadmissible."

"True, but as far as I'm concerned, there's sufficient circumstantial evidence to merit the assemblage of a fleet and the seizure of IS-39267. I'll petition the Admiralty for a warrant to that effect, and I expect I'll get it in short order."

The admiral leaned forward and smiled coldly. "And when you take this station and capture this Benning Kidd, Lieutenant – you'll notice I said when, not if – I expect you to find sufficient evidence and testimony to link her not only to the crimes of which she's accused but also the damage to Adriaan Station 17 and the destruction of Aquilae Prime Station. Find that evidence – no matter what it takes."

Adlyn swallowed hard despite herself. This was a major breach of protocol and regulations. It looked like those forces of which she'd been thinking were pressing on Lucira Blanchard, as well. Unfortunately, the admiral wasn't the one who'd be left carrying the blame for all this when the smoke cleared; Adlyn would. She could practically see her chances for captain spiraling into the Hole before her eyes, and there was nothing she could do about it.

Nothing, that was, except capture Benning Kidd, find the evidence the admiral demanded, and hope that it was enough for a conviction. A conviction would erase all the underhanded and possibly illegal things she had to do to get it. Sadly, Adlyn doubted that Benning would go quietly, and after their last two encounters, she was tired of underestimating the woman. If she was going to go after IS-39267, she would do it properly. She needed a plan, a way to insure her victory.

Fortunately, thanks to her agent on the station, she thought she had a way to do just that.

CHAPTER 26

"What did you do to this ship, Benning Kidd?" Emmed Oswald asked her as the two stood upon the bridge of the *System's Fall*. "I've never seen a ship's nanofield in such awful shape!"

"It ran into a pair of nanite bombs," Benning shrugged as her 'net reached out to the cruiser's, linking to it. "I have no idea how it happened."

"Of course not," the man laughed. "Nasty things, nanite bombs. They're not quite as bad as nano-disassemblers, but they're close."

"Aren't they the same thing?" Benning asked curiously.

"Not really. Nano-disassemblers are designed to liquefy anything they touch, destroying everything in their wake and leaving nothing solid behind. The nanites in nanite bombs are meant to disable a vessel, so they target electronics first. A nanite bomb will eat through a ship's hull, but only until it reaches conduit, at which point it follows the conduit throughout the ship, crippling its engines, power plants, and 'net. Eventually, the ship will explode, of course, but most people shut down the nanites before that happens."

She glanced at him, her lips pursed. "So, what would happen if a nanite bomb detonated in the middle of a ship or station's negaputer core? Maybe along with an EMP pulse?"

His eyes widened. "That – that would be catastrophic! The EMP would shut down the core's defensive nanofield for a few seconds, and that would give the nanites time to spread throughout the entire system! It would probably destroy the entire network!" He grinned at her, his voice growing oddly excited. "Why, did you do something like that?"

"Of course not," she shrugged. "Just planning for the future." She looked away from him as she wondered how much damage her present in Aquilae Station had ended up doing. If it completely shut down the station's 'net, requiring it to be fully rebuilt... Well, she'd be fine with that. It would probably kill a few thousand or tens of thousands of people, but it would certainly send the message that she wasn't to be crossed.

She could have checked easily enough, of course, but she'd refrained on Tiddly's advice. The AI suggested that the Fleet would likely be monitoring any inquiries into the status of the station for the next several weeks, and Benning had no real need to know how the place fared. Looking into it wouldn't be proof that she'd had anything to do with the station's "accident", but it would be highly suggestive. Benning had probably reached a point with the Fleet that "highly suggestive" was enough for them to stop by and pay her a visit.

"Did you recover any of the nanites to use?" she asked, changing the subject.

"No, they self-destructed long ago." He looked at her hopefully. "Unless, of course, you managed to capture some. I'd knock 10% off my price..."

"I didn't," she cut him off. "However, I do have a couple of my own nanite bombs. If I ever set one off, I'll try to grab a few so you can take one – for a price, obviously."

"Obviously," he sighed. "And speaking of price, I assume that you can pay me immediately? That was a lot of work, after all."

"Once the ship's systems are back online," she replied.

"I want to make sure its nanofield is up and running and initiating the needed repairs."

"Of course, it is!" he protested. "When have I ever done less than stellar work for you, Benning Kidd?"

"You haven't, which is why I keep working with you." She eyed him balefully. "But everything happens for a first time, Emmed Oswald. If this happens to be that time, I want to make sure you're here to fix it."

"Fine," he sighed. "It shouldn't be long, anyway. With the upgrades I gave the ship's nanofield, its repair times should be cut in half. It'll also be far more resistant to another attack like the one that crippled it." He shook his head. "Starship Captains are always eager to pay for better armor and grasers, but they never think how effective boosting a ship's nanofield can be."

"Well, I did think of it," Benning said, still monitoring the ship's systems as they slowly came online. "And if it works for this one, I'll be adding that upgrade to the others."

"It will. You'll be amazed at how well, in fact."

<It won't be that good, Benning Kidd,> Tiddly laughed. <He's overselling it as always. You'll definitely notice a difference, though.>

Repair times won't be halved, then?

<No, but they'll probably be cut by a third, which is still a lot in naval combat. The best part is that all of your and your crew's abilities will work faster and more effectively on board.>

What? Why?

<Well, the ship's nanofield helps keep you connected to the Overnet. Remember how hard it was to do things like shoot straight when you were cut off from the Overnet? That's because the Overnet supports and does a lot of the

work for most of your abilities. A better nanofield means a faster connection, and that means the Overnet will be able to provide you with more and faster support.>

That's useful. What about the improved defense against hostile nanites?

<That seems to be mostly true. It looks like he's done some unique upgrades to his nanites, probably based on what he found from the disassembler you gave him. The ship's nanofield should mitigate nanite damage, although by how much, I can't say.>

Benning's attention focused back on the command console as she felt the engine's power plant hum to life. The ship's 'net spread slowly throughout the vessel, linking each part of it and sending its nanofield to smooth less-than-perfect repairs and installations. As the seconds ticked past, power swelled in the ship, and Benning's awareness flowed through more of it as it connected to the 'net. At last, the weapons array powered on, and the command console flickered to life before her.

"She's up and running, Captain!" Graesen Barry said excitedly, his voice carrying from the engine compartment into her ears. "All engine and power systems read green!"

"Weapons are up and functioning normally," Charlo Herrick added just as enthusiastically from her position at the ship's Weapons console. "Capacitors are fully charged, and the new array looks good!"

"Navigation controls are all online, Captain," Brialle Caldwell spoke up. "Dive engines read nominal."

"EM Shield and Dark Shroud are both at maximum," Jezper Shields observed far more calmly. "Static Field generator is online and reading within tolerances."

Benning quickly confirmed her crew's statements with a scan of the ship's 'net, then turned to Emmed Oswald.

"It looks like you did what you promised," she said.

"Of course, I did. I always do."

"So far, at least," she shrugged, then accessed her ship's treasury and transferred over a thousand credits to the man. "Payment as agreed."

"Thanks, Benning Kidd! Do you want me to start on the other ships right away?"

She shook her head. "I'll want to do a shakedown cruise first – and try her out in combat. That might take a few days." She looked at her crew. "Go ahead and power her down. We'll take her out tomorrow for a jump to Frostwise to check the dive engines, then we'll get the fleet together for an excursion the day after to see what she can do."

"Aye, captain," Shields replied, beginning to power down the weapons and defensive systems.

Benning turned back to Emmed Oswald. "I'll walk you off the ship," she told him. "If you need transport back to Sirius, I can have one of my ships take you. Trephor Sands is scheduled to make a run that direction anyway."

"I can wait," he shrugged. "I'm thinking about setting up a shop here, anyway."

"Oh?" she asked, surprised. "Why? I would think Sirius Prime Station gives you plenty of business."

"It does, but there are things I can't buy or sell there that I can here. I'd still be headquartered in Sirius, of course – that's where the steady credits are – but I could keep a small kiosk here to do remote upgrades through the 'net. I think my new nanite defense upgrade would sell much better out here – especially since it would be illegal to sell in most other systems." He grinned at her again. "Plus, when you inevitably need me to reset your field again, you won't have to come to Sirius Prime to get it done."

When they stepped out of the boarding tunnel into the station, Benning was surprised to find both Fodor Hendricks and Tereza Erdeli waiting for them.

"Well, Commodore?" Hendricks asked with a grin. "Is she ready to go?"

"Emmed Oswald's repairs seem to be functioning," Benning nodded. "I'm planning to run her through a shakedown tomorrow. After that, I want to try her as part of the fleet."

"I thought you might," Hendricks nodded. "So, I asked Tereza Erdeli to work up a list of worthwhile targets..."

Benning held up her hand for silence, then turned toward Emmed Oswald. "I'll let you know if I'm interested in moving forward with the other ships after testing this one out," she said.

The man's face fell at the obvious dismissal, but he nodded and turned away. Benning waited until he was well out of earshot before she turned back to the others.

"What did you find?"

"I have several options that seem promising, Benning Kidd," the woman replied. "One is a convoy that claims to be carrying curium-248 but that has far too large of an escort. I suspect it might be actually carrying strange neutronium since the decay patterns are similar."

Benning nodded. Strange neutronium was a highly unstable form of matter, pure neutron matter with a strange quark in place of one of the two down quarks. Outside of containment, it quickly decayed into showers of electrons and neutrinos. Even in containment, strange neutronium had a half-life of a few years. It was incredibly useful as a coating for armor-penetrating weapons, more massive than regular neutronium and doing additional damage through its decay. It was a valuable cargo, and assuming she could verify it, it would make...

Benning's head rang as something slammed into her, hurling her back into the closed hatch of the boarding tunnel. She felt several bones crack and shatter with the impact, and her head smashed against the metal bulkhead, sending stars flashing through her suddenly narrowed vision. She crashed to the deck, pain surging through her body, but she managed to push herself up against the bulkhead and trigger her armor. Too late, the crimson liquid metal flowed over her broken and shattered body. Medigel poured into her, burning through her veins as it hastily worked to patch up the damage, but her resistance hovered at 12% and still dropped slowly as internal bleeding sapped her vitality.

She blinked as her eyes refocused, and she saw a figure in ochre armor with a splash of cyan across the chest walking toward her. The figure held a rifle and raised it toward Benning, pointing it directly at her head. She could see their finger curling over the trigger and tensed her body against the rain of bullets that would inevitably pierce her armor...

A roar of fury made her assailant whip to the side as Fodor Hendricks leaped on them, slamming his heavy, spiked mace into the figure's shoulder. The attacker fell back, and Hendricks swung again, crashing his weapon into their thigh and staggering them. The figure ducked the next blow and slashed at Hendricks with their rifle, but the powerful man blocked the blow and lashed out with his foot, knocking the attacker backward. Benning watched in helpless rage as Hendricks battered their assailant, blood streaming from his wounds, his left arm pressed tightly against his chest. His aura burned a dull orange just a step above red in her vision – he was badly wounded, but his powerful blows showed no sign of it as he rained strikes on their attacker.

Benning's pain suddenly vanished, and she blinked

with astonishment at the absence of agony. She glanced at her resistance bar and understood; it had dropped to 10%, activating I Will Not Fall. She rose swiftly to her feet, unfeeling of the pain in her body as she triggered For Fame. With the bonuses from Strength from Pain, that boosted her physical stats over fourteen, making her entire body stronger, faster, and surer despite her horrific injuries.

She whipped out her Foehammer rifle and targeted her assailant. The figure fell back as her first round slammed into their helmet, knocking their head back, and they spun toward Benning. Hendricks took advantage of the moment of inattention and crashed his mace into the man's elbow. Benning's rifle dropped, targeting the same spot, and the attacker cried out as her bullet ripped through his weakened armor and shattered the joint beneath.

The attacker fired their rifle point-blank at Hendricks, and the pirate collapsed, his aura dimming to crimson in Benning's sight. Rage flared through her as Hendricks dropped, and she let go of her rifle, yanking out her hammer. The attacker stepped back as if to flee, but after activating Flurry to speed her attacks, Benning closed the distance to them in a heartbeat. The attacker turned and raised their rifle, but Benning twisted to the side and slammed her antimatter-coated hammer into their ribs. The armor crumpled beneath her blow, and she spun, spearing the figure's knee with the rear spike. They fell back, their aura dropping to golden yellow, but managed to fire a shot that ricocheted off Benning's armor.

Rage and adrenaline flowed through her body, boosting her speed and strength, and she ignored the assassin's attack. Her hammer flew through the air, cracking into the attacker's rifle and knocking it upward, then slamming down into their stomach and punching through their armor. She kicked her enemy's wounded leg out from under them and smashed her hammer into their helmet, cracking the microthene and launching them backwards to crash heavily into the deck. They rolled frantically to their feet, yanking out a pistol and firing it at Benning, but she raced forward, bringing the hammer overhead and slamming it into their shoulder in a Crushing Blow that crumpled their armor and shattered their collarbone.

"Wait!" the figure cried out, holding up a hand. "I surrender! Enough!"

Benning gripped her hammer, fury raging through her body. This person had come to her station, attacked her, probably killed Tereza Erdeli, and possibly killed Fodor Hendricks. They had taken from her, struck viciously against her for no reason, and she wanted to pound them into a bloody paste on the deck, then hang up their armor as a trophy to remind her enemies not to cross her...

<Benning Kidd, I Will Not Fall expires soon,> Tiddly reminded her. <If you haven't healed some by then, you'll go to respawn, and they'll probably escape.>

Benning took a deep breath and lowered her hammer, then lifted it and slammed the spearpoint into the attacker's hand, pinning it to the deck.

"Flork!" the man screamed, grabbing at the weapon and trying futilely to pull it free from his shattered appendage. "What did you do that for? I surrendered!"

"Stay there," Benning said, stepping back. She triggered another dose of medigel, feeling the nanites flow through her body. Her resistance bar stopped at 8% and began to slowly rise, but not fast enough. Wincing, she hit herself with another dose of the gel; too much of it would actually slow down her healing in the long run, as her nanofield would have to work to undo scar tissue and improperly healed bones, but if she didn't get her resistance over 10%, she'd die when I Will Not Fall ended.

Her resistance had crept up to 12% when pain suddenly crashed over her, leaving her barely able to stand. Cracked bones screamed in protest over the hard use she'd given them, and ripped muscles cramped and spasmed. Her chest and stomach burned like molten metal had been poured into them, and her body trembled as she fought to hold it erect. She wanted to collapse and wait for her healing, but she knew that if she showed any sign of weakness, her attacker would strike once more.

She staggered over to the fallen man and activated her scanning nanites. "Ashtom Gao, Level 13 Bounty Hunter," she said, her voice tight from pain but still clear and strong. "How did you get on my station?"

"I surrendered," the man groaned. "In return, I demand free passage to my ship and freedom to leave peacefully."

"YOU DEMAND NOTHING!" she roared at him as her fury spiked. "You came here, to my home, and tried to kill me! You'll be lucky to leave here alive at all, much less peacefully!"

"I'm doing my job," he grunted. "It's not personal."

"It's personal when someone tries to take my life," she spat. She took a deep breath. "I don't have time for this. Let me show you what happens to people who try to kill me, Ashtom Gao." She sent her nanites forth, and for a moment, Gao just watched her, his face puzzled. He suddenly glanced down as he felt the armor over his crotch melt away, and a second later, he began screaming as her disassemblers slowly shredded his member, reducing it to thick, viscous fluid.

"What – what did you do to me?" he screeched, grabbing his ruined groin with his free hand. That was a mistake, and he realized how much of one when the flesh of his fingers began to blister and bubble as well. He jerked the appendage away and held it up before his helmet, watching as the skin and connective tissue sloughed off in runnels of thick fluid. His screams redoubled, and he wiped the hand against his armor as if he could somehow dislodge her nanites.

Benning withdrew her nanites and waited for the screams to fade. His wails of agony felt somehow appropriate to her. Pain filled her body, and it seemed only fair that she gave him more torment than he'd given her.

"Here's the thing, Ashtom Gao. I can do this to every part of your body, and you won't heal from it. I can turn your arms, legs, eyes, and tongue into splatters of fluid on my deck, leaving nothing but a torso behind, and you'll stay that way until you respawn." She leaned forward, ignoring the screams of pain in her body. "And honestly, I kind of hope I get to. Tell me, Ashtom Gao. Do I get to do that to you, or will you start talking?"

"I – merchant freighter," he gasped, his voice almost frantic. "I hitched a ride, paid them to bring me to avoid the alarms."

"That's how you arrived at my station," she corrected. "You didn't answer my question." Gao screamed as her nanites soared out once more, and his left ear dissolved into a dripping mass of liquid flesh that peeled off his skull and splatted on the deck. "How did you get on my station without my knowing?"

"I – don't know!" he wailed, thrashing his head from side to side as her nanites slowly spread out, tearing more of the skin from the side of his head. "Contract – guaranteed entry! Here, see!"

A contract appeared before her, one that was nearly identical to the one she'd already claimed from the previous bounty hunter. Gao was right; the contract promised that his employer would arrange for his safe entry and offered the full value if he was denied entry. The signature was once more encrypted, and Benning saved a copy of it to work on later.

"I take it you have no idea who hired you, then?" she asked.

"No! Anonymous – I never met or spoke to them." Gao whimpered as part of his cheek dissolved, revealing muscle and the whiteness of his teeth beneath. "Please," he gasped, his voice layered with an odd hiss. "I told you what I know!"

Benning ignored the man's pleas. He had told her what he knew, but her anger wasn't spent. She wanted to make an object lesson of him – no, she needed to do it. Her rage filled her chest, pushing out the perpetual ache there. Fury wasn't a good feeling, but it was better than the endless ache, and she wanted to indulge it, to inflict her suffering on him...

<Are you going to let your anger control you, Benning Kidd?> Tiddly asked quietly.

What? she demanded, her mental voice a scream of rage and frustration.

<You said you wouldn't be controlled, Benning Kidd – but you're letting anger control you right now. You've always used torture as a tool, never something you enjoyed. Aren't you enjoying it right now?>

Benning froze as the gnome's words washed over her like icy water. Tiddly was right; Benning had never taken pleasure in hurting or torturing others. It was something she did out of necessity, not for entertainment. Fury filled her, demanding that she act on it, but Ashtom Gao wasn't the real target of her rage. She was angry at the System, the Fleet, the Noble who must have shut down her alarms on the station – no one else could have done it – but not at Ashtom Gao. He was just doing his job, and he didn't deserve to be tortured to death for that.

She withdrew her nanites, and Gao sobbed in relief as they stopped devouring his face. She pulled out her pistol and leveled it at the man's head, exposed behind the ragged hole her nanites had chewed through his helmet. His gray hair was wet with blood; bone and muscle shone wetly where skin should have been; and half of his long, light brown hair was gone. He wept openly, tears streaming down his face, and Benning felt something new in her chest. A deeper ache pulsed in her, one that told her what she'd done was wrong by her own standards, that she'd caused pain for the sheer joy of it. The man's suffering didn't bother her, but her lack of control did.

<That's shame, Benning Kidd,> Tiddly told her quietly.

Shame. That explained it. She was ashamed, ashamed that she'd let her fury dictate her choices, that she'd broken her own code of conduct. She was ashamed, and it hurt, hurt as much as her slowly knitting bones and regenerating flesh. It was a pain she was determined never to feel again.

"I should leave you like this, Ashtom Gao," she said quietly. "I should send you back to wherever you came from as a message to other hunters of what will happen if they come for me. Instead, though, I'm going to grant you mercy and send you to respawn."

She leaned closer to him. "And in exchange, I want you to make sure hunters know never to come for me. Make sure they learn that, Ashtom Gao, because if they don't, I'll find you and make an example of you the right way next time."

Her finger tightened on the trigger, and the man's body spasmed once as her bullet ripped through his exposed skull and splattered the brain within. As he died, Benning holstered her weapon with a sigh. Killing Gao eased the ache inside her somewhat, but it didn't make her feel better.

"Find out anything useful?"

Benning turned and saw Fodor Hendricks limping toward her, grimacing with pain with every step. The man's clothing and armor were both torn, with blood smeared over them, but his aura was back to orange in Benning's sight. She felt a tightness in her chest suddenly ease at the sight of the man, and some of her anger ebbed and cooled as she realized that he'd survived.

"No," she shook her head. "Just that someone disarmed my alarms on the station."

He frowned. "Who could do that?" He glanced backward, and Benning saw him look at the swiftly dissolving corpse of Tereza Erdeli. "Tereza Erdeli..."

"Doesn't have the authority," Benning cut him off. "No one does, at least no one on the station. Only a Noble could do that."

Hendricks whistled. "A Noble? You have Nobles hunting you, too, Benning Kidd?"

She nodded. "I do."

"The Fleet and Nobles." He shook his head. "You're too young to have those sorts of enemies, you know."

"I don't think they care how old I am," she pointed out. She glanced over at him. "Is this a problem for you?"

"Not for me, no. I think you can tell a lot about a person by the quality of their enemies, and yours are a lot more powerful than most Citizens'. You must be doing something right."

She snorted. "Most would say I'm doing something wrong, I think."

"Only because they don't know what they're talking about. It's easy to go through the Collective without making enemies, you know. Just don't do anything that matters, and no one will care what you're doing." He shrugged. "Once you start doing important things, though, people who don't like what you're doing and how you're doing it will try to stop you."

He turned and gestured at the station around them. "Take this place, for example. You've taken it and turned it from a rat's nest of a pirate base into a real station, one that will become more important and valuable as time goes on. You've built a fleet to defend it and are bringing in credits to upgrade it and make it safer. All those are important things, valuable things, and they matter. A century from now, no one will care what ships you took or how you took them, but they'll care about this place."

He laughed and turned back to her. "And some people like the Fleet – and apparently some Nobles – don't like the way you did it, so they've made themselves your enemies. You did something that matters, but you did it in the wrong way, so you made enemies that matter in the process. Like I said, you can tell a lot about a person by their enemies."

He laughed again, and Benning felt the ache in her chest ease even more at the sound of that laugh. She looked over at him, her thoughts appraising. She realized that being around Fodor Hendricks made her feel – not good, exactly, but relaxed. It wasn't a pleasant feeling, but it wasn't unpleasant, either. He made her feel better about herself and her choices, and the shame that ached in her ebbed at his words.

"Fodor Hendricks, I'm not as good as you with words," she told him after several moments.

"You can be when you need to," he countered. "You've made some fairly inspirational speeches."

"Yes, but I'm not good when it comes to dealing with people one-on-one." She grimaced. "In other words, I'm probably going to say this poorly."

She looked him up and down. "I'd like to share my body with you," she said simply. "I think you're attractive, and I'm comfortable with you. Are you interested?"

He stared at her for a long moment before looking down at himself. "Benning Kidd, I don't think either one of us is in any condition for that," he laughed.

"We'll be healed by the time we reach my quarters," she shrugged. "If you aren't interested, you can say that. I won't punish you."

"That could be its own fun," he replied with a snort.

"So, are you interested?" She stared at him boldly.

He looked at her and took a deep breath. "Yes, Benning Kidd. I'm interested."

"Good. Come with me." She turned and led the man away from the dissolving corpse of the bounty hunter. A feeling of satisfaction rolled through her, mingled with anticipation for what was to come. She'd suffered plenty lately; she was overdue for some meaningless pleasure.

CHAPTER 27

"Elden Rush, status report on the target." Benning gazed at her expanded display from the fleet command chair in the *System's Fall*, her eyes tracking her quarry's images as her Communications Officer read out the information she could clearly see.

"Convoy is one light-hour's distance, continuing on their most recent heading, Captain," the man replied. "Escort is still circling at three leconds radius."

Benning nodded. The distant convoy had to have picked up her fleet's presence, but at a light-hour's distance, they probably weren't too concerned about the cluster of ships. The fleet was running a perpendicular course that would take them well behind the convoy, and they convoy's declared cargo of plutonium wasn't close to valuable enough to induce a fleet of pirates into attacking them. Of course, it also wasn't enough to merit an escort of two destroyers and five fast frigates, either, but its hidden cargo of kulshanium-344 definitely warranted heavy protection. The ultra-heavy element was the first whose inner electron orbitals collapsed into negative energy states and was thus a vital element for the production of negative energy. The half-kig each ship carried was probably as valuable as the entire clipper transporting it, and Benning wanted it badly.

"Fleet, prepare for hivemind linkage," she spoke aloud, her words carrying to her captains. "Ops, activate hivemind."

"Aye, Captain," Jezper Shields replied. "Hivemind linkage is active."

Benning's awareness expanded as the advanced neural net connected the negaputers of all the ships in her fleet into a single processor. She could feel each of the ships as if it were her own, and she knew the captains experienced something similar, if on a much lesser scale. It was a jarring sensation, and they'd had to practice with it for a week before Benning felt comfortable taking her new cruiser-backed fleet into combat. She'd grown used to it, though, and she'd found it to be incredibly useful.

Prepare for rapid dives, she thought silently. The hivemind linkage carried her orders directly to her officers and captains. She felt them echo the orders as the dive warnings went out across her ships. *Rapid dives, light-hour's distance, on my mark – now!*

As one, the ships of her fleet powered their dive engines and soared into the fifth dimension. Thanks to the linkage, they each ran almost perfectly parallel to one another, no longer having to fear crashing or exiting the dive out of formation. She kept her focus squarely on her map screen as the third dimension flattened around her and her ships plunged across a linute of space in ten seconds. The ships emerged from the higher-dimensional manifold only briefly before diving into it once more. Again and again the ships plunged through CY-space, racing across a billion kims in ten minutes.

The third dimension exploded back around her as her fleet erupted into space within five leconds of where she hoped the convoy would be. She'd taken a chance diving so far so quickly – her images of the convoy were an hour old, after all – but they'd been traveling in a predictable pattern for days. Their commander must have been counting on the number of ships in their escort and the perceived lack of value in their cargo to dissuade pirates and didn't bother with random dive schedules or patterns. If she'd predicted correctly, they should have arrived close to where the convoy would be emerging from their latest dive...

"Captain, I'm reading dive splashes," Rush spoke up, still unused to being able to communicate through the hivemind. "Ten of them, four leconds distant – it's the convoy!"

Benning didn't wait for the man's words before she sent her orders. She could hear his thoughts through the linkage; he'd subconsciously projected what he was going to say as the words left his mouth. *Activate warp bubble, Higgs field, and sinkhole generator. All ships, evasion pattern thirty-one. Target vessel Destroyer-1 with grasers; target vessel Destroyer-2 with warheads, spiral pattern. Arcturus, target Clipper-1 with flyboats to disable, then move to the next.*

Her orders took only a fraction of a second to issue, and she heard the silent acknowledgment from her captains almost immediately. As one, her ships moved into a convoluted pattern around her cruiser. The warp generator activated, causing each of her ships' shrouds to condense into a bubble of negative energy that shifted part of their momentum into CY-space and warped spacetime, contracting time around them so that they could react slightly faster than the enemy vessels. She felt the combined grasers of her upgraded fleet firing, unleashing hundreds of pows of gamma radiation at the chosen vessel and utterly drenching its evasion cone with radiation. As the same time, dozens of antimatter warheads streaked forth in a spiral pattern that erupted around the second destroyer.

The enemy fleet responded swiftly, moving into formation and trying to place themselves between Benning and the convoy. The enemy commander understood fleet tactics as well, focusing their fire on a single vessel in Benning's fleet. Unfortunately, they chose the *Fall* as that vessel rather than one of the more vulnerable frigates, and the cruiser was designed to take a beating without damage.

"Fusion warhead explosion, 120 kims declined. No damage," Jezper Shields reported calmly as the cruiser trembled slightly from the explosion below it. Benning's skin tingled slightly, and the officer added, "Glancing graser hit. No damage."

"Destroyer-1's power plant is down to 78%," Rush said. "Engine power at 84%. Destroyer-2 has taken minor hull damage and is venting gas."

Continue firing, she ordered her fleet. *Arcturus, focus on disabling the clippers.*

The enemy fleet continued to pound at the *Fall,* hurling fusion blasts and graser beams at the cruiser. The ship's reactive armor barely took any damage from the impacts, and her power plant and engines were still above 90% as the destroyers took a serious beating.

"Destroyer-1's power plant is spiking," Rush reported. "She's shutting it down and is adrift! Destroyer-2's list is at 35 rpms, and she's venting atmosphere in four places."

Fleet, shift graser fire to Destroyer-2, Benning ordered instantly. *Shift warheads to target Frigate-1…*

"Captain, a message is incoming from Destroyer-2," Rush interrupted her thoughts.

Benning considered for a moment, then nodded. "I'll take it," she said quickly.

The image of a man with a narrow face and a sharply pointed nose appeared in Benning's vision. The man's bright blue hair matched his eyes, and the way it curled forward around his face made his cheeks seem even more slender.

"My designation is Ozkar Clayton," the man said crisply. "I'm the commander of this fleet. To whom am I speaking?"

"My designation is Benning Kidd," she replied with a

cold smile. "Are you contacting me to offer your surrender?"

"Benning Kidd?" the man echoed, his eyes widening slightly, then narrowing in suspicion. "I've heard of you."

Benning felt a touch of pride hearing that. She'd worked hard to build her reputation, and she was glad it was starting to pay off.

"Then you know that if you don't surrender, it won't go well for you," she told him in the same calm voice.

He stared at her for a minute before nodding. "What are your terms?"

"Simple. Your convoy heaves to and allows my cargo vessel to dock, taking what I want from the cargo of each ship. In return, you keep your ships and can continue with the rest of your cargo intact."

"Our ships are carrying nothing but plutonium," he protested. "We don't have anything of value..."

"You're also carrying a kig and a half of kulshanium," she smiled at him. "I'll leave you most of the plutonium; I only need a thousand gigs or so."

The man's eyes widened, and he suddenly looked frightened. "No," he shook his head. "I – I can't let you have that..."

"Then, I'll destroy your escort ships and take it myself," she cut him off. "Along with one of the clipper ships for extra storage. Your employers can lose the kulshanium and a small amount of plutonium, or they can lose eight ships, the kulshanium, and most of the plutonium. Your choice."

He stared at her in silence before he sighed, his shoulders slumping. "Very well. I agree to your terms."

"I'm glad, Ozkar Clayton. Now, tell your ships to heave to, and..."

"Captain!" Brialle Caldwell's panicked voice broke into her conversation. "Dive splashes! A dozen of them! It's...it's the Fleet!"

Benning cut the call with Clayton and pulled up her map, staring at the twelve new icons appearing on it. Four destroyers, three frigates, and five corvettes had appeared from nowhere, their dive splashes rolling across the fleet as they moved to intercept Benning.

Fleet, evasive pattern 19, she ordered. *Graser fire on Destroyer-3! Warheads on Destroyer-4! Arcturus, target Corvette-1!*

Commodore, are we really about to engage the Fleet in battle? Fodor Hendricks' voice sounded concerned in her mind. *We could run...*

We will run, Fodor Hendricks, she cut him off. *However, if we try to dive now, we'll never make it. We need to back them off, first.* She looked at Charlo Herrick at the Weapons station. *Arm the singularity warheads. Target Destroyer-5, box formation. Fire!*

Warmth bathed Benning's skin as the Fleet vessels poured graser fire into her path, hitting her even before her ships could unleash their weapons upon the enemy. The Fleet warships had more powerful grasers than they should have, and they knew how to use them effectively as a fleet. They swarmed in a flower formation, the four destroyers on the inside and slightly ahead of the three frigates circling them, with the corvettes on the outside dipping back and forth into and out of the circle of frigates, making them hard to target. It was an advanced formation, one Benning knew but hadn't taught her captains, and the Fleet officers pulled it off perfectly.

Benning's captains weren't green officers themselves, though, and linked through the hivemind, the fleet moved swiftly and as one. Even as antimatter warheads exploded around the cruiser, rocking the ship in staggered blasts, she felt her vessels firing, pouring high-energy photons into the hull of one of the Fleet destroyers while antimatter warheads streaked toward another. The moment her attacks commenced, a male voice sounded in her ears.

"Citizen Benning Kidd, you are attacking a Fleet warship in direct violation of regulation 14-3-11. Stand down and prepare to be boarded."

"You attacked me first," she snapped in reply. "Self-defense trumps your regulations." She cut the connection before the Fleet ships could reply and returned her focus to the battle. She guided her ships toward the edge of the sinkhole but stopped far short of the boundary, where the horizon's time dilation would slow her vessels down and cut their evasion cones.

"Captain, Destroyer-3's power plant is at 92%," Elden Rush said professionally, his voice slightly numb. "Destroyer-4 has taken minor hull damage."

Continue fire, Benning directed as she felt the hesitancy of her captains. *We need to disable their destroyers enough to make our escape.* Through the hivemind link, Benning kept focusing her fleet's fire on the destroyers, ignoring the burning of her skin as graser fire swept across her cruiser's hull. *Fire dark matter cannons, targeting Destroyer-6, followed by a singularity battery, overlapping pattern.*

Her ship trembled as another salvo of antimatter warheads explode around it. At the same moment, her cruiser fired a blast of dark matter, hurling it close to the speed of light and bathing the area in front of the fourth Fleet destroyer in the heavy particles. The particles did no damage, but the ship's dark energy shroud gathered them and pushed them into the vessel's hull, drastically increasing its mass and slowing it dramatically. Its engines would quickly compensate, but the extra drag briefly narrowed its evasion cone and allowed Benning to focus the fire from her warheads.

"Captain, Destroyer-5 has taken moderate hull damage," Rush reported. "She's venting gas in several places."

The *Fall* shook, and Benning felt a sharp stab of pain in her back.

"Captain, antimatter warhead exploded thirty kims inclined," Shields called out. "Minor hull breach. We're venting gas."

"Destroyer-3's power plant is down to 64%. Destroyer-4 has moderate hull damage." Rush's voice was tense but modulated as he spoke.

"Captain, main power is at 83%. Engines are at 87%."

"Captain, two more dive splashes!" Brialle Caldwell added. "Two more Fleet destroyers!"

"Scrit," Benning swore aloud as she realized she only had only viable way out of her predicament. *Charlo Herrick, singularity torpedo on the center clipper.*

The clipper, captain? Herrick replied, her mental voice confused.

Yes. Fire!

Benning ignored the rumble as the cruiser fired the torpedo, watching as the two new destroyers slipped into the center of the Fleet's formation, allowing the two more damaged ones to fall back. It was a seamless maneuver, one obviously born of long practice, but while it occurred, Benning's torpedo streaked through the formation and slammed into the side of the mostly undefended center clipper. The torpedo's warhead dumped energy into CY-space, creating a storm of Kaluza-Klein particles that almost instantly collapsed into a black hole. The black hole then evaporated, giving up not only the energy poured into it but also far more energy drawn from the higher dimension. The blast of photons ripped through the hull of the clipper, pouring into its cargo holds.

A flash lit Benning's screen as the clipper went photonic with a blast that was far larger and more powerful than it should have been. The blast wave slammed into the ships fore and aft, crumpling their hulls, as well, and a moment later, the other two clippers exploded into twin balls of energy. The blast waves rushed out into the convoy's escorts, and one of the frigates and Ozkar Clayton's destroyer followed suit, ripping themselves to pieces as their power plants lost containment, and all the stored energy within them exploded outward in a nanosecond.

What in the Hole? Trephor Sands' voice over the hivemind sounded shocked as he spoke. *What just happened?*

Kulshanium explosion, Hendricks replied grimly. *The blast carried through CY-space and magnified as it went.*

Fleet, prepare for withdrawal, Benning thought to the others. *Maximum dive!*

Captain, the Fleet's still engaged with us! Avaeyana Roble protested. *If we dive, we'll be vulnerable...*

They've got more to worry about than us right now, Hendricks countered. *The rest of the convoy's escorts are on the verge of going photonic. They'll let us go to rescue them.*

Exactly. Drop sinkhole – dive! As the universe flattened and simultaneously expanded around Benning, she felt a rush of relief. They'd escaped an ambush they had no right to escape, and they'd done so without losing any ships. The loss of the kulshanium hurt, of course, but losing one of her upgraded ships would have hurt more.

They dove randomly away from the convoy until they'd put several light-hours behind them, then soared along to let the dive engines recharge in preparation for returning to IS-39267. As Benning checked the negaputer's dive calculations, a screen appeared in her vision, one she hadn't been expecting.

FODOR HENDRICKS wishes to send
you a message. Do you accept?

Benning frowned. Ever since the two shared bodies, Hendricks had behaved strangely toward her. It was a pleasant experience – Hendricks was strong and not too gentle, which she preferred – and afterward, she'd felt a sense of contentment that she hadn't for a while. It only lasted for a short time, of course, but it was enough to tide her over for some time. She'd sent him back to his room once the act was finished so she could get some training on the Overnet, and all in all, she considered it a positive thing.

Afterward, though, Hendricks had seemed more reserved toward her, even a bit standoffish. He'd left the station quickly after, heading after a target Tereza Erdeli found for him, and he'd only returned when Benning demanded that he participate in the hivemind training. He'd done so, but even she could feel his reticence throughout the fleet's exercises. She didn't understand what was suddenly different about the man. Normally, his behavior wouldn't concern her so long as he still did his job – which he did – but she'd learned that her crew and captains performed better when they were happy. Plus, for some reason, the man's sudden distance made the ache in her chest subtly worse, as if he were somehow amplifying that pain.

Shrugging, she accepted the message, and the man's face appeared in her mind.

Sorry, Benning Kidd, but I wanted to speak to you privately, he said, his expression and voice both neutral.

What is it, Fodor Hendricks? she asked. *I'm trying to check the calculations for the dives back to the station.*

Who knew about this target, Benning Kidd?

Benning frowned again. *All of the captains. Tereza Erdeli. My officers. Why?*

Because that was a set-up, he replied firmly. *A trap set just for you.*

For me?

Yes. I could see the Fleet trying to lure pirates by setting up a convoy and leaking the information that it was carrying kulshanium – we used to hunt pirates like that ourselves, remember? – but that was an actual convoy carrying actual kulshanium. Bait like that is way too expensive and valuable to risk just to catch some random pirates. They must have realized that somehow, you always know the fake ones, so they set that trap up just for you.

Benning nodded slowly. *I hadn't thought about that, but I guessed that it was a trap. The Fleet arrived too quickly and without warning. They had to have been waiting for us, powered down and drifting nearby. They knew we were coming.*

Even worse, Benning Kidd, they knew when *we were coming. We'd been tracking that convoy for days and could have hit them at any time. The Fleet intervened within ten minutes of us attacking, which means they were no more than five linutes distant. How could they have predicted where we'd hit the convoy that closely? We didn't even know until a couple hours before we moved on them.*

The man's face grew if anything even grimmer as he continued. *You know what that means, don't you, Benning Kidd? If they knew where we were going to attack...*

Someone in the fleet told them, Benning finished calmly. *It's the only possibility.*

He stared at her, an odd expression that Benning couldn't read on his face. *I expected you to be a lot more upset about that, Benning Kidd. You usually lose it when someone betrays you.*

I've suspected it for a while, she shrugged. *It's the only way that bounty hunters could have gotten onto the system – and why the Fleet was waiting for us in Van Maanen and Altair. Someone's feeding them information.*

He stared at her, his eyes wide. *You know that? Why haven't you done anything about it?*

Because whoever it is broke their contract with me without consequences, Fodor Hendricks. That means they're working directly for a Noble, and my ways of finding out who they are won't work against a Noble's Designate. Otherwise, I'd have questioned everyone and made an example of the person responsible long ago.

He frowned. *Why didn't you tell me?* His eyes widened, and his expression grew flat once more. *You thought it could be me, didn't you?*

Yes, she said simply.

I see, he nodded. *Well, that explains that. Do you still think it could be me? Even after I pointed this out to you?*

She shrugged. *You could have done that to make me think it wasn't you, Fodor Hendricks. It doesn't seem very likely, but it's possible, so I have to consider it.*

Yes, you would, wouldn't you? He made a face that Benning couldn't interpret. *You don't trust anyone, do you, Benning Kidd?*

I trust myself, Fodor Hendricks, she said honestly.

I understand. He shook his head. *I just wanted to make sure you knew, is all.* He cut the connection, and his image vanished.

Benning frowned once more at the empty screen. She wasn't sure what Hendricks had been expecting from her, but she had a feeling he hadn't gotten it.

She pushed the conversation from her mind. She had other things to worry about, after all. She'd attacked a Fleet vessel and destroyed an entire convoy in their presence. So far, she'd had plausible deniability for everything she'd done, but with several ships' worth of Fleet officers witness to her actions, that wasn't the case. The Fleet wouldn't hold back anymore. They'd come to find her at IS-39267, and they'd do it soon. She had plans to make and strategies to work out. They'd tried to catch her with a smaller fleet and failed. If she were in charge, she'd send a battlefrigate next, and she assumed the Fleet's admirals would think the same way.

When it came, Benning intended to be ready.

CHAPTER 28

"Frostwise Control, this is *System's Fall*, requesting priority refueling," Brialle Caldwell said, her tone almost bored as she spoke.

"*System's Fall*, this is Frostwise Control. You are clear for priority refueling at Station 14, Bay 1."

"Acknowledged, Frostwise Control. Setting course for Station 14, Bay 1."

Benning ignored the exchange. She'd heard it hundreds of times before, and she'd probably hear it hundreds of times again. One of the benefits of her leasing IS-39267 was a large discount on gas purchases at Frostwise, and Benning was fine with saving credits. Hydrogen was hydrogen, after all, and the gas from Frostwise was identical to what she could get at Sol except a tenth of the cost.

Instead, she glanced over her projected flight plan, rechecking the negaputer's dive calculations and matching it to known ship routes. She wasn't traveling with her fleet this time; she wanted to see how the *Fall* would fare in individual combat, instead. The cruiser wasn't meant for that, and it was lightly armed for a ship of its size, but her target had only a frigate as an escort. The brigantine wasn't carrying much, just fifty or so gigs of anti-helium hidden inside a shipment of solid oganesson-313. Benning could sell it for a profit, but not much of one; her aim was more to test her ship's capabilities than to earn a ton of credits.

After the failed attempt by the Fleet to trap her, Benning waited for their expected response. When a week passed without any sign of the Fleet, she began allowing her captains to make short, local runs on small targets; after a second week, she decided to do the same herself. The tiny convoy was only a light-day from her station, and she could be out and back in a single solar day if she pushed her dive engines slightly. It was a decent target, but more importantly, it was a target she could run from if the cruiser turned out to be totally overmatched without its supporting fleet.

That was a real possibility, she knew. Frigates were designed to be escort vessels; they were fast and maneuverable, with powerful shrouds that allowed the ships to make turns up to 1,000 g's, more if the captain upgraded the ship the way Benning had her frigates. Benning's could handle about half that, which doubled her effective turning radius and narrowed her evasion cone significantly compared to a frigate's. As well, around a third of a frigate's total volume was dedicated to weapons and defenses, while her cruiser only used a tenth of its space for the same purpose. That still came out to more total weapons simply because her ship was so much larger, but she could focus fewer of those weapons on a single target at once. Her defenses were stellar, so she wasn't worried about her ship getting damaged in the exchange, but if she couldn't harm the frigate either, she'd simply retreat and call it a lesson learned.

The *Fall* cruised past the ellipse of ships waiting to refuel. It seemed that Frostwise was becoming a popular stop for vessels. She supposed part of that was that more and more merchants used Benning's station as a convenient trading center and outpost, and she wondered idly if that could serve as a basis for a renegotiation of her lease...

"Captain, there's some unusual activity nearby," Elden Rush spoke slowly as he stared at the screen, pulling Benning out of her thoughts. She closed her flight plan and pulled up the local map, showing a swarm of ships moving around her in every direction as they waited for their turn to refuel. She frowned at the map.

"Can you be more specific, Elden Rush? Unusual how?"

"I – I'm not sure, Captain," the man shook his head. "There's something off about some of these ship movements, though."

Benning stared at the ships moving about in various ellipses, trying to pick out some sort of irregularity or anomaly. *Tiddly, do you see anything?*

<No, Benning Kidd, sorry.>

That took Benning slightly aback. *How can Elden Rush see an anomaly that you can't? You're an AI!*

<Well, technically, Elden Rush isn't seeing anything,> Tiddly explained. <The Overnet is doing all the work, and it's telling him what his skill and ability allow him to notice. I'm using your 'net – and the ship's – and those aren't quite as efficient.>

Which means there's something there for him to see, then, right?

<Oh, yeah. The 'net wouldn't give him faulty information. Give me a bit to work on it; I'll figure it out, hopefully before he does.>

"Keep an eye on things, Elden Rush," she instructed. "Brialle Caldwell, watch for groups of ships entering the system at once, and be ready to accelerate to attack speed. Jezper Shields, let me know if you spot any anomalies nearby. Charlo Herrick, power up the weapons and shielding, just in case."

"Do you think something's wrong, Captain?" Caldwell asked curiously.

"If Elden Rush is sensing something, then there's something to sense, Pilot. I'd rather take precautions than chances." She snorted. "Or as Fodor Hendricks likes to say, 'it's not paranoia when people are actually hunting you'."

"Should we refuel later, instead, Captain?" Shields asked calmly. "We could avoid any issues that way."

"No. If someone's hunting us, I'd rather face them here than out in the void." She glanced at the Comm station. "To be safe, though, alert IS-39267 and have the fleet on standby and station defenses powered up. If we need to get out of here in a hurry, I'd rather have the station waiting to intercept anyone who chases us."

"Aye, Captain," Rush nodded.

"Proceed with the refueling, Pilot," Benning ordered. "Let's get some gas and get moving asap."

"Yes, ma'am." Caldwell turned back to her station and began directing the ship toward the fueling bay they'd been directed to. Benning's eyes narrowed as a suspicion occurred to her.

Tiddly, focus your analysis on the area around that fueling bay, just in case.

<You got it, Benning Kidd. It'll take about three minutes to run a full analysis.>

Benning turned back to the map and watched it carefully. Everything seemed normal to her, but she suspected that her all-too-human mind wasn't going to catch anything that Tiddly and Rush both missed. Even so, she kept her gaze fastened on the map, just in case. It didn't hurt to have more eyes on a potential danger, after all.

The cruiser slid up to the prescribed station, and Caldwell deftly maneuvered it into the first fueling port, one that typically stood empty to allow priority ships to refuel. This included the ships in Benning's fleet, of course, but also a number of other vessels whose owners paid for the privilege of fast refueling. Large shipping fleets commonly did this, as saving thirty minutes or so of travel time per visit added up quickly for a corporation with millions of vessels, and the cost was probably less than the gas those ships would waste each solar year waiting for a normal fueling port assignment. The *Fall* shuddered as it connected to the station, and Benning felt the port's slim probe slip into the ship's fuel access and lock into place as pressurized hydrogen shot into her tanks, compressing into metallic form beneath the ship's armor.

<Got it, Benning Kidd!> Tiddly exclaimed. <Here! Look at this!>

At the same moment, Elden Rush straightened at his station. "Captain! We've got incoming vessels! That's what I was sensing!"

Benning's map shifted in her vision as four ships began to glow thanks to Tiddly's intervention. The ships looked to be moving in a typically elliptical fashion, but bright yellow arc leading from them curved inward, taking them in a spiral course that converged on the *Fall.* A frigate, a fast frigate, and two corvettes converged on her, and her ship was a standing target, helpless to defend or evade.

"Pilot, disengage from the fueling port!" she ordered. "I don't care if you have to blast us free, get us moving! Weapons, full power to the warp bubble and static field! Comm, message the station for backup! We're about to have incoming!"

Benning felt as much as saw her point defenses suddenly spring to life as they tracked and targeted a swarm of warheads streaking toward the cruiser. Plasma bolts burned through space, searing the incoming weapons to pools of slag, and hails of kig-mass depleted uranium spheres sprayed outward, slamming into missiles and ripping them to shreds. Even so, her ship rumbled, and her skin burned as three of the missiles slipped past her defenses and slammed into her hull, exploding directly against her armor.

"Three fusion warheads, direct impact," Jezper Shields said. "Minor hull damage, no punctures." He shook his head. "That reactive armor is good."

The ship shuddered as it tore free from the station's docking clamps and soared away, accelerating at max g's. Even with the ship's shroud reducing its inertia and effective momentum, it needed several minutes to get up to a full tock, though – and until it did, the ship's evasion cone was practically nonexistent.

"Direct graser fire against the hull," Shields reported. "Main power plant is down 4%; engines are down 2%."

"Weapons, target vessel Frigate-1," Benning ordered. "Full array graser burst, medium spread along projected arc of approach. AM battery, box pattern around the edge of the evasion cone."

"Captain, those attacks will probably strike other vessels," Herrick warned her.

"Not our problem, Weapons. In fact, if you can hit a ship or two near the projected line of approach, do it. A photonic blast will hurt as much as a warhead."

"Aye, Captain."

"Pilot, divert 25% of max g's to evasion, evasion pattern seven."

"Aye, Captain. That will increase our time to attack speed by one-third."

"Understood."

Her skin burned as more grasers zeroed in on her ship, blasting against the armor. Her upgraded hull funneled away or captured most of the free neutrons released by the blasts, but millions of them still poured into the ship and slammed into her power plants and engines, destabilizing them. The hull rocked as another battery of missiles slipped past her defenses and exploded almost against the hull's surface.

"Minor hull breach," Shields reported. "We're venting gas. Power down 7%, engines down 4%."

"Captain, our AM battery impacted two vessels," Rush reported. "Both went photonic within a lecond of Frigate-1. Target has moderate hull damage and is venting gas."

"Nice shooting, Weapons," Benning said approvingly. "Do it again if you can."

"Happy to, Captain," Herrick replied gleefully. "Let's see how they like this!"

The *Fall* rocked once more as the enemy vessels unleashed another fusion battery around her hull, tearing another hole in it and sending a jolt of pain through Benning's stomach. Her skin burned as positrons streamed against the ship, most deflecting off the EM shield but some slamming into the hull and unleashing more high-energy photons into it.

"Main power down 11%, Captain. Engines down 6%."

"Eleven minutes to attack speed, Captain," Caldwell reported.

"Message from Fodor Hendricks," Rush spoke up. "The fleet is inbound, max-v. They'll be here in fifteen minutes."

We just have to survive that long, Benning thought silently. "Keep fire on Frigate-1," she ordered out loud.

"Captain, singularity warhead impacted a cog half a lecond from Frigate-2," Rush reported. "It went photonic; Frigate-2 is listing."

"Singularity warhead?" Benning stared at Herrick,

who shrugged.

"It worked so well with an AM warhead, Captain…"

"Follow my orders and don't get creative, Weapons," Benning cut the woman off. "AM battery *only*, spiral pattern on Frigate-1."

"Aye, Captain," the woman replied. "Firing."

Pain stabbed into Benning's back as another explosion slammed into the *Fall,* this one impacting the hull directly.

"Direct AM impact, Captain," Shields reported. "Significant hull breach. We're venting gas badly."

"Seal off that tank," Benning ordered, even as her skin burned once more from graser fire. "What's Frigate-1's status?"

"Frigate-1 is down to 63% power and 74% engines," Rush replied. "All noncombatant ships have cleared the area."

"Continue to target…" Benning halted as her ship shook from a series of explosions that sent pain rippling along her left side. "Report!"

"Kinetic blasts from Frostwise Station, ma'am!" Shields said, his voice no longer calm and controlled. "They're firing on us! Multiple hull breaches; we're venting atmosphere."

"*Now,* send a singularity battery at the station, Weapons," Benning said grimly. "Follow it with a pair of singularity torpedoes." Anger flared in her, but she tamped it down. Rage wouldn't see her through this battle; only tactics and patience would. "Keep their point defenses too busy to target us!"

"AM warhead exploded within 200 kims of Frigate-1," Shields reported. "They're venting badly. Multiple warhead impacts on Station 14. They're venting atmosphere." He hesitated. "Torpedo strike to the station's hydrogen tanks. The impact opened the tanks; the entire station is listing."

Pain burned through Benning again as grasers bathed her already damaged hull, followed by showers of antimatter. The four enemy ships were circling around her at the edge of attack range, keeping their distance and pinning her against the station. It wasn't a great fleet tactic – if they worked together more effectively, they could keep her ship under constant attack the whole time – but at her low velocity, it was effective enough.

"Main power down 17%. Engines down 12%."

"Six minutes to attack speed, Captain," Caldwell told her.

"Divert 50% of acceleration into evasion," Benning ordered. "Pattern eleven. Head toward the nearest cluster of noncombatant ships."

"That will increase our time to attack speed by three minutes," the pilot replied.

Benning didn't reply. She needed evasion more than she needed speed; her only hope was to hold out until her fleet arrived, or at least until she could disable one of the frigates. That might give her a chance to run, which was her only other option. She couldn't win this battle alone.

"Continue fire on the station," Benning ordered. "AM battery on Frigate-1, hex formation. Narrow graser blast down the center of the battery." Her ship rumbled again, but this time, the pain was a dull ache as her increased evasion kept her enemies from hitting her directly.

The cruiser soared outward, tumbling slightly as their vented atmosphere pushed the ship in a slow spiral. Grasers glanced against its hull, and stray blasts of antimatter prickled Bennings skin. Warheads exploded all around her, rocking her vessel, but the *Fall* held together.

"Main power down 23%. Engines down 17%," Shields announced.

"No impacts on Station 14," Rush added. "The station's point defenses destroyed our warheads. Frigate-1 took a glancing graser hit. Power is at 60%, engines at 72%."

"Four minutes to attack speed, Captain," Caldwell spoke up.

Her ship rumbled once again, and pain seared down the back of her neck.

"AM battery from the station," Shields reported. "Impact five kims aft. Another hull breach, Captain. Our list is increasing."

"Captain, the reactive armor plant is starting to spike," Graesen Barry's voice sounded in Benning's ears. "Another hit like that, and I'll have to shut it down!"

"Understood, Engineering," Benning said grimly. She was still only a lecond from the station, too close for her point defenses to be fully effective, and close enough that they could blanket her evasion cone with warheads and grasers. If she could take the station out of the battle, she'd have a chance, but there was no way her cruiser could even seriously harm the station at this point. Their armor would shrug off her grasers, and their point defenses made them basically immune to her missiles at this distance. She'd gotten lucky earlier, firing at them from inside their point defense envelope, but it wouldn't happen again.

"Captain, dive splashes!" Rush said, his voice frantic. "Five ships, heading directly for us!" The man turned toward her with a grin. "It's the *Hammer*, ma'am! Our fleet's arrived!"

"Fleet, move into formation three," she ordered instantly. "Activate hivemind linkage and warp field generator once they're close enough." She smiled grimly. "Now, let's see how tough these people are."

Her vessels raced toward her, plowing past noncombatants at three tocks. The enemy corvettes moved to fire on them, but their blasts washed harmlessly through space as the ships wove around one another in a standard formation. Benning's ship rumbled as the station unleashed another blast of AM missiles at them, but a volley of warheads streaked past her as her fleet unloaded their own batteries at the station. The station's defenses targeted as many of the warheads as possible, but the Frostwise stations weren't built for military purposes. They couldn't handle dozens of warheads that each split into multiple smaller ones before impact, giving the station hundreds of targets all moving at 9 tocks. Explosions erupted across the station as antimatter warheads slammed into its hull, tearing holes in its armor.

As her ships moved into position around her, Benning triggered her hivemind linkage, and instantly, her awareness expanded to encompass her fleet. Formation three was a complicated pattern designed to protect a slower, damaged vessel in the center, but with her captains' practice and the aid of the hivemind, her ships slid into it almost effortlessly.

Looks like we got here just in time, Commodore, Fodor Hendricks sent through the linkage. *Your ship looks like it's been through the Hole.*

Did the Frostwise Station really attack you, Commodore? Avaeyana Roble asked curiously.

Your timing was impeccable, and yes, they did, Benning replied. *Time to make them pay for that. All ships, target vessel Frigate-1 with grasers, Frigate-2 with warheads, spiral pattern.*

Grasers streaked out from her ships, bathing the entire evasion cone of the first frigate in radiation. Photons poured into the ship, which had nowhere to flee from them. Dozens of missiles lanced outward, rippling toward the second frigate in a series of explosions that swept over the vessel, slamming into it from all sides. The enemy ships returned fire, but their attacks targeted random ships in her fleet and inflicted minimal damage at best as her ships moved through a convoluted formation, shielding one another from the effects of repeated attacks.

"Captain, Frigate-1's power plant is at 48%," Rush reported. "Her engines are down to 43%. Frigate-2 is listing badly, and her evasion cone is down 31%."

Second volley on Frigate-2, hexagonal pattern, Benning ordered. *Arcturus, target Corvette-1. It's the Elescira; I want her disabled but not destroyed.*

Britella Holland's ship? Fodor Hendricks asked in surprise. *Then the other job she was on…*

Was probably this, yes. Benning turned her thoughts back to the battle. *Keep graser fire on Frigate-1. Once she's disabled, take her, Raelle Muckley.*

The mercenaries continued to fight, but Benning could tell even they knew they were doomed. The ships fought to withdraw, not to win, but Benning didn't give them a chance. Several missile volleys ripped a hole in Frigate-2, opening it to space, and an antimatter torpedo against its hull sent it photonic. Frigate-1's engines dropped offline less than a minute later, and as the *Messenger* sped forward to link to it and claim it, Elden Rush looked back at Benning.

"Message incoming from the *Elescira,* ma'am. It's Britella Holland."

"I'll take it," Benning nodded. A moment later, the familiar face of the head of the Elnu Mohtars mercenary group appeared in her vision.

"Benning Kidd," the woman inclined her head, her silver hair falling back away from her face to reveal sharply pointed ears.

"Britella Holland," Benning answered evenly.

"Obviously, we surrender," the mercenary said with a grim smile. "What are your terms?"

"Standard terms are fine," Benning shrugged. "Half your fee for this job, and you take no jobs against me or mine for a solar year."

"Half the credits is acceptable," Holland nodded.

"No, not half the credits, Britella Holland. Half the *fee*. Someone obviously gave you those two frigates as part of this deal. I'll take the one that's left."

Holland's golden eyes narrowed. "You expect me to just hand over my ship?"

"In five minutes, it'll be my ship, anyway," Benning shrugged. "I've got forty marines en route, and without your ship's plant to power its automated defenses, we can probably take it without losing anyone. This way, you can get your crew off the ship, and I won't have to kill them all."

The mercenary stared at her for a moment before sighing, her shoulders slumping. "Fine. Half the credits and the *Pegasus*. I agree." A contract appeared in Benning's vision, and she scanned it quickly, allowing Tiddly to make sure it was accurate before signing it and returning it to the mercenary.

"Are you at liberty to discuss who hired you for this job?" Benning asked.

"It was an anonymous hire," the woman shook her head. "I have no idea who did it."

"Were you working with the Frostwise administrators?"

"Directly? No. I was told that I would receive their cooperation, though." Holland sighed again. "I almost didn't take the job, Benning Kidd. After seeing what you did to IS-39267 – and to Mildred Joyce – I knew that going up against you was a bad idea. The credits and ships they offered, though, were too tempting to refuse." She made a face. "I did refuse to pretend to want to work with you and attack you from behind, though, the way they wanted. I have a reputation to uphold, after all."

"I understand." Benning looked at the woman with a tinge of respect. Holland was a mercenary, but she was an honorable one. "You know, I could use you for an upcoming battle..."

"I know all about your issues with the Fleet, Benning Kidd," Holland shook her head. "I told you before: we don't do suicide missions. If you survive, I'd love to work with you again, though." She smiled. "You know, you'd make a fine mercenary yourself. You've got the right attitude for it."

"I don't like working for other people," Benning shrugged. "Now, I've got a system administrator to talk to."

Barreth Konishi, the administrator of Frostwise System, refused to respond to Benning's message when she first sent it. After trying three times, she directed her fleet to assault Station 14, and within minutes, the station was badly damaged, its gas storage tanks empty and its weapons systems offline. At that point, Konishi decided to accept Benning's hails at last.

"Citizen Benning Kidd," the bald man spoke crisply, his pale skin flushed red at the cheeks and his mouth and hazel eyes set in thin lines. "Due to your attack on our system, consider your lease of Station IS-39267 revoked, and..."

"Actually, Barreth Konishi, your station attacked me first," she cut him off. "That puts you in violation of our agreement, not me, which means I no longer have to pay rent for the station." His eyes went wide, but she shook her head and went on before he could continue.

"That's moot, though, because you're going to hand over ownership of the station to me. In fact, you're going to grant me ownership of this entire system."

"That's absurd!" he spluttered. "I will do no such thing!"

"Yes, you will," she said coldly. "You betrayed me, Barreth Konishi. If you know anything about me, you should know how I deal with people who betray me." She leaned forward, staring at him with anger flaring in her eyes. "I'm going to make an example of you, Barreth Konishi. I'm going to kill you slowly, over a week or more, then do it again after you respawn. I'll make the next year of your life perpetual torment, and you'll beg me to kill you a thousand times or more.

"That's going to happen, Barreth Konishi. You can't stop it. I have the troops and ships to take Frostwise Prime Station. Frostwise has never had more than twenty Soldiers, and your stations aren't built to withstand a concerted attack. When I do, your punishment will begin today." She leaned back again, staring at his wide and fearful gaze with satisfaction. "However, if you give me the system and IS-39267, I'll give you a chance to run. I'll give you a month's head start, time for you to go to another system and hide. Maybe you'll escape me; maybe you won't. At least you'll have a chance, though."

The man stared at her in silence, and Benning waited patiently for almost a full minute before shrugging. "Your choice. Fleet, target Frostwise Prime Station, full singularity battery..."

"Wait!" Konishi replied, holding up a hand. He stopped and rubbed his eyes. "Fine. I'll give you the system and station for the chance to flee." He snorted. "Not that it matters, anyway. I have it on good authority that the Fleet will be here within three days, and when they come, they'll restore me to my position – and evict you." He sneered at her. "Enjoy your victory, Benning Kidd. It won't last."

The message ended, and a contract appeared in Benning's mind. She scanned it quickly before accepting ownership of not only her station but the entire Frostwise System. She leaned back in her seat and smiled; whoever had set up this ambush would be fuming, knowing that it had only made her stronger instead of weakening her.

Back to IS-39267, Commodore? Fodor Hendrick's voice interrupted her thoughts.

No, Captain, she replied slowly.

No? Where to, then? Are we staying here?

No, we're heading back – just not to IS-39267. She laughed quietly, and her amusement carried over the link. *A while back, you suggested I name the station. I never did because it wasn't mine, and no name I gave it would matter. It is now, though, and I've already decided what I wanted to call it. IS-39267 is now Marauder's Rest.*

The captains were silent for long moments as they processed her words.

I like it, Trephor Sando spoke at last.

So do I, Roble agreed quietly. *It sounds like a place worth fighting for.*

It's fitting, Hendricks said after a moment. *Okay. Back to Marauder's Rest, then?*

Yes, Fodor Hendricks. If the Fleet is arriving in three days, we have a lot we need to get done.

CHAPTER 29

"What sort of evacuation do you have planned, Benning Kidd?" Tereza Erdeli asked as the pair and Fodor Hendricks walked through the administrative area of the station.

"Evacuation?" Benning asked. "Why would I plan an evacuation?"

Erdeli stopped and stared at the Marauder, her eyes wide with disbelief. "The Fleet is arriving in three days, Benning Kidd. Less than that, now. We have to flee."

"We're holding the station," Benning said, continuing to walk and forcing the woman to hurry to catch back up with her. "There'll be no evacuation."

"What about the civilians? Merchants, crafters, Workers... Will you evacuate them?"

Benning shrugged. "They can leave if they want to. I wouldn't blame them for not wanting to get caught in the middle of this."

"What arrangements will you make to get them off the station?"

"Why should I make any arrangements?" Benning asked, genuinely confused. "

"It's standard for the owner or administrator of a station about to come under attack to arrange for transport ships for those who want to leave," Erdeli protested.

"That's a stupid standard, and I won't be following it. They're the ones who want to leave. They can make their own arrangements."

"They'll be expecting it!"

"Then they'll be disappointed. I'm sure I'm going to need all my credits to effect repairs on my fleet and the station after this. Not to mention, I still need to repair Frostwise Station 14 at some point. It's too damaged for its nanofield to fully fix it." She shook her head. "I thought its point defenses would do a little better against the fleet's missiles."

"If you do this, Benning Kidd, people might not come back to the station, even assuming you survive this and retain ownership after," Erdeli warned.

"If we fight off the Fleet, Citizens will flock here," Benning snorted. "Anyone who wants to get out from under the Fleet's laws but doesn't want the anarchy of the Oort Cloud or Wolf will jump at the chance to join us. We might even have to build a second station in Frostwise eventually."

Erdeli stared at her, her eyes wide and her face stunned. "She's insane," she whispered, looking at Fodor Hendricks. "Benning Kidd, you can't believe that if you defeat the Fleet, they'll just leave you alone! They'll come back with more powerful ships until they've destroyed this station and maybe the entire Frostwise System."

The woman halted again and took a deep breath. "Benning Kidd, please, just abandon the station," she said pleadingly. "We can start over somewhere else. You have the Renown and credits to go anywhere in the Collective and find someone willing to work with you..."

"Until the Fleet comes there," Benning cut the woman off. "And then, I'll have to run again, and again, and again. If I start running, Tereza Erdeli, I'll never stop until the Fleet either catches me, or I leave the Collective entirely. I'd rather fight here. If I lose, then I'm in the same place I would be eventually if I ran. If I win, maybe the Fleet will think twice before risking more valuable ships against me."

"There's no point in arguing with her, Tereza Erdeli," Fodor Hendricks said quietly. "You should know by now that once Benning Kidd decides something, nothing changes her mind."

Erdeli sighed, her shoulders slumping defeatedly. "Yes, I should." She looked at Benning. "You don't mind if I let everyone on the station know that if they want to flee, they need to start making the arrangements, do you?"

"Why would I? I don't care if they go, Tereza Erdeli. It's probably smarter for them to, in fact."

"I'll take care of it." The woman turned and stormed off, her boots striking the deck harder than they had to as she marched away.

"Why is she angry?" Benning asked curiously. "She wouldn't be able to leave no matter what."

"She's upset that she might lose everything she's built here," Hendricks shrugged. "And there's nothing she can do about it. It's frustrating when you have no control over a situation. You should understand that."

Benning nodded; she'd felt that same frustration these past several months. She didn't understand Erdeli's response to it, but then, she supposed she didn't have to. If telling the station's residents they needed to flee made Erdeli feel more in control, Benning was fine with it. It didn't really affect her one way or the other.

"Speaking of which," the man cleared his throat. "I need to talk to you, Benning Kidd."

"What about?" she asked distractedly. A hundred things pulled at her attention, from formations she still needed to work on with her fleet to defensive protocols for the station.

"I won't be staying for the Fleet's arrival," he told her, his voice hesitant as he spoke.

She snorted derisively. "Yes, you will. None of my captains have that option."

"No, I won't," he said firmly. "I'm leaving Marauder's Rest with the general evacuation that's about to happen."

She stopped and turned toward him, her eyes narrowed in irritation. "We have a contract, Fodor Hendricks. You can't simply break it and leave – not without penalties."

"No, but I can buy it out," he shrugged. A moment later, a message appeared in her vision.

> FODOR HENDRICKS
> has activated the buyout clause of his contract with you. FODOR HENDRICKS agrees to pay the sum of 16,195 credits and to forfeit the gift of a suitable ship. This terminates your existing contract.

"And I just did," he added a moment later.

Benning stared at the man in mingled shock and confusion. She never imagined that Hendricks might leave her side, never even considered the possibility.

"Why?" she demanded. "Why are you doing this? You've profited enormously from our arrangement, both in credits and levels, and you can keep profiting if you stay. Why leave now?"

"Because some things are more important than credits," he sighed. "Besides, I don't think you're going to win against the Fleet, Benning Kidd. I'm with Tereza Erdeli: even if you beat them this time, they'll just come back stronger until they destroy you. The Fleet has never publicly admitted to losing a battle; they aren't about to let you drive them off without some sort of reprisal." He shrugged again. "I'm getting out while the getting's good."

"You're wrong, Fodor Hendricks," she shook her head. "We can beat them. Together, we can take a battlefrigate, and I have an idea of how to keep it once we take it. With that, the *Fall*, and a growing fleet of our own, we can hold them at bay long enough for them to realize that we're not worth the trouble."

He looked at her speculatively for a moment, then shook his head. "No, sorry. Not interested."

Anger flared inside her, anger at his betrayal of her at such a crucial juncture. "You know I can't let this slide, Fodor Hendricks," she warned. "If you wait until after the battle to leave, I'll let you go. If you leave now, I'll make sure you regret it."

He nodded. "I guessed as much, but again, I don't think you'll be in a position to do anything like that once the Fleet is done with you. At least, not for a long time." He shrugged. "Besides, it's kind of fun being hunted – just not by the Fleet."

Her anger swelled, but even as it did, the ache in her chest began to throb painfully, causing her rising fury to falter. "I don't understand. We're so close to having everything we want, Fodor Hendricks: credits, Renown, and freedom from the Fleet... Why are you walking away from all that?"

"You mean, everything you want. What I want..." He made a face. "What I want, I won't get here. I'll do better looking somewhere else."

"What do you want?" she demanded, stepping closer to him. "Maybe we can work together to get it. We can sign a new contract..."

"I was hoping for the same thing, but I know now that it will never happen. After we shared our bodies..." He looked at her, his gaze curious. "You have no idea what I'm talking about, do you?"

"No," she admitted quietly. "I don't, Fodor Hendricks."

"I didn't think so. When we shared our bodies together..." His eyes grew sad. "Did you feel anything? Anything at all?"

"I felt – content. It was pleasurable, and it made me feel better for a while."

He nodded. "But did you feel anything for me? Closeness? Affection?"

"No," she answered, truly confused once more. "Why should I? We both enjoyed ourselves, I think, and that was the whole point. It was a release, one I needed, but nothing more."

"Why me, then?" he pressed. "You could have gotten that release with half the men on the station."

"Because – I feel more comfortable around you," she said slowly.

"And that's the problem. You find me comfortable, but nothing more – and you never will. There's something broken in you, Benning Kidd. I don't know what it is, but it's something I think no amount of healing or upgrades can fix."

He stepped back. "And that's why I need to leave. I think that the Fleet is going to punish everyone who's helped you, and I don't want to suffer that – not for a woman who'll never see me as more than a useful tool. Goodbye, Benning Kidd."

He turned away, and she felt a spike of panic in her chest. She needed Hendricks; he was her best captain, someone the other captains relied on. She didn't understand what he was talking about, but she had to find a way to convince him to stay. She could offer him the *Hammer* as his own ship, or perhaps a larger share of the credits...

<He doesn't care about credits, Benning Kidd,> Tiddly said sadly in her mind. <He wants something that I don't think you can give him.>

What? Whatever it is, I can find a way...

<You can't, Benning Kidd. He wants you to care about him – maybe even to love him. I don't think you can do that. I don't think you even know what that is.>

Benning stared at the retreating Pirate Captain in shock. She knew intellectually what love was, of course. It was some sort of bond between people, an emotional one that tied them together somehow. She'd never felt anything like that herself, though; she didn't even really understand what it was supposed to be. It always seemed foolish to her – putting someone else's needs ahead of her own felt like a waste of time unless there was a significant long-term gain in it.

Tiddly was right; that was something she doubted she could ever give Hendricks. It was totally alien to her. *I'm broken, like he said,* she thought silently. *Aren't I, Tiddly?*

<I can't tell you if you're broken, Benning Kidd, but that part of you – I don't think it exists. Being a Drone took it away from you, maybe forever. You could probably fake it, but that would make things worse in the long run. Maybe if you could explain that to him, he'd understand and stay, but you can't. You can't tell him that you're a Drone, even if you want to.>

Benning's anger flared again at the idea that she couldn't do something. She was losing something – someone important to her. She wouldn't let the System stop her from trying to keep him around. She stubbornly opened her mouth, willing herself to explain, to make Hendricks see why she couldn't do what he wanted, but the words refused to come out. Her voice wouldn't speak; her lips failed to fashion the sounds she wanted. She felt paralyzed, and she knew the System was restraining her, stopping her from saying what she wanted to.

"Nothing?" he asked over his shoulder, pausing slightly. "You've got nothing to say to me before I go?"

Her eyes narrowed. The System was the problem, but she had a way around the System. The issue was, even if she activated Slip the Net and told him her secret, he'd never hear it. The System wouldn't let him. She could see another way, though. She couldn't tell him, but maybe she could show him. The System could stop Soldiers from entering the Drone tunnels, but it couldn't stop a Citizen who deliberately chose to enter them.

"Come with me," she ordered instinctively, turning her back on him. After a few steps, she realized he wasn't following her; she was no longer his commander, and he didn't have to obey her anymore. She took a deep breath. "Please, Fodor Hendricks. You've followed me all this time. Follow me once more. Maybe I can help you understand."

He looked back at her, his face suspicious but also curious. "Understand what?" he asked.

"Why I can't be that person," she told him. "Why I'm..." She hesitated. "Why I'm broken, like you said."

His eyes softened, but he remained where he stood. "How can you do that?"

"I – can't tell you," she said helplessly. "I just need you to follow me."

He stood still for another moment. "Where?"

"Into the..." She cut off, unable to say the word

"Drone" to describe the tunnels. "Somewhere here on the station. It's not far."

He turned deliberately back to face her. "Why not just tell me?" he asked.

"I can't. I want to, but…" She fell silent again. The System wouldn't let her explain that it was restraining her. "Please, Fodor Hendricks. I won't harm you, you have my word."

He nodded slowly and stepped toward her. "All right. I've trusted you this far. I can trust you one more time. I'll follow you, Benning Kidd. I'm curious to see what you'd like to show me."

She moved briskly through the passages, following the map that Tiddly held before her. The AI had long ago worked out where the Drone tunnels on the station were – after Van Maanen, Benning instructed the AI to map them on every station she entered in case she needed to use them again – and Benning made her way swiftly to the nearest entrance to them.

<It won't work, Benning Kidd,> Tiddly said sadly. <Even if you take him into the tunnels, he's only going to see what the System wants him to see – and that won't include the Drones. He'll just think they're weird maintenance tunnels.>

I think I have a way around that, Tiddly. I'm not sure if it'll work, though. What do you think?

The gnome fell silent as she examined Benning's plan. <It – it's possible, Benning Kidd. I don't know if the System will let it happen, though…>

I'm hoping that it can't stop me. This is my choice, and the System has to let Citizens make their own choices, doesn't it? It might be able to stop me from telling Hendricks that I was a Drone, but it can't stop me from using my abilities the way I want to.

She pulled up before a blank section of wall, and Hendricks stopped behind her, his face clearly confused. "What is this place?" he asked, looking around. "Isn't this just another hallway, Benning Kidd?" His face darkened with suspicion, and he took a step back, his hand dropping to his sidearm. "Did you lure me out here..."

"I promised I wouldn't harm you," she cut him off. "And I won't. You'll see what I want to show you soon enough." Her nano-disassemblers soared outward toward the wall, and he watched curiously as the metal bubbled and liquefied, running to the floor in rivulets and leaving a dark hole behind.

She turned back to look at him. "Whatever you see in that hole, ignore it," she told him. "Just follow me." She looked back at the hole and took a step forward.

"Benning Kidd, what are you doing?" he asked in an alarmed voice, reaching toward her. "That's a live power..."

His voice cut off as she stepped through the wall and into the empty tunnels behind. She stood there for a moment, breathing in the mildewy air, listening to the sound of water dripping in the distance, and letting the memories wash over her. The ache in her chest throbbed once more, but she ignored it; she'd gotten used to it, and while she didn't really understand it, it no longer bothered her. It was just a part of her, something she accepted and dealt with.

Long seconds passed, and she wondered if Fodor Hendricks had changed his mind and walked away. For all she knew, he'd seen her step into a power relay and vaporize. She wouldn't blame him for refusing to follow her through that. She turned, preparing to step back through the hole to show him she lived, when the darkness in the wall behind her shifted, and he stepped through, looking around in confusion.

"Fodor Hendricks," she said in a relieved tone. "I'm glad you decided to follow me."

"Benning Kidd?" he said, his voice puzzled and his eyes unfocused as he continued to scan the tunnel. "You're alive? I saw you turn to ash when you touched that power coupling! I thought I'd join you in respawn one last time before I left."

"No, I'm fine," she told him. He looked toward her, but his eyes refused to focus directly on her. She frowned. "Can you see me, Fodor Hendricks?"

"No, of course not. It's totally dark in here." He frowned. "Where are we? Is this part of the station's maintenance areas? Why isn't it lit? My scanners should illuminate it for me..."

Benning opened her mouth to explain, but once more, the words froze on her tongue. She couldn't tell him where they were. She couldn't tell him that it was actually sufficiently if dimly lit. She couldn't even say that she couldn't explain anything, or why he couldn't see it. The System froze her lips even as it blocked his sight.

Not for long, though, she thought grimly.

She reached out with her nanofield and connected instantly to Fodor Hendrick's 'net. She'd hacked it before, many times, so gaining access was child's play for her. In seconds, she had full access to his gear, status, and credit accounts. She could have killed him in that moment without even trying, shutting down his equipment and nanofield, stifling his abilities, and rendering him all but helpless. She'd promised that she wouldn't harm him, though, and she did her best to keep her promises.

Instead, she took a deep breath and activated Slip the Net. As the ability flooded through her, shifting the patterns of her 'net, she channeled it into the Pirate Captain through their nanite link. The ability resisted at first – it wanted to follow the patterns Tiddly had created for it – but Benning stubbornly held the image in her head of Hendrick's 'net linked to hers, the two joined as one, and demanded that her ability follow that link. The patterns swirled in her mind, trying to ignore her commands, but she drove them into Hendricks, using her understanding of the Overnet and its fields to force his 'net into the form she needed...

Benning inhaled sharply as the ability slid into place. She once again felt that sense of loss as the Overnet vanished from her consciousness, leaving her in a vast silence that stretched interminably. The quiet in her mind railed at her, but she pushed it aside with only minor effort.

Hendricks, on the other hand, reacted far more strongly. He gasped as her ability severed him from the 'net, and his eyes went wide with sudden horror. He blinked rapidly, his eyes focusing as the System's limits on his vision vanished, but he stepped back away from her, his face clearly frightened as he reached for his weapon.

"What – what did you do to me?" he demanded, grabbing his mace and freezing suddenly. "Why can't I use my abilities? What's going on?"

"I cut you off from the Overnet," she said simply, remaining still even as she readied herself in case he attacked. She hadn't considered how he might react to the effects of her ability, and while she'd promised not to hurt him, if he came after her, she'd have to defend herself. He was stronger and faster than her, but she'd fought a lot more than he had recently, and without the help of the Overnet to assist him, he'd be at a large disadvantage.

"What?" he demanded, not attacking but obviously upset. He looked around like a trapped animal. "It's too quiet! Stop it, Benning Kidd!"

"Fodor Hendricks," she said as calmly as possible. She

remembered his panic; she'd felt it herself. Tiddly had been there to pull Benning out of it; she would have to do the same for Hendricks. He ignored her, and she reached out, grabbing his chin firmly and twisted his head to face her, looking into his eyes.

"Fodor Hendricks!" she said sharply, her voice taking on a note of command. "Stand down and listen to me!" He paused, blinking as her words struck him, and she continued. "I know that you feel alone right now, but you aren't. I'm here. I promised I wouldn't harm you; I won't let any harm come to you either." He tried to turn his head away, but she held his chin tightly. "No! Look at me, Fodor Hendricks. You're safe right now, you have my word. Stay calm, and focus on me."

He froze and took a few deep breaths, visibly calming himself. "I – I'm okay," he said at last in a trembling voice. "You can let go, Benning Kidd."

She released his chin and stepped back. She could see the tension that still coiled in him. He looked like a trapped animal, ready to bolt at the first chance, but he slowly mastered himself, and some of that tension leaked away.

"What – why did you do this, Benning Kidd?" he asked at last, his voice trembling only slightly as he spoke.

"Because I had to," she assured him. "The System wouldn't have let you hear my explanation or see what I want to show you."

"What are you talking about? The System wouldn't let me…" He froze and looked around again. "This place was void black a few seconds ago, Benning Kidd – but it wasn't really, was it?"

"No, it wasn't. The System just didn't want you to see it." She gestured past him. "Look behind you at the wall you came through. Does it still look like a live power relay?"

He turned and stared for a moment before twisting back to face her. "It's just a hole. What's going on? Where are we?"

"Drone tunnels," she said, exulting as the words came out of her mouth. "Walk with me, and I'll explain."

She strode off through the tunnel, and after a moment, she heard him following behind her. "How did you know this was here?" he asked curiously.

"Because I lived most of my life down here, Fodor Hendricks," she answered curtly. "Trust me. I'll explain in a bit. Just follow me and don't ask too many questions. It'll be easier to explain all at once."

They passed through the halls in silence, weaving around unseeing Drones int their loose, gray clothing. Hendricks stared at them as they passed, and once he reached out toward one, a woman with short, light blonde hair, but she caught his arm and shook her head.

"They can't see you or hear you," she told him. "If you touch them, you'll only confuse them."

"Who are these people?" he demanded. "What are they doing down here?"

"They're Drones. They live down here."

"But why are they down here?" He looked around. "They all look to be cleaning; I thought the nanofield did that. Are they the station's maintenance staff? Why haven't I seen them before?"

"Because the System won't let you. Just like it wouldn't let me explain what this place was or let them see or hear us."

"That only answers one of my questions," he pointed out.

"I know," she nodded. "But the other questions will be

part of my full explanation. Just be patient, and don't bother trying to interact with anyone you see down here. There's no point to it."

Finding the hive was a simple enough matter. Drones only walked while they were performing their daily duties; once they finished, they rode their helper bots back to the hive to receive their reward of game credits. It still took hours of walking to reach it, though. Benning considered dissolving the door with her nanites but decided to instead wait for a Drone to show up and open the passage for them. They followed the man through the door as it faded away, and they both froze as they entered the Drone hive together.

Benning supposed that Hendricks was probably stopping from surprise, but she had to stop as a swell of memories rushed over her. The hive was identical to the own she'd lived in, down to the last detail. Long tables filled the central space of the hive, and tens of thousands of Drones sat along them in utter silence, eating. Stacks of sleeping capsules lined the walls, rising to the ceiling above and stretched out farther than Benning could see with her normal, non-System-aided vision. A door in one wall led to the pleasure chambers, where Drones could share their bodies with one another, while another wall held the feeding ports where Drones lined up to receive their daily rations of the nutrient pudding that the System gave them to keep them perfectly healthy.

She'd spent countless years in a room just like this one – even with her memories returned, Benning had no way to track the passage of time and had no idea how old she was. She'd lived just as these Drones did, in a haze of perpetual "now", performing pointless tasks designed solely to keep their bodies healthy in return for game tokens that exercised their minds. Part of her wanted to walk over to the feeding port and get her allotment of pudding, then sit down and eat it in silence before retiring to her capsule. It was a habit ingrained over decades, and she had to force herself to stay where she was and simply observe.

"There's thousands of them," Hendricks whispered from beside her. "Tens of thousands! Who – what the flork is this place, Benning Kidd?"

"The hive," she said shortly. "It's the closest thing the Drones have to a home. Every day, they wake up, eat, and go into the tunnels to perform some pointless task the System gives them. Then, they return here, eat again, play games for a few hours, and sleep. The next day, they do it all over again – and they keep doing that, every day, for their entire lives."

Hendricks shuddered. "I couldn't live like that," he proclaimed.

"Yes, you could, because you wouldn't know any better." She gestured at the Drones. "Drones don't have memories, Fodor Hendricks. They don't remember yesterday or the day before. They don't know that every day is the same because they're barely aware that a time before today existed. They don't remember one another; they don't remember what they did today. They just...exist."

He turned toward her, his eyes widening. "How do you know all this?" he asked hoarsely. "I've never even heard of – what did you call them? Drones? I don't understand..."

"Three years ago, Fodor Hendricks, I was one of them," she said softly, wincing as the pain in her chest spiked.

"What? No." He shook his head. "I looked into your background, Benning Kidd. You grew up in a creche, attended Mars Fleet Academy..."

"No. I grew up..." She hesitated. "Actually, I have no idea where I grew up. My first memories were of being an adult in a hive like this one. I lived in one of the Mars hives for years, Fodor Hendricks – how many, I can't say. That time is still mostly a blur."

She turned and looked at him directly. "I was elevated to Citizenship by accident. It was a mistake, the System erring on the side of caution. By all rights, I should still be in a place like this – or dead."

"Dead?"

She nodded. "You're looking at the basis for our immortality, Fodor Hendricks. Every time you die, your consciousness is written into the body of a Drone, and that Drone dies forever. That's who these people are: blank templates, just waiting to be wiped clean and turned into a new Citizen."

His face took on a look of horror that even she could recognize. "Overwritten? Then you…"

She nodded, and anger curled up in her as she spoke. "I was selected to be overwritten, but there was an accident. The System made me a Citizen by mistake." She looked back at the hive.

"This is why I'm the way I am, Fodor Hendricks. Drones barely recognize one another's existence. Without memories, they can't form bonds to one another, can barely understand that other Drones are people, too." She shrugged. "Or maybe the System removes that ability from them. I don't know.

"The point is, I don't understand when you talk about things like caring, affection – love – because I never experienced anything like it. I know what those things are, but I don't feel them. I don't know how to feel them. They're…" She stopped, struggling to find the words to explain.

"Like explaining color to a blind man," he said softly. She looked at him curiously, and he shrugged. "Imagine someone who was blind from birth, who never saw anything in their life. Now, imagine trying to explain what blue is to them, and how it's different from red. You couldn't; it's just something you know, not something you can easily articulate."

"Yes," she said, feeling a sense of relief at his understanding. "That's exactly what it's like. I don't understand these things because I've never felt any of them, not once."

She looked at him intently. "That doesn't mean I don't think you're valuable and important, though. You're the best captain among us; you're dependable and competent; you make everyone feel more comfortable when they're around you and help keep people in line. I still need you, Fodor Hendricks, even if I don't feel any of those things."

He nodded and looked at the hive again. "Let's go," he said softly. "This place is depressing – and it's still too quiet."

Benning was forced to dissolve the door to allow them to leave, and dozens of Drones watched curiously as the hatch dissolved into liquid, but they quickly turned away as their hazy minds forgot what they'd seen. Hendricks watched them return to their silent state and shook his head.

"They've forgotten already, haven't they?"

Benning nodded. "You could go kill one, and the others would forget about it the moment the nanofield scrubbed their bodies. The System doesn't let them remember anything unpleasant."

"What – what was it like?" he asked slowly. "Being a – one of those?"

"Drones are content, for the most part. They don't want for things or worry about things. They perform their tasks and are rewarded with game credits, and they're fine with that. They don't understand enough to be anything else."

"Game credits?"

"Yes. Drones spend part of their sleep cycle each day playing games through the Overnet. They don't have credits, so the System gives them game credits, instead. It helps keep their minds from atrophying, I guess."

He shook his head. "What's the point? Why go to all that trouble when the System could just make a body with nanoreplicators?"

"That doesn't work. When the System tried it, the Citizens it made went slowly insane. I guess only a body with a mind that developed naturally can be overwritten successfully – something about it being able to correct small inconsistencies and tiny errors in the process." She shrugged. "Fyodr Mosin explained it, but I don't really understand. The point is that the System needs Drones to give Citizens true immortality."

"Fyodr Mosin? Isn't he a Noble? Then – they know about this?"

"Apparently. It's the reason that Nobles hunt me, in fact. They don't want me to succeed. I think they're afraid that if I do, the System might elevate more Drones, and the respawn process could be in jeopardy."

He looked at her curiously. "Why did it elevate you?"

"As I said, it was an accident," she hedged, not wanting to explain her abnormally high Willpower. "Unlike most other Drones, I wasn't content with not understanding things. The System tried to stop me asking questions by punishing me or bribing me with extra credits."

He grinned. "It didn't know you well, then. If you were anything then like you are now, that wouldn't have worked."

"It did for years," she corrected. "But eventually, I refused to give in when it gave me pain to stop me from thinking about things it didn't want me to – so it chose to overwrite me, instead."

She hesitated again. "For some reason, the respawn AI mistook me for a possible Citizen. It can't overwrite Citizens – that's a protocol it has – so to be safe, it elevated me to Citizenship and gave me a fake background, along with memories, skills, and education to match it."

"You mean, the System tried to kill you just for thinking things it didn't want," he said in disbelief, shaking his head.

"Yes. And you know me, Fodor Hendricks. When someone tries to kill me, I make sure they pay."

He looked at her, startled. "Wait, you intend to make the System pay? How?"

"I'm going to become a Noble. When I do, I'm going to use that power to find a way to punish the System for trying to hurt me." Rage flowed through her, and it must have showed on her face as she looked at Hendricks because he drew back slightly.

"I never asked for any of this, Fodor Hendricks. I just wanted to live my life and make a place for myself in the Collective – but I can't do that. The Nobles won't let me; the Fleet won't let me; the System won't let me."

"What if they did?" he asked quietly. "What if they all just left you alone?"

"It wouldn't change anything. I'd know that I'd just be existing at their sufferance. What if they changed their minds? What if they waited until I was close to reaching my goals and then tore everything down at once?" She shook her head. "They've declared themselves my enemies, Fodor Hendricks. The only way I know to keep myself safe from my enemies is to make them afraid to attack me."

He nodded. "That's a very 'Benning Kidd' philosophy. If someone hurts you, hurt them back so badly that they're terrified to hurt you again."

They walked in silence back to the exit from the tunnels, which Benning once more had to tear open with her nanites. Once they stepped back into the main passageways, she dropped Slip the Net, and Hendricks sighed in audible relief as the Overnet's presence once more flooded their bodies.

"That's a terrifying ability you have, Benning Kidd. How do you..." He stopped, frowning as he struggled silently, apparently unable to continue speaking. Benning simply nodded; the System didn't want him mentioning that she could cut herself off from it.

"I can't tell you," she shrugged. "The same way you'll never be able to tell anyone what you've just seen and heard. You understand why."

He frowned but nodded slowly. "I do."

"Do you understand now, Fodor Hendricks? Do you understand why I'm the way I am – and why I can't be what you want?" She looked at him intently, her gaze hopeful.

"Yeah, I do." He shook his head. "It doesn't change anything, though. Even if you convince the Fleet to leave you alone, how will you do that to the Nobles – or the System itself?" He sighed. "I can't be part of that, of watching them slowly tear you down. I'm sorry, Benning Kidd."

He turned and walked away from her, and Benning watched him go. The ache in her chest throbbed powerfully, threatening to overwhelm her, but instead of pushing it aside, she let it flow through her, basking in the sensation. She understood it now, knew what it was and what she felt. Being in the hive had crystallized it for her, made the sensation sharp and poignant enough for her to recognize it.

Loss. Loss filled her daily, shading everything she did in her life. She'd lost her identity, her sense of self, her place in the Collective. She'd lost her innocent belief that the System was there to help her. She'd lost her faith in her continued existence. Now, she'd lost the only human she felt remotely comfortable around, the only one she might have considered herself close to.

She turned aside and headed to her quarters. Benning Kidd didn't dwell on her losses. She avenged them. She'd find a way to pay the System back for this one, too.

CHAPTER 30

"The Fleet has entered Frostwise System," Tereza Erdeli spoke without preamble to the gathered captains. "A battlefrigate, as expected, plus two destroyers and three fast frigates. They came out of deep dive two light-hours from the system and are making their way there steadily. I expect them to arrive within six hours."

"They're taking their time, then," Saavi Boguna said thoughtfully, her fingers playing absently with her lavender hair. "They could be in-system in twenty minutes if they wanted. Did you know that battlefrigates create a bubble of CY-space that slows KK particles from forming?"

"They can afford to take their time," Raelle Muckley snorted. "They have to know that the fleet is here at Marauder's Rest, so there's nothing in Frostwise that can really stop them."

"Especially since Benning Kidd ordered the stations not to put up any resistance," Erdeli added a bit waspishly.

"You did?" Trephor Sando asked. "Why in the Hole not?"

"Because it would just get the stations damaged for no reason," Benning shrugged. "I doubt they could take out a single destroyer, not when the Fleet knows how to fight tactically, so it would just delay them by a couple hours at best. After we drive off the Fleet, we'll have to repair that damage, and that cost is too high for a short delay."

"You still think we can win?" Avaeyana Roble asked. "Even without Fodor Hendricks?"

"Yes," Benning nodded, her face carefully calm and composed. "My plan will still work, even without him."

"What is your plan?" Sando demanded. "You say you have one, but you won't tell us what it is."

"It's a combination of the special tactics we've been working on and a new weapon I've recently acquired," Benning hedged.

"Subspace tunnellers won't work on Fleet vessels," Roble pointed out. "Their engines are shielded against them somehow with proprietary Fleet tech."

"No, it's a weapon we've never used in combat before," Benning said. "But it should shut the battlefrigate down completely, and without that, the Fleet ships don't stand a chance."

Muckley snorted derisively. "Shut down a battlefrigate? What, do you have a dreadnought hidden nearby we don't know about, Benning Kidd?"

"We've been talking, Benning Kidd," Roble said hesitantly. "While we've all done well for ourselves working with you – we think that Fodor Hendricks might have had the right idea. We can all afford to buy out our contracts, and I think we should do that."

"It'd be smarter to abandon the station and run," Sando agreed. "A battlefrigate by itself is bad enough, but one with supporting ships accompanying it?" He shook his head. "It's impossible."

"You could run, too, Benning Kidd," Erdeli added. "Once the Fleet regains this place, they'll probably leave you alone for a while, at least."

"Do you really think so?" Benning asked sarcastically. She looked at the others. "Do you really think the Fleet will let any of you alone?"

"They have no reason to chase us," Muckley grunted. "It's you they want." The others looked at her sharply, but she shrugged. "What? It's true."

"Once, it was true. It isn't anymore." Benning touched the table, and a holoscreen appeared above it, turning slowly so that they could all read it.

"What's this?" Boguna asked curiously.

"This is something I took from the Fleet's files earlier today, Saavi Boguna. It's the arrest order for me – and all of you." Benning waved her hand, and the screen enlarged to show the names of everyone at the table, as well as Fodor Hendricks.

"What the Hole?" Erdeli exploded. "'Aiding and abetting widespread piracy'? I was just following the letter of our contract!"

"You all were," Benning shrugged. "The Fleet doesn't care, apparently. Avaeyana Roble, you're being charged with 'Impersonating an Officer'. Trephor Sando and Saavi Boguna are both accused of 'Wanton Piracy and Destruction'." She looked at the green-haired Raelle Muckley, who stared at the warrant in open confusion. "You're being accused of desertion, Raelle Muckley."

"I – no! I got a legitimate discharge!"

"Apparently not, at least according to an Admiral Lucira Blanchard."

Benning closed the screen and stood up, walking away from the table. "You think that running will save you. That warrant shows that it won't. This isn't a Fleet investigation that might last for years without anything happening before they absolve you. It's an arrest order, signed by an admiral and approved by the Admiralty. The Fleet *will* come looking for you, and they'll find you."

"This doesn't make sense," Sando complained. "We

were following orders according to a standing contract! By Fleet law, we aren't supposed to be prosecuted for things we did under those orders!"

"You're right, Trephor Sando. But it's happening anyway – and I don't know why any of you are surprised. If the Fleet is coming after me, why wouldn't they come after you as well?"

"Because, Benning Kidd, you've actually done things to deserve the Fleet coming for you," Erdeli said acidly.

"No, Tereza Erdeli. I've done things to make the Fleet interested in me. I've done things to make them investigate me." Benning turned back to the table and leaned her hands on it, eyeing her captains one at a time. "The Fleet didn't just do that, though, did it? They convinced the governor of Van Maanen to apprehend me. They tried to kidnap me with a neural nullifier. They even lured us into a trap and attacked us all."

"You fired on one of their ships!" Erdeli pointed out.

"After they fired first, Tereza Erdeli," Muckley snorted. "The Fleet isn't supposed to fire first. That's regulations. They'd have needed an admiral's orders to do that." She pointed at the name beneath her warrant. "Looks like they had it, too."

"You're all expecting the Fleet to follow its rules and behave fairly," Benning went on. "It's not – but then, it's not just the Fleet, is it? The whole System is set up against us."

"The System?" Roble asked, her eyes wide. "What do you mean?"

"Tereza Erdeli, you were forced to work for Nikita Mosin, to help him work against me, when I'll bet that you would have been happier to just let me be. Isn't that right?" Benning stared at the blonde woman.

"Yes," Erdeli said bitterly. "I told him that all he had

to do was rescind his bounties on you and let you be, and the whole matter would vanish. No one cared that you beat him in the arena – everyone knows that he's not a good gladiator and relies on cheating and superior gear – and in a year, no one would have remembered that it happened. He wouldn't let it go."

"And because of that, you were forced to come work for me. You were given a choice, but not a real one. Did the System give you any other options?"

"No, of course not."

"By its own protocols, it should have, though. It should have given you a way out. Citizens must always have choices – real choices, not forced ones." She looked at Roble. "You've spent years working to change your path, Avaeyana Roble. Has the System given you anything to help with that?"

"No," the Engineer-turned-captain shook her head.

"No, it hasn't, any more than it's given Trephor Sando something to overcome his low social stat or Saavi Boguna a path that will allow her more exploration. The System is supposed to be designed to uplift humanity and make us into our best selves." She snorted. "Do any of you feel uplifted?"

Silence reigned over the room, and Benning nodded. "I wondered once why I offered each of you a contract over the others who contacted me. None of you seemed like the best captains, after all, and there were people like Fodor Hendricks who had more experience, more skills, and more abilities. Yet, I chose you all, and I know why. We all have something in common. The System has failed us all. It's let us all down, one way or another, forced us to make our own ways in spite of it – or even against it."

She stepped back and walked around the room again. "The Fleet coming here is just part of that. I took this station because my enemies attacked me, stole a ship belonging to me, and left me no choice but to use every weapon I could against them. Yes, I broke the Fleet's rules, but there were mitigating circumstances. I should have paid restitution to the people I sent to respawn, and that should have been the end of the matter.

"Instead, the Fleet has hunted me for months. Now, it's hunting you, too, but that's because the System is allowing it to. It's letting the Fleet break its own rules because the System doesn't give a scrit about any of us. It just wants to keep itself running, to make itself stronger, and to tie humanity to it more tightly. We don't fit into its models, so it's tossed us aside."

She leaned back over the table, slamming her fist down onto it. "Well, I'm tired of letting the System do whatever it wants to me. It wants to send the Fleet after me? Fine! I'll destroy their ships, take their battlefrigate, and come out the stronger for it!"

She took a deep breath and leaned back. "Alone, we're each vulnerable. We have to do what the System wants. Together, though, we're strong enough that the System sees us as a threat." She gestured toward Tereza Erdeli. "Ask her. The last time the Fleet took this station from pirates, it sent a single battlefrigate, nothing more. They had five times the number of ships we do, but the Fleet deployed one battlefrigate to deal with them – and that was all it took. It's sending the battlefrigate plus a secondary fleet against us because it *knows* that we're a threat to it! It *knows* that we'd take down its battlefrigate alone! You see this fleet as a sign that we can't win; I see it as proof that we can, and even the Fleet knows it!"

She moved back to her seat and sat down. "If you want to buy out your contracts, I can't stop you," she said. "But it won't save you from the Fleet – or from me. I'll get through this, one way or another, and when I do, I'm going to find

Fodor Hendricks and remind him what I do to people who betray me." She leaned on the table, folding her hands. "So, do you still want to buy them out?"

"Flork that," Sando snorted. "You're right, Benning Kidd. I think the Fleet's scared of us! I'm not going anywhere."

"I'm staying," Roble nodded, and Boguna assented quietly.

"Where the Hole would I go?" Muckley snorted. "I'm in. Fodor Hendricks was a fool to leave if you ask me."

"Good," Benning nodded, leaning back. "Now, let's all go get some rest. The Fleet will be here soon, and when they arrive, we need to be ready for them."

Benning returned to her quarters and settled onto her bed, pulling the cover over her and dropping into her Overnet domain. She blinked as she opened her eyes and looked around the endless plain, ignoring the golden icon swirling above her head.

"That was a great speech, Benning Kidd!" Tiddly swirled into view in front of Benning, her small, round face excited. "You got them all back on board with you!"

"I did," Benning nodded. "Not that it matters."

"What do you mean? Of course, it matters! You have your fleet, now!"

"Yes, but my plan won't work with this secondary fleet," Benning shook her head. "Not without Fodor Hendricks, at least. None of the others gained the Fleet Tactics skill, so they can't take command. The Fleet will destroy them."

"It can still work, though. It's a good plan, Benning Kidd."

"It can, but it'll cost me everything to gain the

victory." Benning laughed. "Even if I win, I'll lose, Tiddly."

"At least you get to level up!" Tiddly said, obviously trying to distract the Marauder.

Benning sighed. "Yes, I do." She looked at Tiddly curiously. "Level 11 was a lot easier to get than level 10 was, Tiddly. Did you notice that?"

The AI nodded. "I think that it's because your new path is so much more suited to you. You advance your path with just about everything you do, from hacking to using your nanofield to combat. Even that speech you gave to the others bumped you up by a percent. It's a better path for you, so you'll advance faster on it, at least at first. It'll probably slow down after a couple levels."

Benning nodded as she thought about leveling up.

CONGRATULATIONS!
You have leveled up in the Career Path of
STELLAR MARAUDER!
Your new level is 11.
As a STELLAR MARAUDER, you gain
the following with every new level:
All stats +0.2
All path Skills +0.5
3 Standard Credits
3 Skill Credits
Skill credits must be spent before
leaving the Overnet, or they will
be randomly assigned.
Move Ever Forward, Citizen!

ABILITIES GAINED!
As a Stellar Marauder, you gain lesser

versions of abilities from the paths
of Starship Captain, Arena Gladiator,
Cybernaut, and Nanomancer,
although you will not receive every
ability from all of these paths.

HEART OF THE SAVAGE
This lesser version of Heart of the Beast
boosts your physical stats by +50%, gives
you a +50% bonus to attacks, and allows
you to ignore all pain for 1 minute. If
you are out of combat or fail to make
an attack for 5 consecutive seconds
of this time, the ability ends early.

As the leveling euphoria surged through Benning's body, her mind pulled free, allowing her to ignore it. Clinically, she dropped her skill credits into Cyberwarfare, Fleet Tactics, and Nanoresistance, then pulled up her status sheet to examine it.

BENNING KIDD
Citizen Path: Stellar Marauder
Level: 11
To Next Level: 2%
Credits: 21,862.7 Standard Credits

Physicality: 13.5
Coordination: 13.3
Resistance: 13.4

Acuity: 12.1
Willpower: 18.8
Social: 11.7

Renown: +/- 87
Nanodefense: 39.3

SKILLS
Conditioning: 21.6
Cyberwarfare: 19.8
Fleet Tactics: 9.7
Leadership: 23.2
Martial Combat: 22.9
Nanoresistance: 6.7
Naval Tactics: 25.9
Sense Deceit: 6.1
Starfaring: 21.2
Weapons Expertise: 21.4

She grimaced mentally; both Cyberwarfare and Fleet Tactics were very close to ranking up. If she went with her original plan for dealing with the Fleet, she'd probably push both into the next level – but that gain wasn't worth the likely cost.

The leveling ecstasy faded, and her mind rejoined her body. She dropped to one knee as exhaustion swept over her, gasping as she caught her breath. Her muscles still trembled and shook in the aftereffects of leveling up, but her mind was clear and lucid. She waited for the last of the shaking to ease and stood up, closing her status.

"So, what are you going to do, Benning Kidd?" Tiddly asked. "If you think that your plan won't work..."

"I'll have to run," Benning sighed. "I don't have any other choice – at least, not one that won't cost me my ship and probably my life."

"Do you think the Fleet will leave you and the other captains alone if you give them the station?"

"No. At least, not permanently." Benning grimaced. "I was hoping that building a solid fleet would be the way to hold them off, but it looks like that's not the best strategy. It relies too much on trusting other people, and it's pretty clear, that's a bad idea."

Tiddly frowned. "That's not necessarily true, Benning Kidd. Just because Fodor Hendricks left…"

"It's not about Fodor Hendricks," Benning said flatly. "At least, not entirely. I thought I could count on him, but I couldn't – and that taught me that in the long run, I probably can't count on anyone but myself."

"And me," Tiddly pointed out.

"And you." Benning sighed and rubbed her eyes as the ache in her chest intensified. "I don't understand people, Tiddly. I never will, and we both know it. That's the problem, though. I can count on my rifle, my hammer, or my ship. They'll always do what I want them to do and don't need anything but some minor maintenance.

"People are different. They want their own things, and when they don't get them, they go off to find them. That's what Fodor Hendricks did, and it's what the others wanted to do today. They just wanted to keep being simple pirates, staying out of the Fleet's sights. I had to show them that they weren't going to get that, no matter what. Once they realized that, then they were willing to stay – but if the Fleet rescinds that warrant on them, they'll all leave the next time this happens."

"Maybe. Maybe not. Like you said, people are hard to understand. They don't always do what you'd expect them to."

"No, they don't, but at least one of them will do it. Someone will decide that doing what they want is more important than the credits it'll cost or being hunted down by me, and they'll leave." She shrugged. "I would probably do the same thing in their shoes, Tiddly."

"What are you thinking?"

"I'm going to start the attack tomorrow, but once it goes badly – which it will – I'll order everyone to retreat and abandon the station. That way, the Fleet will have to chase all of us, not just me."

"So, you're just giving up?"

"Of course not," Benning said as anger kindled inside her. "I'm just being realistic. I can't beat the Fleet this way – it relies too much on other people – so, I'll have to find a way to do it myself. With Cyberwarfare and Slip the Net, I can probably get into any Fleet base I want, Tiddly. They'll still pay."

She stared out at the emptiness of her domain, and she felt a smile tugging at her lips even as the ache in her chest slowly grew. She'd lost this round to the Fleet – or she soon would – but she knew that ultimately, she'd win her private war. The Fleet would take her station, but in return, she'd destroy one of theirs – and she'd keep doing so until they realized that a war with Benning Kidd wasn't something they wanted to fight.

CHAPTER 31

Adlyn Bechard kept her eyes focused on the screen in front of her as the battlefrigate soared through CY-space. When she'd first left Fleet HQ and set off on her investigation into Benning Kidd, she'd had to work to keep from looking around, seeing the universe from a higher-dimensional perspective. It was a tantalizing view; she could see everything, including inside sealed ship safes and the heart of her starship's computer core. She could even see beneath the clothing of the various people around her, if she focused correctly; however, when she rather salaciously tried, she instead got a deep and detailed look into the inner workings of a nearby Soldier's organs. Seeing the contents of the man's large intestine being slowly broken down by his nanofield wasn't remotely appealing, and the view – and the attendant vertigo looking around gave her – left her nauseated and trembling. After that, she was happy to keep her eyes firmly locked on her reports. A good investigator was supposed to be curious, after all, but that curiosity had to have limits, and she'd found one of hers.

Besides, the reports were interesting enough to hold her attention without needing to play the voyeur on the Citizens around her. She'd collected every account, every witness statement, and every scrap of evidence she could find about Benning Kidd, and she scanned through them meticulously. Captain Harrix Kirwan, her senior and mentor, taught her that a good investigator ignored the scans and focused on the sights; they paid attention not to the larger picture but to the small details. The trick, he'd explained, wasn't to see how the details fit together, but how they didn't, how they didn't match with the story they were supposed to tell. False testimony was like shoddy Molex; find one loose thread and pull it, and more would come free with it until the whole thing unraveled.

And Adlyn was finding plenty of loose threads. Too many things in this investigation simply didn't make sense. The story she'd been told wasn't correct, not completely, and Adlyn was determined to find out what those inconsistencies meant.

The problem was, much of what Benning Kidd was accused of doing, she'd plainly done, but most of it was hard to directly prove. She'd hidden her tracks well, but traces were still there to find if someone looked hard enough. She'd bought a subspace tunneller and a strangelet bomb in the Wolf System, and both of those were used not long after in her capture of IS-39267, the newly rechristened "Marauder's Rest". She'd seized a cruiser after it and several ships nearby suffered damage that looked like a nanobomb attack. The person who'd killed Adlyn was recorded entering Benning Kidd's ship soon after. The attacks on Van Maanen and Altair happened just before that same ship fled those systems.

There was very little direct evidence linking the woman to those crimes, of course. The testimonies of known pirates wouldn't be admissible in Admiralty Court – it would be too easy for the SAD or System-appointed defender to show that the pirates weren't trustworthy, and none of them would allow the Fleet access to their 'nets to confirm their accounts. The few ships that survived the assault on Marauder's Rest belonged to Benning Kidd now, and Adlyn didn't have access to their data recordings without seizing the ships. No security footage showed Benning Kidd near the hearts of either of the stations that were damaged or destroyed. Even so, together, it was powerful circumstantial evidence, and that might be enough for a conviction. Despite what most Citizens believed – thanks to holo-videos and their ridiculous stories about the Fleet, primarily – most convictions in Admiralty Court hinged on circumstantial, not direct evidence. It was only after the conviction that the Fleet gained full access to the criminal's data records and could confirm what they'd done directly.

Except that the only things Adlyn knew she could convict Benning Kidd of were using Fleet-prohibited weapons and piracy. That was an open-and-shut case; the woman had clearly used those weapons to seize Marauder's Rest, and a dozen or more ships' data cores showed Benning Kidd or her fleet attacking and seizing them. Unfortunately, neither of those were considered primary offenses, ones that required the Fleet to actively seek out and punish the perpetrator. Use of prohibited weapons was if Citizens in good standing died in the usage of those weapons, and piracy was only if the pirates seized more than 1,000 H-cubes worth of goods or 100,000 credits worth of ships.

Kidd's actions didn't quite qualify. She hadn't taken close to the minimum number of ships or cargo. Her attack on the station had only killed known criminals; she'd even spared an executive she'd captured and returned them to their corporation. That same executive was killed a few days later, but that came from a bounty that another corporation had put on the man's head for ostensibly misrepresenting their name. If Adlyn arrested Benning for something else, she'd be able to prosecute the woman for her crimes, but they didn't justify hunting her down.

Benning Kidd's arrest warrant didn't mention those crimes, though, and that bothered Adlyn. The woman was being arrested for terrorist acts against Citizens, wanton property destruction above one million credits, mass murder of Citizens, and flagrantly attacking Fleet vessels. Those crimes, if she were convicted, would have her spawn-camped back to level one, stripped of her credits and possessions, and imprisoned for at least a decade somewhere far from Sol. Few Citizens ever recovered from that sort of punishment; most of them gave up and ended up retreating to their domains, spending the rest of their lives in the Overnet and abandoning the Collective.

The thing was, even if they arrested Benning Kidd and brought her in for trial, Adlyn shouldn't be able to get a conviction for any of those things. Was it suspicious that she fled Van Maanen right before some unknown technology wreaked havoc on it? Absolutely, but all it meant was that Benning Kidd knew the attack was forthcoming and failed to warn anyone. That was a crime, but not a serious one; at worst, she'd have to pay a moderate fine of a thousand credits or so. The same was true for Aquilae Station; Benning Kidd likely knew what happened there, but linking her to it required the assumption that some invisible assassin/saboteur worked for her. Adlyn had scoured the Overnet and couldn't find a single clue that Benning Kidd had a contract with anyone who might even loosely fit that description. "Invisible saboteur" wasn't a phrase Adlyn ever wanted to use in Admiralty Court.

And as for the charge of attacking the Fleet vessels – well, Adlyn wasn't given access to the flight records and recorders of the damaged vessels, so she couldn't really say. That in and of itself was telling, though. Typically, those should have been given to her as lead investigator immediately, but they were sealed under Admiral Lucira Blanchard's orders. Adlyn didn't know why, but her best guess was that those records wouldn't show what the admiral wanted – which meant that the Fleet had probably struck first, and Benning Kidd was simply defending herself. If that were the case, the woman would still deserve punishment, but once again, it would be a matter of a fine, not seizure of her ships and imprisonment.

And that was the case for most of the charges against

the woman. Benning Kidd was a criminal, of that there could be no doubt. She'd been involved, one way or the other, in the deaths of billions, millions of credits of damage to one station, and the utter destruction of another. Put together, the crimes Adlyn could tie to her would warrant the loss of a level, six months' imprisonment, and some hefty fines. For some reason, though, the Admiralty was making her out to be some sort of terrorist, a danger to the entire Collective. It was as if Admiral Lucira Blanchard had a personal vendetta against the woman, which was absurd. Fleet Officers didn't reach the rank of admiral by indulging in things like personal vendettas. Use of Fleet resources for personal gain was a court-martial offense, and there were far too many ambitious commodores who would love to move into the flag ranks for any admiral to risk their position over one person.

Something had been wrong about this investigation from the start. Nobles were involved, which always complicated matters, and there were too many things happening out of Adlyn's sight that she couldn't truly understand. She shouldn't be going after Benning Kidd, but she was – and she had a feeling that one way or another, the Corsair would be found guilty by the Admiralty, no matter the evidence or lack thereof. Adlyn felt less like a Fleet Investigator and more like a puppet being moved around, pushed in directions she didn't want to go and forced to act in ways she didn't understand. The admiral might be her puppet master, but it didn't feel like it. Her instincts screamed that even the flag officer was a puppet in this play, and if that were the case – Adlyn didn't want to consider those implications.

The world popped back into normal dimensionality around Adlyn, and she closed her screens and refocused on the bridge.

"Nearing station designated 'Marauder's Rest', Commodore," the young man sitting at Navigation announced. "Distance to projected defense envelope, 10.7 linutes."

"Continue course and speed," the gray-haired woman commanding the battlefrigate replied. "Ops, give me a report on the fleet."

"All vessels are within formation tolerances, Commodore," a young woman answered. "All systems read nominal."

"Tactical, report on their fleet?"

"Fleet remains on station, ma'am. No ships have moved to intercept us."

The commodore frowned and looked at Adlyn. "Are you certain of your intel, Fleet Officer?"

"Yes, ma'am," Adlyn replied respectfully. "My reports indicate that Benning Kidd intends to contest the seizure of the station." Adlyn was in charge of the investigation, but she was only an ancillary part of the fleet's operations and Benning Kidd's arrest. The commodore commanded the fleet and everyone aboard it, including Adlyn. Theoretically, that meant that if things went wrong, the commodore should take the blame – but not if she could claim faulty intelligence from the Lieutenant.

"Then, why are her ships still docked? She should be in formation and waiting for us within their defensive envelope." The woman shook her head. "I thought this woman was supposed to be a skilled tactician, skilled enough to warrant the inclusion of the secondary fleet."

"I can't say, ma'am." Adlyn hesitated. She'd done her homework on the fleet's commander, and the commodore had a reputation as a woman who valued honesty and forthrightness over false respect or having her ego stroked. Adlyn hoped that was true; if she angered the woman, she could end up confined to quarters for the rest of the mission. "I can tell you, though, ma'am, that everyone who's underestimated Benning Kidd so far has regretted it. Badly."

The commodore stared at her, then nodded once. "Point taken, Lieutenant. Fleet, proceed at two tocks, pendulum formation. Keep your eyes peeled for anomalies. We proceed cautiously."

Adlyn stared at the holographic image of Marauder's Rest hanging before them all with a mingled feeling of excitement and fear. Her investigation would be over soon enough; no amount of clever tactics would protect Benning Kidd from the power of the battlefrigate, and once she was in custody, Adlyn would begin questioning her immediately. Hopefully, all her loose ends would be tied up in a neat bundle soon.

Her stomach fluttered nervously. That was her hope, of course – but nothing about this investigation had gone to plan so far. She didn't know what Benning Kidd had planned, but she had a feeling this arrest wasn't going to be as simple as she hoped.

CHAPTER 32

Benning had expected some resistance to her modified plan to deal with the Fleet. As she laid out her idea for a standard defense, the captains responded far more vocally – and angrily – than she'd predicted, though.

"Commodore, you call this a plan?" Raelle Muckley barked, half-rising to her feet. "This is absurd!"

"Watch your tone, Captain," Benning said icily, smacking her hand on the table.

"Forgive me, Commodore, but I have to agree with Raelle Muckley," Avaeyana Roble shook her head. "You're suggesting that we try to fight a battlefrigate and secondary fleet with nothing but standard tactics. That seems…"

"The word you're looking for is suicidal," Trephor Sando said angrily. "We can't use the Fleet's own tactics against them! They've got more ships and more experience with them!"

"We'll be inside the station's defensive envelope, which gives us an advantage," Benning told them firmly. "We've also got better equipped ships and more powerful weapons than they do – and the boosting fields from the *Fall*."

"They have a battlefrigate," Saavi Boguna countered.

"Exactly," Sando agreed. "I'll bet it has abilities like the cruiser's. Once it takes out the station's weapons, it'll destroy all our ships."

"It would be better just to run," Muckley growled.

"Maybe," Benning admitted. "And if it comes to that,

that's exactly what we'll do."

Silence reigned over the table as the others stared at her, their faces shocked.

"What?" Sando demanded. "After that speech yesterday – you're saying we might have to run?"

"We might as well run now, then," Boguna shook her head. "Why risk our ships if even you think we'll lose?"

"You have your orders," Benning cut them off. "I expect you to obey them. Now, see to your ships and be ready to launch."

The others grumbled but rose and filed out of the room, giving Benning more than one dark look as they did. Benning watched them impassively; she didn't much care if they listened or not, in fact. If they all decided to buy out their contracts at the last minute, it would simplify things greatly; she'd have an excuse to run, and she wouldn't need to go through the charade of attempting a defense.

<What if they just mutiny, Benning Kidd?> Tiddly asked. <They might, you know.>

Then I'll make them regret it, Benning said grimly. *After I've convinced the Fleet's admirals to stop hunting me, I'll find them – and Hendricks – and make them understand why they made a poor choice.*

She left the room and headed for her ship, where her crew was already preparing for departure. She hadn't told them that they'd be fleeing; she hoped that none of them took issue with it. They were a good crew, and she didn't want to have to replace any of them. She would if necessary, though. Benning intended to survive the day, and she wasn't going to let someone else's ideas of morality and honor get in the way of that.

As she approached the docking bay for her ship, she froze. A familiar figure stood before the entrance to the boarding tunnel, a tall man with dark skin and tightly braided black hair. He stood nonchalantly, grinning at her, his white teeth gleaming in the relatively low light of the docking ring passageway.

"Benning Kidd," the man said. "Just the person I wanted to see."

Benning reacted instantly. Her hand moved almost of its own volition, reaching down and snatching her sidearm from its holster and leveling it at the figure. He stepped back, his hands held up and to the side, the grin fading from his face.

"Fodor Hendricks," she said coldly. "You made a mistake coming back to my station."

"I never left," he shrugged. "With the evacuation, I couldn't find transportation that wasn't ridiculously expensive – and I recently spent most of my credits, you may remember."

"I don't care," she said flatly, her gun's barrel unwavering as it pointed at his chest. "Find a way off my station, even if it means walking out an airlock into space. You're not welcome here."

"Well, it doesn't sound like it's going to be your station for very long." He lowered his hands, and Benning's finger feathered her trigger almost reflexively. His head jerked back as her bullet creased the side of his face and punched through his ear, leaving a long gash and a hole that slowly oozed blood. "Scrit," he muttered, touching the wound gently. "That wasn't necessary."

"Keep your hands away from your weapons, or the next bullet goes through your eye." He slowly raised his hands once more, but she didn't lower her gun barrel. Fury flowed through her, demanding that she punish him, screaming for his blood, but she ignored it. The Fleet's vessels were close, and she didn't have time to kill him slowly the way she'd prefer.

"What do you want? You think I'm going to give you passage off the station? That I'll give you the credits to buy passage?" Her eyes narrowed. "Or did you think you'd get close enough to me to collect on my bounties and get the credits that way?"

"No, to all of those," he snorted. "I'm not stupid, after all, and I know you, Benning Kidd. Better than just about anyone does, I'd say. You aren't much for forgiveness or mercy." His face twisted in a way she didn't recognize. "In fact, I knew that coming here to see you had a good chance of being a death sentence."

"Then why come?" Her barrel didn't waver in the slightest. "If you know me, then you know you can't convince me not to kill you."

"You mean, *try* to kill me," he corrected. She didn't bother to say anything; she could put a bullet through his brain before he could get his armor activated, but even if he did, she knew the security protocols of his 'net inside and out. She could render him helpless in a second. Hendricks wasn't someone to dismiss or underestimate, and she hadn't. She'd long ago made sure that she'd come out victorious in a fight with him.

When she remained silent, he shrugged and went on. "I came back for two reasons, Benning Kidd. The first was that I got a message from Avaeyana Roble. She told me that you're planning to meet the Fleet with a standard defense, right?"

"It's none of your business," she said coldly, taking a step toward him, her weapons still raised. "Now, I have a defense to organize..."

"You're planning on abandoning the station, aren't

you?" he asked quietly, and she halted once more.

"What are you talking about?" she demanded.

"I told you, Benning Kidd. I know you." He shook his head. "You would never go meet the Fleet with standard tactics. They'd have all the advantages. Not unless you never intended to win. You're going to make a token defense, then order everyone to retreat, right?"

She didn't say a word, but he nodded knowingly. "I thought so." He took a step toward her, and she straightened, her pistol moving to target the center of his forehead. He stopped, his hands still out to the side, but his face didn't look worried or alarmed. Benning didn't recognize his expression, but it was clearly a negative one of some sort.

<It's sorrow, Benning Kidd,> Tiddly said quietly.

"What happened to the woman who was going to punish the Fleet?" he asked. "The Nobility? The System itself?" He shook his head. "What, the Fleet sends a few more ships than you expected, and you give up?"

"Of course not," she snapped angrily. "I just changed my plans so that they don't require anyone else to work." She glared at him. "I've learned that depending on other people is too risky. I can only count on myself."

He nodded. "I agree with you," he said slowly. "Relying on other people is risky, Benning Kidd. They don't always do what you want them to – and sometimes, they make mistakes."

"Is this some sort of apology?" she asked in amazement.

"Hardly," he scoffed. "I'm not much for apologizing, and you wouldn't accept it anyway. No, I'm here because I was wrong, and I don't want you to make the same mistake I did."

"What mistake?"

"When you told me of your plans for the future – about your enemies – I assumed you'd fail. You're talking about the most powerful forces in the Collective, Benning Kidd! No one can possibly stand up to them – at least, that's what I thought. That's why I bought out my contract." He sighed. "I was wrong, though."

"You think that I can win, then? Or are you saying that to try and convince me to offer you a new contract? You found out that the Fleet is hunting you, too, and now you're hoping that you'll be safer with me and my fleet."

"I don't want a new contract. I know that I've burned a bridge with you; I accept that." He took another step toward her, and this time, her finger stayed relaxed on the trigger.

"I wasn't wrong to buy out my contract," he continued. "I was wrong about *why* I did it. It wasn't logic, or making the rational decision. I left you out of fear, plain and simple."

She snorted. "I've never seen you afraid of anything."

"That's because you quite frankly suck at reading people," he laughed warmly. "I'm afraid all the time, Benning Kidd. You scare the scrit out of me on a regular basis." He shook his head. "This time, though, I wasn't afraid of you, or of something you did. I was afraid for you."

She stared at him in unconcealed confusion. "For me? What do you mean?"

"I mean, I still think that you're going to lose, Benning Kidd. I still think that the forces set against you are too strong for you. You might win today, and even tomorrow, but eventually, you're going to lose." He shrugged. "And I was afraid to watch it happen. That was why I bought out my contract. Not because I was worried about what would happen to me, but because I was worried about what might happen to you."

She looked at him with unveiled contempt. "Then you don't know me as well as you say you do," she said scornfully.

"Maybe not. Or maybe I do, but I was just being selfish." He chuckled. "You of all people should understand selfishness, Benning Kidd. You're the living embodiment of it."

"Why are you here, Fodor Hendricks?" she demanded. "What's the point of all this?"

"The point is, I made my decision for the wrong reason: fear. And now, you're abandoning the station for the same reason."

"I'm not afraid of the Fleet," she said firmly. "I respect them, but I'm not afraid of them."

"No, I didn't think you were. You're afraid of something much worse. You're afraid of more betrayal. You're afraid to trust the people around you because they might let you down. You're afraid that if you gamble on them, you'll lose everything."

He took another step closer to her, and while her gun didn't waver, she didn't consider pulling the trigger. He was right; that was exactly what concerned her. She was tired of losing things she valued. She was tired of the pain in her chest, the ache that never faded. She was tired of worrying about who might be secretly working against her, and who might betray her in the future.

"Here's the thing, though, Benning Kidd," he said almost gently. "Everything you've done so far has been a huge gamble. Taking this station was a gamble. Heading to Van Maanen and Altair were gambles. Building this fleet was a huge gamble." He laughed. "Hole, I still don't know how you stole my ship out from under me, but if it hadn't worked, I'd have sent you to respawn, and your plans for revenge on

Argus Leon would have collapsed.

"You've always risked failure, and you've never hesitated to take that risk before. So – why now?" He didn't wait for her to answer. "Because now, you have a lot to lose. If you give it up, it's easier to accept than if it's taken from you."

She remained silent. She couldn't argue with him. He was utterly correct. She had a lot more to lose than she had before, and the thought of the Fleet taking it from her, of the ache in her chest growing even stronger, was more terrifying than any gladiator fight or ship battle she'd ever faced.

However, he was also right that she'd never hesitated to gamble everything before, even when she'd been afraid of losing it all. She'd bet her entire future on her ability to hack the *Relentless'* 'net or fight her way out of a trap many times before. She wasn't afraid of losing or of failing.

She was terrified of the pain of that loss. The thought of the ache in her chest growing, becoming stronger, frightened her more than the thought of imprisonment or going to respawn. It wasn't failure that frightened her. She was frightened of herself, of living with the feeling of that loss forever.

And in doing that, she let her fear dictate her decisions. She allowed it to control her.

"The thing is, Benning Kidd," Hendricks added, his lips curling into a smile, "while I think any plan you have to fight the Fleet is doomed to failure, I've thought that about a hundred of your plans so far. And ninety-nine – ninety-five, maybe – of those times, I've been wrong. I want you to prove me wrong again." He shrugged. "No one can beat the Fleet, Benning Kidd. It can't be done. Which means that if anyone has a chance, it's you. I want to see it happen."

She stared at him for a moment, then lowered her

pistol. She hadn't let anyone or anything control her; she wasn't about to start with fear. Even so, there was gambling, and there was idiocy.

She shook her head. "No, you're right. It can't be done. At least, I can't think of a way to do it. I had a plan that I thought would work, but..." She stared at him, and her anger surged again. "It depended on you, Fodor Hendricks. Without you, even if it works, it'll cost me my entire fleet. It's not worth it."

"Then you've got me," he raised his hands. "Whatever you need, Benning Kidd."

"No," she said firmly. "No, you already abandoned me once. I can't count on you, Fodor Hendricks." That she was sure about. She was fine with taking a risk, but gambling everything on someone who'd let her down before was simply stupid.

"If you'd told me that you needed me for your plan, Benning Kidd, I would have stayed," he said quietly. "I might have left after – and I still will when this is done – but I'd have stayed for this battle." He stepped closer once more. "You have to give trust to get trust, though. I came here, trusting that you'd listen to me and not kill me outright. Now, you have to trust me. What do you need me to do?"

Benning wavered as she stared at the man. She wanted to shoot him, to punish him, to vent her anger and frustration on him – but if he stayed, she had a chance to win this fight. She needed him, but he'd already proven himself undependable. How could she take a chance on someone who'd walked away from her already – especially when her plan would make it easy for him to betray her? How could she know that he'd do his part without something like a contract binding them together?

<You can't, Benning Kidd,> Tiddly admitted. <Trusting people is always a gamble. You'll never know if

they're worthy of your trust – at least, not until they show that they aren't.>

The way Fodor Hendricks already has, you mean?

<Maybe. Or maybe he just wants to feel trusted and important, Benning Kidd. You always ask him to trust you, to follow you even when he doesn't understand, and he did. He didn't know if your plans would work or not, but he went along because it was you. Maybe he's right. Maybe you have to give trust sometimes to get it.>

Benning slowly holstered her pistol. "Fine, Fodor Hendricks. You want to know my plan? Here it is." She quickly laid out what she had in mind, but even as she did, she left out the most critical part. He would still be able to betray her, but not completely. If he did, she'd still have the ability to make him pay for it.

He nodded as he processed what she said. "That – that really could work," he said after a couple seconds. "You're right, though. You need a second-in-command with Fleet Tactics to make it happen." He grinned at her. "Consider me your new second-in-command, Benning Kidd. For this battle at least."

She looked at him, feeling him out with Sense Deceit and finding no trace of deception in him. That didn't mean much; her skill wasn't that high of a level yet, and for all she knew, the Pirate Captain had skills that would counter hers. As Tiddly said, working with Fodor Hendricks was a gamble. She couldn't bring herself to trust him, not really – but she realized that she wanted to. She wanted to be able to count on him the way she once had, to regain at least one thing from all that had been taken from her.

"Fine, Fodor Hendricks," she said, holstering her pistol. "You can have command of the *Implacable*. You know the ship, and the crew knows you."

"Not the Hammer?" he asked.

"Be grateful I'm not putting you in command of the *Orion*." She hesitated. "If you betray me..."

"Yes, I know. You'll kill me."

"No," she said, her voice cold. "No, I won't. I won't give you that mercy. I'll keep you on the edge of respawning for the next year, begging me to push you over – but I never will. I'll leave you broken, helpless, and crippled, your eyes, ears, and tongue gone, unable to heal and trapped in your ruined body." She leaned toward him. "I'm trusting you, Fodor Hendricks. Don't betray that trust – for both of our sakes."

She walked off, pulling up her ship status and adding him to her fleet as a captain once more. She assigned him as her second-in-command, giving him the ability to command if she were unable to, then closed down the screen, ignoring the fluttering in her stomach.

She would trust the man, at least as much as possible. She could only hope that trust wasn't misplaced, but if it was, she swore that generations of Citizens would shudder at the memory of what happened to Fodor Hendricks.

CHAPTER 33

"Helm, take us out," Benning instructed. "Heading 006.3, two degrees declined."

"Aye, Captain," Caldwell responded. "Course 006.3, minus-two degrees confirmed."

"Ops, what's our fleet's status?"

"All ships are moving into position, Captain," Shields said lazily.

"Position of the Fleet vessels, Comm?"

"The Fleet is 4.2 linutes distant, moving our direction at two tocks, ma'am," Rush replied.

Benning nodded. The Fleet ships were coming in a full tock slower than they normally would have. They must have suspected that she'd laid some sort of trap for them. She wished she had, but then, if they came in expecting a trap, it would have been far less likely to work.

As her ship moved into position, she activated the hivemind linkage. Through it, she could feel the disgruntlement of her captains, all except Hendricks, who seemed oddly gleeful.

Marauder Fleet, this is Commodore Benning Kidd, she sent through the linkage. *Move into formation twenty-one. Arm all torpedoes and make them ready.*

Twenty-one? Boguva replied, her voice sounding startled. *Commodore, I thought...*

The plan has changed, Captain, Benning cut the woman

off. Move into position. We won't be abandoning this station today – and we won't let the Fleet win this battle.

Yes, ma'am, Trephor Sando said, his voice eager. *That's more like it!*

You should know by now never to second-guess the commodore, Hendricks chuckled.

Fodor Hendricks, no offense, but shut up, Raelle Muckley said bluntly. *You bought out your contract. I don't know how you convinced the Commodore to let you back on that ship, but you're not part of this fleet anymore.*

Yes, he is, Raelle Muckley, Benning said sternly. *For this engagement, at least. As the only one of you with the Fleet Tactics skill, he's also my second-in-command for this battle.* She felt Hendricks' exultation and added, *Of course, after the battle, feel free to eject him through one of the station's airlocks.*

Sando snickered, and Roble laughed aloud, the sound carrying through the linkage. Benning ignored it and turned her mind to her plans. The secondary fleet was a complication, but she had an idea of how to make that less of a threat. The battlefrigate was the real danger, and her main plan was designed to deal with it. If it worked, she'd be able to win this battle – and maybe even take the battlefrigate as a prize.

The fleet moved out, her cruiser in the center with the *Hammer* under Avaeyana Roble out in front of it, moving in an erratic spiral that would make the larger, less maneuverable *System's Fall* harder to target. The *Implacable* and *Merciless* under Hendricks and Sando moved in elaborate figure-eights behind and around the *Fall,* while Boguva's frigate *Cygni's Eye* wove around the remainder of the ships in a huge sphere. Benning's four corvettes, all with upgraded weapons and armor – the *Slender Dagger, Coyote, Blackbird,* and *Gremlin* – soared at the edges of the formation in weaving floral patterns. The carrier *Arcturus* and the transport *Merry*

Messenger both hovered along behind, while her carrack *Orion* trailed the formation and cruised along slowly.

Marauder Fleet, move to these coordinates, she sent through the hivemind. *Ready all grasers and missile batteries.* She received affirmative replies, but she tuned them out. Her eyes were on the advancing Fleet, moving slowly but steadily closer.

"Enemy fleet now 2.6 linutes," Elden Rush called out. "Maintaining a standard formation, battlefrigate in the rear."

Benning frowned. That wasn't the best formation to deal with her ships, not by a long shot. The battlefrigate should have been in the vanguard, moving to take the station and nullify its defenses, while the supporting fleet engaged hers. Standard tactics would then have called for her ships to engage the battlefrigate to keep the station's weapons active in the battle, which would have allowed the secondary fleet to crush her ships against the battlefrigate. It was the tactic she'd expected the Fleet to use; the one they'd chosen exposed the secondary fleet and made it hard for the battlefrigate to target the station without hitting its own ships. The Fleet either vastly underestimated the upgrades she'd made to the station's armaments – or they had some other plan for dealing with it.

Keep an eye out for dive splashes, she ordered. *Messenger and Arcturus, watch for enemy troop transports. Intercept or disable any that appear.*

Her fleet moved on station and fell into a holding pattern, moving in an elliptical spiral pattern as they waited for the Fleet to draw near. They stayed well within the station's defense envelope, forcing the Fleet to enter that envelope to engage them. Benning plotted her first several attacks while she waited, using the enemy's projected path of approach and choosing her fleet's target priorities based on the formation the Fleet had chosen. She expected them to divert to port as they grew close, moving into a tangential path at around five leconds, outside of effective combat range. She smiled as her images showed them moving into a gentle curve, sliding past her fleet exactly as she predicted.

"Captain, message from the Fleet," Rush spoke up. "A Commodore Laera Morosanu."

"Ignore their message and send them a reply, Elden Rush," Benning said tersely. "Fleet warships, you are approaching an independent station that does not require your services. Remove your ships to beyond one light-hour's distance from Marauder's Rest. Failure to do so will be considered hostile intent and dealt with appropriately."

"Ma'am – did you really just threaten the Fleet?" Brialle Caldwell asked, her eyes wide and her voice slightly awed.

"No, Pilot. I warned them that I'd deal with them appropriately. They can take that however they'd…"

"Fleet vessels accelerating," Elden Rush reported, interrupting Benning. "Moving into a flower formation."

"Is the battlefrigate still in back?" Benning asked.

"Yes, ma'am. It's the center of the formation but trailing the other ships."

Benning nodded. *Activate warp bubble generator, Higgs field, and static field. Fleet, move into attack positions. Ready AM batteries and forward graser arrays but hold fire.*

Are we waiting for them to fire first, Commodore? Sando asked nervously.

No, Captain. We're waiting for them to take our bait.

Benning reached out mentally to the *Orion* and issued it a series of commands. The empty carrack moved forward, accelerating slowly as it caught up with the rest of the ships in the fleet and then soared past, angling toward the Fleet vessels. The vessel moved in an ungainly fashion, but it curved as it crossed the distance toward the enemy ships, moving to within three leconds of them, then two, then one...

Her screen lit up as the Fleet vessels opened fire, pouring graser blasts and warheads into the massive carrack. As the ship registered in her screen as being under assault, Benning turned her thoughts toward her fleet. *Fire all torpedoes, now!* she ordered. *Target the two destroyers!*

The *Fall* shivered as it unleashed a dozen antimatter torpedoes that streaked forth, quickly accelerating to five tocks. At the same time, the huge carrack, 1.6 kims long and 400 ems across, shuddered as weapons fire rained upon it. The cargo vessel was only moderately armored, and its power plants and engines lacked the shielding of a dedicated warship, sacrificing defense for increased cargo space. Benning had stripped even that shielding away, and without it, the *Orion's* power plants and engine plunged from 100% to 10% in seconds, triggering an automatic shutdown – and detonating the neg-bomb she'd rigged to the system's power.

The *Orion* vanished in a flash of light and blast of negative energy. CY-space unfolded all around it, and the photons of its explosion plunged into that space, washing through the nearby Fleet ships and battering them with a hail of KK particles that appeared in the higher-dimensional space. The photons and particles did little damage to the ships – Benning knew that Fleet vessels had some sort of proprietary shielding that made their power plants resistant to graser fire, which included the explosion of a ship – but for a moment, the Fleet's sensors were offline, blinded by the blast of 5-D radiation, and in that moment, her fleet's torpedoes crossed the distance and slammed into the two destroyers.

Both ships' point defenses responded, but without

long-range sensors to guide them, they had only microseconds to react. Even so, they shot down half of the torpedoes, most of which exploded within a thousand kims of the ships' hulls. The other half, though, crashed into the destroyers and exploded in blasts of mingled iron and anti-iron.

"Torpedoes impacted!" Elden Rush said triumphantly a few seconds later as the damage reports came in. "Multiple direct hits on both destroyers! Destroyer-1 is venting atmosphere and has a 12 rpm list; Destroyer-2 has lost port thrusters and is venting gas in eleven places!"

Fleet, move to attack speed, evasion pattern twelve, Benning ordered silently. *Graser fire on Destroyer-1; AM batteries on Destroyer-2, staggered pattern.*

"Captain, the Fleet warships are targeting the *Hammer*," Shields reported. "They've blanketed her evasion cone. Her plants are down 4%."

"What about the battlefrigate?" Benning asked.

"She hasn't engaged, ma'am," Rush reported in a puzzled tone. "She's remaining back, outside the station's defensive envelope. The other ships are within it, though."

"Good. Order the station to open fire, targeting the damaged destroyers. If we can take those out, the battlefrigate will have to join the attack."

Her skin warmed slightly as some of the graser blasts focusing on the *Hammer* washed over her cruiser, but the impact wasn't enough to get through her ship's shielding. Flashes lit her screen as the Fleet's warheads exploded all around her destroyer, but the ship's upgraded armor seemed to hold. Without the battlefrigate, the Fleet ships lacked the firepower to quickly damage her improved vessels. Unfortunately for her opponents, the reverse didn't hold true thanks to Benning's overpowered graser arrays.

"Destroyer-1 is taking direct graser fire," Rush spoke up. "Plants are down 11%, engine is down 6%. Destroyer-2 took a close warhead blast; she's listing at 3 rpm."

"The *Hammer* is still taking direct graser fire," Shields added. "Her plants are at 92%, and her engines are at 97%." He glanced at Benning. "It looks like the improved armor and shielding are holding, ma'am."

Missiles streaked past the *Fall* as the station's weapons entered the battle, hurling a hundred fusion warheads at the two wounded destroyers. The warheads erupted with the flare of myriad tiny suns that shook the ships and bathed them in more radiation.

"Destroyer-1 plant is down 16%," Rush reported. "Engines are down 10%."

Benning's skin burned as her cruiser shook and trembled. "The Fleet is targeting us with their batteries, Captain," Shields told her. "AM warhead explosions in all directions. No hull breaches."

Fleet, shift all fire to Destroyer-1, Benning commanded as she realized that the Fleet ships were too tough and well-built to split her attacks. Her ship shook again, and a sharp stab in her left side told her that she had a hull breach.

"Captain, AM explosion, 10 kims to port," Shields confirmed. "We're venting gas."

Another explosion shook the cruiser as the Fleet vessels sprayed her evasion cone with warheads, but while Benning's skin warmed and throbbed, she didn't feel the sharp pain of another breach. The cruiser's reactive armor was holding. It wouldn't for long, she knew, but hopefully, it would last long enough.

"Destroyer-1's list is at 31 rpm," Rush reported. "Power is down 46%. She's dropping out of formation."

Fleet, shift fire to Destroyer-2, Benning ordered

instantly. The first destroyer was no real danger while out of the formation; if she could get the second one out of this battle, the battlefrigate would engage, and she could move forward with her plan. "Station, shift fire to the frigates."

No acknowledgement met her second order, and Benning repeated the command. When the station remained silent, she frowned and looked at Jezper Shields. "What's going on with the station?"

"Captain, the station's defense and communication systems just went offline!" he replied, his voice no longer calm but tinged with the edges of fear. "All weapons systems are nonfunctional!"

"Captain, the battlefrigate – it's moving to engage!" Rush added in just as worried a tone. A moment later, the ship shuddered as explosions lit up space all around it. "It's targeting us with its missile batteries!"

A message flashed in Benning's vision, and as she accepted it, Fodor Hendrick's face appeared in a corner of her view.

The traitor shut down the station, didn't they, Benning Kidd? he asked solemnly

Yes, she replied simply.

Did you plan for this, too?

I assumed they'd act. I thought they'd shut down their own ship and disrupt our formations – maybe even attack the corvettes or carrier.

What are we going to do?

We continue with the plan, Fodor Hendricks. It's the only chance we have. She cut the contact and refocused her thoughts on her fleet. The linkage hummed with her captains' silent communications, most of which bordered on the edge of panic.

We need to retreat! Trephor Sando stated firmly.

We're so close to taking out that second destroyer, Boguna protested. *If we just keep up our attacks...*

The destroyer doesn't matter, Roble cut in. *Only the battlefrigate does. Without the station's support, we don't stand a chance against it...*

Everyone, be quiet, Benning ordered, silencing the squabbling captains.

What's happening, Benning Kidd? Roble asked. *Why is the station offline?*

Sabotage. Benning felt the shock emanating from the others, but she ignored it. *There's a traitor in our midst, and they somehow shut down the station's defenses.*

Then I was right. We should run, Sando said firmly.

No, Trephor Sando. We fight. Avaeyana Roble is right about one thing: only the battlefrigate matters. If we can take it out of the battle, then this is all over. She's wrong as well, though. We do have a chance against it – a good one, in fact.

What chance is that? Boguna asked.

The final part of my plan, Benning answered.

Which is?

I'm going to be out of communication, Benning said, ignoring the second question. *Fodor Hendricks is in command of the fleet. Switch to singularity warheads, and focus all attacks on the battlefrigate. Nothing else matters. Understood?*

A chorus of somewhat sullen assents met her words as she went into her fleet status and placed Hendricks in command. Her sense of the other ships immediately dwindled and faded as he took over, and she waited for a moment to see what he would do. If her were going to betray her, that would be the optimal moment: she couldn't regain command without his express consent, and he could easily turn the other ships on her cruiser if he wanted.

All ships, move into formation nine, he ordered. *Arm singularity warheads and target the battlefrigate. You heard the commodore; we're not out of this fight yet!*

She felt a surge of relief as she ships soared toward the battlefrigate, moving to engage the kim-wide, spherical ship. She turned her focus back to her crew as she rose to her feet.

"For the time being, you're all under Fodor Hendrick's command," she told them. "Follow his orders as if they were mine." She wanted to add a qualifier about not harming her in any way, but she remained silent. Anything she said like that would cause her crew to distrust Hendricks, and they might hesitate to follow his orders. "Brialle Caldwell, power up shuttle number one, and make it ready to depart."

"Depart, Captain?" Shields asked, his eyes wide. "Are you going somewhere?"

"Yes, Jezper Shields. I'm going to go make sure we win this battle. Ops, you have the command chair until I return."

She left the bridge without answering any questions and made her way to Shuttle Bay 1. The ship shook and trembled around her, but she refrained from looking at her screens to check out the damage or how her fleet was doing. She knew she wouldn't like what she saw; despite what she'd said to the captains, her fleet didn't really stand a chance against the battlefrigate, at least not without her command bonuses and the station's weapons backing them up. If she looked and saw things going badly, she'd be tempted to rush back to the bridge and try to salvage things – but there was no real hope of that. Her only path forward lay in the shuttle bay below.

Her specially modified shuttle waited for her, its engines and power plant both running at full power when she arrived. The small, spherical vessel, only four ems across with just enough space for her inside it, had heavily upgraded engines and defensive armor but lacked any sort of armament or weapons. Benning settled into the single seat and powered up the shuttle's shields and shroud as she ordered the bay doors to open, allowing her access to space. Wind rushed from the bay as the atmosphere escaped into the void, helping her shuttle accelerate as it raced away from the ship and out into the darkness beyond.

The little ship shook as it swept away from the *Fall* and encountered the shock waves of the warheads exploding all around the huge cruiser. Its boosted defenses shrugged off those impacts with no problem, though, as Benning hoped they would. She'd traded speed and weaponry for maneuverability and defense for this ship, and if it didn't pay off – well, she'd find out when she went to respawn.

She programmed the ship's negaputer with its course, locking it into the system, then took a deep breath and triggered Slip the Net. The universe seemed to race away from her as she cut herself off from the Overnet. Silence flooded her mind as the ship's 'net vanished from her thoughts, and when she touched the shuttle's controls, they were dark and unresponsive. Without the 'net, she couldn't connect to the ship to control and monitor it. She was essentially flying blind, and that had to be the case. She thought she could probably link to the ship through her nanofield so long as she maintained direct contact with the console, but that link would also be a connection to the greater Overnet, and it might collapse her ability or even burn it out entirely.

She couldn't risk that; if her identity started beaconing, this battle would end with a marine shuttle intercepting hers and either capturing her or sending her to respawn. Cyberwarfare might disguise her identity, but the Fleet might have realized by now that she could hide herself from them that way. It was a risk she refused to take, not when there was a surer – if far more terrifying for her – method she could use.

The ship shook and rattled as it soared outward, accelerating quickly to three tocks but no faster. The shuttle could handle six tocks, but at that speed, it would beacon as a possible warhead or torpedo to the Fleet's scanners and might trigger their defenses. At regular attack speed, it wouldn't set off any automated alarms, and it was so small that unless a highly skilled officer was looking specifically for it, they'd never even notice it in their scans. The Fleet was known for its skilled officers, though, so rather than trusting to luck, Benning had made sure no one would see her.

The ship rocked crazily as a massive explosion swept over it, nearly tumbling it sideways as its shroud barely compensated and stabilized it. That had been a singularity warhead explosion, Benning guessed. It was the reason she'd ordered her fleet to focus their fire on the battlefrigate, even knowing that such an attack was doomed to fail. The graser blasts, warhead explosions, and incoming torpedoes would blind the ship to Benning's shuttle. Even the highly skilled officer she feared wouldn't be able to pick her shuttle out from all the background noise.

The shuttle shook again, and Benning gritted her teeth, pushing aside her desire to link to the 'net and see how damaged her ship was. That was the downside of her plan. She had no way to know if her vessel was on course, if it had a hull breach, or if its power plant was about to go photonic. She wouldn't know if it happened; the ship would destroy itself faster than her brain would be able to process it. Her only clue would be finding herself in her domain, facing the angry, red notification declaring, "You have died."

The shuttle's shaking increased, and Benning closed her eyes, trying to relax as much as possible. She had no control over her situation, and that lack of control wore continually at her patience, but she forced herself to endure. She had no other choice, not really. This was her only chance to win this battle...

A loud thump echoed through the shuttle, and its shaking stopped abruptly. Benning sat up straight and waited for a moment to see if she'd just passed into an area of calm. Rumbles still echoed through the hull, and she could feel the vibration of shock waves in her feet and the arms of her chair, but the ship remained calm and steady. She removed her harness using the emergency manual disconnect and walked to the shuttle's exit door, laying a hand on it. She felt a touch of nervousness flutter through her stomach; she had no idea what might be waiting beyond that hatch. It could be her destination; it could be a marine shuttle that moved to take her; it could be the vacuum of space. She activated her armor and weapons and pulled out her Arcbar just in case, then manually pulled open the heavy door, sliding it out and up over her head.

Another hatch lay before her, and she yanked it open with only slightly more difficulty to reveal an empty airlock. She stepped into the airlock, took a deep breath, and deactivated Slip the Net. The humming of the Overnet and the clatter of the ship's 'net slammed into her, washing over her and filling her brain. She activated Cyberwarfare at once and quickly modified her designation to that of a Fleet Marine, using her infiltrator suite to match her armor to Fleet standard navy blue. She could only hope that her brief presence in the ship hadn't triggered any alarms. It was a risk, but a necessary one – Slip the Net, she'd found, canceled any changes she made to her identity with Cyberwarfare.

Tiddly, start working on the 'net, she ordered silently. *And get me a map of this ship. I need to get to Engineering as quickly as possible.*

<On it, Benning Kidd,> Tiddly said cheerfully. <Here's

the map – it's Fleet-standard, so that's easy enough – and I'll do what I can with the 'net. Natural Hacking will help.>

Benning nodded and set off at a jog, moving into the depths of the battlefrigate. She hoped her fleet had survived – and that Fodor Hendricks hadn't taken it and run – but she couldn't spare the time or Tiddly's resources to look into it. She had her mission to complete, and if she did it successfully, this battle would be over. If she failed…

She shook off that thought. It wasn't worth considering. She had to succeed, or she'd never be free of the threat of the Fleet.

CHAPTER 34

Adlyn Bechard watched the battle unfolding before her with more interest than she would ever have cared to admit

The fight for Marauder's Rest should have been a brief one, by all rights. The secondary fleet should have kept Benning Kidd's ships occupied while Adlyn's agent disabled the station's defenses. Once that was done, the battlefrigate should have moved in to mop up and seize the station. The whole matter should have been settled in ten minutes, fifteen at the most.

Thirty minutes into the battle, things were still up in the air.

Benning Kidd's trick with the trapped carrack, Adlyn had to admit, had been masterful. With it, she'd blinded the Fleet's scanners and crippled the two destroyers in seconds – and Adlyn couldn't even fault her for attacking those ships. The Fleet had struck first; Kidd had goaded them into firing on an unarmed vessel. It was brilliant, and even Commodore Laera Morosanu grudgingly admitted that.

After that, the enemy demonstrated an excellent grasp of fleet warfare, focusing their weapons to inflict constant damage on their targets while taking very little damage themselves. The *Javelin* was out of this fight, its engines too damaged by an antimatter warhead explosion to allow it to maneuver, and the *Firebird* was barely combat-capable, venting atmosphere to space and listing almost 50% of its maneuverability. The frigates were all fine, but it seemed that Kidd had upgraded her ships' armor and defenses significantly, and by themselves, the four fast frigates wouldn't be able to do more than scratch those ships' armor.

Which was why Adlyn ordered her operative to shut down the station earlier than planned. The original plan was to wait until Kidd's fleet was heavily damaged; her hope was that losing the station's defenses at that point would convince them to surrender at once. That would allow her to reclaim her operative safely and complete her mission, so it was obviously the optimal choice. If the ships tried to flee, instead, her agent would act, delaying the ships long enough for the battlefrigate to trap them in a sinkhole. In either case, Benning Kidd would be forced to surrender, and Adlyn's part in this chaos would be over once she had the woman locked down and under heavy guard.

The enemy fleet did neither of those things. Instead, as the commodore moved her flagship to engage, they attacked the battlefrigate, and they did it well. They shifted formations often, keeping the negaputers from working out their patterns. They concentrated their fire so that the battlefrigate's shielding and point defenses couldn't block all the gamma blasts and warheads. When the *Firebird* tried to lead the secondary fleet against them, their carrier disgorged its swarm of flyboats on the destroyer, and the ship went photonic within minutes, forcing the frigates to withdraw from the battle.

"Singularity explosion, 250 kims ascended, Commodore," the Damage Control officer reported. "Another hull breach. We're venting atmosphere."

"Seal it up," Morosanu ordered. "Keep fire on that cruiser! We have to take it out! What's it's status?"

"It's got minor hull damage, Commodore," the Tactical officer answered. "Main plant is down 11%, engines are down 16%. They've got backup power, though, and their engines are repairing themselves at a rapid rate."

"What kind of shielding do those ships have?" the commodore growled. "With the pounding we've given that thing, it should be crippled by now!"

"As I reported, Commodore, Benning Kidd has significantly upgraded her fleet," Adlyn replied. "Including using proprietary tech…"

"Yes, Lieutenant, I know. That was rhetorical." The commander shook her head. "Just stay silent unless you have something new to offer." Morosanu looked at Adlyn closely. "Actually, belay that. Is there anything your agent can do to help?"

"No, ma'am," Adlyn shook her head regretfully. "Once the *Crimson Cheng* moved to engage, I had them take an escape shuttle and head here. Their last report indicated that Benning Kidd had relinquished command to Fodor Hendricks in furtherance of some plan of hers, which I assume is a cover for her wanting to flee. I thought…" She fell silent, but the commodore finished her thought for her.

"You thought this battle would be done in minutes, and you wanted to save your operative," the gray-haired woman said with a grimace. "You were right. It should have been." She smiled then, catching Adlyn by surprise. "It's been quite a battle, really, one of the best I've had in decades."

"You're not concerned, Commodore?"

"No, Lieutenant. I have no reason to be. There's no doubt how this will end. That commander is good, but eventually, we'll disable the cruiser, and without it, they'll be easy pickings." She snorted. "In fact, I'm glad that they're making such a fight of it."

"Why, ma'am?"

"Because word is that Admiral Danice Kazak is looking

to retire in the next decade or so. She's in charge of Octant 2's fleet, and the Admiralty will want to replace her with someone with heavy combat experience. This little dust-up could put me next in line for flag rank."

Adlyn nodded, keeping her face carefully neutral. She didn't share the commodore's optimism, in all honesty. Morosanu hadn't exactly inspired confidence with her predictions so far, after all. She'd assured Adlyn that the secondary fleet would be more than a match for Kidd's ships. She'd assumed that losing the station would cause the enemy to surrender at once. She'd declared that the *Chang* would finish the enemy vessels in minutes. So far, she'd been wrong on all counts.

Adlyn's agent originally reported that the enemy fleet would face them using standard tactics, but she later claimed that Benning Kidd had some master plan that would take the battlefrigate out of the fight. In response, Adlyn urged the commodore to lock down ship's security, reinforce every airlock, and activate the automated defenses. Morosanu ignored her request. The *Chang*, Adlyn was assured, couldn't be taken by a boarding force. It had a thousand armed defenders, a mixture of Soldiers and Fleet Marines; Benning Kidd had perhaps fifty marines under her command. It had automated defenses placed throughout the ship, all designed to fire on any unknown or unrecognized person. There were checkpoints everywhere, preventing anyone from simply moving through it at will. The ship was secure; if Benning Kidd and her marines boarded, it would just simplify matters, as far as the commodore was concerned.

Adlyn wanted to agree, but her mind couldn't help but remember Kidd's escape from her ship and the destruction of Aquilae Station. No one had seen Benning Kidd leave the ship; no one knew who had attacked the station or how. Somehow, the woman seemed able to roam freely throughout places undetected. If she'd somehow gotten aboard the *Chang...*

"Commodore, there's a power surge in the main engine plant!" the Engineering Officer's voice rang through the bridge, and Adlyn's heart sank.

"Commodore, weapons arrays are fluctuating wildly," Weapons reported a moment later. "We're having trouble targeting – well, anything, ma'am!"

The ship shook suddenly, and the young man at Damage Control looked worriedly at the gray-haired commander. "Ma'am, the shields just dropped, and the shroud's fluxing!"

"What the Hole is going on?" Morosanu demanded. "Did we take a hit of some kind?"

"No, ma'am," he replied with a headshake. "No impacts have been reported, and there are no signs of hull damage."

"Then what's doing this to my ship?" the Commodore said angrily. A moment later, alarm klaxons began blaring throughout the bridge as the lights flickered and died, replaced with dim emergency backups.

"Main power is offline," Damage Control said in a voice tinged with panic.

"So are Weapons controls," the Weapons officer added fearfully.

"Commodore, there's an incursion in Engineering," the older, black-haired Security Officer said. "I'm reading gunfire and explosions in the negaputer core!"

"The core?" the commodore echoed, turning to stare at Adlyn with wide eyes. "Lieutenant, do you know anything about this?"

Adlyn nodded slowly. "I warned you about this, Commodore," she practically whispered. "It's Benning Kidd.

She's aboard the *Crimson* Chang." As the alarms blared and the lights flickered, she stared at the holoscreen showing the enemy fleet that moved to attack the now-helpless ship.

Sometimes, she really hated being right.

CHAPTER 35

Bullets crashed and whined around Benning as she hunched behind her portable wall. She darted up briefly as her nanofield revealed an armored figure moving from cover to cover, working their way toward her. Her rifle tracked the marine unerringly, and her finger pressed down the trigger. Twenty rounds roared from her Arcbar and slammed into the figure's chest, punching through their armor and ripping into their heart. Their aura dropped from green to red in an instant, and she darted back behind her defense as more rounds zipped through the air above her head with audible cracks.

As she switched out her weapons, her thoughts flitted through the *Crimson Chang*'s 'net, slowly working through its firewalls and defenses. Once Natural Hacking had given her a link to the 'net, Tiddly was able to broaden that link and give her rudimentary access to the vessel, but the ship's safeguards and defenses were too strong for the AI to do more than that. It was enough to allow Benning to spoof the ID of an actual marine aboard the ship, allowing her to bypass checkpoints until Tiddly located a Drone tunnel access point. From there, getting to Engineering was easy enough, and Benning had taken the tunnels at top speed. She was certain she'd mowed down a dozen or more Drones in the process judging from the number of times she randomly stumbled or pitched to one side or another, but she didn't care. Time was of the essence.

Once she reached the negaputer core, her nanofield hacked the sealed hatch and allowed her access without triggering any alarms. That was the easy part; the hard part was connecting her field to the negaputer core and gaining a direct link into the heart of the ship's 'net. The direct connection bypassed many of the 'net's security protocols but not all of them, and Benning spent precious minutes brute-hacking her way into the negaputer's command tree. She'd done it, though, and she'd immediately begun destabilizing the ship, turning off targeting arrays, confusing weapons guidance, and sending power spikes to the engines and power plants. When she tried to kill main power, though, she'd triggered an alarm, and marines descended on her in less than two minutes.

If Benning hadn't been holding the hatch to the negaputer core, the battle would already have been over. A few grenades and a rush from the marines would have ended this in a heartbeat. However, the ship's defenders had to be careful in their assault to avoid damaging the negaputer or its console, which limited them to firing single rounds at a time and avoiding explosive weapons. Benning, on the other hand, had no such restraints.

She rose from cover and leveled her grenade launcher at the hallway. She couldn't see the eight marines firing on her, but her nanofield felt them, and it relayed that info to her helmet. Their forms glowed red in her vision, and she targeted a spot in the center of the group before pulling the trigger. The cylindrical fusion grenade blasted down the hallway and exploded in midair exactly where she'd aimed it, forming a new sun in the middle of the passage for a brief instant and sending waves of pressurized air and high-energy neutrons slamming into the hidden defenders.

She switched back to her Arcbar as wounded marines staggered into view, dazed by the close-quarters blast. Her weapon sang as it sent bullets hurtling into the defenders, piercing already-damaged armor and cracked helmets. They quickly recovered and returned fire, but she dropped back into cover, leaving four of their number lifeless on the deck.

Benning had a temporary advantage, but she knew it wouldn't last. More marines swiftly joined their wounded comrades, allowing the injured to fall back. She was trapped in the core, with no exit. She'd already rigged a nanobomb to it – if she died or was captured, she'd set it off and take the ship with her – but she hoped to find another way out. That was why her mind flitted through the ship's net, constantly unlocking new levels of security. She wasn't being secretive, so her efforts triggered alarms throughout the 'net, but with the ship's shields, and weapons shut down and their power plant and shroud both fluctuating too wildly for them to evade effectively, she guessed they had bigger problems to worry about. As if to confirm her thoughts, the ship shuddered and trembled as an explosion of some sort rocked the hull. She smiled grimly; her fleet was still fighting. It seemed like her trust in Fodor Hendricks had been well-placed, at least this time.

The gunfire heading toward her slackened, and Benning used the moment to switch to her Meteor cannon. Before she could rise to use it, though, a voice echoed through the corridor.

"Citizen Benning Kidd, this is Commodore Laera Morosanu of the Collective Fleet," the voice declared in an authoritative tone. "You are ordered to stand down and secure your weapons at once."

Benning snorted and rose above her cover. She wondered if the woman actually expected Benning to obey that order, or if she were just so in the habit of issuing commands that it came naturally. It didn't matter. Benning had only one response for the officer, and it was one that couldn't be misinterpreted or misunderstood.

The marines' images still blazed brightly in her sense, and she aimed her cannon toward one hiding behind the edges of an open hatchway. The weapon bucked in her hands and slammed into her shoulder as she fired, but a hole appeared in the wall where she'd aimed, and the marine behind it crumpled to the deck, their aura crisping to black as their blood poured out a gaping hole in the side of their chest. The other marines responded at once, and she ducked back into cover with a grin. How, she wondered, would the commodore take her answer?

Apparently, the answer was, "Not well."

"There are a hundred marines converging on your position, Benning Kidd," the woman snapped. "You're trapped in the negaputer core with no chance of escape. Surrender is your only option. If you deactivate your weapons now, I guarantee you a speedy and fair trial…"

Benning couldn't help but laugh in derision at that. Even if the commodore meant what she said, nothing about Benning's treatment would be fair if she were captured. She was utterly certain about that. Whatever Noble was working against her would make sure of it. Answering the officer once again with her actions rather than words, she rose and hurled another grenade into the passageway, following it up with more gunfire.

"This is your final chance!" the commodore said angrily. "Stand down immediately, or we will be forced to kill you where you stand!"

"I'd rather die than surrender," Benning spoke at last. "And just so you know, I've rigged the core with a bomb. You may take me, but I'll take the ship with me."

"Spoken like a true terrorist," the commodore snapped distastefully. "What, do you have a list of demands, now?"

"No. I gave you my demands earlier. You turned them down. That was your choice; now, you deal with the consequences." She rose and killed another marine with her cannon, receiving a shot to the helmet that cracked her visor in the process. She ducked back down as more bullets soared around her.

"You leave me no choice, Benning Kidd. Marines, prepare to charge her position on my..."

<Got it, Benning Kidd!> Tiddly said excitedly. <Let's see how they like this!>

Benning quickly dropped her spoofed ID as the turret above the negaputer's core hummed and spun to life. Outside, four similar turrets powered up as well, and a moment later, gunfire roared in the passageway, followed by shouts and curses from the marines. Benning popped back up, her Arcbar leveled, firing at marines as they tried to withdraw from the automated defenses that suddenly turned on them.

"What did you do?" Morosanu demanded, her voice a throaty roar that carried over the gunfire. "What are you doing to my ship, Benning Kidd?"

Nice work, Tiddly, Benning thought as she took down another marine. *Now, they'll be too busy fighting their own defenses to stop us from hacking the ship entirely.*

<There's a problem with that, Benning Kidd,> Tiddly said seriously. <You can't just assume control of the ship like you would any other vessel.>

Why not?

<The Fleet installs an anti-piracy device on all its vessels to make sure no one gets their hands on its tech. If the ship is seized, it activates an automated self-destruct mechanism that overloads the primary power plants. If you hack control of it, it'll explode.>

Benning tuned out the commodore as the woman continued to demand answers, thinking rapidly. *What happens if the ship's captain dies? Does it explode then?*

<No, command just drops to the next ranking officer. If they're killed, it goes to the next, and so on. If every officer on board dies, though, the protocol will activate.>

Benning nodded. *I can work with that.* She glanced upward, toward the railing commodore's voice. *I'll be seeing you soon, Commodore.*

She moved steadily through Engineering, firing at any figure she saw. She killed Workers and Citizens as well as Soldiers and marines already wounded by the ship's automated defenses, which now recognized any armed person other than her as an intruder. Taking over the automatic defenses and putting them under her direct control would have been nearly impossible; altering their friend-or-foe programming was much, much easier.

She re-entered the Drone tunnels and ran through them at top speed, ignoring her impacts with invisible Drones. She needed to reach the bridge; her takeover of the ship couldn't be completed from anywhere else. She stepped out of the tunnels, exiting into a hallway less than a hundred ems from the bridge's entrance. As she emerged into the passage, a squad of marines spun toward her.

"There she is!" one shouted.

"Where in the Hole did she come from?"

"Doesn't matter! Open..."

The marines' moment of confusion passed quickly, but it was a moment too long as Benning's grenade launcher hurled an antimatter grenade into their midst. The grenade exploded with a flash of light and a roar of pressure that swept down the hall, battering Benning where she crouched and scattering the marines like dust. She rushed forward, her hammer snapping into place almost effortlessly. The wounded marines struggled to their feet, but she was already among them, her hammer whirling and flashing.

She shattered knees and crushed elbows, caved in battered helmets and pierced damaged chest plates. In less than a minute, six marines lay dead or dying around her, and she'd lost only 4% from her resistance bar to a bullet that grazed the side of her neck.

She returned her hammer to rod form and took out her Arcbar. As she did, she realized that her battles aboard the ship had gone far more easily than she thought they would. Her scans told her that the marines she fought mostly had better stats and skills than she did, and the majority of the Citizens were higher leveled, as well. She should have struggled in combat with the six Fleet Marines, been badly wounded or even forced to retreat, even with their being injured by her grenade.

And yet, they hadn't stood a chance against her. It was as if they had the stats and skills but lacked the knowledge of how to use them effectively. A high coordination let a Citizen dodge faster, but it didn't tell them when to dodge. Physicality made a marine's melee strikes more powerful, but that didn't matter if they couldn't land a blow. On a screen, the ship's defenders should have taken her apart. In reality, while they probably trained constantly, it was likely that most of them hadn't been in a fight for their lives in years, if ever. She'd spent her entire life as a Citizen in one form of combat or another. That honed her reflexes, sharpened her instincts, and refined her understanding of battle in a way that training couldn't do. She looked less than they were, but in reality, she was far more dangerous.

It occurred to her that perhaps, just perhaps, she was more than her status screen. It was a thought she'd never had before, but it felt right to her. Her status screen didn't tell everything important about her. It didn't tell anyone her actual experience in combat, her ruthlessness, her willingness to do anything to achieve her goals. It didn't show her cunning or her readiness to use unconventional or even illegal tactics and weapons. Her status screen underrepresented her threat level, and she decided that was why she'd been so successful even against opponents who looked stronger on a screen. They didn't give her the full credit she deserved and didn't understand the threat she represented, and they paid for that shortsightedness – just as a certain commodore was about to pay.

The bridge door was sealed, of course, but Benning's disassemblers ripped it open in half a minute. She charged inside behind her mobile cover, slamming it onto the deck the moment she was through the hatch. Bullets and graser fire blasted against the neutronium plate, denting it in several places as the bridge's defenders tried to repel her. She waited while her nanofield spread across the compartment, lighting up her hidden foes, then popped up, her Foehammer leveled and her finger moving on the trigger. Her weapon spat three times, and three unarmored Fleet officers dropped, two with holes in the center of their skulls and one with a spreading, red stain in the middle of their chest. Bullets slammed into her helmet, widening the crack in her visor and rocking her head back. She fell back behind her cover, shaking her head, then paused.

Why in the Hole am I fighting like this? she wondered to herself. *This isn't the arena, and there's a better way to deal with them.*

She focused on the glowing, red figures lit up in her visor, examining each in turn. More than twenty of them filled the bridge, but only four concerned her, the four wearing armor and carrying heavy weapons. She concentrated on those, huddled patiently behind her slowly weakening protection. It wouldn't last long under the concentrated fire it was receiving, but fortunately, it didn't need to.

"Scrit!" a voice shouted, clearly audible above the

clamor of bullets. "What's happening?"

As more voices echoed their cry, Benning popped up once more, this time cradling her Arcbar. Her weapon tracked to the center of an armored figure's chest, where a gaping hole showed through their protection. The hole slowly grew as her nanites chewed into it, widening it and dissolving the marine's armor. Benning's finger feathered the trigger, and bullets ripped into the marine's unprotected chest, dropping them instantly.

More bullets cracked against her visor, but she ignored them and moved to the next figure. Her rifle spat, once, twice, three times in rapid succession, and the three marines fell dying to the floor. Without their heavy rifles and weapons training, the assault on Benning slackened, and she was easily able to ignore the remaining small arms fire. She shifted from her Arcbar to her Foehammer and aimed at the nearest figure, cowering behind a console and unloading their IMP at her almost desperately. Her rifle boomed, and the bullet punched through the console and tore into the person behind.

"Hold fire!" a voice shouted, and the gunfire slackened. A woman with metal-gray hair rose from her crouch, holstering her pistol and lifting her hands out to the sides. "There's no reason for anyone else to die here, Benning Kidd. Let's talk terms."

"You're the commodore, then?" Benning asked, and the woman nodded her head. "Good. Just the person I needed to kill." Her rifle cracked once more, and the officer dropped as the back of her skull exploded outward in a spray of bone, hair, blood, and brain matter.

"Flork!" someone shouted. "Kill her!"

Benning didn't bother to drop back into cover as she moved through the bridge, methodically executing officers. None wore any armor except their Molex uniforms, which offered practically no resistance to her bullets, and their basic IMP handguns barely scratched her armor. These were Fleet Officers, skilled at running a ship but almost useless in combat, and she passed through them like a scythe through grain until the notification she was waiting for appeared in her vision.

> BATTLEFIELD PROMOTION!
> As the ranking surviving officer aboard the *CSS Crimson Chang*, you are promoted to temporary captain of this vessel. This promotion will last until superseded by another, higher-ranking officer or until confirmed or repealed by the Admiralty.

Benning grinned as her awareness spread throughout the ship, flooding along the battlefrigate's 'net. Her skin began to burn and tingle as it responded to the damage her fleet had done to the vessel, and she realized that her ships had been far closer to destroying the battlefrigate than she'd thought. Its main power plant was down to 49%, but several of its secondary plants – including the ones maintaining its reactive armor – were below 20% stability. Atmosphere jetted out into space in six places, and it leaked enough gas that its reserves were just above a quarter full. Several banks of thrusters were offline, and its entire starboard graser array was damaged and barely functioning.

Marauder Fleet, this is Benning Kidd, she sent to Fodor Hendricks quickly. *I've taken control of the battlefrigate. Shift your attacks to the remaining Fleet ships.* She hesitated; this was another chance for Hendricks to betray her, but not a good one. Hendricks could have simply taken her fleet and fled the station if he'd wanted to; she couldn't have done anything to stop him from inside the battlefrigate. He hadn't, and he was certainly intelligent enough to recognize that chance when it came. Still, he might have been waiting to see if she'd take control of the *Chang* or not...

She felt a sigh of relief as her mental map of the nearby area showed her ships shifting, moving to engage the remaining Fleet warships. She quickly ordered the battlefrigate to join them; between the power of the huge warship and the weapons of her fleet, the destroyers and fast frigates of the Fleet wouldn't stand a chance.

"What did you do, Benning Kidd?" a familiar voice spoke, jarring her from her internal thoughts. Benning spun to see the familiar, white-haired face of Adlyn Bechard standing across the bridge from her. The Fleet Officer held her IMP pointed directly at Benning, and her face looked enraged, the deep brown skin purpling and her jaw clenched tightly. "*Captain* Benning Kidd? Commander of the *Crimson Chang*? How..."

She cut herself off and took a deep breath. "It doesn't matter. Whatever you did, it constitutes theft of Fleet property, illegal seizure of a vessel, violation of Fleet command protocols..." She shook her head. "I finally have something I can charge you with, Benning Kidd – and I witnessed it happening myself."

"So?" Benning asked contemptuously. As she spoke, an officer behind her rose up swiftly, leveling their pistol at her back. Thanks to her helmet, she clearly saw the green-haired woman, and she drew her sidearm and fired a single shot into the officer's chest without even glancing back behind her.

"Everyone, stand down!" Bechard ordered. She looked back at Benning. "What do you mean, so? Even if you manage to keep this ship, I'll be back with more ships – maybe a battlecruiser or dreadnought. Eventually, I'll have you in custody, Benning Kidd."

"Send whatever you want," Benning shrugged. "I'll take that ship, too. Every attack on me will just make me stronger, Adlyn Bechard." Her pistol shifted to point directly at the officer's skull. "Enjoy your respawn."

"Wait!" Bechard shouted, her finger moving on the trigger of her own pistol. Benning was faster, though, and her finger caressed the Teravolt's trigger. A single squeeze, little more than a twitch, and the pistol would fire, hurling a 20mm slug directly into Bechard's brain...

The click of her pistol misfiring echoed in the sudden silence of the bridge. Benning's eyes widened as she felt the weapon deactivate, powering down and shutting off in her hand. Her rifle did likewise, and her armor began to slide backwards away from her, pooling behind her back and leaving her totally vulnerable. Bechard must have had some ability to shut down a criminal's gear, something like what she'd used to try and imprison Benning before...

<No, Benning Kidd. This isn't Adlyn Bechard. A Noble just deactivated your gear – or a Noble's command did. It must be...>

"I don't think anyone else will be going to respawn today," a voice spoke from the rear of the bridge. Benning turned toward the speaker, her eyes and nanofield searching vainly for some sense of them, but she saw and felt nothing. She didn't need to see them to know who they were, though; it was a voice she recognized instantly.

"Trephor Sando," Benning said coldly, anger surging within her. "You're the traitor. You're working for a Noble against me." She peered in the direction of the man's voice, but she saw nothing. Even her nanofield couldn't sense him; somehow, he must have been blocking her perception of him through the System. She couldn't imagine too many abilities would allow something like that, but she guessed that a

Noble had that sort of power.

"Correct!" the man laughed. "At least, you're correct that I'm the Designate of a Noble, one who's extremely interested in seeing you fail, Benning Kidd. You're wrong about the name, though." The man faded into view, his reddish-blonde hair and bright blue eyes distinctive in the dim light of the bridge.

Even as Benning watched, though, his light hair darkened and shifted, lengthening until it fell to his shoulders. His round face narrowed, the chin growing sharper and the cheekbones rising higher. His skin darkened from a deep tan to a chestnut brown, and his eyes shifted to match the deep moss green of his hair. *Her hair,* Benning corrected silently as the man's figure slimmed and grew additional curves, breasts and hips forming where none had been before and his shoulders and waist narrowing dramatically.

Benning could change her appearance significantly with her infiltrator suite, but that mod had its limits. She couldn't alter her height, weight, eye color, build, or gender. She could modify her features slightly, but she couldn't utterly change them. She could recolor her hair, but she couldn't make it longer on command. She stared in shock at the woman who now stood before her, a woman whose transformation should have been impossible for anyone but a Citizen who specialized in infiltration or assassination – and a woman Benning knew at once.

"Recognize me, Benning Kidd?" the newly revealed woman laughed again, her teeth flashing in the dim light.

"Yes," Benning said grimly as understanding fell into place. "Welcome on board my ship, Veera Meijers."

CHAPTER 36

"Your ship?" Meijers shook her head. "No, I don't think so. System, suspend current command of vessel *CSS Crimson Chang*."

Instantly, a screen flashed in Benning's vision.

> COMMAND SUSPENSION!
> Your command of the vessel *CSS Crimson Chang* has been temporarily suspended by the order of a Noble.

"So, there is a Noble involved in all this," Adlyn Bechard said, her voice still outraged. "And you've been working for them this entire time? Veera Meijers, what's going on here?"

"A private matter, Adlyn Bechard," Meijers replied with a shrug. "One that need not concern the Fleet. In fact..." The woman raised a hand, and one by one, the remaining officers on the bridge dropped to the deck, their auras flashing instantly to black, leaving only the Nanomancer, Benning, and Adlyn Bechard still standing. "That's better. No need to involve others."

"You just killed Fleet Officers!" Bechard gasped. "Veera Meijers, I place you under..."

"Be silent," Meijers ordered, and the officer's voice quieted instantly. Her mouth moved, but no sound emerged from it, and panic filled her eyes as she realized that Meijers had silenced her with a peremptory command.

"I have to say, both my sponsor and I are highly disappointed in the Fleet, Adlyn Bechard," Meijers shook her head. "I came to you with sufficient charges and eyewitness testimony to descend on Benning Kidd immediately, camp her back to level one, and imprison her for a decade. All you had to do was send the charges to the Admiralty, and this all would have been over months ago."

The Nanomancer's face creased with a sneer. "Instead, you had to do a thorough investigation. You gave Benning Kidd time to become stronger, to mount a defense against you. You allowed her to kill billions through your inaction – and my sponsor will be certain to report that to the Admiralty when this is over."

"Why use the Fleet and bounty hunters, Veera Meijers?" Benning asked curiously. "Why not just kill me yourself? You had plenty of chances." While the Nanomancer spoke, she'd moved cautiously closer to the woman. Her gear wasn't working, of course. Benning felt that she could circumvent that given time, but it was sealed with the same encrypted lock as the bounty contracts she'd never been able to decode, so she doubted she'd have that sort of time. However, she didn't think she needed her gear. If she got within five ems of Meijers, she could kill the woman with her bare hands without too much effort. Meijers was a Nanomancer, not a fighter, after all.

"You think I'm going to give you some sort of explanation, Benning Kidd?" the woman snorted. "No, I'm not. I'm simply going to keep you disabled so that Adlyn Bechard can place you in custody. Then, I'm going to watch while you're tried, convicted, and sentenced. Maybe I'll even get to kill you a few times on your way back to level one, as well."

"You don't need to answer," Benning replied, taking another step closer as she spoke. "I think I know already.

The System gives Nobles almost unlimited power, but it also protects Citizens from them abusing that power. I'll bet it does the same thing to Noble Designates, doesn't it? You never killed me because you can't, not unless I attack you first. The System won't let you."

"Yes, Benning Kidd," the woman snapped as her eyes flashed angrily. "The System won't let me simply kill you, or I'd have done so a thousand times by now." Her grin returned. "However, it also doesn't stop me from using my abilities on you – as long as I'm doing so as a Citizen, not a Noble. Like this."

Benning felt a sudden sense of overwhelming pressure wrap around her, pushing against her nanofield and driving toward her body. A red screen appeared in her vision, confirming what she feared.

HOSTILE NANOFIELD!
You have entered a hostile nanofield. Your Nanoresistance has prevented immediate damage.

Benning slammed her nanites against the field surrounding her, holding them at bay. She furled her disassemblers at the foreign nanites, urging them to rip the invaders to shreds, while she ordered her scanners to link to the field and try to shut it down. As she did, she rushed forward, raising her hands as she activated For Fame and Heart of the Savage. Adrenaline flooded her body, along with a tremendous sense of power – and a flood of rage that washed over her thoughts. Her physical stats all shot up over fifteen, making her almost twice as strong and fast as normal, and she moved with astonishing speed as she leaped forward, twisting so that her extended foot would slam into Meijers' chest, likely crushing her ribcage and certainly disrupting the woman's attack.

Meijers almost flowed to the side, allowing Benning to slip past. The woman's left hand flashed out, striking at Benning's head, and only Benning's combat-honed reflexes allowed her to block the blow. She landed nimbly and spun, kicking low at the Nanomancer's knee while snapping a clenched fist at her throat, but Meijers lifted her foot to avoid the kick and reached up, grabbing Benning's wrist in a lightning-fast movement. Benning twisted her hand free without thought and stepped back, eyeing the woman warily.

She shouldn't be this fast, she thought silently. *Or this good at fighting. She wasn't the last time we met.*

<She has Noble backing, Benning Kidd,> Tiddly said quietly. <Nearly unlimited credits and authority can get a lot of things, including advanced training.>

"Surprised, Benning Kidd?" Meijers laughed darkly, even as she unwittingly confirmed Tiddly's assessment of her abilities. "You shouldn't be. Being the Designate of a Noble has a lot of privileges – including getting to download entire skill sets without needing to train them. I'll bet my Martial Combat skill is higher than yours, now."

The woman seemed to blur as she lunged at Benning, and the Marauder fell into a defensive stance as she dodged and blocked, weaving around and barely slipping past the woman's blows. Meijers snapped a high kick at Benning's head, pulling it at the last moment and dropping it into a side kick that caught Benning in the ribs and knocked her back several steps. Benning blinked as her resistance bar dropped by 10% from that single, low-powered blow and resisted the urge to rub the spot where she was sure a bruise was forming. Meijers wasn't just skilled, she was strong, as well, and Benning wondered if it was possible for her to win this fight.

Meijers rushed at her once more, and Benning again put all her focus into defense. She ducked and wove, guiding attacks past her and responding with lightning-fast counters. Meijers moved as nimbly as Benning, though, dodging these attacks and responding with strikes of her own. A kick slammed Benning's thigh; an elbow grazed the top of her skull; a knee bounced off her hip. None of the blows were dangerous, but their impact added up, slowly dropping Benning's resistance bar to 63%.

All the while, Benning felt Meijers' nanofield pressing closer and closer, working its way through her Nanoresistance. She tore at the nanites with her disassemblers, but ten moved to replace each one she destroyed. She desperately hurled her scanners at them, trying to link up, but the Noble-class encryption shielded them, blocking her from hacking the woman's 'net through her nanofield. Benning felt panic starting to fill her; she couldn't beat Meijers in hand-to-hand combat, she couldn't hack into the woman's 'net, and her Nanoresistance wouldn't last forever.

Once again, the System had placed her in a no-win scenario and expected her to simply fail. It did the same during her level-up, in Van Maanen, and on Aquilae Prime. Each time, it bent its own rules, cut off her options, and put her in a place where she should have had no choice but to surrender, to admit defeat. She hadn't, though – and she wouldn't this time, either. There had to be a way to win. She just had to do something the System would never imagine her doing.

The rage flowing through her focused around that certainty, and her hazy thoughts crystallized in her mind. Realization struck her; there was a way, a way that she could not only defeat Veera Meijers but possibly end her threat permanently. It was a gamble, a huge risk, but it was the only path she could see. Benning steeled herself, then dropped her Nanoresistance, allowing Meijers' nanites to descend on her in a swarm.

Benning screamed and fell to her knees as pain surged through her body. Her nerves were on fire; her blood boiled; her bones felt like they were melting in her flesh. Agony raced through her, filling her, and her resistance bar dropped to 20% in an instant. The rage-filled power of Heart of the Savage drained away as she fell out of combat, but new strength poured through her as Strength from Pain activated instead. She dropped For Fame, as well, and her thoughts sharpened despite the agony that filled her body, freezing her muscles and rendering her utterly helpless – at least, physically.

"Finally!" Meijers crowed triumphantly. She stepped forward and kicked Benning, knocking her to the ground. Bechard took a step forward as if to intervene, but Meijers whipped out her pistol and pointed it at the officer, and Bechard froze, staring at Benning helplessly.

"Last time we met, I tried to be subtle," Meijers said happily, speaking loudly to be heard over Benning's screams. "After that failed, I decided to follow in your example, Benning Kidd. Instead of subtle, I want to make a statement. I want you to remember this moment in your nightmares, to be haunted by it. I want you to live in fear of me ever finding you again, knowing that this is what you'll have to look forward to."

Somehow, the pain intensified, and Benning's resistance dropped to 15%. The pain was too great for Benning to think, too agonizing for her to focus. She hardened her will, but the pain strengthened once more, shattering her attempts to concentrate. Desperately, she pushed the pain back, trying to drive it from her thoughts, and with a sudden lurch, she felt her mind tear itself free from her body, just as it did when she leveled up.

Instantly, silence reigned in her thoughts as the pain became something distant, no longer part of her. In the depths of her mind, she couldn't help but smile, even as her body thrashed and screamed on the ground. Meijers thought she'd won, that she'd trapped Benning in an unwinnable situation, but she'd made a terrible mistake – and now, it was time for her to pay for it.

"Don't worry, Benning Kidd," Meijers laughed. "I'm not going to kill you – not yet. I'll make you wish you were dead, though, then I'll let you heal – and do it all over again. Eventually, your mind will break, and when it does, only then will I send you to…"

Meijers froze, and her eyes widened as Benning suddenly rose to her feet, her screaming cut off abruptly. "If you really followed my example," Benning said coldly, "then you'd know that I learned never to gloat until my enemy's dead, Veera Meijers. You made a mistake; you should have killed me when you had a chance."

Benning moved forward again, striking twice as swiftly as she had before as the effects of All is Lost boosted her stats and skills by a titanic 500%. Her resistance bar hovered at 9%, meaning I Will Not Fall shielded her from the pain of the Nanomancer's assault. Her physical stats hovered above twenty, and she moved with deadly grace as she slammed a fist into Meijer's chest, blocked an elbow strike, and crashed her knee into the woman's side, hurling her from her feet to the floor.

That wasn't the point of using All is Lost, though. Benning didn't want to beat the woman into submission. She had much worse plans for her, and with her Acuity at eighteen, her Willpower at twenty-five, and Cyberwarfare soaring to nearly 120, enacting those plans was as simple as thought. Meijers began to scramble to her feet, then collapsed as Benning's will slammed into her 'net, linked directly to it via the hostile nanites surging through the Marauder's body. That direct link bypassed the Noble encryption holding Benning out, and her thoughts raced throughout the woman's 'net unfettered.

Her vastly expanded mind pinged every system of the Nanomancer's 'net at once, hitting it with thousands of simultaneous attacks. The overtaxed firewall dropped to prevent it from stealing all of Meijers' 'net's resources, and Benning plunged into the core of her enemy's cybernet in less than a second. She shut down the Nanomancer's field with a flex of her will, deactivating all her abilities and gear in the process. Meijers stumbled and cried out in panic as she lost control of her nanites for a moment, and in that moment, Benning twisted the woman's 'net – and the Nanomancer screamed as she found herself cut off from the Overnet, her abilities and Noble privileges stripped from her in an instant.

"What – what the Hole did you do to me?" the woman screamed, holding up her hands. She turned her pistol toward Benning, holding it in shaking hands, but with a simple thought, Benning restored her armor and reactivated her gear. It wasn't necessary; the Nanomancer's gun bucked in her hand when she fired, no longer steadied and stabilized by the Overnet's assistance, and her bullet flew wide as Meijers nearly dropped the weapon. She took a step back and nearly fell, tripping over her own feet as if suddenly clumsy and uncoordinated.

What's wrong with her, Tiddly? Benning asked silently.

<It's like you said before, Benning Kidd,> Tiddly said triumphantly. <All the skills and training in the Collective don't compare to real-world combat. Veera Meijers gained all her skills and stats from the Overnet. Without it, she's back to being a basic Nanomancer.>

And without the 'net, she's a Nanomancer without any abilities, Benning thought grimly. *Time for her to understand the punishment for betrayal.*

"You expect me to give you some kind of explanation?" Benning said mockingly, lifting her own pistol and sighting with it carefully. "No, Veera Meijers. That isn't how this works. I'm going to ask you questions, and you're going to answer them for me. If you don't..."

Benning's pistol spoke, and Meijers screeched in pain as the bullet slammed through her knee, shattering it in a spray of blood and bone. The woman fell to the deck, clutching her leg and screaming, screams that redoubled as Benning fired again and destroyed her other knee in the same way.

"Benning Kidd, stop this at once!" Benning turned to see Adlyn Bechard looking at her, her voice obviously returned now that Meijers' Noble abilities were cut off. The officer pointed her pistol at Benning, the barrel unwavering, but Benning ignored it.

"No," she said simply. "I need answers, Adlyn Bechard, and I'm getting them."

"There are other ways to do this! I can take her into custody, bring her in for questioning..."

"And her Noble patron will have her free before you can blink twice," Benning snorted. She shook her head. "You can't get the information I want, Adlyn Bechard. The System will protect her from you." She looked at Meijers and smiled. "But it can't protect her from me."

Meijers screamed again as Benning's nanites flew outward and enshrouded the Nanomancer's left hand. Meijers watched, her face horrified as flesh ran from her fingers in liquid gobbets, revealing muscle and nerves that sloughed off, pattering on the deck with wet splats.

"No!" Meijers screamed. "Stop! You can't do this to me!"

"Yes, I can, and there's nothing you can do to stop it," Benning shrugged. "I've cut off most of your abilities, and you won't heal from that damage, ever." She stepped forward and kicked the woman onto her back, pinning Meijers against the deck with a boot. Without the Overnet's assistance, the woman's struggles to free herself were pathetic and clumsy, and Benning glared at her in contempt.

She was depending on the System to protect her, she thought scornfully. *She relied on it for everything, and it failed her, just as it fails everyone eventually.*

Bechard rushed forward and grabbed Benning's arm, trying to pull her free, her pistol lifting and firing point blank against Benning's helmet. The Marauder ripped her arm free effortlessly and swiped her fist across Bechard's face, knocking the woman backward and crashing her into one of the bridge consoles. Benning's pistol spoke twice, and Bechard cried out, dropping her pistol as bullets shattered her right wrist and shoulder.

"Don't do that again," Benning said coldly. "You're alive right now because I want you to hear what Veera Meijers has to say, so you can take it back to the Fleet. However, I'm fine sending you to respawn and dealing with the consequences." She looked around at the blood-spattered bridge. "At this point, one more dead officer isn't going to make a difference, after all."

Bechard slumped back against the console, cradling her wounded arm with a look of resignation on her face. Benning turned back to face Meijers.

"Here's what's going to happen, Veera Meijers," she said in an almost friendly voice. "You're going to tell me the names of the Nobles hunting me, of anyone you've placed in my station to work against me, and any plots against me that you know of. In return, I'll send you to respawn."

Meijers screamed again as her left eye bubbled and

dissolved, pouring from the empty socket in chunky rivulets of torn flesh. Benning leaned closer, staring at the woman's one remaining eye.

"You're going to tell me eventually," she said simply. "If you don't, I'm going to leave you like this: helpless, stripped of your abilities, unable to communicate, and cut off from anyone who could help you. The ability I used is permanent, as far as I know; you'll stay like this forever if I don't turn it off, and you can't be healed until I do."

She leaned back, shaking her head. "Imagine it, Veera Meijers. Trapped in your body; your arms and legs nothing but stumps; blind, deaf, mute, and unable to communicate in any way. Imagine being like that for the rest of your existence in the Collective, not even able to flee to your domain to escape it. That's what I'll do to you – unless you tell me, right now, who's backing you."

"I – I can't! They won't allow it," Meijers wailed.

"You can try," Benning said. Meijers shook her head, and Benning shrugged. "As you wish. Let's try your left breast, next. Ready to lose it?"

She raised her hand, and Veera Meijers sobbed in fear, shaking her head. "Lauren Doheny!" she screamed. Her eyes widened, and she stared at Benning in awe and fear. "How – I shouldn't have been able to say that! My contract with Lauren Doheny..."

"Is void for the moment," Benning cut her off. "Who is Lauren Doheny?"

"Noble Lauren Doheny is the matriarch of Malleus Nanotech," Bechard spoke, her voice awed. "She's one of the most powerful and influential Nobles in the entire Collective, Benning Kidd!"

"How did you get her help?" Benning asked Meijers.

"Sh-she contacted me," Meijers said weakly, her body

collapsing to the deck in resignation. "After you took IS-39267, one of her representatives approached me and offered me a way to get my revenge on you."

"How do you know it's really her, and not someone pretending to be her?"

"I met her on several occasions. A Noble can only create a Designate in person."

"Why did she make you a Designate?"

"To let me join your fleet without being discovered or locking myself into a contract," Meijers said woodenly, her voice and face both defeated. "As her Designate, I could command the System to release me from the contract without notifying you. It gave me access to the station's systems and let me communicate with Adlyn Bechard without leaving traces."

"So, you told Bechard where I was going and how to find me? And brought those bounty hunters into the station?"

"Yes, to both. I also placed a bounty for your capture and delivery to the Fleet, then convinced the administrators in Van Maanen and Frostwise to try and claim that bounty when no hunters would take it."

"Were you Trephor Sando the entire time, or did you take his place?"

"There is no Trephor Sando," Meijers snorted. "I created him. I thought that a socially stunted Starship Captain would appeal to you – and it did." She looked at Benning, her ruined face contemptuous once more.

"This isn't the end of this, Benning Kidd. Eventually, you'll send me to respawn, and when you do, I'll start all over again. With the influence of a Noble Designate, I can start my own fleet and come back to destroy this station and everyone on it." Her one eye burned maliciously, and Benning shook her head.

"This is your warning, Veera Meijers. If I ever see you again, I'll lock you down like this and leave you that way forever." She raised her pistol. "Make sure I never see you again."

<No, Benning Kidd, wait!> Tiddly's voice rang out in Benning's mind as the Marauder's finger squeezed the trigger. Veera Meijers' head jerked as the bullet slammed into her forehead, exploded in her skull, and ripped its way out the back of her head. Fragments ricocheted off the deck and plunged back into her brain, tearing through it. The woman's body convulsed once before falling still, her eyes closing in death.

A red screen flashed in Benning's vision, intruding itself on her sight and filling her field of view completely.

> PERMANENT DEATH ALERT!
> A Citizen has died permanently in
> your vicinity! It is recommended
> that you leave this area as quickly
> as possible! Respawn in this area
> is no longer guaranteed!

"Wait – permanent death?" Bechard gasped. "You – you just killed her, Benning Kidd! You ended Veera Meijers – forever! How?"

"It doesn't matter," Benning shook her head, swinging her pistol to face the officer. She hadn't intended that result, of course, but she was content with it. Veera Meijers would no longer hunt her; that was all that mattered. In fact, the woman's death gave Benning new options for dealing with those who attacked her and hounded her. If she killed a few of them permanently, hopefully, the rest would learn to leave her alone.

"What does matter is that you're going to respawn," she continued. "And when you get back to the Fleet, you can tell them everything that happened here, everything you heard. If they want to keep coming after me..." She shrugged and gestured at the cooling corpse beside her. "I can do this again if I have to."

She lifted her pistol, but Bechard held up her good arm, shaking her head frantically.

"Wait, Benning Kidd! I need – I need to know what this is all about." She struggled to her feet, still cradling her shattered arm. "I've known for a long time that something was wrong with this investigation. This fleet never should have come for you; there's nowhere nearly enough evidence to convict you of anything beyond using prohibited weapons." She glanced at Meijers' body. "And now, there's not even enough evidence for that."

"So?" Benning shrugged.

"So, I'm a Fleet investigator, Benning Kidd. I'm just trying to do my job, nothing more. This whole time, I've wanted to talk to you, to hear the whole story." She straightened. "And one way or the other, I'm going to find it out. That's what I do; it's my purpose in the Collective.

"You can kill me, Benning Kidd, and I can't stop you. But it won't stop me, either. If you don't talk to me, I'll just keep digging and hunting. It doesn't matter how many times you kill me; I'm going to do my job, one way or the other."

Benning stared at the woman, feeling a tinge of respect despite herself. She wanted to dislike Bechard, to treat her as an enemy, but she'd always admired people who simply did their job, regardless of the difficulties or challenges. Bechard had just watched Benning kill someone permanently, ending their existence in the Collective, but she was still determined to discover the truth. That was something Benning could respect.

"Fine, Adlyn Bechard. I'll be happy to explain it to you – I can even show you, since this ship has a respawning chamber." She smiled coldly. "You aren't going to like it, though – and you'll never be able to include it in your report, no matter how much you want to."

She walked toward the bridge's exit, watching through her visor as Bechard trailed behind. The Fleet officer would never be Benning's ally, but perhaps, just perhaps, they didn't have to be enemies, either. Benning just wanted the Fleet to leave her alone. If she fed Bechard the right information, perhaps the woman would be able to convince the admirals to back off. Benning hoped so; if that didn't work, she'd take the war to the Fleet, and flork the consequences.

CHAPTER 37

The mood around the captains' table that evening was a mixture of celebration and sorrow.

They'd been victorious over the Fleet, something that none of them believed possible. Under Hendrick's command, her ships obliterated both destroyers and one of the frigates. The other two fled, and Hendricks didn't bother to chase them. Benning didn't blame him; the battle hadn't been one-sided, after all. They'd lost two of their corvettes, the *System's Fall* was badly damaged, and the *Arcturus* was crippled. Even worse, Veera Meijers rigged the *Implacable* to self-destruct, and its explosion heavily damaged the rest of the fleet.

Of course, while Benning lost ships, she'd also gained her new battlefrigate. That more than offset the loss, especially since the ship still had its proprietary Fleet tech intact. She'd already started analyzing it as much as possible. She couldn't create templates from it – the System wouldn't let her – but Charlo Herrick and Avaeyana Roble both felt certain they could use what they would learn from the ship to upgrade the rest of the fleet, and Emmed Oswald was already on his way to Marauder's Rest to study the ship's nanofield – and the new nanites Benning had claimed from Veera Meijers.

The woman's nanofield hadn't destroyed itself or incorporated into the ship's field when she died since it was cut off from the Overnet. Benning now possessed most of those nanites, but she'd only been able to hack some of them, and those barely stayed under her control. She sensed they had advanced capabilities, but either her 'net wasn't sophisticated enough to unlock them, or they were restricted to Nanomancers. Benning hoped for the first, as she could fix that, or Emmed Oswald could.

After Meijers' death, Benning took Adlyn Bechard to the ship's respawn chamber. All is Lost wore off long before they reached their destination, of course, but Benning was careful not to let the Fleet Officer see her weakness. She had a feeling fear was the only thing making the woman so cooperative, and she didn't want to test that guess and have to kill the woman. The ship was mostly empty by that point, as the automated defenses had done away with the defending marines and practically every Fleet Officer aboard, but the Workers were mostly untouched by those defenses and still manned the respawn chamber as usual.

Benning spent the trip silently hacking into Bechard's 'net, and once they arrived in the chamber, she activated Slip the Net for both of them. Someone was in the process of respawning, and Bechard's face grew horrified as what had looked like an empty respawn pod with a body slowly forming in it was revealed to contain a Drone being actively overwritten. Benning explained what Drones were, her own status as one, and how her elevation brought the wrath of the Nobility and System down on her.

"This – this explains so much," Bechard whispered, shaking her head. "Why the Admiralty signed off on your arrest warrant; why so much of your guilt was presumed without evidence." She glanced at Benning curiously. "Is this how you escaped my ship? And how you destroyed Aquilae Prime Station?"

That had been a surprise for Benning. She'd assumed she'd damaged the station, never dreaming that its dark matter generators would drag it planetside and splatter it across the surface. She hadn't admitted anything, of course, but hearing that she'd done that had been a bit of a shock.

At the same time, she now knew a vulnerability of most orbital stations, and she filed that knowledge away. It might come in handy again in the future, after all. She didn't much care about the loss of life – it was a drop in the bucket of the population of Altair alone, and most of those dead were Citizens who would be reborn – but what could be done to one station could happen to hers. She made a note to look into patching that vulnerability in the near future.

"Benning Kidd, while I understand more now – you know that you're still in violation of Collective law," Bechard said at last, speaking slowly and almost reluctantly. "It seems like you've been pushed into situations where you've had to react, but no one forced you to react the way you did. You made those choices yourself, and there'll be consequences for them."

"Of course, and I'm willing to deal with them," Benning shrugged. "Just don't expect me to lay down and accept whatever consequences the Fleet thinks I deserve, Adlyn Bechard. I'll fight to keep what's mine, no matter who's trying to take it from me."

"You can't declare war on the Fleet, Benning Kidd," Bechard protested.

"I don't have to. You've declared war on me. I'm simply fighting back," she snorted. "And so far, I think I'm winning."

Benning sent Bechard to respawn after that – but not before canceling Slip the Net, of course. She wanted the officer to go back to the Fleet, to tell them what she'd learned and how Benning had been responding to attacks against her all along. She hoped the Fleet would get the message and leave her alone, but if not…well, perhaps the permanent deaths of a few admirals would convince them. Benning thought she could make that happen, and in her experience, the people in charge lost interest in hunting her once they realized their own lives were at risk doing so.

"So, Trephor Sando was the traitor all along," Hendricks observed to her as the group sat around the table, talking quietly with one another about the day's battle and what it all meant.

"He was," Benning confirmed. "Or she was, I guess, since she was actually Veera Meijers in disguise, using a Noble's privileges to assume an identity that we couldn't see through."

"I didn't think that infiltrator suites let you change your gender. Must have been a pretty advanced one."

"Nearly unlimited credits and authority can get you a lot, Fodor Hendricks," Benning said, echoing both Meijers and Tiddly.

"Not enough, though, apparently," the man chuckled. "Think she'll be back at some point, or has she learned her lesson?"

"I'm fairly certain we'll never see her again," Benning said evenly. At Tiddly's advice, she'd kept her new ability to permanently kill a Citizen to herself. She didn't know why the AI suggested that, but she trusted Tiddly, so she accepted the gnome's suggestion.

"Good." He leaned back in his chair. "The Fleet, though – they'll be back. They won't take our stealing their battlefrigate lying down. They'll assemble a new fleet to reclaim it, at the very least."

"And when they do, I'll take the most powerful ship from that fleet," Benning snorted. "And I'll keep doing that until I've got my own titanosphere, Fodor Hendricks. At that point, I'm pretty sure the Fleet will get the idea and leave me alone."

"Ha!" he laughed. "Us with a titanosphere! No one in the Collective would be safe!"

"Us?" she repeated archly. "There is no us, Fodor Hendricks. You bought out your contract, remember? You're just here until you can arrange passage off my station."

"I don't think so," he shook his head. "I told you, I made a mistake buying out my contract – the mistake of not believing in you. You just proved that I was an idiot. I'm sticking around..." He made a face. "That is, if you still want me to."

She looked at him for a long moment. "Did you consider running during that fight?" she asked, activating her Sense Deceit skill as she spoke.

"Consider it? Of course," he snorted. "We were fighting a Hole-bound battlefrigate, Benning Kidd. I'd have been a fool not to think about running." He looked at her seriously. "But that's not your real question, is it? You want to know if I thought about betraying you. We both know I could have; I was in charge of the fleet, and I could have taken it for my own at any time."

She nodded. "That is what I'm wondering, yes. Did you?"

"Yes," he admitted simply. "There were a couple moments where it crossed my mind. However, I never gave it serious thought."

"Why not?" she pressed. "You're a Pirate Captain, Fodor Hendricks. You could have had your own fleet. Why not take that chance when you had it?"

"Two reasons, Benning Kidd. The first is that I know you'd never have let me get away with it. You'd have found a way to make me pay, even if it took you decades, wouldn't you?" She nodded silently, and he grimaced. "I assumed as much. However, the other reason..."

He leaned closer to her. "You astound me, Benning Kidd. I admire your ruthlessness and ambition. I'm in awe of your drive and ability to do what's necessary to achieve your ends. And I'm amazed at the things you've done, considering how much the System has stacked the odds against you." He shook his head. "I won't turn on you, Benning Kidd. I can't."

"You know that I'll never feel that way toward you, Fodor Hendricks," she said softly. "I respect you, and you're important to me, but..."

"But only as someone who can help you achieve your goals," he sighed. "Yeah, I understand that. But just because you can't care for me doesn't mean I don't care for you." He shrugged and leaned back. "More the fool me, I suppose, but it is what it is, Benning Kidd."

She nodded; her Sense Deceit skill hadn't triggered once, although it had suggested he'd skirted the edges of the truth a few times. That was close enough for her. "Welcome back to Marauder's Rest then, Captain," she smiled at him, speaking loudly enough for the others to hear and turn toward them.

"Thank you, Commodore." He made a face. "I suppose this means a new contract though, doesn't it?"

"I have a feeling we'll all be getting new contracts, Fodor Hendricks," Avaeyana Roble laughed. "After Trephor Sando – or whoever he was – I'm sure the Commodore is low on trust."

"No," Benning said slowly, tapping her fingers on the table. "No, I don't think new contracts will be necessary, Avaeyana Roble."

"I'd do it," Raelle Muckley snorted. "No one would blame you for it, Commodore."

"No, they probably wouldn't, but..." She rose to her feet, looking at each of them in turn. "We didn't win this battle because of contracts, Raelle Muckley. We didn't win through better ships or firepower. We won by depending on each other, by working together and trusting one another. We won by understanding that together, we're stronger than any of us are individually.

"Together, we've done things that we'd only have been able to dream about separately," she went on. "We've raided convoys that should have destroyed us; we've taken ships that couldn't be taken; we've even faced down the Fleet and won! If we remain together, united, we'll do even more. More credits, more Renown, more power and influence in the Collective.

"I don't want you to follow me because of a contract," she finished. "If that's all that binds us, then we'll ultimately fail in our next challenge. I want you to follow me because you trust me to lead you, because you want to travel the same path, and because you're excited to see what we can accomplish together. If you're simply here because of the contract..." She shrugged. "Then I'll release you from it. Here. Now. This instant. No buyout; no repercussions. You just turn and walk away. I'd rather you do that today than in a month or a year."

She fell silent, and Hendricks looked at the others. "Any takers?" he asked.

Roble simply smiled. "I'm not going anywhere," she said easily.

"Neither am I," Boguna agreed. "I can't wait to see where all this takes us. Maybe beyond the Collective itself..." Her eyes went distant, and Raelle Muckley laughed derisively.

"I'm staying," the rough captain said staunchly.

"Then it's agreed," Hendricks smiled. "We're all on board, Commodore. So, tell us: what's this next challenge you're talking about?"

"The next challenge, Fodor Hendricks, is going to be even harder than the last one," she admitted. "We've dealt with the Fleet; once we're sure that they're not coming back anytime soon, we're going after the person who sent them after us in the first place." She looked them all in the eye.

"Next, we're hunting a Noble – and we'll make them regret that they ever tried to destroy us, one way or the other."

EPILOGUE

"Court is now in session," the ensign in formal dress uniform proclaimed from his spot beside the judge's console. "The Honorable Admiral Kaeler Yessuf presiding. Attention!"

Lauren Doheny watched in amusement as the handful of Fleet Officers present in the courtroom snapped to a standing position as the holographic image of the admiral overseeing the sham of a trial appeared behind the console. Lauren remained seated, of course, as did the three other Nobles who'd chosen to view the proceedings that day.

Deshane Silva was one of those, as she'd expected. The owner of Isullon Industries had a vested interest in the trial before them. The presence of Rosaliya Bucaro, the matriarch of Inception Starcraft, was something of a surprise, as Lauren didn't know the black-haired former Starship Captain had any interest in the Drone. Fyodr Mosin's presence wasn't, unfortunately. He certainly had some interest in the day's outcome, but he likely sought a different ending than Lauren did. She'd hoped her little diversion of arranging for him to receive the incorrect connection codes for the trial would cause him to miss it, but there he was, sitting calmly in the Nobles' gallery above the proceedings, looking down on everything with the same perpetually calm expression that he always wore.

"Remain standing for the members of the Admiralty," the ensign intoned once more. The judge's console sat against one wall of the circular room, with the witness stand beside it. Two tables stood in the center of the room, one of which was noticeably empty, with a few seats behind them where witnesses could sit. Twenty podiums lined the walls to either side of the judge, ten to their left and ten to their right, and one by one, the flag officers of the Admiralty appeared at these consoles. Normally, only three admirals stood in judgment in a trial, but this one had such import and far-reaching consequences that a full twenty had been called. Technically, Lauren and Silva had pushed for the full Admiralty to attend, and even the Fleet had to bow to the whims of the Nobles.

Lauren smirked silently. She'd already arranged for the outcome of this trial long before it happened, but she wanted to make sure no one could ever argue with the result. With twenty admirals calling for Benning Kidd's execution and imprisonment, the Drone would finally be removed as a threat to the Collective. She'd likely spend the next several decades in prison, constantly being spawn camped back to level one, and she'd emerge broken and useless, no longer a concern and proof to the System that Drones couldn't possibly succeed as Citizens.

"At ease," Yessuf said from where he appeared to be seated beside the console. "Prosecutor, you may begin."

Admiral Lucira Blanchard rose to her feet, her long face grim and serious. Again, it wasn't typical for an admiral to try a case like this – normally, the investigating officer would have done so – but when two of the most powerful Nobles in the Collective requested it, no admiral in their right mind would refuse.

"Your honor, the case before us is the Collective versus Citizen Benning Kidd."

"And where is the accused?" the judge asked, staring at the empty defense table. "Or their representative?"

"The accused has not deigned to appear, your honor, and as they have not presented themselves to the

Fleet for questioning as ordered, they were not assigned representation."

"Very well," Yessuf shrugged, even though Lauren knew this went against all regulations. "Let us proceed. Prosecution, present the evidence against the accused."

"Your honor, I call Fleet Lieutenant Adlyn Bechard as our only witness," Blanchard said.

Lauren gritted her teeth at those words. Veera Meijers should have been present, as well, offering direct evidence from her time spent with Benning Kidd. After she'd revealed herself to Benning Kidd, though, the woman had vanished, beyond even Lauren's ability to find her. Bechard's report stated that Meijers died in the struggle, but no mention was made of what happened to her after that. Lauren only knew that Meijers lost her status as Noble Designate, nothing more.

It was an impossibility, really. As a Noble, Lauren could demand the System reveal the location of any Citizen, anywhere in the Collective, and it would, instantly. Only another Noble Designate would be immune to her detection abilities…

She narrowed her eyes at Fyodr Mosin. Had the man somehow made Benning Kidd his Designate? Or even worse, Veera Meijers? Either would explain why Lauren could find no trace of the Nanomancer respawning anywhere in the Collective.

As Bechard took a seat in the witness chair, a pale white shaft of light descended on her, illuminating her in its cool radiance. The light was a sort of lie detector; if it flickered orange, the witness wasn't speaking the entire truth. If it turned red, they were lying, and their entire testimony would be thrown out. Lauren wasn't particularly worried about that happening, though. Bechard didn't have to lie. There was plenty of evidence suggesting that Benning

Kidd had committed terrorism, mass murder, and wanton destruction. Lauren tuned out the testimony; she knew what the lieutenant would say, after all.

The lieutenant finished speaking, and the Admiral nodded. "Thank you, Lieutenant. You are dismissed from the stand, and the prosecution..."

"A moment, if you don't mind." Lauren's jaw clenched as Fyodr Mosin spoke, leaning forward so that his holographic image loomed over the proceedings below. "Lieutenant, there are some things about that testimony that I admit confuse me."

"Are you standing in for the defense in this case, Fyodr Mosin?" Deshane Silva chuckled. "Have you become a Solicitor without anyone's knowledge?"

"I'm merely interested in the truth, Deshane Silva," Mosin smiled easily. "You see, I believe that the Collective's laws apply equally to *all* Citizens, and that they're all entitled to adequate representation. Since the Fleet chose not to provide such – against their own regulations, I believe – it seems that someone must fill that role." He looked down at Yessuf. "If you have no objections, Admiral?"

"No, sir," the admiral shook his head, as Lauren knew he would. A Fleet Officer didn't reach flag ranks by telling a Noble they couldn't speak in an open court. "Please, proceed."

"Thank you." He looked back at Bechard, who shrank under his gaze and looked justifiably nervous. "Tell me, Lieutenant. Do you have any witnesses who saw Benning Kidd use prohibited technology against IS-39267, now called Marauder's Rest?"

"N-no, sir," the woman shook her head. "None whose testimony would be admissible in this court."

"I see," he nodded. "And is there any evidence that

shows Benning Kidd sabotaging Adriaan Station? Or Aquilae Prime?"

"No, sir. Security footage shows no presence of anyone tampering with either station."

"If I may, sir," Blanchard spoke up, "we have reason to believe that Benning Kidd has acquired some sort of advanced cloaking technology that allows her to slip past normal security. If that's true, then there wouldn't be any evidence of her planting any of those bombs."

Lauren suppressed a wince at the admiral's statement. She knew for a fact that the Drone didn't have cloaking tech; she was simply gifted at hacking into security systems and erasing her presence from them. Mosin had to know the same thing, and he would surely pounce on the admiral's mistake.

"What reason to believe might that be, Admiral?" Mosin asked curiously. He glanced at the trembling Bechard. "Lieutenant? Why do you think that Benning Kidd has advanced concealment tech?"

"It – it's the only explanation that fit the data we have, sir. At least, it's the least objectionable one."

"You're claiming that lack of evidence – is evidence?" he replied skeptically. "You honor, is that sort of testimony typically admissible in court?"

"No, sir," Yessuf said heavily. "It isn't. The jury is asked to disregard the Lieutenant's conjectures about concealment technology."

"I fail to see the point of all this," Lauren objected.

"The point, Lauren Doheny, is that it seems the only evidence the prosecution has is that she was on both stations and left them right before they were sabotaged. Is that essentially true, Lieutenant?"

"Yes, sir," the officer replied, hanging her head. Lauren could almost hear the woman's thoughts as she watched her future career washed into the Hole, but she didn't care.

"Are you suggesting some sort of coincidence, Fyodr Mosin?" she scoffed. "That both stations just happened to be damaged while she was there, and she was totally uninvolved?"

"No, Lauren Doheny – although there's a case to be made for that." Mosin glanced to the side as if looking at something. "According to my records, over 200 Citizens visited both of those stations no more than two solar weeks before their respective disasters. Surely, any of them could have sabotaged the stations, and Benning Kidd happened to be present – along with millions of others on each station. With quintillions of Citizens in the Collective, coincidences like that are bound to happen."

"But still very unlikely," Deshane Silva pointed out.

"True, which is why I wonder if perhaps Benning Kidd might have somehow known that each station was about to be attacked and left before it happened. That seems more reasonable than the idea that she eluded both stations' security and attacked them unseen, at least to me. Tell me, Lieutenant, did you consider this possibility?"

"Yes, sir, I did," the officer nodded.

"And do you believe it to be possible?"

"Possible? Absolutely, sir. Reports from my agent in Benning Kidd's pirate band detail that she was very skilled at gaining information that others couldn't find, such as cargoes hidden within a convoy. With those skills, it's possible that she could have learned about those attacks and fled the station afterward."

"And do you think it likely, Lieutenant?" Lauren snapped.

"No, ma'am. I think that Benning Kidd did something to both stations – either that, or she arranged for it to happen to cover her escape." The white-haired woman shrugged. "I have no direct evidence to support that belief, though."

"And yet, there's significant circumstantial evidence, isn't there?" Lauren pressed.

"Yes, ma'am, as I testified previously, there's ample circumstantial evidence linking Benning Kidd to each of these crimes."

Lauren sat back and smirked at Fyodr Mosin, but the man ignored her utterly.

"Not to cheapen the value of circumstantial evidence," he sighed, still speaking to the Lieutenant, "but I personally would like to speak to someone who actually witnessed these crimes of which you accuse the defendant. Didn't you say that you had an agent working for Benning Kidd? A Citizen Veera Meijers?" He looked around. "Why isn't she present in court today? Surely, her testimony would have bolstered your case."

Lauren's heart sank as she noticed the tiny, triumphant smile hovering around Mosin's lips. It was a faint thing, something that the lesser Citizens below wouldn't have seen, but she noticed it, and from the way that Silva leaned back, removing himself from the discussion, she guessed that he had, too. Lauren knew immediately that the entire point of Mosin's interrogation was to lead to this question – which meant he had to have known the answer. She silently seethed; he'd somehow stolen her Designate from her. It was the only possible explanation...

"The witness was unable to be present due to unforeseen circumstances, sir," Blanchard spoke up, rising to her feet. "We have her sworn testimony..."

"Yes, and it's quite impressive," Mosin nodded.

"However, I still want to know why she couldn't make it. What were these unforeseen circumstances, Lieutenant?" The white-haired woman hesitated, and Mosin glared at her. "I might remind you that you're on the witness stand, Lieutenant. If you offer untrue testimony, we'll all know, and by law, your entire testimony to this point will be stricken and removed. I ask you once again. Where. Is. Veera. Meijers?"

"Dead," the Lieutenant whispered, her head drooping as she spoke. Lauren felt a sudden chill; Veera Meijers hadn't died. She would have known if that happened. And yet, the light surrounding the officer glowed the same pale white as it had the entire time; she was telling the truth.

"Ah. She's awaiting respawn, then?"

"N-no, sir. She's dead. Benning Kidd killed her. Permanently."

Lauren's jaw dropped at the Lieutenant's words, and clamor of shouts rose through the courtroom. Dead – permanently? How was that possible? The light around the lieutenant glowed calmly, indicating that she spoke the truth, but she had to be mistaken. No Citizen of the Collective could die permanently…

Apparently, the judge agreed with Lauren. "Impossible!" he roared. "Lieutenant, explain yourself! No Citizen can be permanently killed!"

"I thought the same, your honor, but I saw the System message myself. Here – I can show you." The woman gestured, and a red screen appeared in the air above her head. Lauren read it several times, cursing softly in the sudden silence hanging over the courtroom.

PERMANENT DEATH!
A Citizen has died permanently in

your vicinity! It is recommended
that you leave this area as quickly
as possible! Respawn in this area
is no longer guaranteed!

"This is evidence of murder!" Blanchard said, her face pale. "The prosecution wishes to add the additional charge of murder..."

"Tell me, Lieutenant," Mosin said evenly, not even seeming disturbed by what he saw, "when Benning Kidd killed Veera Meijers, who attacked first?"

"Veera Meijers, sir," the woman said softly. "With her nanofield."

"I see. And in the cases where Benning Kidd attacked Fleet vessels and officers, was she attacked first?"

"Yes, sir – at least, in the instances I saw. The Fleet attacked and destroyed one of her ships before she attacked us at Marauder's Rest, and our marines fired on her inside the *Crimson Chang* before she returned fire."

"Thank you," Mosin said, leaning back. He glanced at Deshane Silva, who sighed and leaned forward.

"If it please the Admiralty," Silva said heavily, "while these are certainly serious charges, I withdraw my recommendation for the imprisonment and execution of Benning Kidd. I suggest the charges of terrorism, mass murder, and wanton destruction be dropped, and she only be charged with piracy and attacking the Fleet in self-defense."

The gallery below broke out in furious murmurs as Silva sat down, and Lauren stared at him in shock. He'd been her ally through all of this, always supporting her efforts to destroy the Drone. Now, he was recommending that she be charged with crimes that would result in her paying a relatively insubstantial fine. It was a knife in her back, a blatant betrayal of her!

Lauren glared at the man furiously. *What are you saying?* she demanded silently.

The only sensible thing, Lauren Doheny, he replied in her mind. *I'm withdrawing my support of your little feud with the Drone.*

What? Why? We could break her, Deshane Silva!

Because of the not-so-subtle point Fyodr Mosin just made. So far, the Drone has only attacked those who've attacked her first. I have no intention of being the one to attack her first, not anymore.

What are you talking about? Lauren snapped. *She's a Drone, Deshane Silva! Are you saying that you're afraid of a Drone?*

Yes, Lauren Doheny, he said bluntly. *And you should be, as well.*

She stared at him in shock, and he leaned toward her, his face grave.

Think about it for a moment. We share the same method of immortality as Citizens, which means that If she can kill a Citizen, she can kill a Noble. Personally, I like living. If you do as well, then I suggest you end this madness. He hesitated. *Assuming, that is, that it's not too late for you.*

What? What do you mean? Lauren's queries went unanswered as Silva blinked out, leaving the proceedings.

She stared at Mosin with open hatred. He'd known this, somehow; he'd known that the Drone could kill a Citizen. And he supported her! If she could end a Citizen's immortality, she could bring down the entire Collective! She was a threat to everyone, a threat that needed to be stopped!

"Lieutenant, one more question," Mosin asked, staring

right back at Lauren. "I assume that Benning Kidd questioned Veera Meijers extensively before killing her. Did she say anything of importance? Anything noteworthy?"

"Y-yes, sir. She said..." The lieutenant swallowed hard, the sound audible in the silence. "She said that she was the Designate of Noble Lauren Doheny, who provided her with the means to infiltrate Marauder's Rest." More muttering broke out at that, and several of the admirals below shot sharp and angry glances Lauren's way.

Lauren's face drained of color as she looked down at the young officer, ignoring the flag officers. What the woman just claimed was impossible! A Designate couldn't speak about or against their Noble sponsor; the System wouldn't allow it. There should have been no way for Meijers to implicate Lauren – but somehow, obviously, she had. If Bechard knew, then Benning Kidd knew, as well. The Drone knew her hunter's designation, now...

"Any decision to convict must, of course, be up to the Admiralty," Mosin spoke up, still looking directly at Lauren. "However, before you render your verdict, I'd like to offer a little evidence of my own. I also scanned the security videos of Aquilae Prime Station and the Fleet warship docked there. I noted in particular that neither one shows any evidence of Benning Kidd after she was freed from her confinement – and yet, the Overnet has no record of her going to respawn, either.

"Your meaning, sir?" one of the admirals asked hoarsely.

"My meaning is that, assuming the lieutenant is correct, and Benning Kidd did play a part in sabotaging those stations, she has a way to do so without leaving a record on the Overnet. She could be anywhere – even in Fleet Headquarters, right at this moment, and no one would ever know. Combine that with her ability to end the life of a

Citizen permanently, and I might consider carefully before issuing a verdict that would make her my enemy." He turned to look at Blanchard, who flinched. "Or charging her with false crimes."

Blanchard's face went blank as she rose to her feet once more, her expression resigned. "Your honor, in light of the testimony and the altered recommendation of Noble Deshane Silva, the prosecution would like to amend the charges to attacking the Fleet in self-defense and piracy. We recommend an appropriate fine and declaring the accused a criminal for a period of one solar year."

"So noted," Yessuf nodded. "Any objections?" He glanced at Mosin, who remained silent.

"Very well. Admiralty, your verdict?"

"We find the accused guilty of the amended charges," one of the admirals spoke up at once, without even deliberating. Lauren simply stared in shock. How could they openly defy her, even knowing that she would seek retribution for this humiliation?

Because they're more afraid of the Drone than you, a voice in her mind whispered quietly in reply.

"The accused, Benning Kidd, has been found guilty of attacking the Fleet in self-defense and piracy. This court decrees that she pay a fine of 1,000 credits and be listed as a criminal in all civilized systems for a period of one year. Court is adjourned."

As the admirals faded away, Lauren rose and stared at Mosin, her face clearly displaying her hatred. "You'll pay for this, Fyodr Mosin," she hissed. "Do you know what you've done? You may have doomed the entire Collective! If that..." She glanced at the spectators still below; even she couldn't mention Drones in the presence of Citizens without repercussions. "If that *thing* is free to act as it wishes, it could slaughter us all!"

"No, not us all, Lauren Doheny," Mosin chuckled. "And I'm not worried about any retribution you might seek to visit on me." He rose to his feet, and his genial face went cold. "You see, I know Benning Kidd, as well as anyone can. One thing I can tell you is that she always finds a way to punish her enemies – and she's just discovered that you're her enemy. If I were you, I'd worry less about me and more about waking up one morning to find her standing over you, ready to end your existence…permanently." He chuckled. "Sweet dreams, Lauren Doheny. Enjoy your life while you still have it. I don't think that will be very long."

As the man vanished, Lauren felt a chill race through her body, one she tried to shake off. She was a Noble, one of the most powerful people in the Collective! She was practically invulnerable – no, she *was* invulnerable. Even the Fleet tread carefully around her; no force in the Collective could truly threaten her, and she had no reason to fear.

So why, as she severed the link to the trial, and the courtroom vanished from around her, did she feel like someone was watching her through a rifle's sights at that exact moment?

Benning's quest for vengeance continues
in Drone Aspirant, coming out in 2023.

Thanks for reading! If you enjoyed "Drone Marauder" (and I hope you did), then please a review to help other readers find out about it. Also, maybe check out some of my other series while you're at it!

Visit me online at The Singularity to see my catalog

of works, find out more about what's coming up, or sign up for my mailing list to get news, promos, and an occasional free short story (from me, of course)!

A big shout-out to RIArtist for their support on Patreon!

To learn more about LitRPG, talk to authors, and just have an awesome time, please join the LitRPG Books group!

If you love Gamelit and want to read more series like this, or to hear about the newest releases and best series, check out the GameLit Society!

BENNING KIDD'S
STATUS SHEET

End of "Drone Marauder"

BENNING KIDD
Citizen Path: Stellar Marauder
Level: 11
To Next Level: 104% LEVEL UP!
Credits: 63,914.8 Standard Credits

STATS
Physicality: 13.6
Coordination: 13.4
Resistance: 13.5

Acuity: 12.3
Willpower: 18.8
Social: 11.9

Renown: +/- 106
Nanodefense: 41.8

SKILLS
Conditioning: 21.7
Cyberwarfare: 20
Fleet Tactics: 10.4
Leadership: 24.2
Martial Combat: 23.1

Nanoresistance: 7.2
Naval Tactics: 26.4
Sense Deceit: 6.4
Starfaring: 21.3
Weapons Expertise: 21.7

ABILITIES
All is Lost
As It Should Be
Better Captain than Crew
Declared Enemy
Flurry
For Fame
From Hell's Heart
Heart of the Savage
Honor the Fallen
I Have the Bridge
I Will Not Fall
Inspiration
Leader of the Fleet
Limitless Body
Malevolent Aura
Natural Hacking
On My Command
Strength from Pain
Weapon Mastery

GLOSSARY OF TERMS

AU – /aw/ A unit of distance roughly equal to the average distance of the planet Earth from the sun. Equivalent to 149,598,000 km or 499 leconds. Not often used in spacefaring.

cim – /sim/ A centimeter

comparm – /komp' arm/ Composite armor, a basic type of armor consisting of plates of HDM held in place with layers of molex and syleather

CY-space – /sigh space/ The space inside an expanded Calabi-Yau manifold. Also called "five-space" or the fifth dimension, although there are multiple dimensions rolled up in CY-space that could theoretically be accessed.

cybernet – The network that links every person and complex object to the Overnet. The cybernet constantly checks the status of its owner and guides the nanofield to maintain and repair and damage found. Cybernets are also used to broadcast IDs, communicate through the Overnet, and upgrade the object or individual as needed. Usually called a 'net.

deep dive – A method of traveling vast distances almost instantaneously using wormholes. Requires negative energy and negative mass to maintain the wormhole. Considered to be one of the more disturbing experiences any Citizen can have in the universe.

dive – The act of using negative energy to unfold the compactified fifth dimension, allowing vessels to travel FTL, or faster-than-light for brief periods. Limited in range to trips no longer than a light-hour, around one trillion ems.

em – /emm/ A meter

enn-steel – A non-Newtonian, or NN metal. When it is struck with force, it partially liquifies, spreading the energy of the impact throughout the entirety of the metal. Far stronger than HDM or transtanium but much more expensive and difficult to fabricate.

entu – /enn too'/ Gaseous nitrogen, a common cargo, usually shipped in liquid form.

foam tungsten – A tungsten alloy with tiny fullerene bubbles that add strength and reduce weight. Much lighter, less dense, and stronger than tungsten or HDM. Stronger and lighter than transtanium.

fulleron – /ful' ər on/ A synthetic fabric made of connected chains of fullerenes, spherical molecules of carbon. Stronger than molex, fulleron is a bulkier fabric and harder to layer.

gas – Hydrogen, the basic fuel for all starships. 'Heavy gas' refers to deuterium, while 'hot gas' refers to tritium.

gig – A gigagram, one billion grams or one million kigs.

h-cube – A cubic hectometer, a million cubic meters, a unit of volume typically only used when discussing extremely large freighter vessels.

HDM – High-density metal, a steel alloy that is far denser and stronger than carbon steel. HDM is heavy, relatively inflexible, and is considered to be a bottom-tier metal for fabrication.

kig – /kigg/ A kilogram

kim – /kimm/ A kilometer

lecond – /le' kənd/ A light-second, a unit of distance equal to about 300,000 kims and the distance light travels in one second. Generally, ship-to-ship combat occurs at distances no longer than three leconds without using diving weapons.

linute – /linn' ut/ A light-minute, sixty leconds or 18 million kims.

liquid metal – A nanite-infused alloy that can shift its density significantly regardless of temperature. Its ability to harden at a single point of contact and liquefy around that point to distribute force makes it an excellent material for armor.

microthene – /mī' kro theen'/ A crystalline plastic that is stronger than titanium but somewhat more flexible and far lighter. Used for many fabrication purposes, microthene has a soft feel to it that belies its strength.

mig – /migg/ A metric ton, 1,000 kigs or one million grams.

mim – /mimm/ A megameter, one million meters or 1,000 kims. Useful in close starship combat, which is considered to be 100 mims or less.

molex – /mō' leks/ A synthetic fabric woven from long chains of silicon molecules. Stronger than steel or titanium, molex is light, breathable, and soft.

nanofield – An invisible network of nanomachines that every person and complex object possesses. A nanofield works to repair damage to its possessor. It can also carry signals from its possessor's 'net over short distances.

negaputer – /neg' ə pyū ter/ A negaton computer. Negaputers use negative energy and mass to process calculations isotemporally, or 'sideways in time'. This allows negaputers to complete incredibly complex calculations in practically no time, although time is needed for the negaputer to input the calculation and output the result. Negaputers are the basis for the Overnet and thus the Collective as a whole.

neutronium – /new trō' nē um/ Neutron matter, matter that has been condensed until its electrons and protons fuse into neutrons. The main component of neutron stars, neutronium is incredibly strong, durable, and inflexible. It is also terrifically dense and heavy and is primarily layered onto objects as a thin coating.

ohtu – /ō too'/ Gaseous oxygen, another common cargo. Usually shipped in liquid form.

Overnet – The all-encompassing network of negaputers that manages the entirety of the Collective. Every human and object is linked to the Overnet through their personal cybernet. The Overnet allows nearly instantaneous communication across interstellar distances and is responsible for the System that Citizens and Nobles use to grow, level, and respawn.

pig – Petagram, one quadrillion or 10^{15} grams. Equal to one billion metric tons.

pijin – /pij' ən/ A petajoule, a quadrillion joules. Most non-photonic main ship weapons operate in the range of a pijin or higher.

planetside – A slang term meaning on or near the surface of a planet. For those who spend their lives in space, being planetside is considered a punishment.

pow – A petawatt, one quadrillion watts. Photonic ship weapons and ship shields are usually rated at a pow or higher.

rimward – /rimm' wərd/ In a system, a direction pointing away from the central star. Usually refers to a direction along the ecliptic, but in regions like the Oort Cloud that enshroud the entire system, this simply means farther from the central star. In the Sol system, rimward also means 'into uncivilized or lawless areas'.

starward – /starr' wərd/ In a system, a direction pointing toward the central star. In the Sol system, starward also means 'toward civilization and the rule of law'.

stim – /stimm/ A nanobot stimulant, restricted in civilized areas, that grants a large boost to physical stats for a short time. This substance has addictive properties and can cause damage that a nanofield can't heal with prolonged use.

stim-down – A painful condition that inevitably results from the use of stim. It causes the nervous system to register pain from every muscle, joint, and bone and can be quite agonizing. Additional usage of stim will counteract stim-down, and this is the main source of the drug's addictive effect.

syleather – /sī' le*th* er/ A synthetic fabric made of woven chains of carbon molecules in three-dimensional lattices. Stronger than molex or fulleron but also stiffer, harder to work, and more expensive.

tic – /tick/ A tenth of a credit.

tock – A unit of velocity equal to 10% of c, the speed of light in a vacuum. Generally, relativistic effects such as time dilation, length contraction, and mass accretion become pronounced around three tocks, which is why few ships travel faster than 2.5 tocks unless there's a significant need.

transtanium – A translucent alloy of titanium that is many times stronger and somewhat lighter than standard titanium. Stronger and far lighter than HDM, transtanium is a very common fabrication material and can be made almost perfectly transparent if needed.

www.ingramcontent.com/pod-product-compliance
Lightning Source LLC
Chambersburg PA
CBHW052349020726
47503CB00001B/172